the summer remains

seth king

For Martin and Island. I don't have to say why. They know.
They will always know

~

For everyone living from behind the barrier of disease and
disability. Let's break it

~

And for Jax Beach and #2 Oceanfront, land of my invincible
July

"In the depth of winter, I finally learned that there was in me an invincible summer."

-ALBERT CAMUS

~

"Every love story is too short. Everyone would, if given the choice, live forever with the person that holds their heart. It is what we do with this too-little time we have been given with our too-mortal loved ones before our too-soon deaths on this too-small planet that makes all the difference."

-ELLA "SAVIOUR" KNIGHTLEY-COLE

Author's Note: the medical condition as particularly described in this book is not real. A person in my life suffers from a similar diagnosis, and so for the sake of discretion, certain words and characteristics were altered. Thank you for your understanding.

A special foreword from Seth King commemorating the one-year anniversary of
The Summer Remains

"Nothing ever ends poetically. It ends and we turn it into poetry. All that blood was never once beautiful. It was just red."

- Kait Rokowski

Grief has been described a million different ways by a million different souls, but I'd call it a neighbor. Grief moves in next door and takes up permanent residence, and you can ignore it, deny it, or even grow comfortable with it and accept it – but it will remain with you for as long as you live.

I didn't really know this when I first set out to write the book that ended up changing my life. I thought I was going to turn sadness into triumph and be done with it. I was two or three years out of the death of my brother at the hands of an incompetent doctor, and his loss was still everywhere I looked. How could it *not* have lingered? His wasn't a typical death. He was thirty years old, he had just graduated from medical school, he had an unparalleled passion for life and adventure and humanity, and he had a young wife and two beautiful children. (And eight months after his death, those two children became three. He never knew about his third daughter.) People who knew him still gasp when they think about what a waste it all was. I thought that sitting down and pouring my grief into the pages of this book would heal me. I was so right, and so, so wrong.

The Summer Remains came to me at a very peculiar moment in my life. Looking back, I was clinically depressed, although of course I did not even know what that term meant at the time. I was going broke, I was one month away from being homeless, and I had no backup plan. So when Martin started calling to me, saying he wasn't finished, I couldn't deny him. I'll never forget where I was when the voice started speaking to me, actually. So I took all my brother's

9

traits – an unusually strong passion for life, a sense of wonder at the universe, a massive stubborn streak – and turned him into a character named Summer. I love her more than anything. She is funny and independent and so, so special, but that's not to say she didn't almost kill me, too. The writing process was so brutal I was often on the edge of vomiting, but I kept going. Today, I suppose this was my own form of bloodletting – I'd gone straight into caring for Martin's children and wife after his death, and therefore I'd never allowed myself to feel anything. In three years, I'd only cried a handful of times. I had to be strong for the kids, and so that's what I did. Until I started writing. I finally opened up the gates I didn't even know I'd closed, and at last I let out all the anger (and anguish) I'd been pushing into the corner.

    At the end of the writing process, though, I hit another closed door. According to the publishing powers in New York, my book was hard to pin into a single category and hit on no current trends, and there was also fear that a book with a female narrator written by a male could be an awkward pitch to publishers. Sick and tired of being faced with dead ends, I held my breath and pressed publish on Amazon's self-publishing platform. I had absolutely no idea what would happen next.

    One person read the book and told ten people. Those ten people then told a hundred more. Through word of mouth the book started trickling across the country, and then the world. It was not a huge hit, but it was enough to transform my life and enable me to move away from my embattled family for the first time in my life. (That sounds strange to say, since I was twenty-five at the time, but the situation was more complicated than I could ever explain here.) It spread across the world in very small doses, but those doses were still enough to inspire readers to email me the most beautiful messages I've ever received. Bearing my pain to the Internet was an uncharacteristic and perhaps impulsive decision, but the letters I got from people in similar situations made all the bloodletting worth the pain.

This is from a note I posted on social media after the book started spreading:

I have no delusions that this book is a megahit, and I know that in the great scheme of things, it is still a speck of dust on the lens of the world. But change is not measured in leagues as insignificant as worldly or monetary success. Every human that reads the book is another human that now knows my brother lived and breathed here on this planet; every soul the story sinks into can be counted as another of his accomplishments after his actual time to accomplish things was cut so short. Now that my brother's lessons are in lights, even dim lights like this, I just wanted to say thank you.

The first stages of grief, for me at least, involved shock and anger and fury. I'm not sure if I believe humans go anywhere after life, but I do know they leave things behind. Everyone who knew my brother agreed that there was a sort of anger around his life and departure – the energy felt dark, stormy, angry; like he hadn't left on good terms. We all knew he wasn't looking back and smiling, not in the beginning at least. But lately, for the first time, we've felt peace. I hope it has something to do with this book. And I hope he's floating on.

Martin's been gone for four years now, and I miss him every day. Of course, there's a sadness that he's not here to see what his life has done. There's a sadness, *period*, that he's gone. As anyone who has ever lost someone knows, I simply miss him. I would give anything for another day, another hour, another walk on the pier under the sun. I miss the way he laughed and the way he waddled when he walked and the way he wasn't afraid to be as goofy as he wanted. But I'm okay. I have accepted grief as my neighbor. And his legacy is still around, in the form of the book you are reading.

The harsh reality of the media business, especially today, means that without friends at publishing houses – or a last name like Kardashian or Jenner – it is almost impossible to get a big project out to the world, no matter the merits of your work. I'm bigger now, career-wise, but I am no Jenner by any means. I've never made a bestseller list, and this book was never even purchased by a publisher. But I don't care. It still made the mark that my brother couldn't. He's found a short second life, and I'm grateful.

  This evening I'm going to walk to Martin's favorite pier where I took the original cover photo of this book while on my first date with the love of my life, and I'm going to drink a can of Martin's favorite beer for him. Because victories don't have to be on a cosmic scale for them to still be victories. He died before his time, but his existence still touched a young medical student in the Philippines and an elderly woman in South Africa and a mother in Chicago. You are all part of the global tapestry that made him matter and turned his blood into poetry. Thank you forever.

  This is *The Summer Remains.*

  - Seth King
  Florida
  March 2016

PART I
SUMMER SINKING

1

On a sunny Tuesday morning towards the end of March, a white-haired man walked into a cold room and told me I might die soon.

I fidgeted on the hospital bed as Dr. Steinberg entered, the late-spring sunlight mocking me as it smiled onto the industrial tile floors. I'd known Steinberg since I was four. He'd handled almost all of my throat problems, and I trusted him. He was like a second father to me, and I knew he would always tell me the truth.

That's why the look on his face scared the living shit out of me.

I listened for the next ten minutes as he gave me the gist of the story. It was all so surreal that my mind could only catch certain phrases before the sentence would run away from me again:

Your esophagus has ruptured again, for good this time...

Your stomach is leaking more and more...

Toxicity levels are through the roof...

Your body just isn't getting the nutrients it needs from your feeding tube any longer...

And finally, *terminal.*

"Terminal?" I heard myself squeak, my throat filling up with that weird, shivery feeling you get when you know your life has just changed. Steinberg suddenly became very interested in a fraying string on the sleeve of his jacket.

"T-terminal," he stuttered. "Summer, the thing is...I'm afraid this is a...well, nobody has ever..."

He finally cleared his throat and met my gaze, tears pooling in the corners of his cerulean eyes. "Sweetheart, I

15

am *so* sorry to tell you this, but this mountain may be unclimbable for you."

My mother let out a small, sharp sob in the corner and then clapped her hands over her mouth.

"Okay, unclimbable," I swallowed, staring down at the floor as I tried to grasp just what that word now meant to me, and my family, and this weird little life I had created for myself. "Okay. Unclimbable. Okay."

But Steinberg wasn't done yet.

"Hold on. I said it *may* be unclimbable, not that it *definitely* will be. I want to prepare you, and I don't want to give you any false hope, but there may be something we can do, Summer. It's a small chance, but still, it's a chance. A Hail Mary, if you will."

I reached up to rub my temples. "Okay, well, survival sounds good. Better than death, I suppose. What is this Hail Mary?"

Steinberg crossed his arms, studied me for a moment, and then took out a chart and launched into a spiel about something called the Porter-Collins Procedure, an extremely major surgery that would perhaps be saving my life in three months' time.

"Nobody has ever survived this particular operation," he concluded a few minutes later, skipping all the medical jargon to keep from boring you to death, pardon my pun. "Nobody. It's been attempted three times, but none of those were ultimately successful. One person survived for three months in intensive care, but she was fifty-one, and in frail health in general. We think you're a much more viable candidate, but then again, there is no way to be sure. We can do it in two, maybe three months, after I've assembled the proper specialists and created a game plan – considering your health doesn't take another nosedive before then, that is. If we're going to try this, we need you in tip-top shape – or as close to that as we can get you, anyway."

"Okay," I said again, sitting a little taller. "And what are the chances that this Hail Mary will even *work,* and that I won't just die a few days after the surgery, anyway?"

"I'm afraid to say that it would be stretching things to even tell you eighty/twenty," he said, peering down at me from over his glasses. I steeled myself and took a breath.

"Okay, well, that's better than a hundred to zero. Let's go out with a bang, then, Steinberg. Let's do this."

He threw up a fist, triumphant, but I could see the fear in his eyes. "It's settled, then. Hail Mary it is."

My mom rushed over to sit beside me and kind of hang onto my shoulder as some counselor woman came in who helped families handle these types of situations – "transitions," she called them, and just hearing that word threatened to pull me under. Dr. Steinberg watched, an apology on his face, as she said things like "preparations" and "options" and "arrangements." I tried to be polite and pay attention, but truthfully I didn't give a damn about what she was saying. It was go time, and things were looking grim – I already knew that. The wet, metallic panic erupting in my stomach was due to an entirely different subject.

"And finally," the counselor lady, Angie, said in a hushed, clipped, polite tone that spoke of years of having impossible conversations with worried families huddled in chilly waiting rooms, "I work very closely with Last Great Hope, a wonderful organization that specializes in situations like this, and if there is *anything* you want before the surgery, Summer – a trip to Tahiti, a cabin in the mountains, whatever – we can do it. Or if-"

"Thanks, but no thanks," I said, making her stop short.

"Wh – *excuse me?*"

"Save the Disney trips for the twelve-year-olds," I told her. "Spend all that money on a cancer kid or something. I know the truth about those fairy tales now. Make someone else happy – I've got everything I need. Or *almost* everything." I paused as everyone leaned in. "I do have one request, actually. First of all, all of you are forgetting something vital."

"Oh no, did we forget your milk?" my mom asked as she reached for her purse. "I thought I put some-"

"No, Shelly, we did not forget the baby milk I pump into my stomach tube every day to keep myself alive because my throat doesn't work, but that does have something to do with it."

As she pouted in my general direction I realized what a complete bitch I was being, and then I realized just as quickly that I probably wouldn't be able to stop myself anyway.

"What is it, then?" my mom asked, stung, and I took a breath and then pushed it back out.

"Frankly, I need all of you to chill the fuck out."

My mom dropped her purse onto her lap. Dr. Steinberg looked at me like I'd just tried to jump out of the third story window. Angie held her pen in midair and stared at me, the sun turning her brownish eyes ocher.

"Excuse me, young lady?" my mother asked. "We need to *what?*"

"Chill the eff out," I said, editing my language the second time around. "Sorry, but all this emotion and drama and doom and gloom crap is already making me freak out. You're all forgetting I've had a broken throat and a tube in my abdomen since I was in diapers, and that I can handle this. I've dealt with health scares before, and I will do it again, no matter how much scarier this Scare is than all the other Scares. Like, I know you're trying to help and stuff, but melting down in front of me is not going to help me deal with this, so *please*, everyone take a deep breath, close your eyes, and get your panties out of a bunch."

"We're sorry," my mom said after an impossibly long and awkward moment. "It's just that we need to prepare you for…for what will happen, and-"

"Prepare me to die?" I asked. "Guess what, Shelly, I'm going to die one day, be it in three months or sixty years, and wasting all my time crying over it isn't going to help. Here's what I want, my one last wish – or my maybe-not-last wish, or whatever the hell this is." A tear appeared in my mom's eye, and I softened my voice as I reached up to wipe the saltwater from her cheek. "Okay. Before the surgery, I

18

want to have a normal summer by the beach," I began as I cleared her eye and shook the moisture from my finger. "I want to go to the sea and go to work and read my books and go about my business like usual without everyone breathing down my neck and treating me like A Broken Person, because if I am treated like A Broken Person for one more month of my life, I will break some faces, no offense. Shelly, if you so much as make *one* special meal – I mean, not that I can eat or anything, because I can't – anyway, I'm burning down the house. There will literally be a pile of smoldering ashes where your kitchen used to be, I promise." Shelly pouted again, but I trudged through. "I'm serious, no special treatment, please. No Christmases in July, no excessive hugging, not even a midnight run to Target for some trinkets from the dollar section. And most importantly of all…"

I looked around and, seeing sympathy in everyone's eyes and knowing this request would be completely futile, said – "No sympathy. *Please.* The sympathy is what breaks me and makes me feel broken. If this is gonna be my last chance to live and have fun and be normal, then I'm going to need to *feel* as normal as possible, and that means absolutely no pity, because that separates me from everyone else and makes me Different with a capital D. And if I don't stay in a good headspace I'm gonna spend the next three months in a fetal position in my closet having an endless anxiety attack about the surgery, so please just work with me here and keep the pity locked up."

A sigh and a smile. Shelly put her hand on mine. "I would never pity you, Summer. You're the strongest person I know, and you always have been. You know that. We *all* know that. That's not what this is about."

I tried to smile back. "Thanks, Shelly."

"Anytime. And can you *please* call me Mom, like a normal twenty-four-year-old?"

"Not a chance, Shelly."

"Okay, fine. So, then…a Jax Beach summer? Is that *really* all you want?"

I paused as her words hung in the overly sanitized air. It wasn't all, and I knew it. As I sat there I thought of the one thing I didn't have, the one thing I'd *never* had, the one thing that screamed at me from the silence and jumped out at me from the shadows – and now that this upcoming summer had perhaps just become Summer's Last Stand, my desire was suddenly more urgent than ever. I knew I wouldn't be able to stop the longing from rising to my face, and as I felt the blood burn my cheeks I caught Steinberg's eyes again, which just embarrassed me even more.

"Well, I mean, since you're asking, there is *one* thing…"

"Anything!" Shelly and Dr. Steinberg said at exactly the same time, and I stared out of the window as my eyes got all weird and watery.

"Okay, well, I know something so sentimental is going to sound crazy coming from someone so…well, you know how I am…"

"Honest?" Steinberg offered, trying to be polite.

"Opinionated?" Shelly said.

"Brash?" Angie asked, even though she'd just met me ten minutes ago and it was literally beyond embarrassing that she already held that opinion of me.

"Headstrong and stubborn and annoying," I finally said, shoving the truth out of the way, and they all nodded. "Anyway, here goes. Since you're asking, the thing is…I'd like to fall in love."

I looked down at the ground again as everyone in the room broke my most important rule already: I could feel their pity descending on me, smothering me just like it had my entire life, snuffing out any chance I had at being treated like a normal, living, breathing human who deserved to love and be loved just like anyone else, as they said in the Hallmark cards.

"Oh, honey…" Steinberg sighed.

"It just wouldn't be fair to someone…" my mother chimed in, just as Angie the counselor lady threw in her two cents, too.

"Sweetie, you have to understand, your situation is very serious – people get irrational during times like these, and if you got involved with someone and the worst happened, well-"

I crossed my fingers behind my back and shook my head. I'd known they'd react like this – why had I even tried in the first place? Some things, I knew, were just better left unshared.

"Yeah," I said. "Okay, yeah, you guys are right. I'll try to…put that off, I guess. For now. God knows I have tons of time to think about it – it's not like I'm dying or anything."

Everyone forced quick, fake laughs and then got back to business. Unbeknownst to them, however, my mind was flying past the barren oak branches outside the window and soaring above the clouds to someplace only I knew. My desires could not be contained by the circumstances in this room, or by sickness, or even by reality in general, really. I wanted love more than anything – this was true, as much as it humiliated me to admit it. I'd wanted love ever since I was a cookie-cutter little girl being brainwashed by cookie-cutter Disney movies about cookie-cutter princes and princesses falling into cookie-cutter love and then prancing off to their cookie-cutter castles to live out their cookie-cutter lives. And strangely enough, this desire had only deepened after the fairy tale fantasies had faded away and melted into a more grown up, real-world entity known as relationship FOMO, when my condition had rendered me an observer from the social media sidelines as everyone else my age paired up and got engaged and married and pregnant and then shouted about it from the Facebook treetops as loud as their keyboards would let them while I sat there single as a nun with the flu. But I didn't want that cookie cutter love from the Disney movies and my social media feeds. I didn't want some run of the mill summer romance that would fizzle out as soon as the sunrays slanted in the fall and the Facebook Official status went to shit.

Because I, Summer Johnson, Purveyor of Pragmatism, Lover of Logic, Ultimate Believer in the Rational, and Person Who Was Maybe Going To Die Soon, wanted to drown in someone.

2

So, before you decide I am a delusional maniac, let me just get this out of the way: the story of my life is not entitled *Broken Girl Feels Incomplete; Seeks Boy to Make Her Feel Whole*. I am not some adorably helpless 1940s movie heroine lying on a couch waiting for a man to plug into me and turn me on like a light bulb. I'm perfectly fine with being me. I mean, yeah, it kinda blows sometimes, and occasionally I wish I was Beyoncé, but I've pretty much accepted my fate of being Summer Martin Johnson, you know? Awkward exchanges with gas station cash register attendants and the whitest of white girl dance moves: this is the situation of Summer. And let's get another thing out in the clear: I know I might not sound like the most realistic person in the world, wishing for this. Because let's face it: quietly attractive twenty-four-year-old girls with stomach tubes and moderately-large facial scars aren't exactly the most desired creatures walking the Earth, especially for shallow guys in their post-collegiate glory days who just want the hall-of-fame blondes with the sparkly lip gloss and the cutoff denim booty shorts. I get that. But something like this had been brewing for quite some time, all thanks to social media, or as I call it, the Public Bathroom Stall of the World.

If you haven't heard of the thoroughly-modern condition known as Relationship FOMO (Fear of Missing Out), let me explain for you in big bold painful letters. There I was a few days before The Big Surgery Bomb, innocently trolling Facebook on one of those late spring Florida mornings when the wind smells like humidity and salt and you know summer is on its way and it thrills you and terrifies you in equal measure, when I was bombarded by not one, not two, but THREE engagement stories on my News Feed. What was wrong with these girls? Didn't they know that it was early, and that my self-esteem was still fragile, and that spacing out their wedding bombshells was the right thing to do, if only until I'd injected my coffee?

But like the masochist I am, I clicked on one of the stories anyway and scrolled through the pictures of the engagement. This one belonged to Misty, this girl who'd sat behind me in high school science class and had always borrowed my pens without giving them back. For months she'd been posting about how Crazy In Love she was and about how this new guy was The One and about how Hashtag Blessed she was and generally just assaulting twelve hundred of her closest frenemies with other completely unsolicited details about her delirious happiness. And now I guess she'd finally gotten her ring in a cheesy outdoor engagement by a lake.

Okay, first of all: I want my pens back, Misty. All of them. Including that one with the dark purple ink that I really liked. And secondly: STFU. You have a guy who loves you. We get it. At the risk of sounding like a bitter old spinster clutching her pearls in jealousy, *you can stop now*. But even my cynicism couldn't overcome my basic humanity, and ironically enough, at the end of the day there was nothing that could make you feel alone like the silvery, artificial glow of your laptop screen. So as I glared at the photos of Misty's boyfriend bending down on one knee underneath their Oak Tree of Love while professing his Undying Devotion to this stupid pen thief, I couldn't help but think to myself: *why can't someone love me like that?*

And then I slapped myself in the face and tossed my phone aside, but not before screen-shotting one particularly heinous photo and reminding myself to send it to my friend Autumn to bitch about it later that day. But seriously, my qualms with the Pen Thief aside, girls were getting married by the boatload, and I couldn't deal with it anymore. At least the Mistys of my mom's generation surpassed her in silence – in this constantly connected age I had to deal with them vomiting their lives onto Facebook all day, every day, reminding me that I was me. I deserved love, too, no matter my present circumstances, and I didn't know how much longer I could watch my frenemies pull ahead on the Highway of Life and live so loudly while I sat in the dark.

On a rational level I knew I was being ridiculous, of course, but still, in some deep and ancient place within me, I felt like a failure, a forgotten loss, a flash in the pan. And unfortunately for my mother, Dr. Steinberg, that random counselor lady, and the boys in my town in general, failure was not something I was accustomed to accepting. Not at all.

~

The days after the surgery news were what the word "blur" had been invented for. The operation was tentatively scheduled for the Monday after Labor Day weekend, so it was official: I was granted one final summer on the beach. Or *not* final summer, depending on the outcome of my surgery, or whatever. There were scores of documents to sign, tons of words to learn, a dozen therapists to pretend to listen to while they spoke to me in quietly apologetic tones, etcetera.

On day three after the big bang, a little Xanax had finally helped my mother's anxiety levels descend to a somewhat manageable rate, and the imminent death of the day flashed a sullen yellow above the ocean to the east as she drove me home after our final consultation for a few weeks. (And I use the word "home" loosely, as I had not felt like I'd had a true home in years. Sure, I may have laid my head at my mom's every night, but it was no longer the dwelling I'd grown up in. Things had changed and evolved and she was always off on dates trying to get remarried while my father had his wife and his other children in Orlando to deal with, which was shitty but understandable, I guess. Even my friends were starting to drift and shift and move forward in ways I seemed to not be. No matter where I went, I never really felt welcome or wanted. I was like a piece of a puzzle that had become so wet and swollen from the condensation of a glass left on a coffee table, I no longer fit anywhere – a new but permanent outlier.)

"Summer, I'm sorry about that request or whatever, with the Last Great Hope lady," my mother finally said as

25

she drove, mentioning the Elephant of Awkwardness we'd both avoided for days. "I didn't mean to shut you down like that, you know. I'm just trying to protect you. That's all I want – what's best for you. But who knows – maybe you'll find love someday."

"Yeah, who knows," I said, pursing my lips together with a secret only I knew. I was going to try.

So, it turns out there was this app called Spark. People my age were plagued by three main questions: *am I ever going to grow up, am I ever going to get my shit together,* and *will I ever find someone, or will I die alone in a pile of cats?*, and since most of my generation had already given up on the first two concepts, they were using Spark to focus on the third. After hearing two nurses gossiping about it the day after the diagnosis, I'd done some digging on Google, and it seemed I'd found my golden parachute. To make a long story short, the app let you "like" photos of nearby guys that you thought were acceptably attractive and/or not murderers, and if they "liked" you back, you could message them. This was perfect for me, and not only because I had the social skills of a rock garden and therefore found the prospect of hiding behind a screen for the unavoidably awkward first few conversations with a prospective love interest incredibly appealing. If the guys declined me, I'd never be notified, which was perfect. (I wasn't *that* fragile, I just liked to avoid bad news – God knows I had enough to deal with already.) Spark was taking the world by storm and making twenty-somethings everywhere have bad dates over overpriced hors d'oeuvres at stupid hipster bars, and you'd better believe I wanted in on that awkward action before fate took me out of it. Not dying in a pile of cats was the most easily-solvable Big Life Question I could confront in the tiny window of time I'd suddenly been allotted, and Operation Find A Boy Before the Operation had officially begun.

Once we got home, Shelly whispered one final apology after a day full of them and then excused herself to her room to "call her sister." I knew she'd really be crying

26

silently into her pillow all alone, and the thought pounded around in my guilty chest like a dresser tumbling down a staircase during a hasty move. As she disappeared down the hallway, I went out onto the porch we'd screened into a sort of indoor/outdoor living room, slammed a comfortable spot into the supremely uncomfortable couch I'd inherited from my great grandmother, and felt my stomach rumble with something that had nothing to do with my health issues. And though the irony of curing that most human of maladies – loneliness – with a soulless app housed in a four-inch piece of glass and metal was not lost on me, my sense of humor was nothing if not morbid, especially now that my condition was now *literally* morbid, and so I smiled and took out my phone.

My bones shivered with a manic, reckless, thrilling energy. This was wrong. I knew that. By joining this dating app I was basically selling someone a ticket to sail on the Titanic. Even if I were to survive the surgery, the next six months of my life would still be rough – there was no doubt about that. But it was also, perhaps, my last chance at love. Life was going to destroy me anyway, be it in three months or sixty years – why not let love help finish the job, too?

And as I sat there, another thought sprung out at me like the old Jack in the Box someone had given me during an extended hospital stay that would jump out at odd hours of the night and scare me senseless: in this age of TMI, I could share *anything* about myself. Should I share the news about my possibly (okay, probably) impending death? Of course they deserved to know, these guys I would prospectively be matching with. But as a human, I also deserved to have someone to look at me and see *me*, Summer Johnson, not the Permanent Death Cloud that now hung over my shoulders like shame during a hangover meal at Arby's. And I knew that would be impossible if someone knew the truth. Besides, I knew I couldn't go one more day as Summer, That Girl You Treat Differently Because of The Throat Thing, and so, like the heinous bitch I am, I decided to do the most sensible thing I could imagine and download the app, take my chances, and hold the information close in the beginning. If I met anyone special I'd share that I was obviously unwell and edit out the death thing, and if things sank down deep with anyone, I'd figure out how to drop the big news then. But would I even be able to *find* love in such a short time?

And then I realized that in all of the madness I was overlooking the simple fact that none of this mattered unless I *actually got a date*, which honestly was still a major question mark for me. (Stomach tube, facial scar, shallow boys, etc.) As usual I was being a cynical, over-analytical, self-doubting mess, and so on that ratty old couch on my ratty old porch in my ratty old life, I took the deepest of breaths and then downloaded the app that would hopefully make me officially un-single for however long my personal forever would last.

3

Welcome, the app said in big red letters. *Create your profile*. I pushed away a particularly frilly pillow and then wrote a short message under the picture Facebook had already linked to my profile:

Hi. I'm Summer. As you can see in my pictures, I'm kinda mangled. Childhood accidents suck. If that's something you can get over, swipe right. If you chew with your mouth open, count NASCAR races among your hobbies, take mirror selfies, or refer to girls as "sluts," "bitches" or "cum catching slut bitches," then swipe left. If not, I'm your girl. I like reading, confetti cake, cynicism, hate-watching the Kardashians, and not much else. Come dislike the world with me.

I submitted my profile and then decided to wait to start getting matches. Or not get matches, either one. No point in fretting when there was reading to be done.

What did the dog say? the first eligible bachelor to message me, a kid with floppy blonde hair named Austin, said after about ten minutes.

I don't know, I responded, perking up. A guy was *really* messaging me already? **You tell me,** I said.

I don't actually know, he typed, **I just wanted to say WOOF to you, because yikes. And PS: I'd shell out for a makeup artist if I were you – you look like a clown with all that white powder and shit**

I hid my face with my hand, blocked the asshole, and returned my focus to the stray issue of *Cosmopolitan* I'd found on a side table, since apparently I was a basic bitch who enjoyed being told how to land my dream job by teasing my hair in a perfectly flirty way instead of, you know, actually going to school and getting a degree like a normal human.

Did it hurt? a kid named Todd asked about five minutes into an article about – you guessed it – VaJazzling. Warily, I typed a short response:

Did what hurt.

When your mother punched you in the face in the womb, he said, **because that's the only way I can imagine how a face like that exists.**

Cringe. Block. Repeat. The next message came soon after, from some hipster-y guy named Richard:

Do you work on a chicken farm?

I knew better than to respond, but my morbid curiosity got the best of me.

No...?

Oh, he said. **Because you sure look like you know how to handle a cock.**

Okay, I thought with a little smile, *at least he gets a few extra points for inventiveness*. I laughed a little, blocked Richard, and then returned to my magazine. But after two more similar messages, one of which mentioned an extremely vulgar act involving peanut butter and a Golden Retriever that I do not even care to repeat, I was starting to get discouraged.

I guess I hadn't really imagined it going like this; the boys being this awful. But then again, my mother had always taught me to never underestimate the shittiness of humans, so I guess I shouldn't have been surprised. And it's not like I didn't know I was damaged. I mean, I wasn't exactly

Unwell, like one of those people you see in the movies who lie in an infirmary all day muttering to themselves about the cruelty of the universe while a machine kept them alive or whatever; I was just sort of flawed. The gist of my issue was that I was born with a particularly annoying defect called Esophageal Intresia, which basically meant my throat was broken. Like, I had an esophagus, it just didn't link my stomach and my mouth in the way that a normal esophagus should have – it just disappeared halfway down my throat. Imagine the pipe linking your kitchen sink to your sewer or whatever, and then imagine severing that pipe in half. Pretty inconvenient, no?

So when I was twelve hours old my doctors went in and tried to fix it and join the two pieces together. And it didn't work. So they tried to fix it again. Eighty times. And after eighty-one surgeries (and counting) to create a throat passage and make my esophagus wider so I could swallow and eat, they still weren't able to fix things that well. They patched things up, if you will, but the whole throat situation never really reached one hundred percent. Throat tissues were flimsy and delicate and notoriously difficult to work with – imagine sewing together a wet sponge – so currently I had a thin mesh tube installed in my throat to keep the narrow, artificially-created passage open, which was exactly as comfortable as it sounded. I could eat some softish foods – *sometimes* – but I didn't really like to because I usually just ended up throwing everything back up ten minutes later anyway, which 1. was gross and embarrassing and inconvenient, and 2. could be damaging to my already-fragile throat tissues. (Funfetti cake was the only thing I would consistently sacrifice potential throat tissue damage for, because Funfetti cake was throat-tissue-sacrificing good.) Anyway, I stayed alive with the help of a little white plastic feeding tube protruding from my abdomen. Four times a day I stopped, hooked up a syringe to the tube, and pumped one can of Instamilk into my stomach, this cloudy, vitamin-y stuff that delivered all the nutrients I didn't get from the food I couldn't swallow. It was a hassle, I guess,

31

but, like, being born as one of those poor featureless blobs you see being wheeled around Disney World by their depressed-looking families would've been even *more* of a hassle, so I didn't think about it too much. The feeding tube was my own version of normal, whatever that word meant, and over the years I'd gotten scarily used to it. I even used to have this joke where I pictured myself having to halt my future wedding as I walked down the aisle (God, isn't that a scary word? *Wedding*?) to pull up my dress and inject myself with Instamilk, but my mom didn't find it funny, and she'd get all quiet and weird and stuff whenever I told it, so I'd stopped telling it.

What was *more* of a hassle was The Scar, as I not-so-lovingly called it, or Scarlett O'Hara when I was in a better mood. During one months-long stretch in the hospital when my doctors had tried to take a piece of my intestines and create a throat out of it (spoiler alert: they'd failed), some nurse had stuck a tube up my nose and run it down my throat to keep the passage from closing again. After I pulled out the tube one too many times, she stitched it to the skin beside my nostril to keep it in place. Well, she messed up badly, because one night I pulled out the tube, including all of the stitches, and sort of ripped a gash in my face from just below the right side of my mouth, up my cheek, almost to my eye. They'd tried to fix this, too, and had failed once again, meaning I currently had a scar the color of my lips running up half the length of my face. The scar didn't feel bad and I barely noticed it, but because of my scar everyone *treated* me like I was scarred, which did feel kind of bad. Strangers' eyes would track away from my face mid-conversation, shopkeepers would say *Hi* a little too enthusiastically when I walked in to look at lamps or whatever, and waitresses often looked at my mother when asking for my order because they couldn't face me without feeling awkward. Over the years it had almost become this annoying, unavoidable buffer between me and the rest of the world. I got it, trust me, but like, I also didn't *get it* get it. It was both understandable and infuriating, but so were lots of things, life included, and like

32

I said, shit happened all the time and at least I wasn't a Disney World Blob, so usually I just bit my lip (get it?) and dealt with the hand I'd been dealt in this fucked-up poker game on acid called life.

My phone buzzed, pulling me out of my thoughts. I picked it up expecting to see another hate message. *Maybe this one will at least be cleverly worded*, I thought as I scanned it:

Hi Summer

Hi, I repeated to myself silently. *Hi*. So informal and breezy. Hi could mean anything. But what did *his* Hi mean?

I pulled up the sender's profile and groaned: another prankster. He had to be. He was beautiful, and I didn't throw that term around. He had a Shy Smile and Sparkling Eyes and Messy Brown Hair and lots of other patented features that were specifically designed to make girls go weak in the knees and spend hours Facebook stalking and get pulled under by their emotions and do all kinds of other crazy things that I'd only ever seen in the movies. It was a face you could fall in love with, that was for sure. And for a moment, just a moment, I closed my eyes and wished that I was a normal girl, a girl this boy could be with, and not just make fun of.

And then I opened them and saw the world for what it was.

Hi, Cooper Nichols, I typed after reading the name on his profile, deciding to just get to the punch line and get this over with. Bizarrely, his response came almost immediately:

So I have news.

I frowned.

Yes? I responded.

33

I both agree with, and reject, your profile, he said a moment later. My head tilted.

Uh. Explain?

Well, he typed, **I also dislike selfies, and also dislike men who refer to women as "sluts" – but not entirely for some Feminist Knight On A Feminist White Horse reason. I'm also just OCD about words, and I hate how that particular word sounds coming from the mouth – it's right up there with "juicy," my other most-hated word. They're just ugly words, IMO.
That's crazy, isn't it?
It's crazy.
I'm crazy.**

I forgot about the stupid magazine and sat up straight. As someone who had fought a lifelong campaign against the use of the phrase "moist towelette" for exactly the same reasons, my interest was piqued.

But still, I waited a little to respond, just so he'd think I was busier than I actually was.

It's not crazy, I finally said. I wasn't good at flirting, but I figured I'd at least try. **You're not crazy. I'm listening.**

Okay, and now for my disagreement with your profile, he continued. **I *would* like to meet with you, because you seem cool and stuff, but I would *not* like to dislike stuff with you. Negative outlooks on the world, even when approached through the prism of humor, are damaging to the psyche, and I steadfastly refuse to engage in any mutual Psyche Damage.
(Although my favorite beer, Guinness, could also be described as damaging to the brain, but I wouldn't mind engaging in that sort of damage with you.)**

I laughed a little, but then I frowned again. This boy was cute and funny and smart, sparklingly so. Why was he talking to *me*?

Okay, I have to be honest, I typed. **I assumed you were messaging me to prank me. So if you're going to do it, why don't we just cut to the chase here.**

I swallowed some air and pressed Send. It was a risky message, and I reached up and bit my nails as I sat on the edge of the couch waiting for his response. Seriously, what was it about cell phones that made us vomit out all our deepest thoughts and most urgent fears and say everything else we would never even DREAM of telling another person face-to-face? It wasn't like I'd ever be able to talk to this hottie in person. (It wasn't that I was quiet, per se; it was just that I was afraid of my thoughts getting out and scaring people.)

Okay, he said.
I'll prank you.
...What did the fox say?

Ugh, I groaned. Not some cheesy pickup line or insult. I thought he was better than this.

I don't know. I typed, hoping my choice to end the sentence with a period would convey my disappointment.

Um... he said.
(Okay, I'll admit it. I actually have no idea what the fox said, I'm just really bad at cheesy pickup stuff, and I just wanted an excuse to keep talking to you.)

So he *did* have a flaw, I thought with a smile. He was a little awkward – but it was *seriously* adorable.

Okay, Cooper. You have my attention.

35

Lucky me!
Even though you should be less hesitant.

Why is that, Cooper?

Just because, he said. **Is it a categorical impossibility that I simply wanted to chat you up?**

I paused.

Love yourself, I kept thinking. Your problems do not place you beneath this boy's attention. Talk to him. Try this.

I've never been good with numbers, Cooper.

That was a good thing to say, I thought after I sent it, even if it wasn't exactly true – I loved numbers. But still: that was a good thing to say that I said. I knew I kind of liked me!

Okay, I'll give you a number, he responded. **Two. That's the number of beers I'd like to buy at Lynch's tonight. (That's one for me and one for you, since you claim you do not happen to be mathematically inclined.)**

Well, I thought as I sat even taller. Well well. I just got invited to a bar. By a hot boy. Me, in a bar, with a hot boy.

But then I told myself to chill. Lynch's was a dark, smoky dive bar, AKA it was probably very easy for someone to get drugged and raped in there, and it wasn't exactly a place to rendezvous with a guy I'd just met on a sketchy iPhone app, however charming and smart he may have been. And wait, was meeting on the first night even *standard* for Spark dating? God, I was clueless about this stuff. And what was I doing, anyway, letting the dangerous vortexes of self-pity known as Facebook wedding albums get to me like this? What if I'd had a totally undiscovered calling in life and I'd missed out on it because I'd spent every damn second of my free time on social media? Like, I could've been destined to cure Alzheimer's or win an Oscar or something, but I'd have no idea because I was too busy stalking Instagram and talking to this boy. Ugh.

Was I too forward…? Cooper asked after I didn't say anything.

No, no, you're fine, I said. **It's just that I thought you weren't good at the pickup.**

Well you tell me how good I was, then. Yes or no?

I bit my lip. Hard. *Love yourself. Love yourself.*

Make it Joe's crab shack and I'm game, I finally said.

Joe's…? he responded, and I cringed. *Joe's Crab Shack?* What was wrong with me? We could've met anywhere, and I'd picked some trashy tourist trap with tchotchke-covered walls and plastic neon crabs hanging from the ceiling?
　　　I tried to cover my faux pas:

You'll understand once you try their Long Island. Sound good?

Better than good, he said. **I'm in a white jacket. See you soon. Here's my number.**

With a dizzying breath of air I saved his number under IMPROBABLY CHARMING AND INTELLIGENT SPARK BOY (PROCEED WITH CAUTION) and then headed inside to get ready to meet this total and complete stranger like the genius I was.

"Shelly, you're gonna have to make dinner," I said as I grabbed my car keys half an hour later. Cooking had always soothed me, even though I couldn't eat, so I usually made dinner – but not tonight. And yeah, living at home sucked, like I said, but it's not like I had another choice. After one disastrous year of sharing a townhouse with a random roommate named Crystal who'd smoked cigarettes in the kitchen and stolen all my bath towels, I'd boomeranged back home and hadn't left since. (My perennially empty bank account was also not helping move the situation along, to be honest.)

"Why?" Shelly asked from the couch, where she was now watching recorded episodes of some show where a bunch of desperate chicks threw themselves at some douchey guy in hopes of landing a six-month engagement that would eventually dissolve into a short-lived tabloid scandal. Lucky girls!

"I'm going out," I said.

Shelly pressed pause and got up from the couch, looking at me like I'd just pledged my lifelong allegiance to the Scientologists.

"But we just got home and…wait, you're doing *what*?"

"Going out," I repeated.

"…Like, at night?"

I turned and pointed to the kitchen window overlooking our tiny side yard and our annoying neighbor Mrs. Duffy's small pink house. "Yes, considering that it is indeed getting dark outside, that would mean I am, in fact, going out at night, Shelly."

"…With Autumn?"

"You know, I do have more friends than just Autumn," I said, who was our other neighbor and my best friend – more on her later.

"Oh, of course you do, I just want to spend time with…wait, are you wearing *lipstick*?" she asked, inspecting me. "And is that my top? I was dry cleaning that, you know!"

I sighed and looked down at my chest. "It's the only low-cut top that still covers all my surgery scars, alright?"

That shut her up. She came up to give me a hug, and I smiled when I noticed that her shirt was tucked into her floral cotton underwear. My poor mom. I returned her hug with one arm and, with a little flick of my wrist, fixed the little embarrassing underwear situation behind her back with my other.

"What was that?" she asked as she looked around.

"Must've been the wind," I said as I grabbed my bag off the counter. "I'm out. I won't be that long, trust me."

"Okay, honey, have fun!" she called, the unabashed hopefulness in her voice breaking my heart. "So glad you're making more friends, even though I'll miss you! Text me!"

"Kloveyoubye," I said as I headed out the door to my car.

Because I was now shivering with a teeth-chattering case of adrenaline, I sat in the front seat for a minute and tried to get myself together. I pulled down my mirror to check my face again. My scar wasn't *that* visible in the dim interior light of my car, but the faint shadow it cast on my skin was, and so I grabbed some concealer off my messy floorboard, did one last touchup on Scarlett just in case, and then prayed to a God I wasn't sure I believed in for a miracle I wasn't sure could happen.

~

I drove the ten minutes to Joe's, a huge tourist restaurant on the beach across from the lifeguard station at First Avenue South, my heart jack-hammering the whole time. I lived in Florida, but not the Florida you think of when you think of Florida – you know, white sands, palmy avenues, shimmering aquamarine waters, people doing bath salts and then eating other peoples' faces off in Burger King parking lots, etcetera. I lived in *north* Florida, the Florida everyone forgets about, far from all the face-eating craziness of Miami and Orlando, in a sleepy little suburb of Jacksonville called Neptune Beach. The sands were the color of those Werther's Originals candies your grandma used to keep in a crystal dish on her side table, the pines and oaks greatly outnumbered the palms, and on most days the color of the sea more closely resembled a rain puddle on a cloudy afternoon than Caribbean blue. But it was home, and it was on the ocean, and the summers were long and hot and humid and stifling in a wonderfully perfect way that made you want to wade into things, and it never snowed or sleeted or blizzard-ed or any of that other nonsense in the winter, which was necessary for a summer creature like me. I loved to get home from work and leave my shoes on my front porch and walk the six blocks to the beach in my bare feet, humming to myself under the oaks on my way to go sit in the sun where the Earth ran out of land. And Jacksonville was also technically in the South, which was nice, because if you ever lost faith in humanity just come down here, where things were slow and people hugged you and everything was enveloped in a fuzzy golden warmth that made you want to hug them back. Oh, and since people were so nice and Southern here they didn't really gawk at others, at least not openly – and that was important for someone like me.

Speaking of looks, I'll never forget what I wore that night – a simple black dress from the Target clearance section – mostly because I instantly felt like a gross, hideous mess the moment my eyes met Cooper's.

Oh, *sheesh*. My thoughts scrambled like a pan of eggs when I saw him. He was even hotter in person. Actually, hot wasn't even the word: beautiful was. He was seriously *so* tall, and his hair was unkempt and his smile was sort of shy but also sort of flirty, if that makes sense? He wore dark jeans and a John Mayer concert tee that peeked out from under a sporty white Nike jacket, and he walked in a way that was so confident it made me think he must've been right about himself. His eyes were a clear, open brown and he had on these weird orange flip-flops, which I guess weren't all that attractive on a guy, but then again when you lived in Florida and it was a humid eighty-seven degrees at seven PM and socks made you sweat like a vegan in a bacon factory, you learned to get over things like flip-flops pretty quickly. Best of all, his sharp chin was softened by a few days' worth of dark stubble, which I loved. I couldn't deny it: he was *aggressively* attractive.

My anxiety reached a panicked crescendo as I got closer and stopped in front of him. He looked at me, and I wondered what he saw when he did so. His eyes fell on my scar and he looked away, just like everyone did.

But then he looked back.

"What's up, Summer," he said with an easy smile. His voice was deep and smooth and made my skin feel all cold and shivery. "Good to meet you in person, or whatever."

I just stared at him. Some kind of static electricity buzzed in my chest, keeping the words in. But before I could even respond he leaned in and hugged me. Hard. His hands were a little too touchy, maybe, and they lingered on my lower back for a moment too long, but after years of people keeping their distance, I didn't hate it. I could still feel my heart thumping when he pulled away. I didn't hate that, either.

"You look great," he said casually. And then he smiled like he meant it.

"Oh, um, thanks. And so do you. Obviously," I added, but I don't think he heard me.

"Ha," he said. "So…shall we?"

He gave me a hopeful look, and I bit my lower lip again. I'd seen enough reality shows to know what came next: this was the part of the whole "online dating" thing where I had decide whether my match was a murderer or not, and whether I wanted to stay and eat with him or run to the police station and file a restraining order instead.

I smiled. "We shall." *Obviously,* I added again, silently this time.

"Awesome."

He turned to the hostess, who had incidentally been eyeing him the whole time. (Just because my face was damaged didn't mean my eyes were.) "Party of two, please," he said, but she just laughed and looked down at her tablet.

"Honey, there's a festival over at SeaWalk Pavilion today, and the beach is packed like church on Easter. You're looking at a seventy-minute wait, at *least*. You should've called beforehand."

Cooper turned and threw a funny look at me. "Holiday weekend! Seventy minutes! This simply will not do, will it?"

I shook my head, trying to mirror his fake disappointment. He turned back to the hostess with a million dollar smile. "So, it seems that we have reached an impasse. How about the bar?"

Her eyes flashed, her face softening. Mine rolled in the opposite direction. "Well, actually," she said in a newly-flirty voice, "I might be able to, like, set you up at one of the patio tables by the bar, overlooking the water, maybe? If you want?"

Cooper smiled again, and I got the feeling he was used to this sort of treatment. This made me roll my eyes *again*, even though it was sort of attractive on some weird level that I didn't want to think about because it was embarrassing.

"So, what do you say about sitting outside?" Cooper asked me.

"Um… I'm not sure?"

But what wasn't I sure of? A table at the bar, or going on a date with this boy while I was maybe/probably going to die?

The tablet beeped, and the waitress looked from Cooper to me. "Looks like I'm getting requests for that table already. Will y'all be needing it, or…?"

I looked at Cooper, my chest feeling like it had shrunken in on itself, my palms all gross and sweaty. "I mean, are you okay with…with *me*?" I asked quietly, so the hostess couldn't hear. He turned his head a little, confused.

"What do you mean? With what?"

I looked down at myself. "You know…with…the way I look, and everything? With the whole scar thing?"

He blinked, shook his head, and then just sort of shrugged. "That? I barely noticed it."

"…Really?" I asked. He frowned and then pointed down at his chest.

"You know, we all have scars, Summer. If yours are only on the outside, you should consider yourself lucky."

I stared at this strange boy, baffled, and suddenly it seemed like my lungs had forgotten how to process air completely. The world had become a vacuum, and I was sucking oxygen fruitlessly. When I finally gathered my wits and slowed the beating of my heart, I considered my options. I could say yes and lead this boy beside me down a path that could lead to…well, God only knew where, *or* I could politely decline and go back to my normal, grey life. Back to winter.

I looked over at the hostess, cleared my broken throat a little, and for the first time in my maybe-waning life, chose danger.

"I think we're gonna need that table."

4

Eight minutes later we sat at the aforementioned table in silence, the gunmetal grey sea stretching out all around us. The Long Island in my hand was sweet – too sweet to be good, really. I didn't drink much alcohol, orally at least, but I'd dabbled enough to know that this tasted more like off-brand cough syrup from a gas station than a cocktail. In fact, something just seemed off about *everything* all of a sudden. The colors of the restaurant were too bright, I felt fugly in my top, and people kept staring at us and then catching themselves and looking away, because ICYMI, the world sucks and people are assholes. Even in the South sometimes. Cooper looked a little embarrassed about it, actually. It wasn't hard to notice. Being around him after meeting him on a phone rather than, say, in a dog park or something, felt simultaneously way more intimate and way more impersonal – like when you get up close to a computer screen and notice the images are really just thousands of little pixels that together constructed a mocked-up visage. I felt like I'd gotten a projected image of him on the phone, all witty puns and virtual winks, but now that I was with Real Cooper instead of Spark Cooper, I knew things could go anywhere.

"So," he finally said with a little smile, "let me just get the whole Spark awkwardness factor out of the way."

"Okay?" I asked, wondering how he'd guessed what I'd been thinking about.

The smile spread into his dark eyes. "Although we met on a dating application that has basically transferred the human mating experience onto a plasma screen that you hold in your hand, that fact does *not* make us desperate, lonely, or insufficient in any way. We are just two normal twenty-somethings utilizing the unusual means of our times to reach out and connect with others in a world suddenly made lonely by hyper-connectivity. Sound good?"

For a long while I just stared at him again. Because I was the most embarrassing individual on the planet, I sort of awkwardly put my hands on the table and then fidgeted and placed them back in my lap – I guess I never did know what to do with those things.

"Well?" he asked. "How's that?"

"Well, then," I finally said. So there *was* truth in the virtual wink. "I think you just about summed it all up. Wasn't really expecting that level of…well, um, that amount of…you're just smart, that's all."

He leaned forward, suddenly looking fascinated by me for some reason. Honestly, it was hard returning his gaze. He was so intimidating. You know those people who just looked like they were *somebody*? Like they had either come from somewhere, or were going somewhere? He was one of those. In all the faded dilapidated-ness of my modest hometown, he looked as out of place as a dolphin in a desert.

"Ha," he said again. "So, what *did* make you do it, anyway? The whole Spark thing, or whatever?"

"Um. Well. I've never really been good at dating, I guess. And this helped, since it makes things less awkward. In the beginning, at least."

"Same," he said, and I felt my eyes narrow.

"Somehow I don't believe that."

"You'd be surprised."

He looked away, and I took a sip of my drink. I was a total lightweight since I never had anything solid in my stomach to absorb alcohol, which was what kept "normal" people from being waste cases every time they drank, but tonight I definitely needed the help. "And, like, what made you download the app and pick me?" I asked. "If you don't mind me asking."

"Something different," he said automatically. My shoulders fell, and he noticed. "Oh, no, I didn't…I didn't mean it like that. I just meant-"

A waitress arrived with a few waters just in time to rescue us. After she left, Cooper turned back to me.

"You look great tonight, by the way. Really."

"Thanks," I said, but I was a little annoyed that he'd said *really*, as if I didn't already know I looked like this. "So do you," I added quietly.

"Ha," was his only response, once again. We heard some people talking about us, and we both looked over at the same time as two girls giggled pretty shamelessly and then cut their eyes and turned red. My pupils met Cooper's for a moment and the next thing I knew, *we* were averting eye contact, too.

"Yeah," I said as he looked down at the table. "So."

Out of nowhere he looked up at me, a question in his eyes. "True or false," he said. "Humans are inherently good."

"Hmm. Heavy subject for a Spark date, but I'd say true *and* false."

"Explain?"

"Well," I began. "I mean, people are garbage, and the world is kinda shitty. But I think *I'm* pretty good on the inside, and so I'm fine with all that, because my goodness is a sort of a shield against a lot of that, I guess? I don't know. What do you think?"

Cooper smiled again; a big, dazzling, goofy sort of thing. A dizzying *whoosh* of a feeling sank into me, pulling me under with it.

"I don't know," he said. "But that's the best answer I've heard yet. I'm leaning towards the whole 'people are good' thing, or at least I'm trying to, but I'm not quite there yet."

"Easy for you to say," I whispered.

"What was that?"

"I said, that's easy for you to say, that humans are good." I motioned at his general glory.

"You don't know anything about me," he said, except the way he said it made it sound like a warning, as cheesy as that sounds.

"What do I need to know, then?"

"Nothing." Something in his eyes changed. "Hey, your name. You definitely don't meet a Summer every day. Where's it come from?"

"Oh," I said, shifting gears. "Um, I mean, the story is a little awkward, but whatever. I was actually, like, the fifth child my mom got pregnant with, but the first that actually

46

survived through to birth, you know? And so when she found out she was pregnant with me it was the dead of summer and it was boiling outside and she was totally miserable and sick and all that, and so she made a deal with God or whatever that if she could just carry me through the summer, she'd name me after the season. And obviously I survived, so that's why I'm Summer. And I mean, I don't hate the name. I live for the summer. Like, for me the rest of the year is just a countdown to when I can spend my days in flip-flops again. I'm basically only happy when I'm under a palm tree with salt on my skin."

"Don't be so hesitant about sharing stuff like that," he smiled after a minute. "Everyone has sad things in their past. Shit, I could write a novel about mine."

"About your name?"

"That too." Something on his face was kept secret, like an embarrassing middle name in middle school.

The waitress dropped by and asked us if we wanted anything to eat while we drank. I could tell she was pushing us to order food and spend money since we were taking up a table or whatever, and I knew I wouldn't be able to dismiss her with a shake of my head like usual. I panicked a little and looked over at Cooper. This was it: the moment in every budding friendship (or whatever this was) when I had to reveal my Other-ness and see how hard the other person flinched.

"I'm fine, I think," he said, and then he looked at me.

"No, thanks," I said. "I, um, can't eat solid foods, or whatever?"

Cooper looked back at the waitress, barely hesitating. "We're good for now, then, thanks."

"You're not going to ask why I won't eat?" I asked after the waitress rolled her eyes and left. He just sort of shrugged.

"It's whatever. That's your business."

"Oh." I was baffled that he wasn't baffled. Where were the weird stares? The awkward pauses?

47

And then I realized what had been making me feel so weird: I didn't want to believe that someone like Cooper was even being nice to me. (Another Scar of mine was that I was so afraid of people mocking me that I rejected anyone who was kind to me even if their intentions were as pure as Caribbean sand, but that was another Scar for another Scar Story.)

Cooper leaned forward again. I inched back, overwhelmed by the reaction his clean, crisp scent gave my body. Honestly, could he, like, *not*, for a minute? To give myself some time off from being dazzled by him, I opened up the good old First Date Line of Questioning.

"So, how come I've never seen you around?" I asked. "Not that I go out a lot or anything, but I know most people at the beach through mutual friends and stuff. Or I know *of* them, at least."

He looked away. "Oh, um, I grew up in St. Augustine, actually," he said, which was this touristy but gorgeous town forty minutes down the coast. "I haven't lived up here for that long."

"Ah! I love St. Aug. I used to go down there with my family all the time. Their bakeries are, like, *beyond*. Not that I could eat much of what I found at them – I just liked to stare."

"Indeed they are, certainly stare-worthy," he said with a smile that was more than a smile. "What about you?"

"Grew up in Neptune," I said, pointing north. "Nothing too exciting."

"Gotcha."

He took out his phone, and because I was a mature, honest person, I refrained from checking to see if he had any texts from any other girls.

JK! Immediately I scanned the screen and saw an unreadable-from-my-viewpoint text from someone named Taryn, along with several starry-eyed emojis.

He swiped away the text and jumped a little. "Oh, shit."

"What?"

48

He returned his attention to me. "So, you know how people use that 'I've gotta go feed my dog' excuse to get out of a bad date?"

"Yeah," I sighed. "Or, like, I've *heard* of it."

"Well, my dog actually *is* sick, like in real life, and I really do have to go feed her and give her some medicine, since my mom can't."

"Oh."

He was leaving. And why wouldn't he be? I couldn't believe I was stupid enough to think he'd actually been having fun with me.

He put a twenty on the table and got up to leave, just like that. But then he turned around, a little nervous for some reason. "Uh, you're coming, right?"

I froze. "Um, I...I didn't know that was an option?"

"Of course it is," he said. "I just lost track of time when I invited you out, that's all. Do you want to come?"

"I mean, yeah...if you want me to?"

He smiled, his face unfairly beautiful. "Don't be silly – you're coming. Just follow me, I live right around here. And I promise I don't live in a murder shack."

I laughed, but then my expression went slack, the word "murder" reminding me what this really was: a girl on her way to the grave, reaching out and calling this beautiful boy to accompany her. So I pumped the brakes.

"But we're going to your totally-non-murder-shack as just friends, right?" I asked, and he frowned.

"Summer, if you're trying to insinuate that this was all some elaborate date-rape scheme, you can breathe easy, because I'm not that kinda guy. And trust me, even if I was, I would've had *way* better style than Joe's Crab Shack." He motioned at our immensely tacky surroundings and then threw me an incredulous look. "I mean, really? *Joe's*?"

"Shut up!" I laughed as I got up from the table with another rush of dizziness I hoped was Cooper-related and not death-related. (Dizziness and weight loss were mostly what had caused me to get checked out earlier this spring, setting into motion this whole stupid surgery thing.) "It was a momentary lapse of judgment, I don't usually come here. And fine, I'll follow you."

As my sternum vibrated with some foreign and wonderful giddiness, I took out my phone and texted my mom:

Change of plans, Shelly. I'm gonna be home later. Maybe a lot later.

5

Cooper's house was just north of mine in Atlantic Beach, in a cute but ramshackle part of town behind Dairy Queen. He apparently lived in a little guest apartment atop the detached garage of a rambling beach house with peeling sea foam green paint, and I loved it immediately. It didn't bother me that he seemed to live with his parents, because half the guys my age did, too. That's what happened when an entire generation grew up into a world that didn't know what to do with it.

Park behind me, on the grass, Cooper messaged me after I pulled up behind him. He drove a black Volkswagen Beetle, which, like, somehow worked for him for some reason? I was beginning to suspect he could make *anything* work. He was certainly doing a number on my heart, sweat glands, and central nervous system already. Or was I just dehydrated?

I took out my syringe and grabbed a fresh can of Instamilk from among all the mess on my passenger's side floorboard.

Give me five, I responded. **Girl stuff.** Then I parked under a magnolia tree and tried to hide myself in the shadows as I transferred the milk into the syringe.

I won't ask, he said, and that was soon followed by a silly, smiley emoji, which should've been weird coming from a stranger but wasn't for some reason. My face mirrored the emoji's as I lifted up my shirt, unclasped the end of my feeding tube, and inserted the milk, giving me the fuel I would need for whatever was going to happen tonight.

"Hey, sorry," I said after I'd hid everything under my seat and met Cooper in his front yard. The sun had set, and the sky was this perfect shade of pinkish lavender broken up by a few golden-orange clouds. You could hear the waves crashing on the sand two blocks to the east, and a middle-aged woman walking her chocolate Labrador across the road smiled and waved at us. God, I loved our forgotten little corner of the world sometimes.

"Oh," he said as he looked into the dim garage, sounding a little worried, "I wanted to remind you again – my mom's here. Is that cool? Play it cool. We're cool."

"Cool," I laughed. What was the big issue? As far as his mom knew, I was just a random friend. And how could *anyone* play it cool around Cooper Nichols, anyway?

We climbed a rickety outdoor staircase and entered a cramped kitchen. You know how when you were little, your senses were stronger and you could practically put on a blindfold and still tell which of your friends' houses you were in just by how they smelled? Cooper's house had this very bold and distinct scent, something like driftwood, dust, and sandalwood. I looked over and noticed his mom, who was reading a book on the couch while halfway watching *Dr. Phil*. She was long and maybe a little on the thin side of healthy, but *wow*, she was pretty. She looked like one of those models from the '70s that my mom used to worship, with the kind of face that made me want to crawl into a hole: high cheekbones, little button nose that curved up at the end like a ski slope, the whole works. Honestly, I was a little mad that she looked too sweet for me to hate without feeling guilty about it. Her only flaw was her slightly weathered skin, which looked almost too wrinkly to be due to the Florida sun alone.

"Hey, Mom," Cooper said. "This is Summer."

I studied him. He didn't say "my girlfriend," but then again he had no reason to call me that and we'd just met and God, I was a psycho for even thinking that. But he didn't say "my friend Summer," either, which was how I usually got introduced, just so people knew not to assume I was dating their kids. But still…hmmm.

His mother looked over and then glanced at the air above me when her eyes were naturally drawn to my scar. I smiled to let her know it was okay.

"Hey, it's nice to meet you. I'm Summer. Cool house, by the way. Very rustic."

She smiled back as she took my hand. She didn't get up off the couch to greet me, which frankly came off as a little rude – until I noticed how thoroughly her arm trembled as she took my hand. I scanned the room, spotted a wheelchair in the corner, and guessed multiple sclerosis. And I wasn't surprised that she still hadn't been able to make eye contact with me, either. Disease did not necessarily make its sufferers any more or less empathetic or able to deal with things than anyone else. Only they could do that.

And just like that, a few things I'd been wondering about Cooper clicked into place.

"Oh, thanks, yeah, I love it, too," she said, stuttering and halting as she spoke. "It's nice to be so close to the water. And great to meet you, as well. I'm Colleen."

She looked over at her son, still totally confused. A little *too* confused, honestly. I was used to even my mediocre-looking guy friends' families being perplexed with a capital *P* whenever I was brought around, but this took the cake. (Mmm, cake. I wanted Funfetti in or around my mouth immediately.)

"Well, I'm just finishing up my reading," she said. "Have fun, you two. How's your birthday going, Coop?"

He blushed and looked away, cringing. I faced him.

"*What*? It's your birthday? Why didn't you...?"

He angled his body further away, and Colleen sort of politely looked at me like I must've been some random chick off the sidewalk for not knowing it was his birthday. This was getting very awkward, very quickly – but at least I now knew the reason behind Taryn's text.

"It's going well, Mom, but I'm *trying not to make a big deal of it*, so let's not do that," Cooper said, and seeming to understand something, Colleen nodded and got back to her show. "The medicine's in the back, Summer. Follow me."

I followed him down a dark hallway, and something told me to look over my shoulder. Sure enough, Colleen was still staring at me, and before she got all startled and looked away, I noted genuine surprise on her face.

"In here," Cooper said as he turned into a back room and bent into a cardboard box with BEACHES VETERINARY HOSPITAL – FIDO'S FIRST CHOICE written on the side.

"Cool. Happy birthday, by the way!" I said after a pause. "Wish you would've said something, I would've ordered an ice cream Sunday or whatever."

"Ah, thanks, but I really wasn't trying to make anything of it. You know how parents are."

"Yeah. Um, is your dad home?" I asked to move things along, but the expression on his face told me I shouldn't have. "Oh, sorry, I didn't know anything about your dad situation, or, like…sorry," I blushed.

"Nah, it's fine," he said. The air suddenly became very heavy and sort of sad – Waiting Room Air, I called it. "My dad situation is that I *have* no dad situation. My mom was stoked when I was born, but my dad, not so much. He pretended to care that I existed for a few years before leaving one day to 'work on an oilrig off the coast of Louisiana' to 'make a better future for me,' or so he said. A postcard from New Orleans was the last thing we ever got from him. I was eleven. We think he's probably dead now, but nobody really knows for sure."

"Wow, that's – I'm sorry about that."

"Don't be. I hated him. He drank himself nearly to the point of liver failure and we had to take care of him a lot or whatever, so his departure wasn't a huge heartbreak. He was so draining to be around. He left my mom the day she got diagnosed with MS, actually, the dickwad."

"Wha – you're kidding me, right?"

"Wish I was," he said, a hard edge in his voice. "She started getting shaky, dropping things in the kitchen, stuttering her words, you know the rest, and then she went in for testing. When she came home from the hospital with the paperwork one day, he got drunk, grabbed his things, and left. Said it wasn't his burden, and that he didn't want to

54

leave even later down the line and make things even worse for her. It happened on my birthday, actually, which is why I'm still weird about it. I feel like I'm celebrating her pain or something."

I tried not to focus on the last part. "Good god – what an asshole."

"I know. Being my mom's sole caretaker was…not easy, to say the least, but we made it work. Anyway, what about you? Family?"

"Yeah, I kinda know how all that can be," I said, thinking of the little brother I was basically raising as my own, since my mom was always off trying to find a boyfriend and get remarried. Or had been, until The Big News, at least. "Sorry again. But what about me? Um, I live with my mom and my little brother, Chase. He's in fourth grade and he's the coolest. He likes video games and reading and kickball. My parents got divorced when I was eight. No dramatic story to tell, they just sat me down in the Florida room one day and told me they didn't love each other anymore. Equitable division of their meager assets, visits at dad's house every other weekend, etcetera. Nothing too interesting."

"Ha," Cooper said as he found two small boxes of something and started removing them from their packaging. I felt a familiar twinge on the back of my neck as I watched. To be honest I still felt guilty about my parents' divorce and knew I was mostly to blame, not that I would ever tell anyone that. Everyone wanted to think that families heroically Banded Together and Rose Up and Overcome the Odds whenever their kid got sick or had problems, but the reality was that it sucked, and that it was hard on everyone involved. My poor parents had probably envisioned spending their first few years of marriage and parenthood going to dog parks and taking me to the aquarium and going to the beach on the weekends and stuff, not sitting with me in a dark hospital room while we waited for throat tissue to grow. I couldn't even imagine the stress of settling down and starting a family and then promptly having your firstborn spend

55

months at a time in a hospital bed. So it all became too much, and they drifted apart. My dad remarried, of course, and moved to Orlando and acquired two young stepsons through his marriage to Cindy, whom I vaguely liked, I guess. She was nice enough, but she was from the North and she wore a lot of beige and shook hands instead of hugging and didn't eat carbs and/or celebrate most major holidays, so…yeah. Not exactly a match for someone like me. My dad was a cruise ship captain for Royal Caribbean, which was, like, one of those random jobs that nobody ever thought of people having, but that had to get done nonetheless. Cruise ships couldn't park themselves, and everyone couldn't be doctors or lawyers, you know? It annoyed me sometimes, actually. Why didn't anyone ever think of the cruise ship captains instead of the doctors, the Esophageal Intresia sufferers instead of the cancer patients?

"Come, let's go get Hadley," Cooper said.

"Hadley?"

"The dog."

"Oh. Yeah."

We hit the stairs again and went into the dank, faintly mildew-smelling garage below his house. Cooper made a kissy sound, and after a minute a decrepit old miniature dachshund with long, light brown fur came limping out of the shadows. Cooper dropped to his knees and held out his arms, and after throwing a fearful glance at me, the dog rested between his knees.

"Come here, little babykins."

"Aw," I said as I watched.

"I've had her since I was thirteen," he said as he scratched her. "She was my aunt's, and after she got too old to take care of her, she gave her to us. And for whatever reason she latched onto me. She has a tumor in her shoulder, and she won't last much longer."

"Oh, no."

"Yeah," he sighed. "We try to keep her in the house, but she always escapes and comes down here – my mom thinks the cold concrete floor feels good on her fur, I don't know. It's not like anyone ever parks in here, anyway. The owners of the house are snowbirds," he said, referring to the term Floridians used to describe Yankees who spent November to March in Florida and then left once the heat and humidity and hurricanes became too much for their delicate souls. "Hadley's a total weirdo, but I love her. This medicine is just supposed to make her transition peaceful. And God, how am I even gonna get her to take this, since I forgot to stop and get some of that beef jerky she likes? It's like my mom says: sometimes you just gotta jump, and then make your parachute on the way down."

I shivered as Cooper awkwardly stuck some pills into a hunk of some kind of weird doggie salami he'd found in a box in the corner and then coaxed Hadley into eating it. After she'd finally swallowed it with a grimace, he smiled.

"Good girl," he said as he patted her. "You know, this medicine should buy her time, but not much. The vet told us she might not even make it to the Fourth of July."

I fought off the shivers and stood tall and tried to act like I wasn't in exactly the same boat as his dying dog. "Ah. That, um, really sucks. I'm sorry."

"It's okay," he said, love flowing out of his eyes as he smoothed her fur. "She's happy. She's a happy girl."

He got up, grabbed a leash, and turned to me. "Come. Let's take her out before it gets too dark."

"With me?"

He looked around. "…Unless there is some other person standing in this garage that I cannot see?"

"*Oh.*"

He wanted to spend more time with me. What a strange and wonderful concept. "But just as friends, right?" I asked, and his beautiful face lit up like the moon. His smile was effervescent; wrapped in so much charisma, you could've surfed on it.

"Friends walk alone on the beach in the dark."

A playful, electric silence followed. "Sure they do," I said finally. "Just let me put my bag in my car."

The sky was almost black when we hit the beach, or maybe more of a deep purple, but the moon was bright and the bars along the beach were spilling light out onto the sand. Our journey was kept slow by the dog, who was barely waddling along, but I didn't mind.

A passing man smiled at us and fanned at his face, joking about how humid it still was.

"Summer and January," Cooper smiled, referring to the local joke about how our only two seasons were Stiflingly Hot, and Too Cold For The Beach. The man laughed and passed.

"So how come I've never seen photos of you around or anything?" I asked Cooper as a way to get him to talk about himself, praying I didn't sound too awkward.

"I don't know. I'm not really on social media."

"Really? Why not?"

"I just think our generation is way too into all that, and it's embarrassing," he shrugged. "Some things should just be kept private, you know? At the end of the day, who really gives a shit about your boyfriend or your lunch or any of that?"

"Whoa."

"What?" he asked, and I realized I was staring at him like a crazy person.

"Oh, nothing," I said as I looked away, "I just agree, trust me. That's an impressive amount of self-control – I should be more like you. Not that I'm loading selfies every hour or anything, but still, the pressure to be *out there* kind of gets to me sometimes, I guess."

"Wow," he breathed as we drifted into some light from a hotel.

"What?"

"You're just beautiful."

I smiled despite myself. Honestly, this was all a little much – it was like he was reading from a script or something. "Why do you say stuff like that?" I asked, clawing at my left elbow with my hand.

"Because it's true. You're beautiful, and beautiful things don't demand attention. It just gravitates to them." He smirked. "*And* I also have a pathological inability to keep my thoughts in my head, so I guess that factors in there somewhere, too."

"Ah, well, that's understandable." And for at least the second time in one night, I wondered if there was a sudden oxygen shortage on Planet Earth. Was the Amazonian deforestation happening more quickly than expected?

But I still couldn't help it – out of instinct, I turned away and hid my scar with my hand. "You only think that because it's dark," I said under my breath.

"What was that?"

"Nothing," I said as I turned back to him, urging myself not to let my insecurity sabotage this perfect night. "You're not bad, either."

He didn't say anything. We passed a large group of people walking along the edge of the ocean, some swigging from bottles of beer in brown paper bags, some looking up at the stars, others talking quietly. Cooper sighed. "God, I love walking along this beach and seeing all these different people. Isn't it weird to think that every random person you see, every stranger you pass on the street or whatever every single day, is their own person with their own life and problems and hopes and dreams and heartbreaks and defeats and triumphs, none of which have anything to do with you?"

I was silent for a minute.

"I mean, yeah," I said finally. "I haven't really thought about it like that. But yeah."

He pointed at a sixty-ish woman in pink capris walking up on the boardwalk. "See, what kind of lady walks alone along the ocean at night at that age? Did her husband recently die? Or was there ever a husband at all? Was she a circus performer who lost her husband in a freak joint trapeze accident? Like, don't you just walk down the street and *wonder* about people sometimes?"

I bit my lip. To be honest, I really didn't. Not very often, at least. Over the years my condition had forced me to deal with what was right in front of me every day, nothing more, nothing less. I didn't have enough wiggle room for peripheral vision.

But like the terrible person I am, I lied. "Yeah, actually. People watching is, like, my thing. It's especially good in Florida."

"I know!" Cooper said, his childlike enthusiasm intoxicating. "I have, like, a master's degree in people watching. You can learn anything you need to know about the world just by sitting on a pier at sunset, opening up a beer, and paying attention." He paused and then pointed a finger at me. "True or false, Summer: ignorance is bliss."

I shivered in the pre-summer heat once again. "What's with all the questions?"

"Just tell me."

"*Well*, setting aside the fact that I cannot stand annoying, oversimplified clichés like that, I would say that it is absolutely, one hundred percent true, unfortunately."

"Explain."

Trying not to let him read my face, I looked at the sea again and thought back to the person I was when I was young and thought the world was mostly good.

"Okay, well, I was kind of a sickly kid," I began. "And I've seen a lot of fucked up stuff in my life. Like, I'd seen things that would've traumatized an adult by the time I blew out five candles, as sucky as that is. And sometimes I wonder what I'd be like if my life had been…normal, for lack of a better word. Would I be, like, *lighter*? Less cynical? And is wisdom a burden? If I could choose to un-see the things I've seen and un-know the things I know, would I?" I took a breath. "And at the end of the day, I do think I'd go back and change it all, because sometimes it gets hard being…like this." I glanced at him. "But in some cases, I think ignorance is a *good* thing, so…who knows."

I stopped myself, knowing I was getting too deep for first date material, or whatever this was. Around guys I had to constantly check myself to make sure I wasn't, like, revealing too much, letting the Floodgates of Emotion open up too early, but Cooper didn't seem to mind.

"Wow," he said again after a while. "You seem very intelligent, Summer Martin. I like that."

"Hey, how'd you know my middle name?" I asked, which was my mom's maiden name, since she'd had no brothers. Cooper shrugged again.

"I don't know, I guess I noticed it when you flashed your ID to the bartender earlier."

"Oh. And thanks, but don't confuse intelligence with, like, world-weariness. I missed a lot of school as a kid and therefore I can't do geometry or tell you about, like, the fall of the French monarchy or whatever to save my life. But, yeah, if you want to know about Life With a Capital L and The Ways of The World and all that, I guess I'm not a *total* idiot."

He flashed that smile again, luminous even in the dark. "Is that so?"

"I guess," I said, my face warming.

"Good, because naïve people annoy me. What annoys *you*, Summer?"

"Hmmm."

I considered bringing up the Facebook wedding thing but then remembered that the word "marriage" was the single worst thing a girl could ever say on a first date besides, like, "I was born a male" or something.

"Lately?" I asked. "Underwear and responsibilities."

"I get you on that one," he laughed. "And what are your, like, hobbies?"

"Are you really asking me about my hobbies right now?"

"Indeed I am. The way in which a human being chooses to spend their down time can be surprisingly revealing. How do you fill your empty time?"

"Hmm. I don't know," I said as I looked out at the sea. Nobody outside a hospital had ever wanted to know this much information about me, and it kind of felt like diving into the warmest ocean around after the longest, coldest

61

winter in the world. "I don't have many hobbies, I guess. I like to read and watch TV? Oh, and I love Scrabble, even though I'm not great at it."

"Blech. Why?"

"I don't know, I'm just sort of obsessed with odds. They remind me that life is a game of chance, and that you can't control anything even if you wanted to. It saves me a lot of stress."

"Interesting," he said.

"What about you? What do you like to do?"

"Fish, for one," he said. "The verb, not the noun."

I gagged a little.

"What? Don't like seafood?"

"No, I just…this is embarrassing, but I sort of feel bad for the fish. Getting hooked in the mouth and then pulled out of the water to drown in oxygen just all seems so cruel and weird."

"Actually," Cooper said, "you would be pleased to know that fish don't even have advanced enough nervous systems to feel pain."

"*I* feel pain, though," I whispered before I could stop myself. "Too much of it."

"What was that?

"Nothing. I just said that *I'm* still being pained, watching their murders. And it seems unnecessarily difficult way to get dinner, too. Why not just go to the fish market and buy it?"

"I don't know," he said. "Life's supposed to be hard. If your life is too easy, that means you're doing it wrong."

I thought about that for a minute.

"Anyway, I also write," he said. "Opinion pieces. Short stories. A little poetry. Anything."

"Is this, like, your profession?"

"Ummm…"

"What?" I asked.

"Well, I used to do stuff for the newspaper, or, like, the online version of it, but I sort of stopped."

"Why?"

"Well, the thing is, I, um…well, you know, the newspaper, it sort of….they let me go, as they say."

He slumped and stared down at the sand, the human equivalent of a collapsed building.

"Oh, I didn't…um, sorry for asking."

"It's okay," he said, looking like it was definitely *not* okay. "They were downsizing, and since I was only a part-time columnist, well…yeah. That was two years ago, and I haven't worked since."

"At all?"

"At all."

"Well, they're idiots," I finally said. "I'd never let you go."

He bit his lip a little, enticed. "Is that so?"

Oh my God. Did I really say that?

"I guess we'll see," I said, trying to save myself.

"Here, let's pause."

He laid his jacket down on the sand for me and then lowered down beside me. We just stared out at the ocean for a minute, watching the reflection of the moon bounce up and down on the surging black waves.

"Well, looking back on tonight, I'm certainly glad I downloaded that app and then weirdly poured my heart out to you," Cooper said as Hadley rolled around in the sand beside us. "This definitely beats Netflix on my couch."

"I'm glad, too," I said. "And don't worry, you didn't rant. If anyone did, it was me. You're just, like, I don't know…disarming."

"Is that so?"

"Perhaps…"

Our eyes met, and, like gravity, our faces started to pull together.

"You know, if I were brave," he whispered, his cool breath dancing across my lips, "I'd stop myself right now, since you said we're just friends and all. But I'm not."

He leaned in to kiss me just as the world lit up. We both turned to see a dazzling firework pop above the sand dunes, casting a golden glow on the sand and sea. People

63

celebrated the Fourth of July in Florida all summer long, and it wasn't uncommon to see fireworks from spring to August here.

I turned back and saw my reflection in Cooper's eyes, but mostly I just saw my scar.

Scar scar scar. I'm scarred. I'm scarred and doomed and insecure and Cooper's not and I shouldn't even be here.

He leaned closer again as everything faded back to black, and I pushed him away with my hand.

"Oh," he said.

"Yeah."

Ugh. This wasn't right. Everything was messed up, most of all me. I was broken and I was dying and I was a heinous bitch for going on a date with someone the same week I'd learned I had a terminal illness. No matter how hard I was trying to act like one of the flirty Facebook girls with the whole world in front of her, I was a broken adult-child who'd spent most of my life in a hospital, and I just wasn't built for this.

"Um, I should go," I said as I got up.

"What? Why?"

I reached down to my left wrist to fumble with the silver bracelet my dad had gotten me on a work trip to the Bahamas, which I did every time I was nervous, but it wasn't there. I'd lost it. *Shit*.

I bent over and started darting around in the sand looking for it. "Because it's getting chilly and I can't find my bracelet and you're cute and I'm not and everything is all wrong and I just want to go home and take a bath and forget the world exists."

Cooper opened his mouth to respond.

"Just don't ask," I said as I stopped and held up a hand. "I can't explain. I'm sorry."

"Well...I mean, I can see you again, right?"

I stared at him. Had this meltdown not done *enough* to push him away?

"Um, sure," I said. "But only if you, like, want to, or whatever?"

"You're delusional, Summer. Come here." He walked over and pulled me into a hug. With a shiver I tried to ignore how good my name sounded on his lips, and how badly I wanted to hear it again, despite tonight. "You're pretty and funny and you're so empathetic you feel bad for catfish. A dude would have to be far stupider than me not to want to see you again."

I just stared up at him for a minute, getting the acute sensation that I was being pulled into something.

"You're *someone*, aren't you, Summer?" he said next, his brown eyes searching me as they flashed against the stars.

"What?" I asked, shifting my shoulders a little. "We just met tonight. What do you mean?"

His bottom lip disappeared into his mouth. "Well, I'm a writer, and I'm big on characterizing people. I get the sense that you're not a supporting player in this world, but a main character – am I correct?"

I smiled at the inexplicable admiration on his face.

Flirt back with him. Just try this.

"I guess we'll just have to see, won't we?" I asked.

"I guess we will."

"Oh, and Cooper?"

"Yes?" he asked, almost breathlessly, as another firework popped in the low clouds.

"Happy birthday."

I never did find that bracelet. So it goes.

6

On my first real Monday back in the real world since the diagnosis, I tried to go about my routine as normally as possible, just as I'd told Steinberg and Shelly I'd wanted to spend my time. I came into work at 1 PM for a half-day, but for some reason I felt totally irritable all afternoon. I spilled coffee from my syringe all over my pants and was accidentally super bitchy to my boss, but since she was so wrapped up in talking about her latest drama with her boyfriend or something, she barely noticed.

I worked at this tiny marketing firm called *Social* that utilized stuff kids used – e.g., social media – to market them stuff they *didn't* use anymore, like day planners and address books and music players and calculators, basically everything the smartphone had made obsolete. Sometimes I felt a little gross, like I was selling corpses to babies, but the pay was okay and it was really easy as far as jobs went. When I was little everyone had always told me I could be whatever I wanted when I grew up, but they'd forgotten to tell me two very important things: 1. how to grow up, and 2. how to figure out what the hell I wanted once I'd done that. So after college had dumped me into a scary and changing world, I'd decided to find something to do *while* I grew up, and that had led me to this job.

Actually, the phrase "growing up" should've been stricken from the English language in my opinion, because nobody ever grew up. I used to think "growing up" was that one moment when everyone looked around and suddenly realized they'd become Miranda from *Sex and the City*, but these days I was pretty sure it meant accepting that the concept of adulthood didn't even really exist at all, and that everyone you'd looked up to as a child had just been elegantly faking it, like a toddler putting on their mom's heels and jewelry and parading around the house with a candy cigarette in hand. Sure, our modes of dress-up changed as we progressed in age, and cheesy pearl necklaces stolen from our grandmothers' dressers gave way to business suits and blowouts and battered old briefcases, but every time I saw my mom send my little brother off to bed and then take off her Adult Mask for the night, slump against the counter with a bottle of wine in our darkened kitchen, and quietly panic about the state of her life, my childhood faith in the authority of the world eroded just a little bit more.

Anyway, my boss's name was Dakota J. Fanning, I am not kidding, and sometimes I suspected she had hired me solely to make me listen to her rant about her personal issues and be a shoulder for her to cry on whenever her love life went south, which was always. After she talked my ear off about her latest problems I went to my desk to work on some ads for a local author (God knows kids weren't reading books, either) and put in my headphones to give myself some time to think about the Cooper situation. Two days had passed and still he dominated my every thought, and I knew that if I didn't get a handle on this soon, I was going to go even crazier than I had that night of the fireworks.

While I thought, I listened to a TED Talk given by this singer called Saviour, creator of my favorite album, *Pop Killer*. Saviour was actually the stage name of an androgynous, auburn-haired seventeen-year-old from Tasmania or something, but age had nothing to do with talent sometimes – I knew that – and she was a lyrical genius nonetheless. She took the most haunting lyrics that simultaneously mocked the state of youth culture and confronted Big Life Questions, and then spit them over these massive, menacing hip-hop beats that rattled your eardrums and shook your bones. Her music was seriously soul-crushingly sad and was mostly about death and disillusionment and the fear of growing old and stuff, but that's why I liked it. Actually, it was so good it made me look at the speakers when I heard it, made me crave some deeper connection to it than I was actually experiencing, like when you finish a good book and hug it to your chest to somehow soak the words into your soul through osmosis. Sometimes it was comforting to know another human was thinking the same messed-up thoughts as me – it made me feel less alone in my awful-ness. And I guess I liked when something made me feel deeply, while having no real-life consequences. I enjoyed reading words that attacked my soul and made me question everything I thought I knew about the world, and I liked that I could get my heart broken by Saviour's music and then get up and walk to the sea and feel nothing at all. I found it healthy to seek temporary heartbreak in art, especially since real life gave you such a hell of a hangover. After all, wasn't that what constituted humanity in the first place? Seeking out some pretty bullshit to insert the knife and remind us of why we're different from the beasts?

I opened up Photoshop to start ~~obsessing over Cooper~~ doing my job. "This age has turned us into a billion little superstars," Saviour began in her odd, high, crystalline voice. "If you eat it, post it. If you're feeling it, rant about it. If you love it, shout it from the heavens. If you hate it about yourself, hide it with a filter and move on. The truth means nothing if the lie is pretty enough. We run to our glowing screens and throw our edited lives under the lights and bam – it's seen, it's heard, so it matters and it's true. Nothing that happens in the dark actually happens – a tree falling in the forest has to be observed, shared, dissected, backlashed against, and then accepted again, or else it was never a tree, not at all. So hide your broken hearts and smile for the camera phones – we are the new monsters, and the whole world is our stage now."

I turned off the speech as quickly as I could. That was enough Saviour for today.

After Dakota Fanning let me off work I stopped by Publix to get some stuff for dinner. I wanted to make lasagna from scratch and didn't exactly know what you were supposed to put in it, which sounds dumb but oh well, and so I grabbed a cart and got out this cooking app I used for recipes and stuff. On the way into the bowels of the store I passed a rack full of magazines about famous people, and these people had a *lot* of problems. Even more than my boss, actually.

"JEN FIRED FROM NEW MOVIE: PARTYING TO BLAME FOR PREMATURE AGING?" one read. "JULIA GOES UNDER THE KNIFE AGAIN: 'I'VE NEVER LOOKED BETTER!'" another proclaimed. "KATE'S FAMILY WORRIED: TOO THIN, TOO FAST?" a third screamed. "INSIDE EMMA'S NEW DIET: GET THIN FAST!" another read, confusingly. How wrong had I been in my assumption that people were either fat or skinny, ugly or pretty? In the "before" picture of the girl losing all the weight, she looked like a beauty queen and weighed probably 115 pounds. In the "after," she was borderline anorexic. Figures. Our culture forced perfection on you and then told you you weren't perfect enough once you attained it. *Nice fad diet and plastic surgery, but still fugly! Try harder next time, fatty!*

Out of instinct I reached into my bag for my mirror to make sure my scar was still nicely concealed under the ever-present layer of makeup I'd caked over it that morning.

Ten minutes later I was looking for cheap tomato sauce while thinking about what outfit to wear next time I saw Cooper, if I'd even see him again at all. I had this purple dress I looked kind of good in, but then again it showed a rather large surgery scar, and I knew I'd feel self-conscious in it. Or maybe I could just play it cool and wear jeans and a cardigan. Or maybe I could stop being such a callous fucking bitch and stop trying to date someone while I was dying. Whatever. As I browsed, a mother and daughter passed by, and the little girl, who looked about three, pointed over at me from her cart.

"Mama, what's wrong with that girl's face?" she asked as her mom pushed her. "It's broken."

I turned as red as the sauce in my hand as I tried to look away, but I made eye contact with the mom just as her eyes popped out of her head.

"Ana Elizabeth Flores, how *dare* you say-"

Once the mom realized I had noticed, she paused, arranged her pretty features into a desperately apologetic and embarrassed smile, said a quick "sorry," and then pulled her daughter away, muttering under her breath at her until they were out of sight.

"Wow, sorry," someone else said, and I jumped and saw a lanky guy standing behind me. The Publix clerk loading boxes of off-brand seasoning onto the shelves had seen the whole thing. "Babies," he said, shaking his head. "They just don't know any better."

"Yeah, um...yeah."

I tossed the sauce back onto the shelf and darted away, mortified that he had heard.

Mortified that my makeup hadn't worked.

Mortified that I lived in my scarred broken skin.

Mortified that I was me.

Mortified that I was mortified.

Just mortified in general, basically.

I had the house to myself that night since Chase had gone to a sleepover after dinner and my mom was at a "coffee meeting with a friend," which I'd quietly suspected was actually a date from this Christian singles website she was obsessed with, although I didn't say anything. It was gross outside, a light, windy rain falling in sheets against my shingled roof, and because everything else in my life was going to shit, I cuddled up in bed and opened up my Kindle app. My life could be kinda sucky sometimes, and there was nothing that comforted me more than sinking into a good book and immersing myself in a world I knew nothing of and feeling things I would never otherwise feel. If eyes were windows into the soul, books were rabbit holes into the imagination. But my brain was on overdrive and I couldn't concentrate on my book for the life of me, as it was one of the sixteen thousand other books where a petrolifically-named bad boy called Slade Stonewood or Rock Rockford steps away from his greasy motorcycle and/or cage fighting arena long enough to be redeemed by the love of a bookish brunette. Seriously, all the books were the same, and I was *so* ready for something new. Anyway, because I would rather stick rusty pins under my fingernails than let myself be alone with my thoughts for too long, I went into the Florida room and put on last week's episode of some *Real Housewives* type show I was trying to get into. During this episode this one woman I couldn't stand, Gina, was supposed to get drunk and have a meltdown and punch a bunch of people at a fundraising gala for an anti-bullying charity or something, and so I grabbed a bottle of white wine from the fridge and laid myself out on the couch. I injected not one, not two, but three syringes full of wine into my feeding tube, and soon I was doing that thing where you accidentally get drunk alone at home.

To make myself feel less pathetic I grabbed my mom's black-and-white cat, Socks, and tried to get her to snuggle with me so I could at least say I was accompanied by one other soul during my pathetic drinking exploits, but she sniffled – she'd been sick lately – and then marched away with her tail in the air. She'd been having nonstop allergies and her doctors were starting to think she was allergic to feline hair, which would literally mean she was allergic to herself. She had no idea how much we had in common.

As the situation onscreen devolved into chaos and Gina started stumbling through a mansion yelling at people and overturning furniture, my thoughts wandered to Cooper once again. I tried to ignore it, I really did, but soon he was everywhere.

I thought I could do this, fool someone into dating a dying girl. I really did. But I hadn't anticipated feeling like such a lying sack of shit in his presence, and I wasn't sure if I was strong enough to overcome my guilt about my fate and reach for his love. And it wasn't just the surgery thing. It was also a Me Thing. I thought I'd come to terms with myself in middle school, but now that I'd been subjected to Cooper and his almost inhuman perfection, antique feelings were starting to rise within me, floating up to the surface like bad indigestion. I'd always longed to be one of those people who had that weird spark about them, that verve that shifted the gravitational field around them and just attracted good things, made them *pop* and *crack* and *whiz* like lights in the July sky, but I wasn't. And Cooper was. He glowed on the edges like a cloud that blocked the midday sun. And maybe we were too different. The other night had proved that. He was headed for forever and I was headed for an operating room, and we would never be able to close that gap. No matter what my phone had told me, the first few Spark boys who'd called me ugly had been right: I was unlovable, and Cooper and I were not a match. I could press my emotions into my keyboard and send them off into the fiber-optic cables of the world for the sake of dilution and distraction all I wanted, but at the end of the day the too-ancient truth in my too-modern world was that I was all alone and somehow Less Than everyone else and that nobody in the world knew just how cold that felt.

Gina ended up getting arrested for throwing a random Buddha statue at someone's face, and I started to drift off to sleep as the eerie purplish police lights from the television danced across my walls, the opulent violets pulling me into the dark. You know, being strong during the day is easy. Everyone is strong in the light. But when the silence arrives, with no phones or tablets or headphones around to drown out the Human Noise reminding us that we are not enough, bravado falls away and the truth comes. And as the warm fuzziness of sleep started to wrap around me, the rain whispering and tapping at my windows, I was left with one final and ruinous thought: if humans were colors, Cooper was the most dazzling gold in the world and I was a million different shades of the same boring grey.

7

The next day my best friend Autumn stopped by after work, which I guess lifted my spirits a little.

"And speaking of Tyler, did you *see* his ex Michelle Braun's wedding album?" she asked ten minutes into a rambling story about the latest guy she was trying to date. "That girl is *so* over the top. I mean, a dove release after your vows? *Really*? Ugh."

"Yes, unfortunately my eyes were assaulted by that album the other day," I told her as I flipped channels from the couch.

"Ugh. I swear, if that girl were any more low-rent, she'd be a spring break destination!"

I laughed as Autumn took another dramatic sip of her Diet Coke in an attempt to send her quip off into history with appropriate flair. Autumn was…interesting. She was about my age and was a year past her second round of chemo for an outrageously vicious, and early-striking, form of breast cancer. She was sort of in remission, but her doctors had been worried lately, and you know what that meant. We'd met at the hospital when she was first diagnosed and had clicked immediately. Even though her mouth sometimes moved faster than her brain, she was my best friend – one of my only friends, come to think of it, since adulthood seemed shrink my Circle of Friendship smaller and smaller every year – and I loved to meet up with her at Panera and listen to her bitch about life. Basically she was unsinkable, the cancer doing nothing to her famously buoyant personality, except perhaps make her sense of humor even more pointed. She was always going on about the latest gossip, but a lot of the time I felt like she was talking *at* me instead of *to* me. And this might sound mean, but she had a lunch lady body and wasn't exactly as pretty as she thought she was, but that was sort of the point of Autumn in the first place: her delusions of grandeur were strangely endearing. (And I know – best friends named Summer and Autumn? That only happens in impossibly-twee YA novels with cupcakes on their covers, right?! But our seasonally-themed names were one of the first things that had drawn us together, and besides, her name wasn't even really Autumn at all, but Atushmati or some other Indian name that had proved so unpronounceable to Americans that she'd had to Americanize it after moving over at age six.)

"And *why* does it seem like there's a new wedding or baby announcement literally every time I check Facebook?" she asked, and I frowned. Bitching silently was one thing, but I was kind of annoyed that Autumn would talk about this to someone who was obviously nowhere near attaining marriage, either.

"Because we're twenty-four and that's the logical next step," I told her. "To some people, at least."

"Yeah," she said vacantly, picking at her lilac nails. "I guess. But whatever, screw everyone and their dumb weddings. I wanna go to Key West."

"Why?"

"Because I'm miserable here and everyone was just posting spring break selfies from the Keys and I'm dying of FOMO and I just really wanna go to Key West."

"Comparison is the enemy of happiness," I said, as I simultaneously wished I could take my own advice and stay the hell away from Oak Tree of Love girl's profiles. "Stop measuring yourself against the world. And you can't just run away somewhere to get away from yourself. If you go to Key West and sit on a beach with a pina colada in your hand, you're just gonna be unhappy on a beach in Key West with a pina colada in your hand. That's just relocating misery. Not to mention the whole cancer thing."

She blinked and shook her head. "Whatever, Therapist Johnson. I'm sick of staring at a screen, watching strangers live the life I wanted to live. And anyway, I was-" she paused and leaned forward. "Wait. You're distracted, and you're acting all weird and stuff. Or, like, weirder than usual, at least. Are you hurting?"

I fidgeted with my arm and then pawed at my scar out of habit. I'd put myself on strict orders not to tell anyone

74

about the seriousness of my diagnosis, meaning Autumn knew only that there was a surgery, and that there would be a long hospital stay involved. I hadn't mentioned the mortality rate to *anyone*. After all, there was a chance I could survive, and freaking everyone out by telling them about the stakes involved would just be needlessly placing a burden on them, even though to be totally honest I found myself craving the attention at times. Sometimes the grosser parts of me almost wanted to draw people into dark rooms and confess my life-changing news and then soak up the sympathy and tears while they reacted. Growing up, I wasn't the girl all the boys chased around the schoolyard, and eventually I formed some sick, parasitic relationship with sympathy, because sometimes it was the only kind of attention I could get. I guess that's why I shunned all sympathy and emotion now – my disgust at my own attention-seeking ways had forced me to veer in the other direction, perhaps too forcefully.

"No, no," I said. "I'm fine."

She looked down at my chest region. "Um. I just noticed you've lost some weight. Or some *more* weight, I should say, you skinny bitch. Are you sure you're fine?"

I wrapped my arms around myself. The truth was, I kind of *was* hurting, but I always hurt, so I'd learned to ignore it, and if not ignore it, then overlook it.

"Autumn, the whole 'not being able to eat solid foods' thing doesn't really lend itself to morbid obesity," I said, and she blinked again.

"Oh, yeah, sorry, I just...oh my God, *Spark*!"

I jumped and hid my phone under my shirt. Oh, *shit*. Since I'd been reading and rereading Cooper's messages all day, I guess she'd seen the app's telltale red-and-white messaging bubbles on my screen.

"I can't believe it!" she cried. "You're one of *those*."

"What's wrong with Spark-ers?"

"I mean, don't get me wrong, I have one," she scoffed. "I've just accepted the fact that you are better than me in every way, and I do not approve of you using a

75

hookup app. The big sister in me wants to take you out back and spank you, actually."

"But you're younger than me," I said.

"Uh, yeah, by like three months. Anyway, why did you get it?"

"I don't know. And, actually, um…I kind of met up with a guy off it the other night – nothing sketchy," I added after she threw me a look, deciding to just vomit it all out, "just for a drink, and we didn't *do anything*, or whatever. We just talked. But he was really cute and nice and funny, and I think I kind of embarrassed myself at the end, and I don't know how to fix it, or if I even *want* to fix it. Like, I'm not sure if I should let myself be with him. *Because of the stomach tube and stuff,"* I said quickly, to keep from tipping her off about the whole death thing.

"Oh, shut up," she scoffed. "We have just as much of a right to get laid as anyone else out there, healthy or not. But no matter what you do, do *not* use a winky face."

"Why not?" I asked, thinking of the winky emoji Cooper had sent me that night.

"Because a winky face is a universal sex invite, everyone knows that. You'd might as well say 'Hey, I'm just lying in bed in some trashy lingerie, wanna stop by?' Which is fine, obviously, but you don't want to give it up too quickly. Personally, I wouldn't have sex with him until your second hangout session."

"*Second?*"

"Is that too long?"

"Ugh," I sighed. "Never mind. Calm your tits, I haven't even said anything to him yet."

"Gross, don't say 'tits.' And who is this boy, anyway?"

"Nobody special," I lied. He was totally special, but for some reason I didn't want to say his name out loud. He was *my* secret to creepily obsess over.

"Well just wait and see what happens. You've got nothing to lose, right?"

I looked away.

"Oh, I didn't mean it like that, Summer, I just, like…"

"It's fine," I said. "I fully understand that I am the most single person that ever single'd."

"No, no, Spark is good for you! Because they don't have to meet you right off the bat, and-"

She stopped again. This reminded me of another facet of Autumn, besides her perkiness: she also had some serious problems in the whole "accidentally being horribly offensive" department.

She walked up and gave me a hug. "I'm gonna stop while I'm behind," she said quietly. "I know we face the same issues. We're 'sisters in sickness,' to quote that annoying chaplain lady at the hospital, God bless her soul. But my foot is so far up my mouth, I'm choking on my knee. I'm taking my fat ass to the elliptical, or I'm gonna try to, at least. See ya later. Text me if you need any more advice."

"I think any more of your 'advice' would make me end up pregnant and in a halfway house. But hold on. Before you leave, check the top shelf of my fridge."

Autumn went into the kitchen and then came out with a trembling bottom lip, holding the Funfetti cake I'd made for her with the words RIP GRANDPA written in yellow icing on top.

"Summer," she said. "You remembered."

"Of course I remembered," I told her, referring to the one-year anniversary of the death of her grandfather who'd basically raised her, since her parents hadn't been able to emigrate from Sri Lanka with her right away. "I mean, you made such a production out of the funeral, it was hard *not* to remember it."

"Seriously, Summer. You are such a good friend. You're the best person I know and I don't deserve you. I'd hug you if I didn't have this cake in my arms. So go out and slut things up, babe. You deserve someone. You deserve *love*. And not to mention that you've always been the cute one out of this friendship, and I harbor a deep resentment towards you for it, so you'd might as well take advantage of that."

"Whatever, stop being a weirdo. You know I like making cakes more than I like eating them. For obvious reasons," I added with a giggle, which she mirrored.

"Okay, well, thanks, and don't ask for a piece, because this cow is eating the whole thing by herself. Fuck marriage, I'm hungry."

"Couldn't if I wanted to!" I called after her, and at precisely the same moment as the door slammed behind Autumn, my phone pinged with a message that made me feel like I'd just been drenched in a bucket of ice water:

It's Cooper. I know your secret

8

So, here's the thing: as I mentioned before probably a hundred times, when you basically grew up in an ICU, where you're woken up two or three days a week by the wailing of parents whose kid had just died, you learn to see the world for what it was, not for what you wanted it to be, or what you hoped it would become. This had served me quite well so far. I was logical. I was levelheaded. I could tell you everything there was to know about bedpans and IV drips and how to dress a stomach bandage.

Unfortunately this life had taught me nothing about how to text tall cute boys with messy hair and goofy smiles and muscular forearms and improbably good taste in music.

After I regained the ability to breathe, I huddled on the couch and wrote (and then rewrote) about ten different messages to Cooper with trembling fingers, scared shitless of what he knew, and how. What I was doing terrified me, sure, but I was sick of being scared – I felt like a coward or a weakling or a shut-in or a closeted Evangelical or anyone else who was ruled by fear. Autumn's words – *you deserve someone* – had been ringing through my head for an hour, and I wanted to agree with her.

You do? I finally asked, and by this point the sun was setting.

Indeed I do, he said, and for a moment it felt like all the oxygen in the world had evaporated yet again.
You've been driving yourself crazy because you can't stop thinking of me, and all you want is to see me again.

My relieved sigh was audible even to Socks, who glared at me for making a ruckus and then sneered his way off to find somewhere quieter.

Am I right? he asked after I didn't respond.

79

You may be right. You may be wrong. Some things are just better left unshared.

Meet me at the Ritz tonight, and tell me in person, then, he said immediately, which was one of the nicer bars in town.

Why? I asked as my whole body vibrated with something between panic and excitement.

Because it's a beautiful night and I'm alive and I would like to be standing in a chilly bar next to you?

For a while I just sort of stared at the screen. I felt warm and funny and a little dizzy, like I'd just jumped off a roof and was falling through warm air. I really *had* to train myself to stop acting like such a moron with him, I told myself silently.

Too much? he asked a moment later.

Oh, no, no, I typed after I'd snapped out of it. **I was just caught off guard.**
I'd love to, I said, the word *unclimbable* ringing in my head as I typed, **but right now I'm busy :/**
Sorry

Can we at least text then? he responded.

Why? I asked.

...Because I like talking to you?

Well, then. Suddenly I remembered that my face was covered in tiny little hairs, because they all stood on end at the same time, giving me this weird feeling like I'd been kissed by a cold phantom wind.

"Who are you texting?" Shelly asked as she breezed into the kitchen, a bag of groceries in hand. "And what is that look on your face about?"

"Nothing," I said after a pause that was a bit too long. "Autumn wants info on a guy who lives down the street. What's for dinner?!"

So Cooper and I texted. And texted. And texted. We didn't talk about much, just the usual stuff you have to get out of the way with someone you don't really know: siblings, interests, how horrifically awkward it was that you'd met online, etc. Of course I would've already known all this if he'd had a Facebook to stalk, which he didn't, which I kind of loved. His distance from the rest of my generation just made him even more attractive. He was twenty-five, had no siblings, and was still sort of vague on a lot of other things, just like he'd been on the first night. But I didn't care. We mostly talked about me, actually, which was, like, really unusual and cool for some reason. I'd never had anyone besides hospital administrators ask me so many questions about myself, and I kinda loved it.

Wait, I said half an hour into a conversation about the best bars in Jacksonville Beach (or Jax Beach, as the collection of local beach communities was called), not that I had much insight into the matter. **It's one in the morning.** How had time gone by so quickly? **I have work at nine. I need to crash soon.**

But I'd rather keep you up, Cooper responded, making my whole body jump.

Enticing, but I'd rather not fall asleep at my desk tomorrow, I said, trying to keep it cool.

Fine, he typed. **If I must, let me bid you adieu. Goodnight, Summer.**

81

Goodnight, Cooper.

I'm kinda glad I downloaded Spark, he said next, and I smiled with everything in me and then threw my phone across my bed so I wouldn't say anything else and betray my feelings, cutting him off before I could cut myself off. (After all, who would I be if I didn't run from what drew me in?) I didn't want to go to sleep – that meant there would be eight more hours until I could talk to him again – but I knew I had to, and so I put on one of Saviour's more upbeat tracks (if that is even possible), called *Blood on the Dance Floor*, and hoped to quell the happy chaos in my head long enough to let Saviour's crystal voice carry me into the oblivion:

I hate all these assholes and the feathers in their hair
Liquor in plastic cups, disco ball sparkles, but idiots are
everywhere
Why does it seem like all I got to offer is this vacant stare
Ugh, I just can't take me anywhere

But tonight I'm gonna dance 'til there's blood on the dance
floor
Until I believe you don't mean a thing to me anymore
And tonight I'm gonna dance 'til there's blood on the dance
floor
Until I don't hate you and me and my friends anymore

My father tells me tomorrow's no guarantee
Be young and wild, baby, run free
But if this is all I have, this one ride
Then why's it feel like my heart's on ice?

So tonight I'm gonna dance 'til there's blood on the dance
floor
Until I forget that you're the one my pulse beats for
And tonight I'm gonna dance 'til there's blood on the dance
floor
Cut me open, baby, I'm yours, don't push me away anymore

(Blood on the dance floor)

~

Cooper texted me first the next morning, which was a huge relief, since I obviously didn't want to do it myself and come off like some overeager psycho. I was distracted at work all afternoon, and he was deliciously to blame. I screen-shotted (is that even a word? Or is it screen-shat? Oh well) some Facebook pictures to him and we made fun of Oak Tree of Love girl, whom we'd both worked with in the past, and soon we agreed that her Public Displays of Matrimony were both unnecessary and embarrassing. After I got home and made some pork chops for Shelly and Chase, I retreated to my room and got deep into a very serious text war with Cooper over the merits of regular coffee vs. decaf (of course decaf *had* no merits, but he said regular made him too jumpy, so I indulged him in the debate) when suddenly the convo changed course:

Can I call you? he asked.

Sure, I typed with a feeling I'd only previously gotten after injecting champagne into my stomach tube last New Year's Eve and feeling the little golden bubbles rise up into my broken esophagus. **Call away.**

I smiled for the millionth time that day. Calling someone was creepy unless you scheduled it out beforehand; I knew that from work, and just from, like, being alive in the 21st century. But it was cute that he actually played by the rules. I *liked* following the rules sometimes, even if "the rules" themselves were kind of stupid and weird and archaic.

"Hello there," he said when I answered. "How goes it?"

"Hmm. It's going."

83

"I would like to hear more about these goings-on, but in person, perhaps?"

I paused. "Are you asking me to hang out?"

"Oh, come on, did you really think I'd be content talking to you on the phone forever?" he asked. "I am, indeed, asking you to meet up. Or not so much asking as telling, actually. Come to the Ritz with me tonight, Summer."

I got this happy/panicky feeling as soon as he said my name. As I picked at my cuticle I wondered when this butterfly-ish stuff would go away, and then I wondered if I wanted it to.

"That sounds quite demanding," I said.

"I am nothing if not a demanding tyrant. Couldn't you tell? No, seriously, come. I was meeting some friends, but they bailed on me."

"So that's it?" I asked, laughing. "I'm just a replacement hangout partner?"

He paused. I could hear that he was nervous. "It's not just that. I don't know, I kind of, like, enjoy talking to you, and I'd like to do it some more, I guess."

I gave myself a chance to back out, but I knew I wouldn't be able to: my whole chest suddenly filled up with this cool, breezy, giddy sensation that felt like letting go of something. "Okay. Why Ritz?" I asked, trying to hide the smile in my voice.

"…Because we live in a beach town in Florida and it's almost summer and there's nothing else to do?"

"Touché. I'm sorta busy now," I said as I looked around my empty room, "but I can meet you there at, like, ten. Is that good?"

"My mind has been read. Can't wait. But first, let's make some ground rules."

"Ground rules?"

"Yep. Did you not hear me say I was a tyrant? Let's start with number one: no storming off this time. Sound like a plan?"

I laughed from the bottom of my stomach. "Okay. Tonight will be a storm-off-free zone. I promise. Unless you turn out to be a psycho criminal, or something."

"Point taken. And number two: you must promise to actually let me in, instead of shutting me out again."

I hesitated a little. Why did he even care? "That's one's negotiable," I said. Although I had a PHD in Pushing People Away with a minor in Putting Walls Up, I told myself to think about it. "And besides," I went on, "we're just friends, so none of that matters. Any more diva demands?"

"Yes. When you forget about this ridiculous 'just friends' bullshit and inevitably become overwhelmed with physical desire for me and attempt to sexually molest me, I hereby vow not to tell your friends about it and embarrass you."

"Okay, I'm hanging up now," I said, even though I didn't want to hang up at all. "See you soon, you diva."

"Oh, and speaking of that, I actually have one other demand: wear a bathing suit under your clothes."

"Huh? Why?"

"Just do it, please?"

"Fine," I said. "I usually do that anyway in the summer, but not to go out. But whatever, Mr. Prima Donna. Only for you."

When I got into the car a few minutes later I stopped to feed myself some milk. As I maneuvered around in the dark car, some of the liquid squirted all over my stomach (PS: "squirt" is such a gross word), and I had to find some wipes and clean myself, cursing under my breath all the while. I couldn't hide the stomach tube forever – how was I going to tell Cooper about all this stuff without revealing the news about the big surgery? I mean, sure, my scar had told him that something had obviously gone wrong in Summer World, but how did I tell him about the rest? Everyone had baggage they inevitably had to lay out after a few dates: their parents were divorced, they'd gotten arrested for underage drinking at the beach when they were seventeen, they made a really weird

85

sound whenever they yawned, etcetera. But my baggage was on another level. How did you say, "*Hey, Date. I was born without a working throat, and I have a tube sticking out of me, and I have a life-threatening surgery scheduled for the end of the summer?*"

And why did I even care in the first place? Usually I tried not to worry too much about my health, as I found worry to be a dreadfully useless emotion, the equivalent of drowning in a kiddie pool on a clear day. Either fix a situation, or accept the unfixable – that was my viewpoint. And I'd mostly accepted mine. Some girls got married, and I just got milk farts. And that was okay! Or it had been, at least, until this mental break of the past few days.

I gripped the wheel with both hands, closed my eyes, and gave myself a silent pep talk. Despite the odds, I'd found a beautiful, funny, kind boy who was not grotesque in any way and who came from a sick mother and was therefore somewhat able to look past my health issues, and I did *not* want to fuck it up now. I literally couldn't afford to.

Stop fucking second-guessing yourself, Summer. Your situation does not make you inferior to this boy. You are worthy of love. This hot guy totally wants to hangout with you tonight, as crazy as that sounds. Wait – d'oh! That's not crazy! Worthy of love! Worthy of love!

I took a breath, threw my car into gear, and headed for whatever was waiting for me.

9

I met Cooper at the street corner by the Ritz in downtown Jax Beach at precisely 10:09. I'd been noticing little details like that lately, I didn't really know why. More little details I couldn't help but notice: he wore khaki pants and a dark green shirt, and his hair was combed and looked much sleeker than last time. He looked beautiful in an almost irritatingly easy and carefree way, and once again it baffled me that he was even meeting me.

"Well, hey," he said after he hugged me. He looked weirdly happy to see me, or maybe that was wishful thinking on my part. "You look great."

I wondered if I would ever get used to him lying. I was wearing a lackluster blue dress, and my dark-blonde hair looked like it always did. A disastrous attempt at a trendy bob last year meant that it was currently just past shoulder-length, with super long bangs that I often found myself trying to drape over my scar when I felt embarrassed. But I smiled anyway.

"Thanks, sir. So do you."

"Ha." He held out his arm. "Shall we?"

I locked my elbow with his as a thrilling little shiver ran up my side. "We shall."

And off to the bar we went – but not before flirting with disaster. I looked away when the bouncer took my ID and inspected my face with the flashlight, and he got all mad and told me to look back at him because he suspected I was avoiding him because I was underage, and I couldn't bring myself to do it because I felt awkward, and the whole thing was just generally an uncomfortable mess on every level. (And was it a job requirement for bouncers to be the the the most deplorable cretins on Earth, or was that just at the Ritz?) But Cooper barely noticed, thank God, or at least he pretended not to notice, which I've learned is the same thing. After the bouncer finally let us in, we made it to the bartender, and Cooper ordered us two Bud Lights without asking me what I wanted. I didn't really like that, but then he paid for them, which I did like. Next we found a quiet-ish spot in one corner of the winding bar that populated the center of a huge, wood-paneled room. Then the silence came. People were walking by and glancing from Cooper to me and then giving us weird looks, and I felt a little strange. Seeming to notice, he gave a furtive little look and turned to me.

"So, I have a confession to make: I lied."

"You did? About what?"

He smiled. "When I agreed to come here as just friends, I was lying. I don't wanna be just friends with you, Summer."

I turned away. "Oh."

Could he see what I was feeling? To plow through the weirdness I sipped my beer. It wasn't easy, and it kind of felt like trying to squeeze a large boulder through a Chinese finger trap, but somehow it stayed down. "Thanks. And thanks for the beer." I took a breath. "...And sorry for my little meltdown the other day, by the way."

"*Meltdown*? There was no melting down involved. You were fine, Sum. We all have our moments."

"Sum? My mom calls me that!"

"Damn it, I thought I just made it up."

"Not quite." I looked around a little. "So, do you Spark a lot? Is that even a word? Or should I say Spark-ize?"

"Yeah, no, I believe the verb is the same as the noun, like fish. And no, I don't use it much. What about you?"

"You're the first," I said, and he smiled. "Why is that a good thing?"

"I don't know – I just like being the first, for some reason."

I looked away, praying I wouldn't vomit from either nerves or butterflies or Intresia, as another Saviour song came on called *I'm Here*, a more hip-hop sounding one where she murmur-rapped over a gigantic beat. I watched as Cooper mouthed every single word along to the song:

I'm coming

Fuck what you thought, I'm coming
Fuck what they said, I'm coming
Laugh at my youth all you want
I'm coming

I'm not what you think I should be
Girl in the clothes of a boy, with the brain of a freak
But fuck y'all, and fuck what you think
Your prescribed notions of what a human should be

Just 'cause I'm young doesn't mean I haven't been knocked
off my feet
And just 'cause I'm small doesn't mean I haven't been out on
these streets
I came up from nothing, and that is no small feat
'Cause the chase for glory is what makes the muscle in this
chest beat

So I'm coming

With this thing here I wrote, I'm coming for the future I'm
owed
You may think I'm owed zero, but my talent made it so
Got a hum in my bones, a rumble in my ears
Gonna be brave like my brother, rise up, face these fears
So I'm coming

Fuck it

I'm here

"You're really interesting," I said, letting it spill out before I
could stop it, the beer already in my bloodstream.

"Thanks. So are you."

"No, like, really." I knew that in the morning I was
going to regret this like I regretted my first email address,
but I pressed on. He was a twenty-five-year-old guy who
knew a Saviour song, for God's sake. "I mean, like, a lot of

89

people you meet every day are the same. But you're not. I know we just met, but from what you were saying over texting and whatever, it seems like you…see things differently. It's almost like you're seeing the world through different glasses, or something? I don't know."

"Well," he laughed, "for the record, my eyesight *is* remarkably bad."

I took a breath. Suddenly I wanted to know everything about Cooper, and see everything he had ever seen, and experience every feeling he had ever felt, and that scared me. A lot.

"So what did you do today?" I asked him.

"Helped with my mom, pretty much. We had a hospital bed installed, so I was pretty busy with that."

For someone who had been raised by a team of nurses and counselors just as much as my parents, that seemed a little off. "Oh. Didn't insurance install it? Don't you have, like, helpers?"

He avoided my eyes. "Well…it's a weird situation. That's part of why we moved here, actually. She lost her insurance last year, and we couldn't afford our house anymore, so we had to find a place up here that was closer to her new Medicare hospital."

"So you're the *only* one who helps? Wow. I can't imagine."

"Yeah," he said with a distant frown. "I love my mom, and I would never complain, but…yeah. It's hard. Middle-of-the-night errands, grabbing things for her all day, it goes on and on. She pushes me to the edge sometimes, bless her heart, but God, I love her."

Suddenly a drunken guy stumbled into the wall and then fell hard at my feet, knocking his head against the wooden base of the bar.

"Oh my God," I said, leaning down to help him. I brushed off some of the beer he'd spilled all over his leather jacket and then helped him up. "Are you okay?"

"Thanks," he slurred, his eyes vacant. "Turns out forgetting Jobeth wasn't as easy as I thought it'd be."

"Huh? Jobeth?"

He mumbled another thanks and then went on his way, and as I watched him go I thought about how *Forgetting Jobeth* sounded like the title of some tragic, poetic novel about a man escaping to the mountains to get over his dead girlfriend or something. Then I felt eyes on me and turned to see Cooper watching me, some weird look on his face.

"What is it?"

"That was just nice of you," he said. "Most people would've scoffed at that guy and looked away."

"It's whatever," I said as the last of *I'm Coming* faded away.

"No, really, it was. You're a good person. Why are you cringing so hard?"

"Oh, um…sorry. I'm just not used to people looking at me like that, I guess. Or at all. Sorry."

He tilted his head. "You know, I don't get the way you talk about yourself, Summer. Not at all. You'd think you were Quasimodo or something."

"Ugh," I said as I shook my head and motioned at myself. "That's not it. It's just that, like, I know I'm not pretty, and I have this scar, and sometimes it gets awkward. I'm not trying to get all Debbie Downer on you, but, like, I have some issues, and I'm not attractive. I get that."

"I know you're not attractive," he said. "You're above that: you're hot. You've got that whole hazel-eyed, dark-blonde, freckled, beachy girl thing going on. I'm into it."

"What? I-"

I paused. I had never been called "hot" by a boy before, and *especially* not one that I would call hot, too. Was it crazy that I didn't hate it?

…And that I actually kind of loved it?

"Thanks," I said. "But it's fine. I get the whole 'scar' thing. It's just weird sometimes. You're probably used to the platinum blonde Jax Beach bimbos. Girls that…I don't know, girls that *glow*," I said as I impersonated their prissy little arm movements.

"Is that right?" Cooper asked, looking amused for some reason. "Girls that glow?"

"Yeah, and it's no big deal, but, like…"

"Come on," he said as he headed for the door. "I already paid for the drinks."

"What? Wha – where are we going?"

He turned around with some weird smile on his face. "Do you trust me?

"I mean, yeah, I guess?"

As much as I can trust a total stranger I just met on some dating app, I added to myself.

"Come, then."

"But *why*? What is with you and your physical inability to stay in one place for longer than five minutes?"

He smiled down at me just as *You Know I'm No Good* by Amy Winehouse started thumping from the DJ booth. "I'm gonna make you glow."

~

We walked down to the boardwalk along the beach and then turned south. It was super dark, the surf shops and touristy restaurants mostly closed up for the night, but I felt pretty safe. Outside the only crowded bar, a group of Jesus people yelled stuff at the partiers on the porch and waved signs reading "GOD FORGIVES – REPENT NOW, SINNERS" and "EVEN THE WICKED LIKE YOU CAN FIND REST IN HEAVEN." Hailing from a shadowy corner of Christianity, the group came to Jax Beach to scream and hand out Jesus pamphlets about one night a month, and their habit of attempting to recruit people to join God's ranks at a *bar* of all places struck me as equal parts bizarre and hilarious. Cooper and I exchanged knowing glances as we passed them, and I giggled despite myself, wondering if he knew how badly I wanted him to take my hand. We finally turned at the entrance to the fishing pier that jutted out a quarter of a mile into the waves of the Atlantic.

"We're going fishing?" I asked.

"Shh," he said. "Brenda," he nodded as we passed the large security guard, who sat on a flimsy chair reading some sort of romance novel. She looked up, smiled, nodded, and waved us in.

"Cooper, the pier is closed, and it's really dark," I said. Somehow his name felt well-worn in my mouth already, like a sweet old lady's hands or a cruise ship comedian's jokes. "What are we doing?"

"Just wait and see. Walk with me."

There was a jump in his step, and it was cute. We walked out into the night, and the sounds of town faded away. Halfway out I looked back and gasped a little: the view was beautiful. The towering condo buildings piled up against the shore like runners at a starting line, their lights blazing white and yellow, as the waves shined a silvery blue in the moonlight.

"Wow," I said as we walked.

"What?"

"The view. Haven't you seen it?"

He turned around and looked at me. *Really* looked at me. I felt even more exposed than when you have to stand in those X-Ray machines at the airport and hold your hands up and try to act like a group of men isn't staring at an image of your naked body.

"My eyes have been busy doing other things tonight," he said darkly.

Oh.

When we reached the end of the pier, he stopped and began removing his clothes without explanation. He motioned for me to do the same, and I tried not to look at his thinly athletic body as he took off his shirt.

"Um, explain, please?"

"We're jumping," he said.

"Jumping?"

"Yeah, jumping. I've done it a million times, it's fine. You wore a bathing suit, right? I was thinking of going hot-tub-diving later tonight, but this is way better."

I looked down at my dress. "Um. Yeah. But my clothes, and my phone, and my-"

"Your stuff's fine," he said as he stood in his boxer-briefs. "Brenda won't let anyone else out here. We can walk back out and get it all. It's fine."

I stared at him. "You're seriously trying to get me undressed on our second date, or whatever this is?"

"Of course it's a date," he said. "And…wait, why are you looking at me like that?"

The wind whipped between the pilings below us. "Well, it's just that…um…nobody has ever taken me out on a date before, that's all."

His head turned. He wasn't expecting that, I guess. "Really? At twenty-four?"

I stared at him for what felt like forever, feeling stark naked. Finally he turned, shook his head, and approached the railing. "And fine, don't take off your clothes. Have fun sinking to the bottom when you are overwhelmed by the weight of soaking wet cotton! Just come on, trust me. I won't even touch you or look that hard, I swear."

I hesitated. The thing was, in my haste to get ready, I'd put on a two-piece instead of my usual one-piece, meaning I'd have to show my stomach. But oh well: he was asking for it.

I reached down and lifted up my dress to just below the white tube sticking out of my lower left abdomen and the surgery stars crisscrossing my trunk and lower neck area. The truth was, I was technically disabled, although I had accepted this fact to varying degrees throughout my life. Because being disabled makes you Other, and that erases you, because nobody in the world wanted to be Other. Your genes told you to find a suitable mate, and that meant someone who was strong and capable, someone who carried good genes – not someone defected like me, because I would produce less-than-perfect offspring. So I literally repulsed

94

people on a genetic level – I was logical enough to acknowledge that, and human enough to admit that it broke my heart. But I hadn't always been like this. By a certain age I'd started trying to hide and deny my disability by doing anything I could to be seen as One Of The Normal Kids. During one particularly pathetic period of denial, I tried to join the track team in high school and then saw my two-week career as a runner go up in flames when I fell on my face during a track meet with the Florida School for the Blind, single-handedly making my school lose the entire meet. Now, losing a running contest to a bunch of kids who could not see was a very specific kind of humiliation that I would not wish on even the most distant of frenemies, but it did lend me a certain humility that I carry with me to this day.

But I was done hiding, if only because I no longer had the energy. So I closed my eyes, took the dress off completely, and waited for his response as I stood there in all of my scarred glory.

"And...?" he finally asked. "What are you waiting for?"

I finally opened my eyes. "This is a feeding tube. I get milk through a tube. I can't eat, Cooper. Like, at all. Anything. It makes me barf. Just so you know."

He just stared at me and then grabbed my hand, pulling me to the edge of the pier. "Summer, if you wanna scare me, you're gonna have to pull some hidden tentacles out of your bra or something. My mom's in a wheelchair, so a little health issue or two is nothing for me. Anyway, you ready?"

A smile rose from somewhere deep within me and parted my lips. And I couldn't explain why, but suddenly I felt like the lightest person alive. "Tentacles? Ew. And I guess. I mean, yeah. Let's do it."

We climbed the railing. I held my breath. And together, we jumped.

Now that my life had a possible expiration date, why did it feel like I'd only just started living?

10

We freefell for a few moments, and just as my stomach got that gross falling feeling, we hit the water with dual thuddy-splashy sounds. Immediately we started rising and falling with the waves, out in the middle of the sea. It was weird, and fun, and I had never done anything like it before. There was this greenish glow on Cooper's face from the stars, and he was just beautiful.

"Look down," he whispered, and so I looked down and gasped again. "It's phosphorescent plankton," he said as I stared at my glow-in-the-dark skin. You know how little bubbles form on the inside of a champagne glass and then rise to the surface? That's what was happening, except they were forming on my skin in a beautiful neon green color, and then they'd, like, zigzag away from me whenever I moved. My skin was sparkling, and for all the world it looked like I was emitting little green champagne bubbles. "My friends and I learned about this the first time we broke into the pier after dark and drunkenly jumped off," Cooper explained. "We looked down and noticed that we'd lit up like fireworks. It was crazy, and we've been doing pier jumps every year since then." He paused and licked his lip. "But anyway, now you can see what I see. You were wrong, Summer: you *do* glow."

The subject of my scar left my brain, along with all the hatred I regularly pointed at myself, and suddenly it was just me and Cooper. Us. All at once the cruel words of supermarket strangers and gawking passersby faded away, and for the first time in my life, I truly believed I was beautiful.

Cooper reached up and touched my face.

"You said you wouldn't touch me," I whispered.

"I lied. Sue me."

He ran his finger along my lip and then started going up my cheek, and I took a breath as he brushed over my scar. For the first time ever, I didn't flinch.

And neither did he.

"You're beautiful," he said quietly as we treaded water like puppies under the night sky. "Really. You have this…I don't know, this grace. You carry the light, my friend."

I rolled my eyes.

"Come on," he said. "Haven't you noticed how people act around you?"

"Um, by staring?"

"No, not at all. It's the craziest thing, but they, like, act *better*. They pull up their shoulders and speak softly and mess with their clothes. I noticed it both nights we've hung out, with waitresses and bartenders and just random people and stuff. It's like you make them feel inferior just by being yourself."

"Is this your '*thing*?'" I laughed after a minute. "Like, do you just go around doing crazy things like this for shy, vulnerable girls? Is this what you *do*?"

"You're not vulnerable, not really," he said. "The way you look at people, the shine in your eyes…there's a strength under there, whether you know it or not."

I tried to push down the golden feeling I was drowning in. *Come on, Summer, you're acting like the annoying Facebook girls.*

He laughed a little and then pulled away and started swimming ashore. I was dreading getting out of the water again, because that meant he'd be able to see my stomach in all its splendor, but I followed him anyway, trying not to think about all the sharks and stingrays and eels and feelings and all the other deadly, terrifying things that were circling us at that very second, maliciously plotting our bloody deaths.

"Doesn't this scare you?" I asked Cooper as we swam.

"What?"

"Oh, I don't know, this whole '*swimming in the pitch-black ocean in the middle of the night*' thing?"

He turned around. "I fear the unknown. And I know what's in this ocean. Therefore, it does not scare me."

"Oh. What *is* the unknown to you, then?"

"Everything else. The future, mainly."

"Okay then," I said, and kept doggie paddling. As we swam I thought of the stars, and whether anyone up there knew or cared that I was floating in a sea of surging liquid on a doomed planet with a boy I liked and enjoyed and wanted desperately to like me back.

"Are you okay?" Cooper asked after we'd sloshed our way through the surf and collapsed on the sand. In truth, I didn't know if I was. I had a vague pain near my feeding tube and I was incredibly out of breath, but I lied.

"Yeah, I'm fine," I panted as I hid my chest with my arms, angling my face away so he couldn't see my makeup-free face. "I think. Ugh, that was cute and all, but you're lucky my ankle wasn't bitten off by a shark or something. Then this would've definitely been un-cute. Like, the opposite of cute."

"You know it was more than a little cute," he said, his face a little too smug to be adorable. "Admit it."

"Nope." I shook my head. "I refuse to participate in your ego-building exercises when it already seems big enough to begin with as it is."

He laughed and then just sort of stared at me.

"Why are you looking at me like that?"

"I don't know, I just like you," he said. "Do you know what a turn-on it was when you turned me down the other night? Seriously, *so* sexy, Summer."

Ughstopsayingmynameyouaredrivingmecrazy. My emotions were becoming too much to deal with, so I turned away again.

He looked up at the stars. "Looking at this, I almost believe in God again," he said, and then he smirked. "True or false, Summer: God exists."

"Why are you asking me all this?"

"Because the Jesus people back there got me thinking, and because you seem smart, and I want to hear your opinion."

98

"Okay, but you first."

"Where would I begin?" he exhaled through his teeth, puffing out his cheeks. "Okay. Well. I was raised in the church, and I built my whole identity around God, and my relationship with Him, and all that crap. But then life happened, and I had that same identity crisis when I was like nineteen that everybody has, and it just leveled me, pretty much. I felt like I had been sold a lie. If God wasn't real, then what *was* real? If there was no order to anything, then why was I even trying? If we were all just monkeys on a rock spinning in space, then why did anything matter at all? Why not just crawl into a hole and die?" He met my eyes. "So that's where I am. I want to believe. I really do. But I just need something to believe in."

"Yes, I agree with all that," I said. "There is no destiny or order or ledger in the sky deciding what your life is going to be – which is exactly the reason you should start living your life, exactly how you want to live it, right now."

He stared at me. Because I just wanted him to know things about me for some reason, I continued. "Like, I guess I'd call myself an optimistic nihilist when it comes to all that. Nothing matters, so everything matters. You can find joy in the nothingness, and silence in the chaos. I've been thinking about this stuff since I was a kid, and I think this world was just one big accident, and that we create our heaven and our hell by the way we live our lives."

"Um, explain that last bit?"

"Okay," I said. "Okay. So, like, in every neighborhood there was a miserable old cat lady who closed her curtains and hated the world and threw stuff at the kids who crossed her driveway, right? You didn't have to wonder whether she was going to hell, because she was already in hell. Her life was miserable, whether she'd admit it or not. She'd created her own hell for herself, and she lived in it every day. But, like, that other lady two streets over who volunteered her time and checked on local sick children and, like, de-wormed African orphans on her work vacations and stuff? She was happy and free. She'd created heaven already.

Who was to say that wouldn't last forever? Who could say that disappeared as soon as she was done borrowing the set of bones she'd been leased?" I paused. "So anyway, I just try to create a good life for myself and the ones I love and forget about the rest. That's what I try to do."

"Well," he said after a moment. "You're deep. That's kinda hot. Scratch that: really hot. I like smart girls."

"Yeah right," I laughed. "When's the last time you checked out a girl's cranium?"

"Point taken, I guess," he said, shrugging. "But you know, right now I'm reading this book by this singer you probably don't know, it's essays and poetry and song lyrics called *Strange Fiction*, and-"

"Wait," I said. "Wait just a minute. You fuck with Saviour?"

"I do, indeed, fuck with Saviour," he laughed. "Float on, my friend."

"You know 'float on?!'" I cried, which was sort of Saviour's catchphrase and the slogan of her fans, since it was from a poem of hers saying 'even dead fish like us still go with the flow, so let your heart die and fly like a crow.' She signed all her blog posts with the phrase, too. It was also a dark inside joke about how we were all "floating" toward an inevitable death anyway and therefore none of this crap even mattered, but that was obviously too dark to bring up now.

"Yeah, I love her music," he nodded. "Now *there* is a smart girl. Her songs are like X-rays of the human psyche or something. She simultaneously describes all the things I loved about being a teenager, while reminding me that I'd never, *ever* want to be that person again. What's the latest on her, anyway?"

I paused and scratched at my elbow. Since I was a total Saviour fangirl and followed her on all the embarrassing celebrity blogs I read, I practically knew what she ate for breakfast every morning – but obviously I didn't want him to know that. Caring about celebrities was, like, weird and lame. And actually, I had to make sure not to get *too* immersed in Saviour's world of albums and blog posts and opinion pieces and *Strange Fiction*, because in my boring life, the prospect of sinking into her beautiful dark fantasy land and losing interest in my *actual* situation, all darkness sans beauty, was all too tempting.

"I think she got arrested at an airport for heroin again," I said nonchalantly. "Or so I heard."

"'*Again*?' Isn't she, like, sixteen?"

"Yeah, but she's also a genius, and as she says in that song *Bones*, intelligence and happiness are-"

"Infrequent companions," he said, finishing the quote for me. "I know that all too well. That sucks though, she's so talented. Anyway, yeah, I've been reading the book over and over, and I think I've internalized pretty much every word in it – so *clearly* I like smart girls," he joked.

"Strange," I said, shivering a little. "I've memorized the book, too. I wouldn't have expected that from you. She's so...dark."

"She is, but she describes everything so perfectly. Sometimes I just wonder, like, *how could anyone else possibly be this lost, too*?! Sometimes the words are so beautiful and true and unsettling I just want to hug my book and make sure nobody else in the world ever reads those words, because they are *mine*, Goddamnit, and they apply to *me*, and damn it if anyone else is going to steal *my* words and plug them into *their* lives!"

I laughed harder than I had in months. It was so rare to meet anyone who made me laugh like this, or anyone who made me laugh at all, actually, and didn't make me shiver with disgust and decide that they were Not Like Me, But One Of Those Others; those people who chewed with their mouths open and didn't care for animals and thought white sunglasses were an acceptable life decision. You know, muggles. But Cooper was just...acceptable, in the best way.

Something else came to me. "In the water you said the future scared you. What did you mean?"

"Well maybe not the future," he said, "but, like, how I'm even going to *get* to the future at all. *That* scares me."

101

"Ahh," I said. "The age-old plight of the twenty something. *What the fuck am I doing with my life?*"

"Yes!" he cried.

"Mhmm. I feel like your teens are all about those big, cheesy questions: you know, 'who am I,' 'why am I here,' etcetera. But then your twenties are when you have to actually put those answers to *work*. Like, in a larger context. Like, I'm here, and I sort of know who I am, but who am I in the *world*? What do I do now? And am I doing it right, this whole *life* thing?"

"Yeah," he said, "your twenties are definitely a weird age. Children in adult bodies being forced to make adult decisions with their child brains. It's all a big mess if you ask me."

"Exactly!" I said, and then he laughed.

"What is it?"

"I'm just like everyone else," he said. "I have no idea where I'm going, but something tells me I'd be fine ending up wherever, as long as you were with me."

I hesitated audibly. Something told me he was sincere, but I still didn't want to believe him. I'd already seen too many rides around the block end when we'd gotten back home; watched enough flirtatious little texting relationships fizzle into radio silence. This was all too perfect. I felt like I was in a movie. Something needed to go wrong. And so, like the idiot I was, I *made* it go wrong again.

I crossed my arms and turned away a little, like anyone whose mouth was about to deliver a message their balls couldn't back up. "Okay, you're talking cute, Cooper," I said. "No doubt about that. But what you're doing is speaking so loudly, I can't hear it over what you're saying."

"What?"

I thought for a moment. We weren't nineteen anymore. The time for bullshit was over. Life was now a game of musical chairs, and I was still standing. It was either wear your emotions on your sleeve, or watch the object of your affection go off and make a Facebook engagement album with some other girl. As far as love went, this wasn't exactly my first chance, but it might have been my last chance. I know I was probably being too honest and revealing too much, but this diagnosis had blown me open, and everything I'd never been able to say or even think before was suddenly spilling out of my soul with reckless abandon. (Key word: reckless.)

"I love hanging out with you so far, obviously," I said, "but, like, it also makes me feel really inferior. Because you're...perfect. Almost *aggressively* so. And it's almost, like, offensive to me."

"What are you talking about?"

"Come on. I have these, these *issues*," I said.

"And?"

"And I have issues! That's all I need to say!"

"So what? Everyone has issues. The key is finding someone whose issues mesh well with your issues."

"But you don't *have* any issues!" I said a little too loudly. "You're, like, perfect, and your house is adorable, and you could charm a fire hydrant, and I don't know why you like me, and-"

"What is it, Summer?" he interrupted. "What's wrong?"

I pointed back at the bar. "Like tonight, when I got into that little thing with the doorman at the bar, you didn't even notice, but-"

"Oh, I noticed," he said as he looked away.

"You did?"

"Yeah, I did. I have no idea what kept me from breaking that guy's face, but somehow I controlled myself. I guess I didn't want to say anything and, like, attract any more attention to it, or whatever. For your sake, you know."

"Oh," I said. "Oh."

"And you know what?" he asked. "I'm scarred, too. Why can't you see that? Everyone is. We're all wounded animals zombie-ing around the Earth with our arms out looking to find our way and make a connection. So what if your scar happens to be on the outside?"

103

"Because it matters, Cooper, and stop acting like it doesn't," I said, resisting his cuteness. "People are shallow selfish assholes, and looks matter, and unless you're the Mayor of Underarockville, you know that."

"You matter," he said quietly. "You're smart and pretty and funny and cool. I just wish you would see all that."

I looked at him hard. The eye contact was awkward but I kept it going. "Okay," I finally said, with a fake smirk. "I'm a hot, cool genius. I get it now."

His face broke into a big, loopy smile that made me excited to be a human. "Don't let your head get *too* big," he laughed, "you're not *that* smart. You *did* just jump off a pier into a dark ocean with a Spark guy, after all. Don't push your luck, young lady."

I frowned up at the stars, wondering just what they had in store for me this summer. "I already am."

"What?" he asked, and I just shook my head at the sky.

This wasn't fair. I knew I had to tell him about my surgery, and about Intresia, about all of it. But I couldn't. I was already growing addicted to the version of myself I saw in his eyes, and I couldn't turn away just yet. I was too weak and I knew it. Never in my life had someone looked past the scar, the feeding tube, the bitterness that came from a lifetime spent in hospital gowns, and just seen *me*, Summer Martin Johnson. Even the way he was looking at me right now just swam with some unquantifiable emotion that said: *I am fine with you. I like everything you already are.* Never in my life had I seen a look like that. Never.

Cooper reached over for my hand, and as my soul rioted within me, I let him take it. Simply put, he was a goner, and I was the executioner. Hook, line, and sinker: my lies were deadly, and he was done.

Because right then and there, for the first time in my life, I decided to tell my brain to shut the fuck up and let my heart take the wheel instead.

11

We hung out the next day. And the next. You get the picture. Caution had officially been thrown to the summer winds. On Wednesday we walked the pier again and watched an old man rant to a flock of seagulls about the cruel ways of the world, on Thursday we went to Rita's Italian Ice and sat on a bench with an Orange Dream while I filled Cooper in on my work drama, and on Saturday he took me on a real, actual date, to a hokey but cute Mexican place near my town's main strip of bars. He got food poisoning halfway through and had to go home and puke all night, but still, Summer Johnson was being taken on dates – that was a thing that was happening. *Score!*

Four days with Cooper faded into a week. The last of late spring was exploding into summer, and my depressed little town was off to the races. The sidewalks clogged with tourists, the restaurants and bars filled with local surfers trying to wash the ocean out of their mouths with cheeseburgers and craft beers, and the beaches overflowed with sunbathers trying to worship the ball of fire in the sky. Surprisingly I never got sick of Cooper or found anything wrong with him, like I'd usually done whenever I'd liked someone in the past, just to kill the relationship before it had the chance to kill me. *Hey, you just smiled at me and you're cute and normal and in no way unacceptable in any discernible form – time to friendzone myself and/or run for my life!* I called it the 10/90 rule: you know how after you charge your phone, the first ten percent of your battery life is strong and glorious and it fades so slowly you think it's gonna last forever, but then once it hits 89% it starts plummeting faster and faster and before you know it, you're at two percent and you're having an anxiety attack looking for a charger? That's how my precious two flirtations had gone: spark, explode, and then slowly fizzle out. I'd notice the guys losing interest and then decide they were messy eaters, notice they were rude to waiters, whatever, and then push them away to keep them from eventually leaving me and breaking my heart. Then I'd curl back into myself to keep myself cold and alone and safe and sound.

But with Cooper I found this urge slowly falling away like an iceberg sliding into the sea. I liked him so much it terrified me, actually. We didn't do anything, like, *physical* just yet, and it's not like we hung out 24/7, either – we both maintained our separate lives – but it was good to have someone on my team. And soon I found myself sinking into his world like I'd only sunken into books. He was so interesting, and it was really nice to hangout with someone who was just so…cool. Shockingly, we never ran out of things to talk about. We spoke of life and food and health and Saviour and what scared us and what made us feel alive. We also talked about Funfetti cake. He knew so much about so many random topics, too. At the Mexican place that night, pre-vomit, I mentioned how my uncle lived in California, and Cooper looks up and goes "Did you know that if California broke away from the States and became its own country, it would have the fourth largest economy in the world?" I couldn't stop giggling. I mean, who even *knew* things like that?

So, side note: during one of my mom's more dramatic episodes a few years back, she claimed she'd gone colorblind and had demanded that I drive her to church, since she "wouldn't be able to read the stop signs." In reality she was fine and just didn't really feel like driving that day, but I mention this because it was like Cooper was disability blind. He liked me. He seemed to really, actually like me. I was dumbfounded in the best way.

And speaking of Shelly: one evening Cooper accidentally met her while picking me up after work, which was nerve wracking for obvious reasons. I swore he was just a friend, but I could see the skepticism in her eyes. He literally could not have been sweeter, though. Shelly was a little icy and closed-up at first, as she always was around my guy friends, but Cooper wore her down quickly. By the end of the visit, she was shoving food down his throat and giving him even more to take home to his mother, whom Shelly demanded to meet and befriend ASAP. Since I didn't want my quickly-evolving double life to get even more complicated, I rushed us out the door and bid her off. He was mine, at least for now.

~

One night towards mid-April I walked to the Ocean Avenue beach access after work to watch Cooper surf. Although it was a little boring to sit there on the beach and watch him bob up and down amongst all the other dots also bobbing up and down waiting for waves, I thought it was really cool that he had a "thing." Most people didn't have a "thing," you know? And he was really good, by the way. When I got super bored I took out my iPad and halfway watched a seagull trying to pull out a crab that was burrowing into the sand. Even though the waves were getting closer, about to sweep the crab away, the bird stayed put and tried to get what it wanted. But I never saw if it was successful or not, because Cooper suddenly plopped down on the sand next to me.

"Looks like we might have to get out here soon," he said, pointing at the gathering storm over our shoulders. I tensed up at having him so close to me – being next to him was still so hard sometimes – but I was trying.

"I wouldn't mind the rain," I said. "Actually, the beach when it's raining is probably my favorite place in the world."

He grimaced. "Really? Why?"

"I don't know. Because it's deserted, and nobody can see me."

He thought for a second. I could tell he didn't really know what to say.

"Gotcha. What were you writing?"

"Nothing," I said as I hid my iPad under my shirt.

"No, really, what was it?"

"Um, this might sound weird," I said, "but I know this girl named Kim who has spina bifida, and I heard she's

108

been really down lately because she's single and stuff, and I was just writing her a Facebook message telling her that she looked pretty in her recent pictures, and that we should get together soon. But it wasn't a charity message or anything – I genuinely do like her. She's sweet."

"Somehow I'm not surprised," Cooper sighed. "You make me feel like shit just by being *you*."

"*Welcome to my world*," I said under my breath. "But anyway, what happened? Why'd you come in from surfing?"

"Got bored," he said.

"Why? You're, like, really good."

"Thanks, but I hate it."

"Surfing? Why?"

"I just don't like it. I mean, I'll do it, but I think it's boring, and I'd rather be fishing. I usually only surf to hangout with my childhood best friend, Kevin, actually. He's a big surfer around these parts, and it's all he does. He's sponsored and everything."

"Oh. Cool. Where is he?"

"He left, he's gotta go on a date. With someone named Jeff," he added with a glance at me. "Is that, like, cool with you?"

"Of course."

"Good. Some people think it's weird, or whatever. But our families are super close and he's been like a brother to me since I could remember. Or a sister, I guess, come to think of it."

"Too bad I didn't get to meet him," I laughed.

"It's fine. You'll get a lot more chances. And plus, this just gives me more time alone with you." He leaned against my leg and then got serious. "Oh, and I have something for you."

Soon he produced a crumpled-up paper from his backpack, smoothed it out, and placed it on my towel. I picked it up to find a photo of a gorgeous teenaged girl with red hair and striking hazel eyes.

"Yeah?" I asked as I held it. "She's cute. Who is it?"

"You just read her book for the sixteenth time," he said, and I jumped a bit. The most remarkable thing about Saviour was that nobody had a clue what she looked like. She went everywhere in elaborate bejeweled masks from Paris fashion houses, and her true appearance had been a mystery ever since her first album two years ago.

"Wait, *what*? Saviour's face is nowhere. Where did you…?"

"It wasn't easy – I spent all day at the library," he smiled, "but the reference computers proved useful. Turns out she won an international poetry contest in New York when she was thirteen, and I found this somewhere in a competition log."

I didn't know what to say. "This is amazing, Cooper, but…*why*?"

He bit the inside of his cheek, brown eyes burning. "To show you the subjectivity of beauty," he said. "A mask can make a beautiful face invisible, and beauty can make a scar invisible. It's all just a bunch of beautiful bullshit if you ask me."

I just stared at him.

"And also, *I* wanted to see her face, too," he blushed. "Hiding in plain sight these days is a pretty admirable feat."

"Agreed," I said when I could talk again. "By the way, I have something for you, too. Are you done surfing?"

"I guess. Why?"

I reached into the Publix shopping bag I'd brought and carefully took out the Tupperware box containing the mini-Funfetti cake I'd baked for his mother earlier that day. I was a little nervous and didn't want him to think I was like, weird or stalkery or anything, and so I didn't know how he'd take it, but for some reason a tear squeezed out of his eye.

"It's for your mom," I said as he took the pan. "You mentioned how tomorrow was her birthday, and I just wanted to make sure she had a good one, and…yeah. Hope I'm not overstepping any boundaries or anything."

"You are," he whispered, "but not the ones you're thinking of."

110

"What?"

"Never mind." He just stared down at the cake. "God, this was really nice of you, Summer. My mom's been really depressed ever since getting stuck in the wheelchair, and she doesn't really have any friends anymore since none of them knew how to deal with the whole MS thing, and, well…"

He grabbed my head and planted a kiss on my bangs. "Your heart is as big as the ocean we live on, Summer. I am very glad I met you. And for the record, my birthday's in March, as you know, and I like Key Lime Pie – any cooking activities on my behalf would be greatly appreciated." He sniffled and shook his head. "And enough serious stuff. Tell me about your day at work, why don't you? I absolutely *must* hear more about this crazy boss of yours!"

~

Not all sailing was smooth, though. About a week later I discovered I had the day off from work and decided to indulge in Morning Movies, my favorite past time, to clear my rip-roaring head. For some reason I just really liked the movie theater in the mornings, when everything was cold and empty and sterile. I went at 10:40, but at that time they were only showing the most depressing movie ever, some weepie about a WWII bride who got left alone at home while her man went off to fight, and I had no choice but to watch it. And in the end it turned out being way worse than depressing: it was just totally unrealistic and full of stupid clichés, and it even made me mad for some reason. All the bride did was sit around waiting for her man. Why were some women so desperate? Did someone left alone *really* have to lose their identity? And, like, falling in love was dangerous. Why would this girl just hand over her heart to someone who was about to leave? Didn't she know how stupid that was?

And why on Earth had I agreed to watch this movie in the first place, again?

One line in particular toward the end of the movie chilled me to the bone. "And in the end," the bride whispered at her groom's body as it lay in the casket upon returning home, "I suppose the only way to find happiness is to risk total destruction."

I shivered the whole way home.

That night I settled into a game of Scrabble with my mom and Chase on the dirty living room carpet. Hanging out with the two of them had always been a little awkward – it was usually either just me and Chase, or Chase and my mother. It'd been this way ever since his second birthday, when we'd both burst into his room early in the morning to sing him the birthday song and give him a donut. After taking the donut, he said, "Thank you, Mommy, love you," pushed Shelly aside, and reached for me instead.

She didn't get out of bed for a week.

To escape the awkwardness I sneakily took out my phone and started scrolling through Facebook. Misty the Pen Thief was shouting about her engagement again, sharing every single detail about her meetings with her party planners and her latest dates with her fiancé. He looked miserable in every picture, and if I didn't know them I would've guessed they were on the rocks, or at least well on the way there. But like Saviour had said, I guess the truth didn't matter as long as the lie was pretty enough. *Look at my love!* all her posts seemed to shout, regardless of what they actually said on the surface. *Look at this man love me! I am so much better than all of you bitches!*

I was preparing to send a gossipy message to Autumn trashing Misty the Pen Thief to shreds when Cooper texted the following:

I want to continue this text conversation, but I'm going to eat, and I want a companion. I'll text you the address. Meet me there, if you are so inclined. Let's redo my Night of A Thousand Trips to The Bathroom before I die of embarrassment.

I smiled, bit my lip, and then drifted into a fog of *Battle Bride*-related anxiety.

It's been four minutes, he said four minutes later, apparently. **Four minutes is an ETERNITY in texting time. Yes or no?**

I told myself to chill. First, I was lying to him, and our whole relationship – or whatever this was – was based on that lie, no matter how much fun I was having. And the second reason was a slightly more classic one: I wanted to impress him by coming off as impossibly busy and nonchalant. Because I really liked him. This could be something, really *something*, and I didn't want him to think I was some Debbie Desperado who crazily waited by my phone all day for him to text me and invite me out. His next text came soon after:

I had a bad day and I really need to hangout with someone. Please?!?!?

"So I've been thinking about things we can do this summer," Shelly said while passing out supplies. She was still mad at me from this morning, when she'd caught me watching *Maury* in the Florida room. "I will *not* have the Devil's work under my roof!" she'd said while wrestling the remote from me. "If you want to watch this trash, you can go find your own house!"

"But Shelly," I'd said with wide eyes, "without reality shows, how else am I supposed to be reminded that there are people out there who are worse-off than me? I may have a broken throat and a leaky stomach, but at least I'm not twerking on a soundstage somewhere in Connecticut because I've just discovered my child's actual paternal lineage!"

She gave me a funny look, but only for a second. "Twerk somewhere else," she finally said while marching into the kitchen, the safe sounds of Kathie Lee Gifford now flowing from the flat screen. "This is a Methodist home."

"So," she said, back in the present, "what about an Amelia Island weekend? You love all those antique shops. Or maybe Universal Studios? I hear they have some new rides, and the drive isn't too long. You can stay with your dad, and I'll get a hotel."

I motioned at Chase, who was still oblivious as to Operation 80/20, and did a throat-cutting motion. "Those are nice offers, but you do remember what I said about wanting to be *normal*, right?"

"That is normal. How is wanting to spend time with my only daughter not normal?"

Cooper texted yet again, and I started to get nervous.

"Look, Shelly, that sounds great, but let's continue this another time," I said as I got up, which took more effort than usual for some reason.

"Where are you going?"

"Out."

"Out with…?"

I picked at my shirt. "With a friend."

"Does this friend happen to possess a Y chromosome?"

"Yes, Shelly, he is a guy."

"I *knew* it! Your skin is all pink and blushy and your eyes aren't focusing on anything. Who is he? What's going on? Is it that boy from the other day, the one you said was a friend?"

I tried to scoff, but no sound would come out.

"You're crazy," I finally said. "The only thing I'm falling in love with is Funfetti cake. I'll be home later. See ya."

"But I never said the word *love*," she said darkly, and I froze. Before she could turn it into too much of a drama, though, I turned back and smiled.

"Oops. Brain fart. Gotta go. Bye!"

"So, what was on our agenda tonight?" Cooper asked after dinner, which consisted of steak for him and a tube of milk discreetly pumped into my stomach during a trip to the bathroom for me. The restaurant Cooper had chosen, Salt Life, was quiet and deserted, so thankfully nobody had walked in on me.

"*Our* agenda?"

"You and me," he said, like our hanging out was a foregone conclusion. "Us."

"Oh," I blushed, "I, um, I didn't have any-"

"God," he said quietly.

"God, what?"

"God, it just feels good to see your face, after today."

"*Oh*." And then: "What was your bad day about, anyway? You never did tell me."

"Just stuff with my mom, I don't know," he sighed. "She gets depressed sometimes, and it gets hard."

"Yeah. I'm sorry."

"Me too." He just stared at me. "That color looks so good on you, by the way."

"Thanks, weirdo," I said. "And tonight?" I chewed on my lower lip and gave myself a chance to turn him down and save him from me and my dubious fate. I failed.

"Well, I was gonna watch this hideous Netflix romance, but I don't have anyone to sufficiently mock it with. Care to join?"

"Hmm," he said. "*How* hideous?"

"Pretty hideous. I've seen it before. The couple meets after the girl trips on a puppy and helplessly falls into his arms. Drama ensues."

"How *much* drama?"

"I remember seeing tears fifteen minutes into the movie."

"Hmm," he repeated. "Any horrible clichés yet, besides what you just said?"

"The main character is a bright young writer named Lola who works at a fashion magazine called *Flaunt* and wants to expand her horizons and get serious about her career."

"Yep," he nodded, "only dogs and celebrity babies are named Lola, and writers haven't been paid to write in a decade. I would know. Sounds bad enough. I'll follow you home – you're worth the drive. Hopefully this movie won't kill me with its cheesiness, because this night has already been amazing."

I felt my face slacken with horror.

"What is it?"

"No-nothing," I stammered, trying to recover myself. "Just please don't joke about death with me, okay?"

"You got it," he said a little suspiciously, as he got his box of leftovers and headed to his car. I let him follow me home in the humid night, the word *unclimbable* ringing in my head in an endlessly hellish chorus all the while.

~

I snuck him into my bedroom through the back porch to keep from dealing with my mother. The movie was just awful; a total hate-watch. Actually, you know when you hate something so much that you watch it just to make fun of it, but it's so frustrating it just ends up making you even madder than before? It was one of those. It starred Kate Hudson or Katherine Heigl or whoever, and it started out with the spunky blonde heroine tripping over a leaf or a book or something and falling directly into the arms of a scruffy male lead with a name like Josh Trent or Trent Josh or Trosh Jent or whatever. After some affable banter and maybe a few coffee dates with the female lead's adorably zany best friend named Zoe or Roxy tagging along as third wheel, they fell in love. Eventually they hit some road block, but just some cutesy problem that could be wrapped up in a bow, not a real-life issue like a demanding career or families that didn't mesh well or, you know, an incurable medical condition or something. It ended with the couple coming to their senses and quitting their jobs and running towards each other on the

116

Brooklyn Bridge at sunset, Josh Trent giving up literally everything to chase down the object of his love.

"Why do all these endings have to be *happy*?" Cooper asked as the credits – which were of course pink – started to roll. "Why do all the movies end with the couple running off into the sunset? That's so boring. Where are the sad stories? That's why I like Saviour, you know. Life isn't neat, it's dirty. I like to be reminded that fucked up stuff exists. It gives me…feelings. Doesn't feeling stuff, even if it's bad, make you remember that you're…I don't know, *alive*?"

"Agreed," I said, trying to roll away from him in a way that was not awkward. "You have no idea how much I agree, actually. Let's make a pact: no more rom-coms ever again. If there is a cupcake, a puppy, or a pastel-colored balloon on the cover, we are not watching it."

"Deal."

I got up to turn on the light. "And the worst thing was that they were calling each other 'soul mates' – that idea is just *so* not realistic."

He gave me a weird look. "Wait, I didn't say I was *that* cynical. You don't believe in love?"

"I believe in love," I said as I returned to the bed. "I just don't believe in soul mates."

He blinked a few times.

"Okay, well, I do believe people can find the 'love of their lives,' or whatever, but I don't think that's the same thing as a soul mate, and I don't think that 'thing,' whatever it is, has to last for both of their lives."

"Why not?"

I took a breath. "Because rarely do those people end up together. I've watched my mother suffer for years because of my dad. She's still in love with him and everyone knows it. But are they together? Nope."

"How do you know she feels that way?"

I felt my eyes track away from him. "Because when he's on his way up from Orlando to visit me and my brother, she gets a glass of sweet tea and just sits by the window in the living room, watching for him, all day. Waiting for him to come back. It really is the saddest thing."

A long silence filled up the space between us. "God," he finally said. "That's depressing. No matter what happens with us, let's never be like that, okay?"

"Okay," I smiled. "And sorry, I'm not trying to be a Debbie Downer. My reason for not believing in soul mates is more about numbers and odds than anything – as usual."

"Explain?"

"Okay, so, like, I look at life as a game of circumstance, right? A play at odds. There are seven billion people on Earth, I think. How many of those seven billion people do you think one human encounters in a day?"

"Hmm. If I stay in bed all day watching Netflix, zero. If I go surfing or fishing, a couple dozen. If I go to the bars, maybe a few hundred."

"Yeah. And what about in a year?"

"Tens of thousands, maybe. Perhaps a hundred thousand."

"And a lifetime?"

"Um. Maybe a few million or so?"

"Exactly," I said. "And so the amount of people in the world – seven billion – divided by the amount of those people you will actually *see* in the world during your lifetime – a few million – is, like, so infinitesimal a number that I don't even want to figure it out. So the whole 'soul mate' concept, the idea that there is one person out there who is 'made for us' and 'meant to cross paths with us' or whatever is ludicrous enough on its own, but the chance that we would actually *meet* that person, even if they existed? The chance that we'd share a class with them or move down the street from them or pass them on the sidewalk and spark some instant connection with them, out of so many other billions of people out there to meet? Those odds are laughable, and all those people watching romantic comedies and posting Facebook statuses about their One True Love need to eat shit."

For one long moment he just stared at me, studying me. Finally he leaned forward and smirked, looking thought-rearrangingly gorgeous. "Here's a number for you," he said. "One."

"What's that?" I asked, and he smirked even harder.

"The number of times I need to look into your eyes to know everything you just said was bullshit."

I gasped, totally gasped.

"But I don't know, I kinda just think you're too cynical for your own good," he said soon, talking himself back from the Edge of Awkward Profundity a little. "And that's coming from someone who listens to Saviour. From what I can tell, sometimes it's like you mask cynicism as logic and use it as a weapon."

"*I have to*," I whispered as some strange sadness bubbled up from some chasm deep within me.

"Why?"

"I don't know. What if I *had* to turn cynical to protect myself? What if I had to turn all my edges in on myself and fold myself up to nothing just to defend myself from a world that seemed to have it out for me?"

He said nothing for a long while.

"You know, the world is more beautiful than that," he finally murmured. "I don't know what happened to you to make you like this, but I swear, goodness exists. You just have to find it." He blinked at me and shook his head. "And who knows – maybe the soul mate concept doesn't have to be some be-all, end-all thing like it is in the movies. Maybe the whole world is made of love, and we're just supposed to bump into love and feed off love and contribute to love and then break off and drift somewhere else and start all over again. I mean, I fall in love with things all the time – I love books and music and beer and the sea. Maybe there are all sorts of things and people for me to fall in love with along the way, and if I do, that doesn't mean they have to be my One and Only – maybe they're just one wave in a sea of love."

I saw the opportunity and jumped for it, like the crazy person I was. "…And what are your thoughts on marriage?"

He rolled his eyes. "Same as your thoughts on getting out of bed on Monday morning: it's terrible and awful and torturous, but for some reason, people still seem to do it anyway. I said I believed in *love*, not the government-sanctioned version of it. And don't look at me like that – you'd be this cynical on the issue, too, if you'd grown up watching my parents' pathetic excuse for a marriage. I want love, sure, but that doesn't mean I want a piece of paper to *tell* me I'm in love."

"Let me read something of yours," I said suddenly, probably to mask the disappointment sinking into my chest.

"Huh?"

"You said you're a writer, and I wanna read something you wrote. Anything."

His jaw clenched. "No."

"Why?"

"It's just embarrassing."

"Then how do think you could ever become an author if you never let anybody read your stuff?"

"Because those people are…strangers," he said. "And I don't really care what they think. But you're…you, already. You don't understand how personal it is. Writing is like throwing your soul onto a page and then going, 'Here, everyone, hope you love it!' I don't really care about that faceless audience out there, but it would crush me to not have *your* approval. I already think you're the smartest person I know."

He looked away, and my insides caved in for him. He was twenty-five and unemployed; letting his life slip by because he was too afraid to chase his dreams. And as I noticed how warm his last comment had made me feel, I realized how much I wanted to make him feel warm, too, in return, and I started thinking of ways I could do that. By looking at me the way he did every day and making me feel the way I was feeling, he was giving me a gift. But how could I give *him* a gift?

"You *should* show people," I said. "You're obviously very smart, and you should take advantage of that. Put your brain to work."

"How do you know I'm not the worst writer to ever put fingers to a keyboard?" he asked, trying not to smile.

"Trust me, if you write half as well as you speak, you'll be fine. So stop being cat shit and let me read something, you overgrown toddler."

"And you wonder why," he said.

"What?"

"And you wonder why I like you. You just used the phrases 'cat shit' and 'overgrown toddler' in the same sentence. You speak my language, Summer."

He slept over. Or more accurately, I *let* him sleep over, which was stupid and reckless of me, because every one of these Big Relationship Steps we passed just made me fall deeper into like with him. When my work alarm jolted me awake at seven the next morning, I found him gone. And even despite it all, I felt empty and disappointed, I can't lie. And also super embarrassed, because I always slept with my mouth hanging open and looked totally fugly, and that meant he'd seen me at my worst. Oh well.

There was a note on my desk, and when I reached over and grabbed it I laughed: Cooper's handwriting was beyond awful. Hopefully he wrote his newspaper stories on a laptop, I noted to myself as I read, because this was damn near illegible:

It's 2 AM and you're too cute to mess with. I'll let myself out. Check your mailbox when you wake up, though – I changed my mind. Just left you a little something I happened to have in my car. Nothing big. -Cooper

My whole body went numb as I finished reading. I tried to turn off my feelings, but it just wouldn't work. Then I said a silent prayer that my mom hadn't seen him leaving last night – as she was devoutly and irrevocably Methodist, I'd

121

probably never hear the end of it. And because I am an impatient fool, I immediately walked out to the mailbox and found a blue folder with a story inside printed out from Microsoft Word, along with another note from Cooper:

Okay, don't judge this too harshly – it's a first draft. You'll get used to my typos eventually. Hope you love it. Float on, my friend.

I put the folder under my arm and went back inside, the word "eventually" ringing in my head like the bells that sometimes chimed from my mom's church down the street. The way he spoke about us hanging out in the future like it was a *given* or something was astonishing to me for some reason. No one had ever done that before. Not even close.

I tried to be cool and tell myself I'd get around to reading the story once I was free, but in reality I was free right then, and was super excited to devour it. I was kinda scared, too, that it would be terrible, and that my view of Cooper as some dark, twisted genius would be ruined forever. So as I sat down to read, I prepared to lie to him if it was bad, and keep the secret to myself.

To soothe my nerves I put on my favorite song, *The Road* by Saviour. *And so it goes,* she sang as I started reading. *Just because you're lost on life's road / doesn't mean you can't find someone else to wander beside you and help lighten the load.*

And from the first sentence alone, Cooper's story blew my mind.

"We don't get to choose how much time we get in this life, but we do get to choose how we spend it," the story began. "And I am here today to tell you I have made all the wrong choices."

Called *Eighty Eight*, the book was about a boy our age who sat around all day worrying about the future while doing nothing to help his current situation – you know, obsessing over his career and family and all that while his bills piled up on the counter, etcetera. Then one day he woke

122

up as an eighty-eight year old man and realized he was stuck in that body for good and was going to die soon, and so he frantically ran around trying to do everything he'd planned on doing as a young man, except he was too old and frail to carry out anything on his bucket list. In the end he died with no experiences under his belt, no stamps in his passport, and nothing to show for his life, all because he'd wasted his youth stumbling through the tense fog of anxiety. The book wasn't totally perfect, and there were some typos and clunky paragraphs he could've smoothed out, but the bones of greatness were absolutely there. It was only about sixty pages, but by the last sentence I was in tears. It was flat-out devastating, and it made me realize just how much I hid behind hoping for a better future instead of improving my present, telling myself I would fix it all one day and never actually fixing anything at all. In only sixty pages I had become completely attached to the old man, feeling every ounce of his heartbreak and every inch of his joy. And as I turned the last page, I just looked outside and felt empty and full and exhausted and pumped up all at the same time, but mostly I just felt hopefully heartbroken.

In the mid-morning light I saw a mom walking with her little son and their dog, and I wanted to lean out of the window and shout, *What's wrong with you freaks?! Why isn't your world stopping? Why aren't you heartbroken? Why aren't you lying on the floor, broken and sobbing, because a totally fictional character in a totally made-up story is dead?* I was furious that the world wasn't broken by a story it had never read, and I wanted to gouge out my eyeballs so I could read it all over again with brand new eyes *–that* was the mark of a good fucking book.

After all this I found myself totally in awe of Cooper, and even *more* confused. Cooper was a writer to the floor of him, that was obvious. But why didn't he know that? And how could I convince him of his talent while I still had time?

And also: why was he even *thinking* about these things? I'd thought *I* was the most morbid twenty-something to ever exist, but this book had out-doomed me in spades.

Just what, exactly, had happened in his past to make him this dark? Things were starting to add up about him, and they weren't making sense. I'd thought he could look past my scar and all that because of his mother, but now I was suspecting there could be more. Why did he act so weird in public sometimes? Why had a gorgeous boy been alone on his birthday, turning to a dating app for companionship, warning me about his internal scars?

As I closed the folder and reluctantly headed for the shower to get ready for work, I couldn't help but ask myself: was I *really* the only one in this relationship who was being haunted by something?

13

Three weeks later, I fainted.

It went like this: I was just getting out of my car at a beach access to watch Cooper surf, which I'd been doing more and more. I'd just gotten out of the car when a strange, silvery, lightheaded feeling struck me, and the last thing I remember was noticing a crushed can of Sprite lying next to a fence lined with overgrown sea plants when everything went out.

When I woke up a few moments later, I was staring at the sand dunes, my cheek against the grass. I'd simply fallen sideways onto soft soil, but I'd missed a metal bench by inches. I brushed myself off, got up, and walked towards the sea. I wasn't going to let my issues stop me, whatever they were. Not yet. After a lifetime of winter I was finally stepping into summer, and I would let no one – not even Dr. Steinberg – make me go back.

I had an early-morning checkup meeting with Steinberg a few days after the fainting incident. In all the Cooper business, I was almost forgetting that I was, you know, maybe going to die. (Almost is never enough, unfortunately.) It was so good to see him, even under the circumstances. His hair was white like the snow I'd only seen in books, and his eyes were warm and crackly like a summer bonfire. He said my team of doctors were fine-tuning their approach and asked me how I'd been feeling, and I kind of embellished the facts a little. Skipped over a few details, you could say. I didn't mention the fainting, the fatigue, the mental fog, the way it was starting to take all the effort in the world just to open my car door, and so forth. I didn't want him to get concerned and throw me into a hospital room out of caution and lock away the key when I was having the time of my life out here in the world. And besides, I was as fine as I ever was.

I hoped.

But best of all, Steinberg had news for me: it seemed he'd found a girl in Germany who'd survived a surgery very similar to mine. I checked out her blog on my phone after I left the hospital, and sure enough, she was now my age and – *get this*! – married to someone she'd met after the procedure. She could eat food and run marathons and do everything she'd only dreamed of as a sick person. And for the first time since March, I really let myself imagine a future for myself. Not necessarily with Cooper, just in general. As I drove down Third Street after the appointment I imagined all the events of a normal life, all the Facebook milestones like an engagement and a marriage and a baby and a mortgage, unfurling themselves out in front of me like waves on the ocean. It was really possible after all – *life* was possible. Cooper was possible. And imagining the possibilities of what he and I could build this summer left me, for the first time in my semi-adult life, absolutely giddy with excitement.

I shivered at a stoplight and let the surgery melt into the shadows of my mind just a little bit more.

And the summer of my dreams barreled on. I worked part-time, I injected myself with milk four times a day and spent as much time with Shelly and Chase as I could, but besides that, Cooper was becoming my whole routine. If I wasn't working during the day, we'd surf or fish – or rather, *he'd* surf or fish, while I'd sit in the tide pools getting lost in my Kindle. When the afternoon rains came we'd run back to his house and get ready for lunch. Sometimes he'd eat at home, and sometimes we'd go to local Jax Beach spots like Angie's Subs or TacoLu or this little Filipino place on Lemon Street. It rained every other day in Jacksonville in the summer at, like, four PM, and not just passing showers, either, but these giant, black super cells that invaded the city like those alien spaceships from *Independence Day*. I loved to go sit on my driveway and watch the rains come in, the slate-grey clouds spilling in from the west, the olive green oak leaves on my street throwing up their silvery undersides to welcome the storms; I lived to feel the balmy breeze on my face and breathe in the scent of distant rain falling on distant marshes and watch the way the electricity in the air made my arm

126

hairs stand at attention. Then I'd go inside and lay on the couch to read a book or watch TV while the storm hit, the *pitter-patter* on my windowsills lulling me into some kind of summer-storm-induced nirvana.

After one of these weirdly heavenly afternoon storms, I was getting dressed in my room when I saw Cooper pull into my driveway through my window. As he got out of the car, I gasped, because he looked *good*. Like, I mean *goooood,* with five O's. A cashmere black sweater than was just tight enough, a pair of dark jeans, and brown suede shoes. All of this was set off by his tan, which was exactly the color I imagined the color of a villa in Tuscany to be, weirdly enough. That was Cooper: lighting up my world so thoroughly, I was imagining things I'd never even given two shits about before.

"Who's here?" Shelly asked after I came out into the living room. "I thought you had Anti-Support tonight."

My mom's affection for him aside, she was getting more and more frantic and scatterbrained as the surgery loomed closer, and she was growing increasingly suspicious about my absences. I'd try to claim that I was meeting Autumn for coffee or doing anti-support group stuff or whatever, but I'd never been a very good liar, and I was also quickly running out of excuses. I could tell she was onto me.

"I do have Group tonight. And I don't know who it is," I lied.

"It's that tall boy with the crooked smile," she said, peeking through the curtains. "Tell me the truth. Who is he?"

"A friend," I said.

"A friend that makes you blush and giggle and forget things?"

She pointed down at my top, which I noticed wasn't even buttoned at all.

"Friends blush at each other," I said as I reached down to fix my mistake and hide my scars.

"Okay, well, then, when am *I* going to get some of this time you're giving this *friend*?"

127

I sighed and dropped my shoulders. "Shelly, listen. I am living my life while I can, and I need you to back off. I can make my own decisions. Can you do that, please?"

A tear unexpectedly came to her eye. "Just be careful, Summer. That's all I'm asking. You remember Travis Gibson and-"

"Yes, Shelly," I interrupted. "Of course I remember Travis Gibson And His Bet."

In sixth grade the worst thing ever happened. Like, the *worst* thing. A cute, popular boy named Travis started flirting with me and telling me he liked me and stuff, and I fell pretty hard. He asked to be official and everything, and we'd even hold hands when we walked down the hallway, which was like a totally *huge* deal in a middle school relationship. But anyway, about a week into things, I found a note from Travis' friend Logan asking him how much money Logan owed him that day. It turned out Travis was being paid to date me all along as some sick kind of joke for the popular kids to laugh at. He even got a bonus for every time he touched me, since I apparently grossed him out so much that he couldn't bear physical contact. I spent two weeks in bed after that.

That was also the year I started covering up my scar with concealer full-time. The Asshole Deflector, I called my little jar of makeup. If I couldn't control people's reactions to me, I could at least hide myself as best I could, as a preemptive strike against douchebaggery. (Which had made my choice to download Spark all the more strange for me, I guess. But desperate times, desperate measures, desperate-for-attention Facebook brides, etcetera.)

"Shelly," I said, trying to close down the conversation before it got even more embarrassing, "I appreciate the concern, but I am twenty-four. Please stop micromanaging my personal life like I'm some slutty tween getting felt up in the back of a movie theater. I've got it covered."

128

"Oh, baby," she said in her faint Savannah accent as she stepped forward. "I'm sorry. I really am. I just don't want to see you, or anyone else, get tricked or hurt again."

Hot rage licked at my scarred chest. "So that's what this is?" I asked. "I'm so thoroughly unlovable that the only reason a boy would like me is to make fun of me, like Travis?"

Her jaw fell open a little. "No, I...I love you, Summer. I love you. And I don't want to see any hearts being broken. That's all. And by the way," she said pointedly over her shoulder as she turned for her room, "it wasn't *you* getting tricked that I was worried about."

"If you're gonna look so good," I said after I shook the Shelly drama off my shoulders and opened the door, "can you at least tell me the occasion?"

I was getting a lot better at talking to him, and at pulling off this double in general: Broken Woman-Child at home, Healthy Femme Fatale with Cooper.

"Whaddyou mean?" Cooper asked, rubbing his hands together and bouncing up and down on the balls of his feet. His excitement reminded me of a five-year-old before a soccer game. "I thought we were going out to eat tonight, for the holiday weekend?"

I racked my brain and came up empty. I had no idea what he was talking about.

"You...you agreed the other night, remember?" he asked, his shoulders falling a bit. "You said you wanted to watch me eat at Outback while cursing the Throat Gods for not letting you participate in the greasy carbfest of glory known as the Bloomin' Onion?"

This rang a bell.

"Oh, damn," I said. "Yeah, I thought we were talking about doing that on Monday."

He sort of turned away a little and motioned at his car. "Um, I mean, I can leave, if you want...?"

"No," I said, "no, it's not that, it's just that I…I had plans already." But how in the world could I tell him about the Anti-Support Group?

His eyes lost their sparkle completely. "Oh. Were you hanging out with someone else, or…?"

"*What*?" I asked. Why would he even think there could possibly be someone else? I was clearly, embarrassingly obsessed with him, and everyone knew it. I was also, you know, not very attractive, so there was that to take into account, too. "No, it's this thing I do every Thursday night," I said quickly. "I, like, didn't want to say anything because I thought you'd think it'd be weird or something."

"Well," he said, a little relieved, "*weird* is a relative term for me. Is it, like, Scientology meeting weird, or tetherball practice weird?"

"No, none of those. Um, it's just that I hold a meeting for people with health issues every other Thursday night, called the Anti-Support Group?"

"*Anti*-support?"

I hesitated. Most people couldn't handle this stuff. I knew that. A quote-unquote "normal" person was just not equipped to go sit with a bunch of ill and broken people, some of them terminally so, and listen to them complain. Because that's what we did in my group: complain. I just wanted to create a space where other people like myself could complain about their problems without exhausting people, and so I'd banned all inspirational sayings, cheesy pep talks, sappy quotes, over-the-top Jesus stuff, etcetera, and instead I just let them vent to me. Because venting was an *extremely* important part of being a damaged person. Most people didn't want to sit there listening to others bitch about their health situations, for many reasons. They didn't understand, it grossed them out, and saddest of all, most people just didn't care about other peoples' problems that much, *especially* when someone's whole life basically revolved around One Big Problem. And if people *did* want to talk about this stuff with you, they were usually Church Lady types with big crazy eyes who circled hospital waiting rooms like vultures and feasted on drama and pity and despair and heartsickness like most people feasted on Thanksgiving dinner. Not cute, in my opinion. So once a week I simply invited a bunch of people my age in varying states of unwellness and/or disability to sit in a room for an hour and bitch at me.

But to be honest I wasn't sure if I wanted Cooper to know about all this. For one, he already saw me as Different enough, and the other day he'd even walked in on me as I'd fed myself in his laundry room. He'd tried to act like it didn't bother him, but I kept seeing his eyes tracking toward my abdomen the rest of the day, and it had bugged me to no end. We'd revealed a few embarrassing things about ourselves in the past month or two – I'd let him see all the celebrity gossip magazines peppering the floorboard of my car, and he'd shared his weird habit of watching Cartoon Network every morning – but this was a little much. I didn't like to tell "normal" people about my problems, mostly because that was weird, and also because I hated people who sat around moaning about all the things that had "happened to" them, in passive tense. Living actively   e.g., happening to the world instead of letting it happen to me – was a big priority for me.

And plus, I just didn't want to be one of those people who always had to have A Story, with a capital S, you know? Everyone knew of someone with A Story: like, say some girl on your Facebook's dog dies or something, which is admittedly sad and terrible, but then she never lets it go and makes literally everything about the dead dog for the next year. Like six months later she'll post a sunset selfie and caption it "This is so beautiful, just wish my baby could see it ☹," or post a random Buzzfeed video and be like "My dog would've loved this soo much." Like, it sucks that your dog bit the dust, but children are dying in Sudan and get the hell over it, you know? At the end of the day I guess I just didn't want My Story to be *That Girl Who Didn't Eat Food*. Like, make me *That Quiet Girl in the Corner Who's Always Reading* or *That Girl With The Fashion Sense of a Blind*

131

Substitute Teacher, whatever – make me *anything* but *That Girl With The Medically Induced Anorexia.*

So I sort of explained what I could to Cooper, minus a few of the more intense details, and when I finished, he stepped forward and grabbed my face. My entire body went tingly at his touch, just like they talked about in the books.

"Summer Martin Johnson," he said as he planted a kiss on my forehead, "I would like nothing more than to spend my Thursday night listening to people complain about their problems with you."

"You would?" I asked as I got the succinct feeling that my skin had melted. He hadn't kissed me like that since a walk to Dairy Queen a few days before, and I was starting to miss his touch, and want more of it, in different ways.

"'Course," he said. "Something tells me I'd do almost anything if it involved you."

I didn't need any more convincing. I grabbed a sweater and told him to get in my car.

After a jittery drive to the converted fire station that served as our community center, I stocked a flimsy card table with some pretzels and Diet Coke and then put up a sign saying *SUMMER'S ANTI-SUPPORT GROUP: POSITIVITY FREE ZONE, BITCHING WELCOME* on the front door and waited. Someone barged in looking for a gardening club meeting and then saw me and politely said "Oh, sorry, this is the room for that cancer group," and left the way he'd come. I glared after him, because this fed into another issue I had with my issues. Don't get me wrong – cancer sucks, and watching my great aunt Tess slowly die of breast cancer was one of the worst things ever. *Ever.* But, like, people *understand* cancer, right? People *grasp* cancer. People have heard of cancer. You hear the phrase "cancer patient" and you immediately get this image of a bald-headed warrior sitting in a chemo clinic Fighting the Good Fight, Not Giving Up, etcetera. Like, it's terrible and random and it strikes anyone, but people *expect* that cancer can unexpectedly come at any second, you know?

But there is no gallows glamour in somebody's body not working correctly. It seems like every few months there's a sweetly melancholy movie about some dude finding out he has eight months to live before a brain tumor makes him bite the dust, and then he sets off on a sweetly irreverent journey where he Chases His Dreams, Checks Off His Bucket List, parasailing on that beach in Australia like he'd dreamed of as a snot-nosed kid, etcetera. Either that, or the tried-and-true tale of adorable cancer-stricken teens finding love. But there are no darkly funny stories about a girl with no throat and a death sentence just trying to live her life. There are no books entitled *Esophageal Intresia And Me: Living a Full Life with Half a Throat and Three Months to Live (And You Can, Too!)*. When people broach the subject of People Who Are Not Entirely Well, they want a story they've heard of, something they can understand, something they can wrap up in a cute little Ribbon of Disease and keep on their shelf for a rainy day. *Cute White Kids With Cancer Fall Into Doomed Love in the Suburbs* is the title of the story they all want. When family members of other sick people look over at me in waiting rooms and ask me about My Story, they sort of perk up, half-expecting to hear some tale about a heroic battle against an evil tumor in my heroic sinuses or something, but as soon as I explain that no, I'm not Fighting the Good Fight, and yes, this is my real hair and not some chemo wig, it's just that my body just sort of doesn't work correctly, I watch their eyes glaze over immediately. There was no drama in being born incomplete, with parts that didn't work, pieces that didn't add up to a whole. Even the phrase "birth defect" struck me as almost unbelievably callous – like, I'm a human, and you're calling me "*defected*," like some flawed model to be sent back to the factory to be fixed or something? Guess what: there was no factory. It was like the hero of an action movie dying in the middle of the film from a stray bullet: so senseless, it was just boring. Every sad story had to have rhyme or reason. Mine had neither, it just *was*. And sometimes that made me feel more broken than anything. Once I was even exiting my doctor's office with an Intresia pamphlet in my hand when a girl and her father commented that it "must be one of those cancer books." I wanted to turn and tell them that fuck no, it wasn't a cancer book, that there were other maladies in the world besides cancer, and that my condition had nothing at all to do with cancer, but I turned and left like the coward I was. But still, deep down, I kind of wanted my boring story to matter. I wanted people to care that I had something other than Cancer with a capital C. I just didn't know how.

Guests slowly started to trickle in, but the turnout wasn't great. I guessed people were busy with summer, or just busy getting dead, either one. So I got going. Although we didn't have any new people, we always started the meetings by going around the circle to tell our stories and share anything new about our conditions, and so at 7:10 I welcomed everyone, mentioned that Cooper was just a curious friend tagging along (the intensity of the stares coming from the girls in the group warranted an explanation) and asked the member closest to me how he was doing.

"Alright, I guess," said Victor, who'd been paralyzed in a car crash when he was just a kid.

"That face you just gave me doesn't look alright," I said. He swallowed.

"Well, it's…it's my girlfriend. It was fine at first, and it seemed like she didn't really care that I was immobile, but I can tell she's sick of reaching for things and getting my TV remote for me and stuff. She's sort of pulling away."

I nodded. "Yeah. That sucks. And I hate to say this, but there's a chance she might dump you."

His mouth fell open.

"Victor, sorry, but being broken makes us different," I told him, throwing an uneasy glance at Cooper. "You know that. That's just how it is. Whenever we walk into a room – or roll into one, in your case, sorry – people glance. It's their nature to glance, just like it's our nature to slow down when we see a really bad car wreck. We are the car wreck, and we just have to accept that, or else we'll never get anywhere in this world. Do you get that?"

134

He just sort of nodded. "Yeah, I get it. It just sucks."

"Welcome to life," I said. "It sucks. And by the way, this girl sounds like a total bitch, so she wouldn't be much of a loss anyway."

A few people laughed, Cooper included. I didn't even want to wonder what he thought of all this, so I kept going.

"Who wants to complain next?" I asked, and Scotty raised his hand. He was around my age, had "beaten" leukemia at around fourteen, and came to the meetings to help others who hadn't yet healed and were still stuck in their problems.

"Not a problem, just a contribution," he said. "People suck. Get used to it."

"Why thank you for that uplifting comment," I said, and he sort of bowed in his seat. I looked to his left. "Hey, Kim."

"Hi," she said, typically shy. Because of her spina bifida, she was in a wheelchair, too, and couldn't do much.

"You doing okay?" I asked.

"I mean, yeah, I guess."

"What's the 'I guess' for?"

"I don't know. There is one thing. Feeling pretty is a struggle every day."

"Well that's stupid," I told her. "You're gorgeous."

"Agreed," Cooper smiled, and I looked over at him. "Your hair is beautiful, by the way. Are those highlights?"

Kim blushed, reached up, and patted at her dishwater blonde hair. No hairstylist in the world would've given someone that color, and he knew it.

"No, this is all natural, I swear."

"Could've fooled me," Cooper told her casually. "Looks professional. Where'd you get it done, anyway? Can I have the stylist's number? My hair's been looking a bit shaggy lately, and my mom teases me relentlessly about it."

Kim laughed, and they went on and on. And the thing was, his interest in her didn't come off as condescending or patronizing in any way at all – he was just talking to her, in the same way any human talked to any other human. It's just

135

that Kim was never spoken to like a human – in the eyes of most people, she was a pile of pity in a wheelchair. *Compliment her, do your good deed of the day, and then move on and forget she's an actual human who wants to talk about anything other than her issues* – that is what most people thought when they looked at Kim.

But not Cooper.

A lull finally came in their conversation. Before I could tear up, I turned to the guy next to her.

"Anyway, Hank! Hi."

"*Hiiii*," Hank groaned. Hank was a dead-eyed soldier a few years back from Afghanistan with a missing arm and a major hole in his psyche to show for it. He had a dark, vaguely irritable demeanor, like a dog that had been rescued from a bad owner. I grew up around the corner from a nasty dive bar called Ginger's and I knew Hank because I grew up watching its patrons come and go whenever I got bored. They were all just like him: broken, carved-out people who sat around looking to the past because they were haunted by their present and resigned at best about their futures.

"Anything you wanna bitch about?"

He shrugged, as usual, so I turned to Autumn. "Okay then. Hey, Autumn. How's it going?" (For the sake of inclusiveness, Autumn and I tried not to be too buddy-buddy at meetings. I knew she was confused as hell about Cooper's presence and would be cornering me about him as soon as she could, but I tried not to think about it just yet.)

"Shitty," she said, deadpan. "Like, shittier than a Mormon who accidentally walked into a porn convention. *That* shitty."

"Explain."

"It's just so fucking unfair, *all* of it," she began. She usually saved her biggest rants for these meetings, so I settled into my chair and braced myself. "Like, I'm twenty-four years old, and all my friends are looking forward in life, buying rings and wedding dresses and baby cribs and starter houses, while I'm having consultations with plastic surgeons about potentially having my breasts removed. Give me hot guys, give me a wedding, give me Key West – give me *something*. Shit, I'll even take an unwanted pregnancy at this point. I just feel like I'm…stuck, you know? I'm sure *you* know." She looked right at me as she said it. I bristled, feeling Cooper's eyes on me.

"Um…yeah. I know." The conversation was hitting too close to home, so I moved onto someone else. "So, hey, Ethan, let's talk about-"

"Like, seriously," Autumn said, refusing to let me drop it. "Why me? Why now? I'm sick of being the heroic cancer fighter. This has really been bugging me lately, especially now that literally *everyone* in my life is coupled up. Or so it seems." She threw me a mean glance, and I looked away. "Like, if my family had stayed in Sri Lanka, I'd still have cancer, but at least I wouldn't be getting bombarded by engagement stories every week, since they're so conservative about marriage or whatever. But still – I'm jealous. Like, I really want the chance to buy a fucking overpriced wedding dress and select ugly centerpieces and get into passive-aggressive email fights with my bridesmaids, you know? Why can't I at least get the *chance*?"

My lips curled into my mouth. I felt vaguely dizzy but I pushed it down. "I don't know," I finally said. "None of us knows. But that's why we're here. To find some sense in a totally effing senseless situation."

"Oh boo hoo," Hank suddenly said. Because he barely ever said *anything*, everyone looked at him.

"Go on," I said.

"You're sitting here moaning about not having a boyfriend?" he asked in Autumn's direction. "Well, get over it. I know you have cancer, and it sucks. But at least you're alive, unlike some previous members of this group, and at least you have two arms."

"*Excuse me?*" Autumn asked after a brief, and very shocked, silence. "Um, I'm complaining about a *lot* more than being single. There are new wedding albums being posted every weekend. This is a major problem! And for your information, I'm not even totally single. I'm talking to someone!"

"Is this like the last guy you tried to date, who barely knew your name?" he asked. "Just because I'm quiet doesn't mean I'm not paying attention."

"'*Tried to date*?'" Autumn asked in disbelief. "We spoke! In person! Twice! And he even gave me his Snapchat username! He didn't exactly add me back when I friended him, but I'm optimistically waiting!"

"I rest my case," Hank said.

"And…so do I!" Autumn cried. "I forgot what my case is, but I rest it! It is very well rested, trust me!"

"Whatever."

Autumn crossed her arms and looked away. Hank tried to do the same, remembered he only had one arm to cross, and then sort of awkwardly hugged his shoulder while everyone else stared at the walls.

"Well," I said. "So! Moving on. Um, Ethan, how about you? Anything new in Ethan Land worth complaining about?"

Ethan was seventeen and fighting a rare blood cancer that was famous for the almost unendurable pain it inflicted upon its sufferers. He broke my heart to pieces every time I looked at him. I'll never forget the first thing he said to me when we met a few years back, after his parents had heard about the group and asked me to go visit him in the hospital to talk some fight into him. After I walked into the darkened room where he was being partially subdued by straps to keep him from dis-attaching himself from the torture machines keeping him alive, he politely greeted me, pulled me down to his eye level, and asked me in the softest, most angelic voice I had ever heard if I would please kill him.

He was a tad better now, and had been weaned off some treatments, but I still cursed the world every time I saw him and thought of everything he had to deal with. He would be lucky to grow old enough to one day be legally allowed to drink in a bar.

"I'm doing, like, okay, but the thing I hate more than anything is the guilt," he said, and a few people nodded. "It feels like all I am is a problem or something. My dad can barely be around my mom because she cries so much about me, and my friends are pulling away from me to save themselves from my death. I just feel like, I don't know. Like I'm not worth the trouble."

"Have you ever had a dog that died?" Cooper suddenly asked. I looked over at him, confused, but he nodded ever-so-slightly to signal that it was okay.

"Um. Yeah, I think?" Ethan said. "My family poodle, Pork Chop. When I was, like, twelve or something."

"And did you love him?" Cooper asked.

"I mean, yeah?"

"And when Pork Chop died, were you furious at him for dying? Did you punch the dirt at his grave and curse him for daring to grow old and leave you? Or were you grateful for every second you got with that little dog?"

For a moment Ethan just stared and blinked.

"I...I get it now," he finally said, his blue eyes large. "I get it now. Thanks."

Soon Autumn started to complain about destiny again, and patience was wearing thin. I was feeling weirdly barf-y, too, so that wasn't helping me pay attention, either. Why was boob cancer Autumn's destiny, she wondered aloud, while every other girl's destiny was to prance down an aisle at twenty-three? "And I'm starting to think that I'm just like, *doomed*," she ranted, "and I don't even know how to-"

"Or you can just accept that that there's no sense in anything," Cooper interrupted. Everyone looked over at him again, myself included.

"Care to explain?" I asked.

"Okay, well, my health is fine," he said, "and I don't want to feel like I'm, like, speaking to your situation or whatever, but I've been re-forming some of my opinions lately due to some new insight from the smartest person I know-" he winked at me- "and for me, things started to feel a lot less terrifying when I accepted that life is a happy little accident. Optimistic nihilism, I call it." Another wink.

"Go on," I told him, trying not to blush.

"Well. Like. We are not the descendants of two naked creatures created in a garden for the amusement of some bearded man in the sky," he began. "I'm pretty sure of that now. We are one cell that evolved into another cell that evolved into a creature that learned to live in water and then crawled out of a pond and then started walking and then turned into lizards and other animals that adapted into monkeys and then those monkeys happened to leave home and evolve into humans, and now here we are. All of those coincidences and accidents and random occurrences led to us sitting here, in this fire station, young and beautiful and damaged, trying to rise up into a sunken world, and so we'd might as well stop trying to find any sense in the chaos and just deal with the particular set of accidents we've ended up with. That's my advice, at least."

Silence fell upon the room. That is, until Autumn cleared her throat and raised her hand a little.

"So, um...are you *sure* you're not single?"

The drive home was tense. I could feel my feelings for Cooper, like, *deepening* in a really weird way, putting down roots. And it terrified me, to be honest.

He reached over and absently ran his fingers up and down my arm, making me wince and pull away. He looked over at me.

"Sorry," I said, "I'm just not used to that. Here, do it again."

I returned my arm to where it was, and he got right back to it.

"And I'm sorry about Autumn," I said to break the quiet. "She's the only person I know who would go to an illness support group to pick up guys. Sorry."

"Ha," he said. I could tell he wasn't really listening.

"Where are you right now, Cooper?"

140

"Listen," he said suddenly, throwing me the most nervous glance I'd ever seen. "I want you to tell me the truth about something."

Oh no. He's dumping me. He snapped out of this trance where he finds me attractive, and he's done with me.

"Yeah?" I asked, as he fidgeted with his shoulder.

"Well, the thing is…if you hated it, I just want to know, so I can…so I can throw it away, and just forget about it, and…yeah."

"*What?*"

What did that mean? Was he trying to push me away so he could shake the blame from himself? Was this leading to this classic *it's not you, it's me* bullshit conversation?

"The book," he said, looking like he hated himself. "If you hated it, I just want to know. Just lay it out there, please."

I felt like my body had melted into my seat with relief. We hadn't discussed *Eighty Eight* yet, or even mentioned it, really – I got the sense that he felt too awkward to talk about in person.

"No, Cooper," I said. "Nooooo. No no no. It was amazing. I mean, like…yeah. I cried like a baby. It was good. Really good."

"You think so?" he finally asked, stupefied. How could he be so oblivious?

"Yes. It's amazing. Trust me, I read hundreds of books a year. It's like you painted a portrait with words instead of paint. Why aren't you pursuing this?"

He said nothing. When he did speak, his voice was shy and quiet, his head turned down, towards the floorboard. "Because I just, I already tried once, at the newspaper, and I blew it, and I don't think…I don't think anyone would want to read a book by a loser, or whatever. I already put my thoughts and fears and desires out there once, and I failed and got fired. Why do it again?"

My chest shattered for him. I wanted to reach out and take his hand, but I couldn't. I was still too locked up within myself. "Cooper," I said. "This story is as good as, or better

141

than, ninety percent of the stuff I come across. You have a gift. Use it. Live your purpose. Don't let one failure stop you. And of course people would want to read something by you. You're…you. Humans try things, and we fail sometimes, and then we get back up and try again, and then we win, hopefully. That's what we do."

"So you *really* think it's good?"

I shook my head. "Ugh. Are you *serious* right now? I'm not a good liar. You should see when my little brother shows me his watercolors. I try to be nice, but my reaction is…yeah. Slightly less supportive, you could say. Seriously, though, how do you not know how good you are?"

He angled himself away, a *V* between his brows, and my insides caved in for him. "I don't want to talk about this anymore," he said. "I was wondering something else, too. Something I noticed."

"Yeah?"

He bit his lip. "What makes you angry, Summer?"

"Um, I don't – what do you mean?"

"Your anger," he said. "That thing that bubbles up sometimes. Like back there, when you were talking to that one kid. You got kind of…rude, to be honest."

I thought hard. Honestly, being happy for me wasn't that easy most of the time. In my eyes, empathy was the ultimate double-edged sword: I was blessed with the ability to care deeply for people, and cursed with the knowledge that they would nearly always choose the worst for themselves.

"So much makes me mad," I said. "Everything. Mostly suffering. And the knowledge that the world is unfair. The fact that somewhere out there some kid is crying in the rain with no family and no hope. The fact that the world contains hatred and bigotry and injustice and hunger and Justin Bieber. All of it. I literally sit there being angry at the planet sometimes, just because of how unfair it all is. That's probably why I started the group. And I'm not saying I did it out of some obnoxious, self-serving Mother Teresatype quest to be better than everyone, either, I just – I don't know. I wanted to do *something*, you know? *Anything*."

"I can see that," he said, and then he let out a long and lazy sigh. "You are a remarkable person, Summer Johnson. Better than me, that's for sure. Honestly, what I saw back there was the most amazing thing I've ever witnessed. You were wonderful."

"I was?"

He ignored me. Instead of responding, he picked up my hand and kissed the back of it. "Did you know there are about 7.94 million seconds in a summer, Summer?"

"No," I breathed.

"Well there are. But the thing is, you don't get to spend *all* those seconds actually enjoying yourself. So, take out a couple million seconds to sleep, maybe a few hundred thousand to eat, and subtract another couple hundred thousand for running errands and whatnot, and a few thousand in August so you can watch *Shark Week*, which I never miss, and then that leaves me with…still not enough seconds to spend with you." I froze and looked over at him. "You've lit up my summer, Summer, as horrifically cheesy as that sounds. I was just…*dark* before you came along."

The panic was rising up, threating to blow me open, but I swallowed it. Instead I pulled into my driveway and opened my door to make the interior lights come on, lighting up the car. "Now you know how I feel," was my only response.

He kissed me on the cheek and walked to his car. I hurried to my bedroom and slammed the door, too dazed to think anything other than *Cooper Cooper Cooper Unclimbable Cooper*. In my haste to get ready for bed – or at least several hours of lying in my bed, swimming in my thoughts – I shifted my portable speaker looking for my phone charger and knocked Saviour's book to the floor, which Cooper had leant me after I'd lost my copy in the depthless pit of doom that was my car. When I cursed and bent to pick it up, my eyes fell on a single sheet of paper on the floor, which I guess had fallen out of the book. I grabbed it and crawled into bed, noticing once again how awful Cooper's handwriting was. It was obviously something he'd only meant for himself to see, and so like the terrible beast I am, I read it immediately:

So. The world kinda sucks, and sometimes it's important to remind yourself of stuff that makes your soul feel young and alive, because when you hit about twenty, The Feels start to die and your heart goes numb and you sort of forget what you're breathing for. And in my opinion, it's important to seek out ways to resurrect those Feels from time to time just so you don't become depressed and end up, like, killing a bunch of people in a mall or whatever. So, in no particular order, here are the REASONS FOR COOPER NICHOLS TO BE HAPPY AND FEEL STUFF AND NOT MURDER HIMSELF AND/OR OTHERS:

- **Nutella**
- **Pancakes**
- **Nutella pancakes**
- **July**
- **Florida**
- **July in Florida**
- **Country ham**
- **Good music + good beer + good people**
- **Netflix and a couch while the late afternoon rain rolls in**
- **The way I can still perfectly remember the theme song from Zelda, my favorite childhood video game, even though I haven't heard it in years**
- **The fact that I know enough about life to know how important it is to hold onto that memory with everything in me**
- **That thrill you get the night before leaving for a big trip**
- **A day of fishing under the pier with nothing to do but a bait bucket to empty and a sunset to wait for**

144

- The unpopped kernels at the bottom of the popcorn bag
- The fact that I'm gonna be a dad one day, and have a doctor hand me a baby and tell me it's all mine
- My mom, and the way I feel when I'm around her. Like I'll always have a place there
- My sweet Hadley
- Sweet tea, and grits, and driving through long country roads surrounded by open fields on a Sunday morning, and the South in general
- That thing that happens when you think you've forgotten how to feel, and then the feeling comes back
- The thing that makes the feeling come back

And then, at the bottom of the page, an additional few lines had been added in a different-colored ink:

Post-Summer Addendum:

- Her
- Her doe eyes
- The way she looks at me
- The way I feel when her doe eyes look at me
- The fact that she's making the feeling come back

As a growing buzz roared in my ears I looked out of my window and stared at the pale pink roses blooming in my front yard, their petals glowing rose gold in the burning sunset, and that's when I realized I couldn't run from it any longer. The impossible had happened.

There comes a time in every relationship when you look over at the other person and suddenly realize: *this could break me.* You look into their eyes and feel the ancient lonely bones within yourself start to rearrange and shift into something new and golden and thrilling and good, and you know that this person has sunken into you, perhaps irrevocably, and that their happiness is now intertwined with your happiness, possibly forever. And right then you realize there will be no turning back from this, whatever "this" is, because to send them off into the night now would wreck you. And tonight, sitting in the car in front of my house, I felt myself reach that moment – and it scared the living shit out of me. Because the Me he knew, the Me I felt him falling for more and more every day, was a lie. Quite simply, she did not exist. And I had no Earthly idea what to do about it.

A very long time ago I had decided the world was generally a bad place and subsequently locked my soul away for good, figuring the only way to avoid being broken by this cold cruel planet was to turn myself off and drift unfeelingly through the icy meadows until death came, *whenever* it would come. But all at once, Cooper was making me come alive again – and that wasn't good. Because we were building a palace on pebbles, and every passing moment was just another moment closer to when it could all fall down. No matter how much my brain had told my heart to run away and save him from my fate, I had let myself drown in Cooper Nichols. Shelly was right: now that he was drowning in *me*, I needed to get out of fantasy mode and fix this mess before my dream collided with reality and exploded like fireworks in the summer sky.

14

So, above all, I was still a rational person, and the way I saw it, I had three options: I could turn away from Cooper for good, cold turkey, just delete his number and forget I'd ever known him. I was also rational enough to know that this would make me go fucking crazy. I was in too deep now. So, option two: I could always just tell him about my diagnosis and confess about lying and see what happened. He would either get mad at me for lying and then ditch me, or…

Or. That was the key word: there was no *Or.* I didn't really see an option besides that. I had misled him by not telling him, and that was wrong, and he'd probably never forgive me for it.

But there was also a third option. A dangerous one. And that option was to say nothing and hope the surgery would be successful and therefore make all of this worrying unnecessary. I'd disappear for a few weeks in September, and then poof, I'd be back, cured and mended. The German girl was proof – maybe the procedure could fix me, and maybe I was getting all worked up over nothing.

And maybe, just maybe, my health was cratering and I was ignoring the signs and I wouldn't even make it long enough for any of this to matter, and trying to find love before death was as futile as a crab trying to stand against the rising tides and hope to stay in place.

I gave myself a week to decide.

Sure enough, Autumn was furious with me for neglecting to tell her about the Cooper thing, and she called me in the middle of the week and ordered a Starbucks session to investigate. After she commandeered a prime corner table in the coffeehouse, she peered through the window toward the passing cars on Third Street, but it seemed like she was looking *through* them instead of at them.

"So what's up?" I asked after a moment. "I thought this would be an interrogation session, but you look totally weird. You didn't like him?"

"No, no, of course I liked him," she said, snapping back to the present. "I mean, God, have you *seen* the kid's forearms? Holy shit. You could carve wood with those tendons. No, it's just that that night, like, made me sad for some reason, that's all."

"What? Why?"

She sighed. "I don't know. The way he looks at you…I just want someone to look at me like that. To love me like that."

"*Love?*" I asked. "Um, we're not using words like that yet, Pollyanna. It's been, like, a month or two, at most. Who do you think I am, one of the Facebook psychos we make fun of?"

"Yes. Apparently you are. I mean, come on – sneaking around, showing up at Anti-Support with someone like *him*? I feel like I barely know you. And it *is* love," she continued, searching me, as she shook her head. "I could see it. I could *feel* it, almost. Do you know what you're doing, though?"

"What do you mean?"

Her eyes strip-searched me down to the bone, and suddenly I wondered just how much she knew. "You know what I'm talking about, Sum. Your surgery and everything – it's pretty big, and maybe he deserves to know. I told you to be slutty and everything, but this is clearly becoming…*something*. Does he know what he's getting into?"

"Stop." I ignored the shiver that ran up my back at her words. "I'm figuring it out as I go, I promise. Lay off me. You got to have all the fun forever. Please don't tell him anything – I just want to enjoy him for a bit, especially since the Fourth is coming up and all."

"Okay," she said, glancing away again, the far-off look in her eyes making a whole new ocean of anxiety well up within me. It's not like I thought she'd run off and tell him everything to purposely hurt me, but that was the thing about Autumn: sometimes she couldn't help herself.

After I sat with her for a few more minutes we started drifting towards the door. "Here," she said as she threw away her empty cup, "take a hug before you go off with Cooper again and I lose you."

"Thanks," I said as she embraced me with a Patented Autumn Hug. "I needed that."

"You needed what? Hugs, or your boyfriend?"

"Both," I said. "Always. And that kind of terrifies me."

The Fourth of July in Jacksonville Beach was absolute heaven, even for a Cynical Cindy like me. Thousands upon thousands of people hit the streets on bikes and skateboards and scooters, parties and cookouts and Slip N Slides filled every driveway and yard in town, and fireworks popped in the sky from sunup to midnight. Usually I rode the back of Autumn's bike from cookout to cookout until we got tired and went to take a nap, and then we'd walk down to the pier at sundown and watch the fireworks shoot off the end. They'd zoom up and explode over the shimmering black seas, burning red and blue and gold and white against the dark sky for one brilliant moment, and at the end of the fifteen-minute firework show I'd always find myself convinced that there was beauty in the world again. Then I'd take that hope and fortify myself with it for the next year until I could see the fireworks again on the next Fourth and refill my dwindling Hope Reserves once more.

And the prospect of never experiencing all this again just broke me in the worst way. Not in the way Cooper's smile broke me or a photo of a baby Yorkie broke me – just broke me, thoroughly and senselessly, like when you drop a glass bowl from pretty high up and it doesn't even bother with cracking or shattering, it just makes that *pop!* sound and explodes into a million tiny shards. And since my self-imposed deadline was Monday the Fifth, I figured I'd try to let myself enjoy one final weekend before making the big Cooper decision. I had to. I couldn't live without the summer.

The first Thursday of the holiday weekend I went over to his place while his mom made a late breakfast. This may sound creepy, but I loved to watch the way his mom looked at him, and admire the way her eyes lit up when she did so, and think about why they did. And as he picked at a Nutella pancake a while later, his mom watching *Discovery* in the next room, I kind of gently asked about her prognosis. Long story short, it wasn't good – her MS was advancing quickly, and it wouldn't be too long before she'd have to be sent off to some expensive nursing home. The only thing keeping her out of one, I guessed, was Cooper's presence. Barely anyone in her situation had an able-bodied young man at her beck and call, and I got the sense that he knew it, but still couldn't stay there and wait on her forever. Nobody would be able to. I'd seen the same silent battle being waged in my mother's eyes my whole life – *should I sit here with my child and nurse her for another week, or should I go out and get back my life before it's too late?*

Anyway, Colleen's disability checks from the government were helping to keep both of them afloat, but Cooper's savings from his newspaper days were about to run dry – which was all the more incentive for him to take his chances at getting a book published, in my eyes. But what did my opinion matter?

"But it's fine," he said after he finished explaining, as he pushed around the remains of the pancake on his plate. He ate *a lot*, and very often, and although I had no idea how his body stayed so perfect, I kind of hated him for it. "She's fine as long as I'm here. That's why I got her that geode necklace."

I smiled. I'd noticed the necklace before, actually, a beautiful geode with purple crystals inside that had been sliced in half and then strung from a fine silver cord that dangled from Colleen's neck.

"Just wanted to remind her that beautiful things can grow in ugly places," he told me. "She lived in a bad situation for a long time, but she has me now, and she always will. At least...I hope she will."

150

Cooper sank into himself, his frown shading his features. He did that a lot, disappear in front of me, and lately he'd been doing it more and more for some reason. He'd done a good job of acting sparkly and light and happy-go-lucky, that dazzling boy from Joe's Crab Shack, but now I knew the truth: he was lost. I could see it in the shadows in his bottomless eyes; hear it in the silences he let drag on for far too long during our conversations about his life. He was just better at hiding it than I was. It all made so much sense now: of *course* he wrote stories about people who dreaded the future; of *course* he constantly obsessed over these Big Life Issues like death and fate and legacy. He was stuck in the past, dwelling on the ruins of his dreams and dealing with his ailing mother every day, unable to move forward. They said that people stopped maturing at the exact age of the onset of their health problems, frozen in time by the pity that suddenly descended upon them like molasses, but I'd never imagined the same being true for that person's family members, too. Perhaps this explained my dad's flight from our family like a college student who had impregnated a one-night-stand and then run for the hills; my mother's shaky emotional state; my little brother's immaturity and lack of self-confidence and weight issues. Cooper was exactly like me, a girl frozen at the age of her diagnosis, held back from truly experiencing adulthood by a smothering but well-meaning mother and sympathetic strangers and by having to literally feed myself milk every day like a baby. In a world of already-stunted growth, we were practically children. I'd had no idea we were so alike.

"That's so sweet. But are you calling yourself beautiful?" I asked to swivel the conversation toward a heart-melting direction.

"Of course I am. Have you *seen* this ass?"

"Touché. And sorry for asking about your mom," I said, and he shook his head.

"Don't be. It's whatever. But seriously, like I was saying before, I really want you to have fun today when we go to the beach."

I gave him a weird look. "We've gone to the beach, like, ten times. Of course I will."

"No, like, *really*," he said. "We've done what you like to do, now it's time to do *my* routine. It's Florida, and it's summer, and that's what people do in Florida in the summer, Summer. Swim, boogie board, run around – they don't just sit there in their clothes reading books, like you."

I swallowed hard, imagining a crowd of beachgoers awkwardly staring at my many surgery scars and the plastic tube protruding from me. "Thanks, but you know I....I can't do that," I said. "I have a one-piece, but my tube still pokes out, and it's weird. People stare, and it gets awkward and stuff. Like, *I* don't care, but I don't want *you* to feel weird or anything."

Cooper looked away. "Oh, um, well, speaking of that, I, um, got you something." He went into the living room and then brought back a bag from Dillard's, the local department store.

"Cooper! It's not my birthday or anything," I said as he put it on the table in front of me.

"Yeah, but I saw it and I, like, thought you might like it, or whatever."

I took a box out of the bag and opened it. Inside was a brown one-piece bathing suit with a white sarong.

"I just know you can be self conscious about your feeding tube and whatever," he said, looking away from me, "and I, uh, got you something to maybe help fix that."

I took out the bathing suit. It was *super* brown, and nothing I would ever buy for myself or anything – but it was still the most perfect thing I'd ever gotten.

"It's great, Cooper. Thank you. I can't believe you did this."

"You don't think it's weird or anything?"

"It's not weird, Cooper, it's..."

Suddenly I spotted a handwritten note in the box and took it out. *All I want is to show you off,* it said in his trademark awful script. *Please let me now.*

I looked up and smiled. "It's not weird. It's perfect. *You're* perfect."

"Good," he said. "And before we – wait. Are you okay? You're looking a little pale. You're almost green, actually. Everything good?"

"I'm fine," I said, messing with my arm in a weird little way. "This whole 'not eating' thing does take its toll every once in a while, I guess. But I'm splendid." I took the bag and stood up. "Okay, I'm gonna go out to the car to get something and change and stuff. I'll meet you downstairs in-"

"Hold up," he said as he held out a hand. "I know where you're going. You're getting your makeup kit."

My shoulders fell. "Um...yeah. And?"

"And I refuse to allow you to keep hiding under all that stuff. You're beautiful. You don't need it."

"Oh," I said. "But-"

"There is no *but*," he said as he got up and kissed my cheek, his stubble scratching against my skin, reminding me that I was a human capable of feeling things, no matter how hard I'd been trying to avoid that fact up until now. "You're hot and you need to show it. And plus, it's the beach. Who puts makeup on to go to the *beach*?"

"You do have a point," I smiled. "I guess it is kind of tacky."

I turned for his tiny bathroom with the fake wooden walls. After I changed into my new super-brown bathing suit that I loved completely, a spare tube of concealer fell out of my bag and rolled under the sink. I turned and left without picking it up.

I followed Cooper to the pier and waded in a tide pool while he fished. In Jax Beach the water was usually a muted slate color, but sometimes it changed with the light of the sun like a pair of hazel eyes, and today it happened to be a beautiful shade of dark green, like an emerald in the shadows. The beach was crowded but not many people were by the pier – they were too afraid of the sharks that congregated there

153

because of all the bait in the water. (Typical of us to head straight for the danger.) The weather was on the humid side of comfortable, as was often the case in northern Florida in the summer, and after I got out of the water I sat right on the edge of the sand and put my feet in the cool sea to fool myself into thinking it wasn't so gross out. By now I'd figured today's "fishing trip" was actually just an excuse for me to meet Kevin, Cooper's best friend. I'd told Cooper there was no rush, that I was sure I'd meet him eventually, but for some reason he was, like, weirdly insistent on introducing me to all his different friends and family members, which was cute I guess.

"I'm so sick of pretending I care about fishing," Kevin said as he dropped beside me. We'd already been introduced, but I guess I had to acquaint myself now. With dreads protruding from the half of his blonde head that wasn't shaved, weird hipster tattoos all over his arms and chest, and gauge earrings, he looked more like an attendee at a Grateful Dead concert than the trendy surfers that populated Jax Beach. I found that odd, since Cooper's easy confidence had made me picture him as coming from the popular crowd in high school, the kids who sat in the middle table in the cafeteria, soaking up all the attention. Kevin looked more like an emo kid from the corner table where all the skateboarders and rocker chicks sat, shooting spitballs at the popular crowd instead of sitting with them – to be more specific, he looked like *my* kind of person.

"You mean to tell me a champion surfer doesn't like fishing?" I asked. "Isn't that, like, against the rules?"

He gave me a weird look. "Oh, didn't Coop tell you? I do love surfing, but I'm also totally gelaeophobic, and fishing doesn't exactly help that. I'd rather not know what was out there if I had the choice."

"Come again? What-a-phobic?"

"Fear of sharks. I have it."

"Wait. You're a surfer with a phobia of sharks? What?"

154

"Not just that, I'm deathly afraid of the water in general," he said. "I saw a little girl get bitten by a shark while standing in waist-deep water down in Cocoa Beach when I was ten, and I've never been the same. But by that point I had already fallen in love with surfing and there was nothing I could do about it – I was a goner."

"I know what you mean," I said under my breath, a chill running up my leg even though the temperature currently hovered somewhere between Inhospitably Muggy and Suicide-Inducingly Hot.

"So what's your love life like?" I asked to move things along. "Any boy news to report?"

"Oh, no," he said. "I wish. I'd let you know if I had some. The last guy I dated ended up cheating on me with a Spark guy. How tacky is that? Like, as if relationships weren't hard enough before, now we have to deal with our boyfriends being able to get on their phones and sext whoever they want in secret. Why couldn't I have been born in the '20s, so I could dress like a flapper and not have to worry about Spark?"

"Agreed," I said with a nervous little laugh. "Even though…"

"I know," Kevin said as he gave me the side eye. "Coop told me all about the Spark thing."

I cringed hard. I didn't think Cooper had been telling people about me, and *that*. I shriveled into myself a little as I wondered what *else* Kevin knew.

"It's fine, though," Kevin said. "So you had a lonely moment. Who hasn't? I bet you don't regret it for one second." He motioned at Cooper.

"True. I don't."

"But seriously, you're good for him. Better than anyone I've seen, actually. He seems…different now. Happy. Less stressed. And it's good that you're, like, handling all his baggage – his devotion to his mom and whatever. Most girls are annoyed by it, since it leaves no time for them."

155

I watched Cooper's back muscles ripple in the sun as he tossed out his fishing line. "Something tells me they all got over it."

"True again."

"How many girls *have* there been, by the way?" I asked as matter-of-factly as I could, since I am a monster and sometimes I don't even know how I live with myself.

"Um, a good amount," Kevin said, sort of halfway apologetically. "Not by his doing, though. Coop's the guy who always made all the girls fall in love with him by being so nice and charismatic and, like, smart, and whatever, but trust me, he was clueless beyond that point. He's the most oblivious guy I've ever met, actually. He never really had a male role model in his life, and that sort of hit his confidence hard, I think. He only dated anyone when *they* pursued *him*. But, I mean, just look at him – he *did* get pursued a ton."

"Yeah," I said. In my peripheral vision I could see the judgy look Kevin was giving me.

"Does it change your view of him to know that you're not, like, the first girl to take him for a ride around the block, or whatever?" he asked, and I couldn't tell if he was testing me or not.

Cooper shifted the angle of his body a little as I watched him, his rippling abdominal muscles casting shadows on one another. I felt my face warm up as I turned to Kevin. "Something tells me I'll get over it."

When the sun sank behind our heads, the shadows cast by the palms and hotels along the shore creeping ever closer to the water as the day wound down, Cooper finally came and sat beside me. As I rubbed my leg against his I wondered if there was anything in the world better than this. His hair was getting golden like his skin, which looked spectacular against his warm brown eyes. I guess I was getting sort of sun-kissed, too. In that moment I wished very much that I could sit right here next to him, being that young and that beautiful, forever.

"Sorry," Cooper said, "this one shark was eluding me and kept eating my bait and then swimming off."

"Oh no," I said, mocking disappointment. I liked him so much more when he was unburdened, acting young and easy like this. "How tragic it is that you didn't get to reel in a deadly shark while standing five feet away from me. The horror!"

"Hey, I like catching them!"

"Why, though?"

He looked out at the sea, puffed out his chest, and exhaled. "I don't know. They're trash fish, you can't really eat them or do much with them, but lemme tell you, they fight like hell."

"Ah. The fight," I said. "That explains it. You're such a guy."

"No. I'm just a human. And I fight. That's what humans do. We have to. There is no other option."

He stared off into the clouds for a long time as I thought about this and watched him. I noticed something in his eyes that reminded me of myself – the sadness, the insecurity, the fatigue. And suddenly I knew exactly how to help make him happy.

I tucked it away into a giddy little corner of my mind and returned to the sea.

I was just about to say something when a wild shriek caught my ears. I looked around, half-expecting to see a shark attack victim limping ashore, when a blonde girl under the pier jumped up and down and accepted a ring from a quite attractive guy kneeling in the shallows at her feet. Of course there was a crowd of friends taking photos from behind one of the pilings supporting the pier – because if Facebook doesn't see it, it never happened at all – and once the couple made out in front of everyone, the friends stopped taking photos and jumped out to congratulate them.

I shivered a little and then noticed Cooper staring at me.

"What's wrong?" he asked. "You look...sad."

"Oh, no, nothing," I said. "Good for them! Weddings! Marriage! Yay!"

He said nothing, his gaze suspicious.

"Hey, you wanna try your luck before we leave?" Kevin asked me. "My pole's over there against that trash can."

"Nah," Cooper said casually before I could respond, waving his hand. "She's not big on the whole fishing thing. Feels bad for 'em."

I opened my mouth and then closed it. I'd told him that exactly one time, on our first date.

"And wait," Cooper told Kevin. "You've never offered your pole to any of my girls before. Why now?"

Kevin smiled at me. "Let's just say that I trust my pole would be in good hands with her."

"Great," Cooper said, "now let's stop talking about your pole being in my girl's hands and look at the sunset. God, isn't this view awesome?"

Kevin checked out Cooper from behind and then gave me a knowing smirk, eyebrows raised. "Yeah," he said as I tried not to laugh. "It is."

A little wave surged up around us as we sat there, the tide rising quickly, the words *girl girl terminal girl* repeating in my head. Cooper reached over and splashed me.

"Hey!" I said as I wiped my face, but inside I was suddenly panicking. I didn't want him to wash off *all* my concealer and see my scar in all its glory, here in the fading but still impressive July sunlight. "I just straightened my hair!" I lied. "I can't get wet."

"You did, huh?" he asked as he got up and stared down at me. "So you wouldn't mind if I did...*this*?"

He stuck his leg into a tide pool and kicked water at me. I screamed and rolled to the side.

"Cooper Nichols, how *dare* you!"

That was it. I pushed myself up – which took more effort than ever – and started chasing him like a child. He ran into the water and I followed, jumping through the waves to catch him, ignoring the dull ache in my side as I did so. I

158

finally reached him and pushed him down under the surface, but he grabbed my arm and pulled me under, too. That's when I remembered my makeup. I stood up and turned around, hiding my face, as another surge made the water rise up to our shoulders. This wasn't like the night at the pier – it was still light out, and my scar was totally visible.

"What is it?" he asked. "What's wrong? Did I hurt you?"

Figuring that there was no hiding now, I turned around with my right hand over my cheek.

"My scar," I said quietly. "It's just showing now, that's all."

The look in his eyes changed; softened. He crept closer, grabbed my hand, and slowly pulled it down, revealing me – all of me. I had never felt so exposed. I wanted to flinch and turn away because I was a monster, an ugly defected mess-up, but somehow I resisted. Finally he leaned in and planted a kiss on my upper lip.

"No," Cooper said, a few inches from my face, as my nerve endings went wild with electric delight. "*You* are showing. And it's okay. You're alright, Summer Johnson. You're okay."

I could tell him, I suddenly thought. I could totally tell him right now – that I'd been lying all summer and that I wasn't the person he thought I was and that my days were as numbered as the waves were relentless and that, oh God, I wanted more than anything for him to forgive me and stay.

But like the coward I was, I said nothing.

"I know you've been nervous," he suddenly said, and terror sank into me all over again.

Oh no. He already knows. I won't even have to tell him.

"I have?" I asked.

"About the way we met, on that dating app," he said, weakening my knees with relief. "I'm not blind – I see it in your eyes, in the way you pull away from me sometimes. Kevin told me you were talking about Spark. It's freaking you out that we met on some shallow, promiscuous app – it scared me a little in the beginning, too. But I don't care at all anymore."

As we waded along with the current, we stumbled into a deep hole in the sand and fell into neck-deep water. When we made it to the other side he stood up and laughed, but then he pulled me closer and got serious again.

"See, that's the thing about this world, Summer – you can find deep places, here in the shallows."

I breathed, in and out, in and out, my terror subsiding. We waded there in the sea for a moment, rolling deep in the emerald waves, and suddenly I saw the scene through Saviour's eyes. For one golden moment we were submerged in a weightless ocean of love, a girl on the way down and a boy on the way up, meeting in the middle for one fleeting summer by the sea before cruel fate would yank us apart again – or hopefully not.

"But we still don't know each other that well," I said, making one last attempt at pushing back against this thing that was overtaking us with more force than anything I had ever known before, "and-"

"I know you," he whispered. "I see you, Summer. I know you."

I just stared at him. This was it. The moment of truth, from an honest boy and a lying girl. I knew what I wanted to say, but did I really know what it meant? Was I old and adult enough to know what it was? Did *anyone* even know what it was? My mother was in her middle ages and still had no idea what it meant, and how to get it, or keep it. I knew this was moving too quickly, and I knew I was perhaps headed for the end of the world, but I couldn't run from this anymore. All I knew for sure was that in the still of the night, in the quiet of my mind, in the shimmering sea of my soul, my thoughts would always run back to him – I figured that was a good enough explanation.

"I love you," I finally said, tossing out the words like a hot dish from the oven, too exhilarated and terrified to even look him in the eye.

"I love you, too," he said, a smile in his quiet voice. And then we kissed.

We'd kissed before, obviously, but never like *this*. My body lit up as he explored my mouth, and then other parts of me with his hands, underneath the water. We only stopped when a few kids tut-tutted near us, making us giggle and come to our senses.

"God, what kind of sick fucks *are* we?" he asked, shaking his golden hair free of the saltwater, as my heart rate crashed and burned.

"The kind that make out in front of innocent families on summer holidays, apparently."

Finally he took my hand, and together we trudged through the waves before collapsing onto the sand again. I looped my elbow around his big arm and leaned into his shoulder, thinking about how we were different but sort of the same. We were little crabs scurrying around on the sand trying to find a hole to sink into before a wave came up and swept us away, lost and scared, but no longer alone. The wave was life.

I reached for my towel and checked the date on my phone. Only two more days until I had to make the biggest decision of my possibly-waning existence.

15

The next day, Autumn got the biggest news of *her* possibly-waning existence: her doctors could not find any more traces of cancer. When she called me to share the news, her voice sounded triumphant but muted, like someone whose oceanfront home had just survived a hurricane when there were three more still headed straight for it. But still, this was Autumn, and she know how to celebrate the moment more than anyone. It turned out she was having a day-drinking party under the pier to celebrate, but I politely brushed off the invitation – I was feeling weirdly tired, and besides, I had other things to do.

  Cooper didn't text me all day, which I found a little odd, but it was fine – like I said, I was busy, and I wasn't the type to desperately wait around on *anyone*, even someone as swoonworthy as him. That night I was sitting in my kitchen, having spent the afternoon at Office Max preparing Cooper's surprise I'd come up with under the pier, when I got the following text:

Hadley is dying. I need u

My heart skipped a beat, literally speaking. (It had been doing that lately, dizzying me and making me plant my feet firmly on the floor to keep from swaying or falling, but I didn't really think much of it. That was just what love felt like.) Within a moment, Cooper texted again:

Or maybe I don't need u. Idk.

Huh?

  I sent him a series of question marks, and when he said nothing, I really started to get nervous. That night I was supposed to help Chase with his summer reading essay questions while my mom went out with some dude from a dating website for one of the first times since The Big News – or at least one of the first times she'd admitted to, anyway.

Before that, this had been a near-nightly occurrence, me babysitting Chase while she ran around trying to reclaim the years I'd taken from her by being sick. She'd pop her head into my doorway at around six PM, and the conversation would always go like this: *Hey, Chase has a fever and needs a babysitter, and I'm wiped out from taking you to the hospital yesterday, so would you mind?* I wanted her to be with someone and live her life, but I also wanted her to watch her own kid, so…yeah. It was complicated. She was already texting me about how miserable her date was and how badly she wanted to leave, but it wasn't like I could leave Chase to go bail her out, so I'd kind of rudely told her to deal with it herself.

I can't be there, like, now, I told Cooper. **But I can come later?**

Ok, he said. **But come. Don't bail on me. I'm a mess** And then, two minutes later: **Wait. Don't come.**

I frowned as I read the latest texts. He was being weird. And needy. But I didn't want to let the darkness govern me, and so I chalked it up to the dog situation to save myself from having a heart attack.

I wouldn't dream of bailing and you know it, I said. **See you soon.**

"Where are you going?" my mom asked from the foyer fifteen minutes later, her date having ended awkwardly early. Because of Cooper's weirdness, I'd put on my best dress to impress him, this ice blue thing Shelly had gotten me on special at some department store last summer. I'd also done some makeup tricks I'd learned from this YouTube tutorial thingy I'd watched a few days ago during a spell when Cooper was busy and wasn't talking to me, and all in all, I was starting to feel just a *little* bit cute, if I could say so myself.

"Out," I said as I grabbed my bag and Cooper's surprise.

"Wait," she called as I hit the door to the garage. "Stop, Sum. What about me? Don't you think I want to see my daughter during her last-"

"During my last what, Shelly?" I interrupted, turning around. "My last…summer?"

The second I'd said it, I wished I could unsay it.

"Wait, I just…sorry," I told her. "I'm sorry. But please let me live my life. I need this. Do you understand? …Come on, don't just stare at me. Do you?"

I turned and left before I could hear her start to cry.

Ten minutes later I pulled into Cooper's driveway and walked into his garage to find a total mess. An empty bottle of whiskey lay at his side, and some of it had spilled out onto the concrete, staining it with loopy amber veins. He was next to Hadley, who looked fine, if a little tired, and his shirt was soaking wet with liquor and what I determined to be tears.

"Oh my God, did you drink all that?" I asked as I fell at his side and started to pull off his shirt. He was drunk, that was clear. And crying.

"I don't know," he said. His body language was distant and weird and I tried to ignore it. "One sip turned into a lot more sips and now I don't know where my shoes are. And why are you so pale? You look strange."

"Um," I said as I lifted his arm out of the puddle of alcohol. "Come on, let's get this shirt off and talk. You're drunk."

He glared past me. Figuring he was just wasted, I helped him clean up in the outdoor shower, and then I found his shoes under a ladder across the garage and grabbed him a robe. When I was done he grunted something, and I asked him to repeat himself.

"What?"

"It's Hadley. We have to fix her."

"Okay then," I told him. "Go sit in the garage again, by the wall. I'll handle this."

164

Soon I got an assistant from the vet on the line, even though Hadley seemed no different than she had the other night when I'd dropped by to pick up Cooper for a movie. Then the assistant put us on hold. Twice.

"It's a twenty-four hour place and it's priced like one, too," Cooper slurred from beside me. "Those bitches had *better* answer."

"Shhh!" I said as I finally got the assistant back on again. I helped Cooper explain all of Hadley's symptoms, and soon the assistant decided Hadley probably wasn't going to die immediately, because her body was still strong enough to try to fight. In the end the assistant told us to hold off on taking Hadley to the emergency vet, and to wait until at least morning, since she probably had a few days left in her.

"Okay, fine, I overreacted," Cooper said after I'd thanked the assistant and hung up.

"It's okay," I said as he glared at the wall again with that weird, far-off look on his face. "She *is* breathing slowly, I guess, which isn't good. Just try not to freak out."

He stared ahead, breathing heavily, and since his defenses were lowered I figured this would be as good a time as any to spring something on him. (See previous statements re: me being a shameless bitch.) Autumn's friend's wedding was the following week, and before meeting Cooper I'd figured I'd just go alone, but now I was beginning to imagine more. I saw Cooper and me laughing at a softly-lit table in the corner of the venue; dancing under the hipster-ish Christmas lights strung from oak tree to oak tree along the dance floor; drinking champagne together by a river while we made out like teenagers.

"So," I said with a smile and a blush, "I have this thing next week, this wedding, and I was wondering if you wanted to-"

"Autumn told me," he suddenly blurted out with dead eyes, turning to me.

"What?"

"Autumn told me. Your mom told her mom, and her mom told her, and she told me."

My chest vibrated with pure, yellow panic. I tried to swallow it down. "She told you what?"

"I can't believe you," he said, emotionless. "You're a liar. My heart is broken."

Hadley yawned. I said nothing. I couldn't. Nothing in the world made sense anymore.

"I could've dealt with it, you know," he said with a trembling lip, his voice starting to shake. "I could've understood. You should've told me. But I cannot deal with this. You've been lying to me this entire time. You're a *liar*."

I stared at him.

"Was this your plan all along?" he asked, his voice falling in on itself, getting harder, as he hated me with his eyes. "To find some boy and trick him into falling in love with you before you died? Was this all just some joke – some last laugh, some last summer fling before it all went to hell?"

"I...I don't know what to say," I finally croaked, my vision flickering. "I didn't think any of this would..."

"That's it," he interrupted. His eyes were now closed doors, and all of my ivory taffeta dreams were seeping out of the cracks. "That's exactly it – you didn't think. I can't believe you led me on like this and didn't tell me, and now I might lose you, and...and..."

He turned back to me, his eyes suddenly wild. "Actually, here's a secret. Secret reveal time! Bombshells for everyone! Ready? I've been clinically depressed my whole life, and I got addicted to antidepressants and anxiety medication when I was twenty-one."

"Wh...*what*?"

Some sick kind of glee took over his face. "Yep! I actually know your friend Hank, from the group – we've been to Narcotics Anonymous together. When I was twenty I buckled under the pressure of working for the newspaper and taking care of my mom and being scared shitless that I would eventually leave her like my father did, and I started stealing her pills when mine wouldn't fuck me up enough to escape the worry. One night I got blitzed on Xanax and drove a

166

company car into a ditch and then walked home, and when I woke up I had no clue what had happened or where it was, and I was caught. I went to counseling with my mom after that, but I still never recovered, not really. The version of me you know is an act – I am damaged, Summer. Fucked up. Every time you talked about people staring at you, every time you said it made you feel awkward, you were wrong. They weren't looking at you, they were looking at *us*, because they knew my past and didn't understand why anyone would date such a loser. I'm a *loser*, Summer. A reject. A failed writer. There you go! I'm a liar, too! Any more secrets?"

"Um…I didn't…"

He took a breath and steeled himself. "Actually, I don't care. I don't care what happens with *anything*. I hope I never see you again. Good luck, or just die, either one."

I winced like I'd been hit by a gust of wind on a winter day. The room started to spin, but I fought off the dizziness and pushed myself up to leave. All I knew for sure was that I had to get away from this place, and be anywhere else than here. In the corner of my eye I saw his face crack, and he sat up and reached for me.

"Wait, Summer, I didn't mean it."

"No," I said faintly. "No. I have to…go. Leave."

"Don't leave," he called, louder this time. "Summer, I didn't mean it. Stop. Come back. I love you, Summer. Stop!"

I staggered out of the garage and vomited into the bushes. I could hear him calling my name, but I wiped my mouth and kept stumbling until I reached my car, throwing it into reverse and speeding away as if on autopilot. All I could think as I sped down the street, ruined in my best dress, was that I'd been caught. We were over. This was over. I was broken. I hated him. I hated Autumn. I hated the world.

Just give me the stupid surgery now – I wanted to die.

At precisely the same moment I turned onto Third Street, I knew Cooper would be running around his garage to come up with plan B, and that's when he'd notice the book I'd made at Office Max that day and had accidentally left on the garage floor like a moron. His story had been turned into a real-life book, printed, bound, and covered, with *EIGHTY EIGHT by COOPER NICHOLS* written in elegant black lettering on the cover, along with a simple Post-It note inscribed with the following message:

You told me you'd never write a real book, Cooper. I beg to differ. This book is as real as the love I feel for you.
-Summer

~

I got home at eleven after almost falling asleep at the wheel twice. I was beyond exhausted and just wanted to sleep more than anything in the world, but my mom's voice stopped me.

"Where have you been?" she asked. She was sitting in the dim kitchen with a half-empty empty bottle of wine and was clearly furious. I didn't even want to imagine how long she'd been there.

"I was at the Nichols' house," I said faintly, because it was true. "I had to help them…do something. With their dog."

"Which one is Nichols? Is it that boy you've been going around with?"

I paused. Something about the way she'd said "that boy" triggered some deep fury within me.

"No, one of my *other* boys," I said as I turned and looked in the cabinet for a new carton of Instamilk to make this weird feeling go away. "You know how I am. Different boy calling me every night. There are never enough for me. Their thirst for me is literally more insatiable than Niagara Falls' thirst for water. They just love me and my scar and my fucking feeding tube. That's me!"

"I...I didn't mean it like that," Shelly said. "And please don't talk about yourself like that, it hurts me. But tell me something: does he know?"

"That I'm getting life-threatening surgery?" I suddenly asked, turning to her. "Yes, Shelly, it was the first thing I said when I met him. I was like, 'Hi, I'm Summer. I like pretentious literary novels, long walks on the beach, and oh, I might die soon, but love me anyway. What looks good on the menu?'"

She winced. "Sum, I wasn't saying that. Please chill out. And don't talk like that, you'll be fine. If you're hungry there's some milk in the – wait, actually, you are looking *beyond* pale. Do you want me to make you some gravy?"

I glared at her. For some weird reason, probably because it was fatty but also kind of liquid-y and I could eat it sometimes without barfing, my mother had spent my entire life laboring under the bizarre delusion that I liked gravy. I never usually made a fuss about it when she shoved it down my throat, but tonight I was in no mood to beat around the bush. Some truths you just had to put out there, even Gravy Truths.

"I don't like gravy," I said. "I don't like it and I don't want it and I will never want it and I did not just get my heart broken by Cooper and that fucking bitch Autumn."

"Huh?" Shelly asked, squinting at me as she stepped closer. "Summer, what happened? Are you okay?"

"I don't have time for this right now," I said, the kitchen blurring around me as I lifted up my shirt to insert some milk. "I just wanna lie down."

"Don't shut *me* out, Summer Martin. Don't be like that. Look – I know you're dealing with a lot, and you're trying to live your life."

"Yeah," I said. By this point the room was spinning.

"But just please stop running away from me. From us. I like having you around. I want you around while we...while I still can. And it's not just that. You think you're all grown up but you're so young, Summer. You don't know it. You're *so young*. Didn't you get my voicemails about the carnival tomorrow?"

"No," I said absently. *Sleep Sleep Sleep Cooper left me Sleep.* "I don't even check my voicemail. Voicemails are awkward."

"Well, I needed you around today. Chase has the flu and I've been so stressed out with work and-"

"Chase doesn't have the flu," I said. "I saw him this morning. He's fine."

"He's practically on death's door, Summer, and you denying it isn't going to help."

Even though I was getting groggier by the second, I felt my body shiver with that weird thrill you get when acidic words rise into your throat and you know you won't be able to keep them there.

"Why do you want him to be sick?" I asked, letting the acid out. "So you can stay in denial about me and shove all your anxieties onto him and live in your fantasy world where you make me babysit him while you go off on dates looking for a replacement for Dad?"

Once again, I regretted it the moment I'd said it. I turned around, and my mom's eyes were filling up with tears.

"You...you really think I do that?"

"I don't know what I think anymore," I said as I looked away, my vision going in and out for some reason. "Sorry."

"Sweetie," she said, "I feel weird even talking to you about this because I feel inferior to you and you make me nervous for some reason, and I would *never* blame anything on you, but...you have no idea...you have no idea how hard it was. Caring for you became my whole life, and I let everything else fall away, including my marriage. And sometimes I...sometimes I think I waited too long, and it's too late for me."

The pain grew. "Shelly, it's not too late for you, but I..."

"No, I *need* you to hear this," she said. "It's just that I wanted to take care of you, but I also wanted a life, but I forgot about myself, and now I have nowhere to direct my energies, and-"

"You think I don't know all this?" I asked as I leaned forward and propped myself up on the island's countertop, growing delirious from the pain. The light was fading but I needed to get this out. "You think I don't know that I'm the reason you're broke, and alone, and obsessed with Chase's nonexistent health problems? You think I don't feel like a mistake, a flawed model, a scar on the face of humanity? News flash, Shelly: I'm fucked up, and I might die, and my existence is going to fuck up the lives of you and Chase and everyone else I love. It is my destiny to ruin you, and there's nothing anyone can do about it."

A shocked silence followed.

"Do you...do you *really* feel that way?" I was vaguely aware of Shelly asking next. She turned on the light to see me better. "Do you – oh my God, you're white as a ghost, Summer! What's wrong? Are you okay? What's wrong?!"

I clutched the edge of the counter and then felt my knees buckle under me. All the pain and light shrank into one pinprick of unbearable misery before everything fell away, and my mother screaming Chase's name was the last thing I heard before I sank into the warm, comfortable darkness of sleep.

16

There was a river. That much I knew. I did not know if I was dreaming or if I was dead or if any of this was even real or just my shutting-down soul imagining what death might look like, but I did know one thing for sure – a river ran through me, submerging me, until I was trapped in my own mind between life and whatever lay beyond life. The trees on either side were big and deciduous and reminded me of North Carolina where I'd gone every summer as a girl, young and broken but brave. I bobbed in and out, fluttering on the edge of two worlds. Underneath, everything was grey and muted and comfortable. Safe. I knew nobody could ever hurt me here. Every time I fell under the surface again I would feel my breathing slow and hear the voices in my head subside and I knew I would be protected there.

But then the current would force me up into the sun again, out into the air, and I'd see or imagine all the things I wasn't so sure about in the world: my mother, with ancient fear in her eyes. Hordes of doctors staring down at me, murmuring to one another about my prospects. And finally Cooper, the stormy-eyed boy of my dreams and nightmares. I could sense it down to my invisible bones: he was deliberating.

And I was the deliberated.

The wheels in my brain, wherever or whatever it was, started to turn, and soon I knew I had to choose. I could feel the currents pulling me back below, trying to sweep me off to somewhere only the angels knew, but soon I decided I didn't want to go just yet. I wasn't done here: I wanted to comfort the terror out of my mother's soul. I wanted to stand tall and prove to the doctors that I was worthy of undergoing the surgery. But most of all, I wanted one last chance with Cooper; one last breath on the surface of the river that was my summer with him. And so I made my decision.

I wished my way up to the surface and woke up in a sweaty hospital gown on the fifth of July.

~

The endless machines surrounding me buzzed and beeped as Dr. Steinberg walked into the room early that afternoon. Upon his arrival I'd been sort of exhaustedly humming a favorite Saviour song, *Stars and Stripes*, while thinking of the strange, watery dream I'd been having upon waking up that morning.

I could love you
That's what I thought when I first saw you
But now that I'm drowning in you
I'm wonderin' why you didn't banish all my blues

You are my only god now
My Stars and Stripes, the thunder in my chest, pow pow
The star of my show, boy, take that bow
But now that I've fallen into you, why's it feel like we're
doomed somehow?

What goes up comes back down
Camelot, Jackie O, burn that crown
But I am standing here asking you to break the tradition
Don't let me down, boy, success is my only condition

I stopped humming and looked at him.

"Hello there, Summer," he said quietly.

"Hi."

"So. I think you know why you're here."

"I actually have no idea. Nobody has said anything yet, so I thought I was just here for fun."

"Yes," he nodded with a sad smile, "unfortunately this hospital *is* known for its exceptionally uninformative nurses."

"Ignorance, bliss, etcetera." I closed my eyes for a second and took a breath. "Okay, Steinberg, I know I've been neglecting my health and this is probably bad and

173

whatever, so just lay it all out there, please. Get it over with so I can go home."

He cleared his throat, but the sound was empty and forced. "Home is no longer in the cards, Summer."

I stared at him. "Wait – what? Why not?"

He sighed. "Summer, you are here because your toxicity levels were through the roof two nights ago, and your body shut itself down to prevent any further damage. You were almost in a coma-like state when you arrived here. You were already in bad shape because of malnutrition, but then the stress of the other night, with those problems with your boyfriend that Shelly mentioned-"

"He's not my boyfriend," I said, the word *boyfriend* suddenly seeming so stupid and trite and useless after all this. "I don't have a boyfriend."

"Well, okay then. *Whoever* he is. All the stress brought on by your *friend* made your body go haywire when it was already damaged, and it shut down as a preemptive measure. But you will not be so lucky next time." He stepped forward a bit. "You know, it troubles me that you didn't come see me earlier. You skipped two checkups last month to get weighed and get your blood tested, and even Shelly said you've seemed a little out of sorts lately, until you came home the other night white as a ghost and collapsed. What's going on with you? This isn't the Summer I know."

I looked away. "I mean, yeah, I didn't exactly feel great over the past month or two, but I'm used to not feeling great, ya know what I mean? I was just dealing with a lot, and I figured it was nothing, and I…I didn't want to cause a fuss, to be honest. I should've said something when I noticed my weakness and the fact that I haven't really been able to keep liquids down at all, but I didn't want to make waves. My neck was sore, too, but it's always sore. I'll be totally forthright or whatever from now on, though, I promise."

"I'm afraid you won't have that luxury, Summer. You're here until the surgery."

"But *no!*" I said, sitting up straighter. "You promised I could have one last summer or whatever, and I met someone, and-"

"I'm sorry," he interrupted. "There are no questions. I know I said I'd allow you some time to enjoy yourself, but we no longer have that time. One of the stipulations of performing this Hail Mary operation on you in the first place was that you stay healthy enough to actually survive it. If you leave and something goes wrong and you are not within reach of care, you will die."

He looked out the window, his eyes wistful. "Sum, spending a summer on the beach is great and all, but you should've been paying attention to your body. And hell, I had a summer of love myself. It was probably the best thing that ever happened to me, actually. There's nothing wrong with being young and in love – just remember to check your damn vitals sometimes."

"Yeah, I love Ann," I said, who was his wife.

"I'm not talking about Ann."

"*What?*"

"Her name was Rachel," he said as something in his eyes collapsed. "She was visiting her grandparents for the season down in Palm Valley. We met at some old bar that's probably long gone now, and that was it. Falling in love with her was like being hit by a wave just after you've come up for air and your eyes are still closed. You're minding your own business when a little splash hits your nose and you duck for cover, but you don't move quickly enough – or maybe you don't *want* to move quickly enough – and suddenly you're being knocked off your feet by the weight of the world. She swamped me. I am so grateful I kept my eyes closed and let her hit me, though. I loved every second I spent drowning in that girl, let me tell you."

"...So what happened after the crash?" I asked after a long, quiet moment.

"She went back to Virginia and never talked to me again."

"Oh."

He blinked three times, his smile wistful. "But it's alright. I still have the memories. And other things. Don't tell anyone I said this, but a summer like that can stay with you forever, kiddo. Even if it's short." He winked after that, and I didn't understand why.

"Yeah," I said. "I'm certainly hoping so."

But I knew the truth. My summer of sepia-toned love was over. I couldn't broadcast the fake version of me to the world anymore. This was my reality: the jig was up, and my time of fooling Cooper into thinking I was someone worth loving was over.

Ugh. It was so unfair. All of it was. I'd been happy with Cooper, finally and truly happy. And not to mention confident. At last I could walk into a room without shrinking into a corner and sliding my bangs over my face; at last I was starting to like myself, *all* of myself, even the plastic parts I had to pump milk into. And now that I'd finally gotten to happy, life was just going to toss in a wrench like this and take it all away, and end it even sooner than it was going to end before? It didn't make any sense. Nothing did. I was so angry. I wanted to be stoic and strong and graceful and all those other things that sick people were supposed to be, but the truth was that I was pissed.

Fuck. This was so unfair. *Life* was so unfair.

Steinberg went over some plans with me next, and when he finished, something caught my eye. I frowned.

"That's all good, but can I ask you something personal?"

His face became more thoughtful. "Anything."

"Okay. Well, you're a smart, logical, professional, levelheaded person. Why do you wear that cross necklace?"

He smiled down at his cross, fingering it delicately as it glinted in the sunlight. "Ahh, so *that's* where your thoughts have been all this time," he laughed. "You think I'm too smart to believe in all this malarkey, right? You think there is too much misery and sickness and unfairness and Esophageal Intresia in this world for a God to possibly exist, and you think that if he *does* exist, he's a mean old bully focusing bad fortune on you like a snot-nosed kid focusing sunlight on an ant pile with a magnifying glass, correct? You think I'm a right old idiot for wearing this and believing in this Mean, Bullying, Ant-Burning God of mine, don't you?"

I gulped. "Well, I mean, in no uncertain terms, pretty much."

His eyes sparkled with something between love and wonder and frustration. "Summer, child, there is still *so* much you don't know about the place you live in. This world is anything but fair, and God knows you've dealt with things nobody should ever have to deal with. You're sad and angry and overwhelmed and you have every right to be. But the universe has a way of settling the score and making people like you get the goodness they are owed. I promise. I know you don't want to hear it now, but one day when you least expect it, the clouds will open up and what's fair will fall into your lap. Eventually you will get the heaven you deserve – never stop fighting until then."

"And what if I die before that day comes?" I asked, still trying to process everything.

"Then your life will still mean something. Someone out there will make sure of it. I promise."

Something else came into his eyes, something playful. "And I know what you're thinking: I wasn't born with any health issues, besides this damned arthritis, at least. How would *I* know, right?"

I nodded.

"Well, you know my daughter Margo, right?"

"Yeah, she's pretty cool. I saw you guys eating at TacoLu once and you came up and introduced her, remember?"

"I'm afraid I'm too old to remember that, but yes, that was probably my daughter. Anyway, Ann is not her mother."

I felt like I'd fallen a few inches even though I hadn't moved an atom. "But...but what? You mean..."

"Yes. My first love, Rachel, left Florida with more than just my heart in her hands. She was pregnant. That's why she was spirited away from me – her family was Catholic, and, well…you know how that goes. But four years after she gave birth to Margo, she was hit by a drunk driver on the way to work, and social workers found my name in some old documents. I got every summer with her after that. She was the best gift I never asked for, and every time hug her, I can feel Rachel, and the sea, and that one eternal summer we spent down in Palm Valley, a summer that begat so many more eternal summers." He smiled. "Miracles are everywhere, Summer. All you have to do is stay positive enough to notice them."

Steinberg called in Shelly and Chase after that. Shelly was everything I expected and more: weepy, apologetic, more dramatic than a soap opera, etcetera. She was sure the hospitalization was her fault because she'd failed to see the signs, and yadda yadda yadda. It was nobody's fault and she knew it. Then she called my father and put the phone to my ear, and I spent ten minutes listening to him halfheartedly apologize about how he hadn't been able to make it up yet, but he would be here as soon as his wife recovered from the flu and was able to watch the kids by herself, and so on. I told him that I was fine, and to take his time. I felt absolutely full of guilt that I hadn't told him the extent of things before, but I just didn't want to disrupt his world any more than my stupid existence already had.

None of this was to mention how torn to pieces I was about Cooper. But that grief could wait.

"I am so sorry," Shelly said after my dad hung up. She fell to my side again, and thankfully the nurses took Chase to a playroom to avoid the Shelly Show. I let her lay beside me and hold me, and as she cried into my gown, an orderly came in and waved around a paper with something written on it that I wished I hadn't seen. It was our bill for the portion of my stay that my family's insurance wouldn't be paying, and it was for sixteen thousand dollars. My mother had been broke my entire life because of hospital stays and Instamilk, and she'd been fired from nearly all of her jobs for skipping work to stay with me whenever I was in the hospital or couldn't get of bed. I couldn't do this to her anymore, but I didn't know how to fix it. Even as she touched me, I wanted to pull away. I could feel that there was some sort of disaster intrinsically tied to every single one of our interactions, and through her loving me, I was leading her down a path of certain doom. I was already feeling the instinct to push her away and protect her from myself – I already had been doing it for years, to be honest. And not just with her, but with everyone. I was a time bomb and I knew it.

Finally Dr. Steinberg came in one more time, his eyes twinkling, as they did. "Ms. Johnson, could I interest you in sharing a mug of coffee outside so we can go over the latest news?"

I flashed him a small but grateful smile. He knew I was tired and was trying to get her out of here to let me rest and think.

"Oh, yeah, o'course, yeah, she needs to sleep," Shelly said before giving me one more kiss on the forehead, smelling just as she had since I was a girl: like Estee Lauder perfume and oily Revlon lipstick. She was a mess, that was for sure, but I loved her for it. "Bye, babe."

"Bye, Shelly. Oh, and Dr. Steinberg?" I asked. He turned back around. "I feel really bad that you've been on call for so long just because of me, especially around a holiday, so why don't you just go home when you're done talking to my mom? I'm sure your family misses you and everything."

He just smiled down at me. "Typical."

"What's typical?"

"You just got life-changing news, and you're worried about *me*."

~

179

So when were you going to let me in? Cooper texted me after everyone left.

Ohhh, sorry, I'm not home yet, I responded, cringing at our night of disaster in the garage. **I won't be for a while. There's, um, a key under the potted rosebush if you need something?**

His response came quickly:

I'm not at your house.

I looked up at this nurse, Cassie, who was cleaning my feeding tube while rambling away, asking me question after question.

"…And by the way, Summer, when was your last general checkup? We'll need documentation of that, since they're bumping up the surgery and all."

I paused, and suddenly I got really nervous. Wasn't that one of those things you were just supposed to just *know,* as an adult? Why was what I did and didn't know about myself suddenly so terrifying?

"I'll find out for you," I said. "But hey, have I had any visitors?"

"You mean besides that boy?"

"I already saw my brother, remember? Earlier?"

"Not your brother," she said as she walked over to the dry erase board. "The other boy."

"What boy? What?"

"The boy who's been waiting for you nonstop in the second floor waiting room." She sort of tittered and glanced over at me as she said it, like all the nurses had been talking about it and had been waiting for the gossip. (Over the years I'd learned that patient gossip, romance novels, and Sun Chips were the primary time-passing methods of the nursing community.) "There's also been some other girl, Annie, I think?"

180

"Autumn?" I guessed, waiting to feel outrage at her name, but honestly I felt nothing – Cooper deserved to know. Autumn was just being Autumn, and I wasn't even really surprised. I was more annoyed with Shelly for blabbing to half the town.

"Yeah, her, she's come and gone, bringing your mom Burger King and whatever, but that boy won't leave."

Suddenly my face felt all warm and weird and tickly. Oh, Cooper. It didn't even occur to me that Cooper – I mean, I *assumed* it was Cooper – would even care about me after his discovery, much less come visit me, much less stay here. This wasn't his battle to fight, and that was fine.

Only now was I starting to think that maybe, just maybe, he wanted to fight it with me.

"I...I didn't know anyone was waiting," I said as Cassie fussed around with my charts, a quiet joy settling into my bones.

"Well this boy's hot, so I wouldn't suggest making him wait long," she said, and I raised an eyebrow. "*What*? He is."

I scoffed at her, held my breath, and looked down at my phone. What the hell could I possibly say to him after all this?

I started to text a response, but my phone told me he was typing, and so I erased what I'd written and waited until I received the following message:

I know I broke your heart, but you are the only thing on Earth to me now, and I really wanna make this right.

"Cassie?" I asked after I'd caught my breath.
"Yeah, sweetie?"
"Do you happen to have any makeup I can use?"

17

My teenaged dream walked in half an hour later, after I'd let Cassie dab some foundation on me and gloss my lips and, okay, yeah, hide my scar a little. I didn't want him to see me like this, because I knew he would pity me, and pity is my least favorite thing in the world to deal with besides, like, falling off a building or unrest in the Middle East or whatever. But I also wasn't going to keep him waiting alone outside like a bitch, and there was yet another thing, too – I was excited to see him, in this weird and giddy and destructive little way. I missed him.

He appeared in the doorway, staring at the floor and looking somewhere between terrified and exhausted. The brave, golden boy of this summer was gone, replaced by this ghost, pale and scared in his Polo. He was still beautiful, though, his dark stubble enhancing his already-perfect bone structure. And that's when I realized it was official: my eyes would *never* get used to him.

"You look like a hangover," is the first thing I said after he walked in, and he finally looked up at me.

"Ha. Hey, kid. Sorry, it's been a rough day or two."

"Tell me about it."

The machines beeped and the nurses murmured outside, but he said nothing. I decided to push him along. "So, um, yeah…you wanted to talk?"

He swallowed hard and finally sank down next to me, onto one of those weird reclining chairs upholstered with the world's cheapest vinyl that hospitals seemed to order by the boatload. "First of all, how are you feeling?" he asked.

"I've been better."

"Ugh. I…yeah. Well. What can I say?" The silence stretched between us again. "I can't even really describe what an idiot I feel like, Summer, facing you after our last…meeting, or whatever that was."

"It's okay, Cooper. I understand."

"No you don't," he said, and when I tried to interrupt, he raised a hand. "Look, Sum. I am *so* sorry. All I could think about for the past few days was my meltdown that night, and what I said, and how stressed I got you, and...yeah. You have *no idea*. I've been blaming myself over and over, and if you didn't make it, I would've...I couldn't have..."

I waved him off. "Stop, Cooper. It's not your fault. I've been sick for a very long time." I laughed a little. "And now you know that, thanks to Autumn."

His face fell, *literally* fell, that's how pronounced his frown was. "Don't be mad at her, please. It's not her fault. I basically pulled it out of her, and-"

I waved my arm again. "Trust me, she's called six thousand times in the last hour, but I don't care. I'm too exhausted to keep being mad. Someone needed to tell you anyway, I guess. It is, as they say, *what it is*."

He slumped even further. "Well, *I* still feel like a pile of shit, and I want to make this right."

I paused, the words I couldn't say hanging in the air. What was it about hospitals that made you want to pour out your soul and lose your words in your mouth all at the same time?

"Cooper," I began, "you don't have to—it's fine. I understand. I get it. None of this matters anymore. I don't need some pity trip. Shit hit the fan for me, and it sucks. And I lied to you, and it wasn't fair. But this isn't your problem. You have your whole summer in front of you, and I have hospital visits and surgeries and feeding tubes and-"

"You're right," he said, nodding and sitting taller. "You do have all that to deal with. But you also have me, no matter what I said the other night, and I want you to prove that to you."

I just stared at him again, confused. "What? With all due respect, Cooper...no. Just, no. You don't get it. You will never know how this feels. I am...different. I am other. And you're not. And it's not fair. It's been fun, but you don't have to do...this, whatever this is. And I don't want to do this to you."

"You don't want to do *what* to me, Summer?"

I met his eyes as the bottom fell out of my stomach. "I don't want to do *me* to you."

He frowned, exhaled, and then scooted the chair closer, motioning at the room around us.

"Hey. This hospital room. It's nice, huh?"

"What?"

"The room," he repeated. "It's nice. Pretty spiffy, huh? Wouldn't you agree?"

"I mean…yeah, as far as hospitals go, it's okay, I guess."

"Okay. Well, why don't you just stay here forever, then?"

"What?"

A ghost of a smirk crawled across his beautiful lips. "Like I said, it's nice. So just stay. You're safe in here – no germs, dim lights, comfortable bed. It's easy in here. Nobody can mess with you, or, say, fall into your soul and destroy you."

I gasped. What was with this boy and his gasping powers?

He put a hand on my arm, and for probably the first time, I didn't take it away. "That's why I lost my mind the other night, Summer. You came in a few months ago and turned my world upside down, and it terrified me. I was so used to everyone in my life leaving me that I made a safe little spot in my mind where nobody else could reach me, and I told myself I'd just be alone forever. My dad walked out, my friends disappeared, even my mom leaves me more and more a little day, as her health fades. But you came in and got close and wrecked all that, and…well, when I talked to Autumn and she told me what was up, the scared little boy within me got all frantic that you were going to leave, too, and I just…well, lost my fucking mind, to be honest. I didn't think I could deal with that again." He locked eyes with me, and I was knocked senseless by the burning intensity of them, like those wispy clouds that huddle in front of the sun at sunset and catch fire from the inside out. "But then I remembered something important: I'm in love with you."

184

I looked away and swallowed as hard as my broken throat would let me.

"I'm not afraid of speaking that truth anymore," he told me, and I could feel his eyes on my face. "Not after all this. I'm in love with you, Summer. I know that now. *You* know that now. That's not going to change. So get over yourself. We've been through the wringer already and we won't stop now. This won't be easy – you lied like crazy all summer, and I was a huge fucking douchebag who broke your heart. And it's not just that. I'm clingy and I need you too much sometimes, and you let me in and then push me out again, and that's just what we do. It's our Thing, like smoking cigarettes on the porch is my mom's Thing and farting in the kitchen was my dog's Thing and lying like a bastard is a politician's Thing and, oh God, I don't even know what I'm saying anymore, but I'm in love with you and I'm not leaving."

"Cooper," I breathed, "I'm-"

"So you're facing some problems," he said, sitting even taller, looking like he was bracing himself for a hurricane. "So what? I've found someone I want. You're it. That cake you made for my mom, the way you acted at that support meeting, the way you always know the right thing to say to pull me out of myself, the general way you carry yourself through this fucked-up world...I've found what I want, so who cares about what comes next? Who cares about the odds? Statistically speaking, it's perfectly possible that you could walk down the sidewalk tomorrow and get run over by an ice cream truck – does that mean I'm gonna stop loving you all of a sudden? Does that mean I need to step away? No. I need you too, you know. And I know you need me, no matter what you tell yourself. So let yourself be happy, Summer. Stop doing this. Let love destroy you – God knows life is going to, anyway."

I had to grip the metal bar along my bed to steady myself. He knew my favorite Saviour poem about love and destruction? How were all these similarities between us even *possible*?

"Okay, Cooper, let me process what I can process," I began, gulping for air. "You just referred to Hadley in the past tense. What happened?"

He nodded sadly. "Yeah. It happened late last night, after I got home. But it was peaceful, and it was just like she fell asleep, between me and my mom's wheelchair, down in the garage."

"Oh, no…God, I'm sorry."

His eyes filled up with the past. "It's okay. She was happy. She was a happy girl. She had a good life."

"I'm really sorry, Cooper."

He shrugged, and I waited for him to get his thoughts together. "And that book…*God*," he finally sighed. "It's the nicest thing anyone's ever done for me. I have it in my pocket, actually. I've been reading it over and over again in the waiting room. I can't believe my words are on a real page." He took it out and looked down at it almost reverently. "This is a dream, Summer. A real-life dream. I had let go of those when I met you. With my depression and my mom's issues and – with all that going on, I thought life had beaten my dreams out of me. But seeing my words in real, physical form – I could *never* repay you for the feeling this book gave me. Never. You're making me want to fight again, and that's huge." He exhaled again. "And honestly, the dog situation affected me, too. When we took her in for cremation this morning, the vet told me not to cry, because although she was only around for part of my life, I was her *whole* life. And it really got me thinking."

He got all weird and serious and watery-eyed and took my hand again, acting like he'd rehearsed this moment – which he probably had, I realized. "So, look, Summer. I know this might be the end of the road for you. You can't hide that from me anymore. But I'd like to be here for the rest of your whole life, however long that may be, and it would be an honor to only have you around for part of mine."

For the longest moment I just stared up at him. Finally I laughed and wiped my nose.

"Cooper, that was beautiful, but did you just compare me to a *dog*?"

He set his jaw. "Maybe I did, but it was goddamned adorable and you know it, so you'd better get over it and let yourself love me – *or else*."

I looked out of the window at the oaks, and that's when I finally got over the obstacle plaguing me and accepted the unthinkable: Cooper loved me back. It was true. He wasn't just some beautiful Spark prankster, trying to fool me into some one-sided summer affair, and this wasn't Travis Gibson And His Bet, version 2.0. Cooper Nichols loved me. He couldn't run from this any more than I could.

"Tell me," he said, "do you remember the lyrics to *Freedom* by Saviour?"

"It's only my favorite song in the Milky Way and several other galaxies," I whimpered. He recited them as I listened:

"My father once told me freedom was being in charge of your own destiny
And that my glory would be solely of my construction
But I just smiled and reached for his whiskey
Because I knew freedom was really being in charge of my own destruction."

"I'm sad about this, Summer," he said, biting his lower lip. "And I'm a little mad. I can't lie. I wanted more time with you. *Real* time, not hospital time. And I wish you would've prepared me for this. But what rips me up even more than my anger is the idea of turning away and not having you around. So if destruction is what this is, if that's what we're headed toward, then I'm happy, because I really wouldn't mind destruction at your hands, Summer Johnson. Not at all. Remember that scene from *Battle Bride*, where the girl says the only way to find happiness is to risk total destruction? You're worth the risk, and I'm all yours. Be careful with me."

"Ugh, Cooper," I said, feeling heavy as a burden and light as the wind all at once. "You are *such* a writer. Can you stop being so damned poetic for a second? It is *so* distracting."

"Speaking of that, I'm gonna write a book for you, to return the favor. A new book. I'm not confident enough yet to write one for publishers or anything, but I would totally write one just for you in a second."

"Okay," I smiled, "but make it about a girl named Summer, and make her super hot, and super smart, and the funniest person on Earth, and-"

"I will," he said blankly. "That's what it's gonna be, if you want."

"I was kidding!"

"We'll see," he said seriously. "You gave *me* a book, and now it's my turn."

Suddenly he pulled away and looked down at me. It was still so hard to maintain eye contact with him – he dazzled me so thoroughly it was like staring into the sun – but I tried.

"Can we just start over?" he asked. "No more secrets, no more evasiveness, no more whispers in the dark – just us?"

"Sure." I held out my hand. "Hi, my name is Summer Johnson, and I'm twenty-four. I like Funfetti cake even though I can't eat it, I often think myself to the point of craziness, I have no idea what I want to be when I grow up even though society tells me I'm already there, I hate the way my sentences always curl upwards at the ends like I'm asking questions, and, oh, yeah, I might die soon. And who are you?"

A glimmer in his brown eyes, he bent down and took my hand. "Hi. My name is Cooper Nichols, and I am absolutely swimming in love with a girl named Summer Johnson."

He stood up and picked up a bag I hadn't noticed him bring. "And now that we've made our introductions, I think I'll settle in before you have another change of heart. And

188

even if you *do*, I'm much bigger and stronger than you are – especially now – so you can't get rid of me now even if you wanted to. These four walls contain everything I need, including you, and I am staying here indefinitely, so now if you'll excuse me, I have to fucking pee before I humiliate myself any further by acting like a begging, groveling bitch for one additional second."

He turned, marched into the bathroom, and slammed the door behind him.

~

The next day I had a videoconference with Steinberg and Dr. Dill, the specialist from Alabama who'd volunteered to do the surgery under Steinberg's supervision, to go over the new plans. Listening to them talk about my possible death was on a level of awkward that I did not even want to comprehend, so I tried not to. But Dill did talk me through everything he'd be doing, and on a rational level at least, it all made sense. My impression of Dill, the man who was going to cut my body open and try to save my life, was...nothing, actually. He was being so clinical and using so much medical-speak that I couldn't really get any glimpse of his personality at all, which wasn't that unusual. He was going to split my flesh with a scalpel, not meet me for coffee and some gossip. Doctors were there to fix you, not befriend you. Steinberg was just a rare, friendly gem, and I didn't expect his level of personality from the others. And in the end, it was decided: because my health was plummeting so quickly, we were out of time, and the surgery would happen in eight days. In eight days I would undergo the procedure that would determine my fate. I could not stop shaking for the life of me.

"You understand the stakes, and what you need to do, right?" Steinberg asked me afterward, during a private moment.

"I think," I said, and his eyes narrowed.

189

"No, really. We are going to move heaven and Earth to save you in eight days, Summer, and things are actually looking much better than they were before, but still, this is a maybe-goodbye thing. I want you to know that, and be ready for it."

I nodded as some ancient sense of purpose settled into me. "Right. A maybe-goodbye thing. I understand. I do. I promise."

If things had felt surreal before, the next few days were in dream territory. I literally didn't even have time to think, things were happening so quickly. I didn't know how to prepare myself for what was coming because I didn't know *how* to prepare myself – getting ready for an eighty percent chance of death was not something I was not exactly accustomed to. I assured my mom over and over that I was young and strong and would perhaps emerge from the surgery in one piece, but her theatrics knew no bounds, the parameters of logic included, so I just dealt with it.

Most of my time was taken up by the army of well-wishers that descended on me like mosquitos at sunset. (Well-wishers – what did that phrase even *mean*? Who would show up at a hospital and *not* wish the sufferer well, except if they were an evil stepmother with a billion-dollar will or something?) Anyway, aunts, cousins, neighbors, all sorts of family members I had forgotten existed – and not to mention my boss, awkwardly – either called or came to the hospital, and greeting them all and pretending like I remembered meeting Aunt Linda's new husband and that yes, I totally noticed the Facebook news about Cousin Gina having twin granddaughters, was a total blur. How had so much gone on while I was wrapped up in Cooper Nichols world?

But through it all I sat there in my bed, often with Chase, helping him with Fast Track, the online program he had to do over summer because his reading wasn't yet on par. Why I cared about something so trivial, I had no idea – I just did. In the eye of the storm, sometimes you reach for anything you can, no matter how small. I guess I just needed to know that something, somewhere out there was real and normal and not revolving around My Problems. Autumn groveled her way into the room and apologized in five thousand different ways, saying she'd spotted Cooper at the beach after a day of drinking at the pier and flagged him down to talk. Her mom had just told her the big news that morning, and, totally heartbroken, she'd blabbed to Cooper and tried to take solace with him about how I'd kept it from them both. I told her I didn't care, and that I wasn't mad, because for the most part I really wasn't. He needed to know, and besides, I wasn't going to spend my last week before the surgery being angry at people.

Speaking of Cooper, he didn't leave my side the whole time. Literally: he wouldn't leave the Plastic Recliner of Uncomfortability beside my bed. Steinberg had confined me to a wheelchair for good, which was fine because A: I was quickly becoming so weak and thin that walking anywhere was becoming crazy difficult, and B. I'd had enough surgeries and been in a wheelchair enough times to know that although it is extremely fucking annoying, it's also a great way to get people to reach for things for you. And Cooper had to reach for a *lot* of things. I felt ten kinds of terrible that our time together had gone from sitting in the sun to lying around in a fluorescent hospital room, but what could I do? He was an absolute godsend, shooing Shelly away when I needed a moment, acting as a middleman between me and the rest of my huge extended family when I needed to be alone. Our time together had an eerie urgency to it now, and I didn't really know why. I could guess, though.

When he wasn't helping me he sat in the corner scribbling away into some notebook that he said was his diary. I didn't question it. His constant presence created some awkwardness, for sure, and he let his lingering anger about my Summer of Lies slip out more than once. I didn't question this, either – after all, I was lucky he hadn't sworn me off forever that night in the garage. He also had to pretend he didn't see a lot of things he did see, like the nurses stripping me down to perform tests, changing my catheter, and walking me to the bathroom where I would vomit for twenty minutes straight. Being sick wasn't like what you saw in the movies, where an actor in full hair and makeup lay in a rosy, well-lit hospital room surrounded by flowers and cards and loving family members. In the real world sickness was a messy, gruesome, disgusting, and above all embarrassing business, not for the faint of heart or stomach. It was humanity at its most basic level, which wasn't even really humanity at all, just animalism. We are animals, and there's nothing to remind you of that like spitting bile onto your chest because you didn't have time to grab a cup. But since humans fear oblivion above anything else, we've elevated ourselves in our own minds to these God-like creatures in order fool ourselves into thinking we're headed for somewhere better than the rest of the beasts walking the Earth. After all, why do you think people found fart jokes and poop stories and husbands' horrified tales about witnessing their wives' C-Sections so funny? Humans hate being reminded that they're just animals, carcasses made of water and melanin and bone and blood, and so they laugh nervously at the fart joke to avoid that little voice that reminds them *oh God I'm no better than the animals in the safari videos oh God I'm gonna die one day and nothing will be left of me but this rotten carcass Oh god it's all futile just kill me now*. We want to believe we are gods walking a doomed planet, both originated from and heading for somewhere else, and so we dart our eyes around and laugh about the joke reminding us we're animals with organs suspended in blood headed for oblivion. We're nothing but monkeys toiling away on a watery rock we decided to name Earth, and nothing can save us from that non-fate.

So, like I said: shit was embarrassing. One night I looked back and realized I had left the bathroom door open as I wretched horrifically, splattering whitish bile all over the tile walls. Cooper was crying as he watched me.

I pretended I didn't notice him.

But through all this, I was grateful, even though I would never admit it because I know it would just piss him off. I loved to feel his warmth and his presence next to me, I loved to wake up in the middle of the night all disoriented and hear the comforting sound of him snoring on the little day-bed across the room, and I loved to watch the nurses flirt with him and then see him refuse them and pay attention to only me, as miserably childish as that sounds. The forced intimacy of it all made us closer than ever before, and he told me all kinds of things about his family and childhood that made me feel like I knew him that much more.

A few days into my stay I did try to say something, though. It wasn't lost on me that he was wasting his summer with me. I felt sort of guilty and dirty and heavy; like a lawyer or a reality television star or a mom who fights loudly with her children in public without trying to hide it, or any other garbage human. He was playing Scrabble next to me on his iPad, a habit he'd just picked up from me, and I reached over and touched his arm.

"Hey. I just want to say, like, thanks, or whatever. You don't have-"

He held up a hand as he returned a text from Kevin. "Stop. No mushy stuff. That's my rule."

"No, Cooper," I said. "Listen to me, seriously. You don't have to do this, and it's not your problem. You should go home and take a shower or something. Have some fun, and-"

"Take my phone," he said, barely looking up, as he placed his phone into my waiting hand. "Now break it."

"What?"

"Break it. Throw it on the ground and shatter it to pieces."

"No!"

"Why not?" he asked, looking up at me. "I'm sure you could put the pieces back together if you tried."

"Yeah, but it still wouldn't work the same after that," I said, and his expression turned to stone.

193

"*There*. Now do you get it? *Now* do you understand what you'll do to me if you push me away again?"

I just thought for a moment. He put his arm up and held it next to mine. "I am you, Summer. You are me. You're not a problem, you're a gift. A gift that talks about emotional stuff too often, is a bit too stubborn, and snores extremely loudly, but a gift nonetheless."

"Oh my God," I said as I covered my face with my hands. "I really snore?

"Pretty badly," he nodded. "I could barely sleep sometimes."

I clasped my fingers together harder. "Why didn't you tell me?"

"I don't know, I thought it was funny." And then: "You may have farted a few times, too."

My mouth fell open, and then I reached over and pawed at the wall for the nurses' button.

"Okay, you can take him out now, Cassie."

~

By the next day, cabin fever was setting in. My room was getting hot and crowded and it smelled faintly of rotting flowers left in the sun, Shelly was starting to annoy the hell out of me, and Cooper, bless his heart, was starting to get fed up with Chase's constant requests to join him in playing racing games on my TV set's XBOX. At around lunchtime I excused myself to get some coffee and have some time alone, and on the way back one of the nurses from my floor looked up from the break area and approached me. Her name was Noelle and she couldn't have been much older than me, and she had a no-nonsense air about her that I really liked.

"So what are you doing with Last Great Hope?" she asked offhandedly as she scanned a dry erase board.

"Nothing. We denied them, pretty much. I said to save the Cinderella stuff for someone who-"

"That's not what I heard," she interrupted.

"Oh. Well, what did you hear, then?"

She studied me with mascara'd eyes. "They sent over a dossier this morning. It says you've requested a trip."

"*Oh.*"

I bit my lip as I thought of my mother going over my head to arrange some dramatic Last Trip To Disney World for me. If I wasn't in the stupid wheelchair, I would've marched to her and yelled at her right then and there. Noticing my agitation, Noelle came closer and sank down to my level. It didn't seem so much an act of condescension as an attempt to, well, level with me.

"Guess someone was meddling, then," she said. "I figured. But Summer, seriously, I've been doing this for a couple of years now, and don't tell anyone I said this, but if the worst happens, like, you don't want any unfinished business to be left behind. Not that 'the worst' will happen, anyway – this is an excellent hospital, and I've heard all good things about Dill. But you know what I mean. Wanna know what I recommend? Just to help you, like, deal with things, mentally speaking?"

"Alcoholism?"

"Nice try," she smiled. "No, you really do need to go somewhere. Escape for a day or two. Or I would, at least. Somewhere close, but where you still feel comfortable. Your mom will probably be a lot to handle before surgery, no offense, and you're gonna need a break from the action."

"Okay, um, I get what you're saying."

"Good. And Summer?"

"Yeah?"

She raised an eyebrow. "Bring that boy. If you don't, then one of the nurses is going to snatch him up, and I am including myself in that hypothesis. He is magnificent."

Five minutes later I wheeled into my room to find Shelly and Cooper sharing a Subway foot-long on the daybed in the corner. They stopped talking immediately when I entered.

"Shelly, why did I just get asked about Last Great Hope filing papers with the hospital?" I said, and they exchanged sweaty glances. I didn't want to throw a fit in front of Cooper, but at the same time I was kind of beyond caring by this point. "See, this is *exactly* what I didn't want. You going over my head to send me off to Epcot, treating me like a sick little child, giving me anxiety with your theatrics. I told you the first day this happened, please, just let me act normal and keep all this out of my head, and-"

"It wasn't me," Shelly interrupted, and I paused.

"What? Then...*who*?"

Slowly she looked over at Cooper, whose face was as red as the meatball sub on his lap.

"Wait, really? *You*?"

"Well," he said, "we weren't gonna tell you yet, but...I just thought it'd be great to get you away from the hustle of the hospital for a few days, and so I called them the other day...it's nothing crazy, no penthouse in New York, but..."

"Listen, Cooper," I said, trying to let him down softly, "that's sweet of you, it really is, but like I told my mom the day all this day started, I really don't-"

Just then Steinberg turned into the room, focused on the clipboard in his hands.

"Steinberg, is this true?" I asked. "Have you all been conspiring behind my back?"

He halted and began to back up the way he'd come.

"Please, someone just tell me what's going on," I whined, even starting to annoy myself. "I'm not mad, I just hate surprises."

"Yes, well, uh, unfortunately," Steinberg stuttered, "Dr. Dill won't be available until next Thursday, and so that leaves us a bit of grey area in between, so when Mr. Nichols here came to me, I was, uh, obliged to listen to him."

I swallowed, or tried to, at least. "But...my hair is falling out, and my ribs are showing, and I can barely wheel myself to the bathroom – how can I leave?"

Steinberg smirked. "Indeed, all that is true. You are very fragile, and you're being watched very closely, and as you're one of the oldest living Intresia patients, several doctors around the country are very interested in your case and don't want you stressed before the surgery. *However*, I have a feeling that I am about to forget to request that the nurses forward me your visitor logs every day, as I have been instructed to do. Furthermore, as long as you cooperate with me on the no walking or eating rules, I have a hunch that I will *continue* to not care who you admit into your room, or who *leaves* your room, as long as you are within an hour's drive of me. And coincidentally, the place you've requested is just under fifty-five minutes from here."

I tried not to smile at the man who saved my life every day. "But where am I going?"

"I'm afraid that's up to Mr. Nichols," he said, and I turned to see the most dazzling smile I'd ever seen on Cooper – and considering that this was Cooper Nichols we were talking about, that was saying a lot. I thought I saw a strange look of understanding flow between him and Steinberg, too, but maybe I imagined it.

"It's a shame you can't eat right now," Cooper said, "because I heard from someone very close to me that the bakeries down in St. Augustine are absolutely to die for – no pun intended."

"Cooper   really?"

He walked closer and bent down to shield our words from our prying public. It was awkward to be so intimate with him in front of all these people, but I tried to meet his completely overpowering gaze. "Summer, I want to take you somewhere, and I *know* you want to bust out of this joint. It'll make me happy, and besides, if I smell one more whiff of lavender disinfectant spray, I will lose my mind. But please give me this. Whatever *this* is, whatever is happening between us, I want to finish it." He wiped my eye and smiled. "Hey, remember when I told you how many seconds of summer there were?"

I nodded.

"Well, get your bathing suit ready – I think I just gave us a couple hundred thousand more.

18

Over the centuries St. Augustine, Florida has been the home of Spanish conquistadors, Caribbean pirates, Minorcan religious refugees, Civil War soldiers, the richest industrialist in America, and Cooper Nichols. It was an oddity, an anomaly, as if God himself had picked up a little European town, cobblestone streets and all, and dropped it onto the marshy coasts of northern Florida. It was maybe a little kitschy, sure, but I loved it to death anyway. (Side note: taking recent events into consideration, I *really* needed to start finding new sayings that didn't involve the word "death." Oops.) An oak-filled square ringed by museums and cathedrals sat at the heart of it, and that connected to a long main street called St. George lined with little touristy boutiques and ice cream shops. I guess some of the buildings in St. Augustine weren't even that old, actually, and you could see the plastic underneath the plaster, but all that just made everything even more charming in a weird little way. The focal point of town was a rambling colonial Spanish fort (*actually* old) at the top of a windswept hill that looked out over a cute little harbor that filled with sailboats and yachts and dolphins in the summer. This town held more memories of my childhood than anywhere, and on weekends when I wasn't in the hospital and the weather was palatable, my parents and I would drive down and walk around town all day, window shopping and going to museums and eating strawberry ice cream. (Okay, my mom would eat the ice cream while I watched her. Same thing.) It was perfect for my current situation, I guess, since it was beautiful and had lots of stuff to do, but it wasn't so far away that I'd be out of reach of the hospital if anything went wrong. Cooper was thrilled to get away from that awful place and show me his hometown, and I was kind of weirdly intrigued at the prospect of seeing it through his eyes, too, and so I finally let myself get excited about the trip.

As we left the hospital in my mom's green minivan on Friday morning, though, something bad happened – like *cringe-worthy* bad. Shelly leaned into the car, over Cooper's chest, and said: "Have fun, Summer. Looking back on it, I'm *so* glad you disobeyed Steinberg's orders and found someone."

I got away from her as quickly as I could, but Cooper had still heard, and he pulled away from the hospital with a clenched jaw. He'd known I'd kept the surgery from him, sure, but knowing that I'd actually *gone against my doctor's explicit orders* to find him? That was on a new level of low that made his eyes shut down and his lips fold into his mouth. I had *no idea* how to move forward.

On the drive to St. Augustine we passed a few little burnt-out beach towns still reeling from the migration of tourists to fancier resorts in south Florida. The abandoned aqua-hued motels were almost cinematic in their faded seaside glamour, mirroring the broken-down feeling within me. For some reason Cooper kept playing one Saviour song in particular on repeat called *Chasing Glory* as we drifted southward, mouthing all the words as he drove, looking distracted and detached as he stared out at the road:

I can tell that you're lonely
I'm the daughter of a bad man, you can't hide those scars
from me
You're smilin' big in that American flag tee
But the ghosts show their teeth from underneath

(So come with me)

You know who my flames burn for
I can't hide that either anymore
You say you don't know
That you're the one I'd lay it all down for

(So come with me)

Don't got no money, no plans

199

Just dreams to chase and this pen in my hand
So come hop in this faded van
Let's go win some glory, baby, make one last stand

(So come with me)

They say we're the new lost generation
And with my burned-out eyes, I can't deny that
So let's drive and drink and play the Replacements
'Til the future we're running from doesn't look so black

(Just come with me)

I must've heard the song ten times by the time Cooper pulled off A1A and headed towards the bridge to St. Augustine. He was still acting weird and tense, and when he stopped at the gas station by the marsh and hopped out to get gas, I saw him scowling in the rearview mirror.

"Do you want anything?" he asked as he stopped by my window after pumping, the earnest boy from the bedside speech nowhere to be found. "You said you liked Strawberry Mentos once, or was that a lie, too, just like the rest of them?"

"…I'm fine," I breathed. With angry regret in his eyes, he turned and stomped into the gas station, leaving me alone and reeling in the car.

So, side note: when I was in Sunday School, my teacher talked a lot about original sin. She said humans were constantly trying to go around and look for salvation because in the end everything went back to one simple fact: we had been born sick. She likened it to doing something really bad and breaking our parents' trust: once you crossed that line, you could never go back, and every fight you might have with them afterward would really be about the original sin of your first transgression. And this is what I thought of as the minivan climbed the steep, tall bridge to St. Augustine, a spongy marsh stretching out under us, a coffee-brown river ribboning out to the horizon in the midst of the sawgrass.

The original sin of our relationship was that I'd told the biggest lie of all: I was healthy. Maybe everything would always go back to that, no matter what happened in the present. No matter how forgiving Cooper claimed to be, perhaps I would still never be able to scrub that sin off my skin.

"Cooper," I finally said as we got into town, "listen." I was addicted to his magic, even when it stung, and I wanted to make this right again. "I'm really glad I came here with you, and I'm excited, but still, I can't be punished for lying to you forever. I'm trying to enjoy my time before the surgery, and rude little comments like that aren't going to help. Trust me, all I want is for us to drift back into summer world and have it be like it was before the hospital. Please help us get there."

Finally we rounded a corner and pulled up to our hotel, the Casa Monica. The fanciest place in town, it looked like an old Spanish fortress and had multiple turrets and towers jutting up into the blue Florida sky.

Cooper turned to me. "You're right," he said with an expression like he'd just swallowed half a lemon and was trying to pretend it wasn't sour. "I shouldn't have said anything. I'm sorry. I want to get back to how it was the last few months, too." He sighed. "Let's just try to forget about the surgery, forget about your issues, forget about everything and just have a beautiful weekend under the oaks. Can you forgive me for being such a massive anus head? Is that feasible?"

I smiled. "It's more than feasible. You have a deal, sir."

"Have you stayed here before?" the concierge guy, Frank, asked as he waited for our keys to print in the lobby.

"Not really, but I've been to the bar a bunch," Cooper said as he looked around at the Moorish Revival space (I'd taken an interior design course during one particularly misguided semester of college and had retained a bit of information). His eyes were huge and filled with this weird, boyish excitement, and it was pretty adorable.

"Nice!" Frank said. "We've got a lot of history here. At different times this building has been the fanciest Gilded Age hotel in Florida, an infamous courthouse, and then finally the remodeled hotel you see today, which is famous as a honeymoon retreat because of its romantic suites overlooking the town square. They say people either come here to face death, or fall in love."

"What about both, at the same time?" I asked before I could stop myself. Cooper looked over at me, looking equal parts heartbroken and admonishing. It was the heartbroken half that shut me up.

"Uh," Frank said after throwing us a weird glance, "yeah, anyway, let's go check out that suite."

"But we don't have a suite," I told him. "Last Great Hope arranged for a standard room with a pool view, or whatever?"

Frank took the keys and turned to me with a tight smile. "That has been changed at the request of Dr. Michael Steinberg. Shall we?"

Our room was beyond beautiful, of course. Actually, I don't even know if I can call it a *room*, because it was more like a palatial New York apartment, a three-story situation on the corner of the hotel in one of the towers. The first floor was a plush lounge area with a little bar and a few antique couches, and after climbing a steep staircase we reached the middle bedroom level, with a giant bed with a red velvet headboard that looked out over the town square. Up another stairway was another bedroom, this one with two large beds that you could jump across. And we did just that, or at least Cooper did, jumping from bed to bed while I took iPhone pictures from the edge of one of them. Finally he fell next to me and sort of nuzzled me with his leg to test my mood, and after I looked at him to assure him I wasn't mad anymore, we started making out like teenagers drunk on love and Natty Lite. I knew my breath probably smelled like hot garbage after being in the hospital for so long with barely any sink access, but what could I do?

Before we could get very far, though, he pulled away. I noticed how alive my body still felt at his touch, and wondered if that feeling would ever go away.

"Gah," he said, "we've got all weekend for that! You're so distracting. Let's get ready for me to show you around. I can't wait to be your cheesy tour guide."

He got up and started rustling through his bags. Of course he did. I reminded myself that I now looked like more of a Hospital Patient than ever, and that hooking up with me would've been more of a chore than anything else. I had to give him time to adjust to my quickly-eroding looks before jumping his bones.

"But I've been to this town a million times," I told him, trying not to sound too crestfallen. "What can we do what we both haven't done before? And hey – what's in that box?"

A small, rectangular velvet box fell from his backpack – a *definite* jewelry box. Panicked, he bent down, retrieved it, and stuffed it back in.

"Nothing," he snapped. "We're just here to hangout, okay? You've never been here with a native St. Augustinian. Let's just go get ice cream before dinner, and then come up here and use the beds for trampolines until we get sleepy. Then I'll push them together and make one giant bed for us."

"Okay," I said, shivering a little for some reason. I was getting *very* thin, sure, but something told me nerves had nothing to do with my sudden chill. What was going on? Was that box the reason for this trip?

And suddenly my doubts jumped out at me. Was actually Cooper still furious with me, and had my mother simply guilted him into making up with me and taking his Sick Little Wheelchair Girlfriend on one last trip where he'd give me some cheesy proposal in the Spanish district or something? Was that why he was so angry? Is that what everyone thought I wanted? To force him down the aisle before I bit the dust?

I told myself I was acting psycho and tried to calm down. Cooper and Shelly could've been talking about *anything* the other day over that Subway sandwich. Once again I was being the Queen of Self-Doubt and needed to tell my brain to shut the hell up.

"Ice cream and jumping on beds," I said as I looked up at him again. "Sounds great. You know, I'm so glad I never grew up."

"And I'm so glad I found someone to stay a kid with," he said as he kissed me on the forehead with chapped hospital lips and then headed for the bathroom.

To kill time, I pulled out my phone and scanned the latest Facebook engagements. Spoiler alert: it was the height of summer, and there were four.

As afternoon fell into early evening, busting a hole in the oppressive heat blanketing the city, Cooper walked me across the square to the head of St. George Street. We weaved our way down the cobblestone path through the tourists and sightseers, stopping here and there to check out a boutique or little tchotchke shop or candy store or whatever. I wasn't really embarrassed to be in the wheelchair in public, but I still felt like a total burden, and I was embarrassed on Cooper's behalf that everyone was staring at us. Because that was the nature of humans, to stare at what didn't make sense to them – and this tall, strong boy pushing around this frail girl who no longer looked young nor beautiful definitely did *not* make sense. He didn't seem to mind, though, and that kind of just made me sink deeper into love with him than before.

"You're *sure* you're fine with the wheelchair thing?" I asked him for the tenth time after sweat started to show on his forehead. "I think I can rent a little motorized scooter thing from the visitors' center if we need to."

"Sum," he said, "I played football for a year in high school. I was a defensive end, which meant I spent my afternoons pushing against three-hundred-pound lineman at scrimmages. You are a feather compared to them."

"Point taken."

As Cooper pushed me I tried to notice everything in the world, but mostly I just wanted to notice *him*. I liked noticing him. There was so much to notice, after all. The hint of swagger in his walk, his broad shoulders, the tendons and muscles in his forearms that flexed as he moved, his dark hair, and the way it shined gold in the sun. And as I sat there I said a silent little prayer that I would get to notice him for a lot longer.

As we walked (or wheeled, in my case), Cooper pointed out all these things I'd never known about the city, and his enthusiasm was adorable. "Oh, see that dormer window up there?" he asked, pointing at the slanted roof of an old wooden building. "They say the ghost of an old woman waits there every night, waiting for her soldier husband to come back from the Civil War. Needless to say, it's been awhile." He pointed down the street. "Oh, and see that Minorcan flag over on that porch? One of the original groups of settlers here were from a Mediterranean island called Minorca. I'm actually partly descended from them – that's why I get so tan in the summer. And that old building at the end of the street down there? Most people call it the oldest school in America, but it's actually only the oldest *wooden* school in America. Disappointing, eh?"

"I'm crushed, really. *So* unimpressive. Get me out of this dump."

I tried to pay attention, but soon it became clear that my body wasn't going to cooperate. I was cold even though the summer air was warm and wet, and I was getting so bony, it hurt to go over every little bump in the road.

"What's wrong?" he asked half an hour into our journey, turning into an ice cream place called YE OLDE ICE CREAM SHOP. Where the plaster was chipping off the faux-aged walls, you could see Styrofoam underneath. "Getting warm?"

"No, I'm fine. Maybe just hungry. Could you push me to the bathroom, please?"

We squeezed by a group of women waiting in line to pay for their ice cream, and they apologized profusely for blocking the way to the bathroom while simultaneously not moving because they didn't want to give up their spots, and soon the whole thing turned into a mini-spectacle. That's the thing with wheelchairs: people go so out of their way to not turn your condition into a "thing," they turn it into an even bigger "thing" than it was before. In the end, Cooper and I sort of got pushed into the bathroom together. I tried to reach down and grab a carton of Instamilk, but it hurt something in my abdomen, and I winced.

"I've got it," Cooper said as he grabbed the milk. I reached up and tried to protest. "I've *got* it," he said again. "Just relax."

He filled the syringe with milk and then brought it over to my tube and started pumping it into me. I guessed he'd seen me do it enough times to know the basics. I was humiliated, but I let him continue. As he pumped, he brushed a strand of my thinning hair from my face and smiled down at me.

"You look great," he said with a forced smile.

"So do you," I said, doing my best to return it.

"Shall we?" he asked when the syringe was empty, echoing what he'd said to me that first night back at Joe's Crab Shack, back when I was healthy and our future seemed brighter than this.

I smiled anyway. "We shall."

We window shopped into the evening and then headed back to the hotel. We were scheduled to have dinner at some fancy Spanish restaurant called Columbia with absolutely legendary sangria, and so I put on my best dress and let Cooper push me all the way there, since he'd insisted. When we got to the big white restaurant with the blue tile roof right on St. George Street, however, we bypassed the main dining room and went down a side hallway.

"Where are we going?" I asked, but he kept pushing. He turned us into a dark, private room with oak-paneled walls, a rustic chandelier, and a single table with three chairs. Upon closer inspection, I saw that sand had been laid out under the table atop plastic sheeting, and little umbrellas decorated the tropically-hued drinks already adorning the table. Since we couldn't go to the beach anymore, I guess he'd brought the beach to me. All this made that strange feeling rise up in me again, like I'd do anything in the world for him.

"This is amazing, but three plates?" I asked. "Who-"

That's when Autumn came busting out of the shadows and wrapped me in the biggest hug ever.

"You little rats!" I said as Autumn pulled away and smiled down at me. "Awkward" wasn't the word for what I felt around her for nearly wrecking my relationship with Cooper, but wine could fix that. "You know I can't handle surprises."

"Well get ready to handle more," Cooper said, and then he pointed at the corner, where a girl with long brown hair sat on a wooden stool holding a guitar. He nodded at her, and she nodded back and started playing one of my favorite Saviour songs, *The Fall*.

"Obviously, Last Great Hope couldn't afford Saviour." Cooper said as her soft voice filled the room. *What's done is done/you've fallen into me, I've come undone/two hearts now beat as one.* "I looked into it. Apparently she charges a quarter of a million just to leave her country, but they *could* afford a wonderful local cover artist to come in her place and play some of her songs while we ate, so…yeah. Compromise. Say hello to Fake Saviour!"

I almost cried like a bitch, but I stopped myself. "That is *so* cool, Cooper. And how did you get this loser to come?" I asked as I slapped Autumn on the leg a little too hard. "Besides with the promise of free food, I mean?"

"He called me," she said as she darted away. "Turns out he can be *very* persuasive. Not that I needed persuading."

"I know what you mean," I said, trying not to focus on how obsessed with him she was, and together we all went to the table to eat. Or not eat, in my case.

Having Autumn around went surprisingly well, I guess because her presence gave us a break from all the death-pondering intensity of the past few days. The cover singer was actually very good, too, even if her voice lacked the same strange, slightly childlike quality that made Saviour so unique. But I was in heaven anyway. Autumn talked, mostly, regaling us with tales from the frontlines of her disastrous love life. I didn't eat much, obviously, just swallowed bits of Sangria, but I enjoyed the company. By dessert, I was a little drunk. I just couldn't believe I was sitting with Cooper, my best friend in the world, and a Saviour lookalike all in the same room. Cooper tried to pay attention, but I saw him drift off a few times. He had every right to be exhausted, though. Whenever he'd notice me watching he'd snap out of it, smile, and reach over to squeeze my knee under the table. At the end of dinner the cover artist played one of my very favorite Saviour songs, *Flower Crown Ruins:*

Got flowers in my hair and ruins on my mind
Wondering what'd be left of me if you left to find
Someone new, someone who isn't me
Since they all say you're trouble, you're bad news, you'll set me free

(But fuck that)

The best souls I know are a little crazy
Something in their eyes a little hazy
So fuck all those normal ones, they scare me
Give me broken, God, give me crazy

In the end the only kids having any fun are the lost ones
Those fools out there in the real world, they slave away at the cost of their souls
So grab a PBR, boy, and pull up a stool
And tell me about your dreams and your monsters, you beautiful little fool

"Selfie time," Autumn said, crouching behind us and whipping out her Android.

"No!" Cooper and I both cried at the same time, turning away and hiding our faces.

"What is wrong with you guys?" Autumn asked, gaping from me to him. "What's wrong with a little selfie action? And by the way, you're not even FBO. When is that going to change?"

"FBO?" Cooper asked.

"Facebook Official," she said. "Summer's profile is as barren of activity as it ever was. If I found a guy like you, I'd be shouting it so loud, they'd chop off my tongue."

"And you haven't seen what I can do with my tongue," Cooper said, and I shoved him in the shoulder as Autumn got an expression like Jesus himself had descended from heaven.

"And thanks for the suggestion, but tonight was just between us three," he continued, meeting my eye and smirking.

"I agree," I said.

"But isn't that why you wanted someone in the first place?" she asked me, and I raised my eyebrow to tell her to shut up and stop embarrassing me. "To show up the Facebook girls screaming about their stupid weddings, and whatever?"

I glanced over at Cooper, mystified. "I mean, yeah, maybe in the beginning I kind of did, but suddenly I don't really care about all that anymore." I winked at him. "Maybe some things are just better left unshared."

We left Columbia and headed out for a nightcap. On the sidewalk along the bay, we passed some drunk-looking bar hoppers stumbling from one place to another, and I instantly smelled trouble along with whiskey. They gave us funny looks as they passed, and when they thought they were out of earshot they decided to share their brilliant analysis with one another.

"Hey, what was up with that hot dude pushing the wheelchair chick?" one of them laughed. Cooper stopped immediately.

"Yeah, that was totally weird," the other one slurred. "Maybe I should become paralyzed, too, so I can get a boy that hot."

I reached up and put my hand on his tense arm. I was somewhat familiar with wheelchairs, and I knew they were an even more visible form of disability than just my scar – people literally veered out of the way when they saw me now. If my scar was a barrier, the wheelchair was a force field, and ninety-nine percent of people were just too uncomfortable to pierce that force field and get to know the person behind it, for whatever reason. But rarely were they as outright rude as these bitches were being. And suddenly I wondered who was freer: me, wizened from the inside of the barrier, or them, ignorant on the outside of it. Everything to me was ugly and illuminating; everything to them was beautiful and empty. Maybe I *didn't* have it so bad.

"Let it go, Cooper," I said. "They're stupid and drunk."

"*And* they smelled like cheap Kmart body spray, so their opinions are invalid anyway," Autumn added.

Cooper opened his mouth as he looked back at them, ready to rip them to shreds, but then he stuttered and closed it again. Finally he sighed and dropped his shoulders. "You know, ill-mannered young ladies like you two are exactly the reason I think spanking should've *never* been outlawed by America's court system!" he called after them, loudly but politely. "A belt would've really done you two foul-mouthed troublemakers some good as children, in my humble opinion!"

They glanced back and kept laughing.

"And for the record," he continued, "you should know that Summer Johnson is the sexiest 'wheelchair chick' to have ever traveled via wheelchair! *Period*!"

The girls laughed at each other again and stumbled across the street to a bar, totally ignoring the words coming out of my wonderful boyfriend's mouth.

"Come on," Autumn said in my ear as she grabbed my chair and started pushing me away. "If we don't get out of here now, I'm gonna rape him *myself.*"

~

The next morning we woke to a brilliant blue sky. It was weirdly cool and breezy for July, and after Cooper got some coffee from the Starbucks in the lobby we decided to go antiquing. Getting ready had been quite the ordeal, and even though I'd felt super tired for some reason, I'd refused Cooper's help in taking a shower. I was so weak that it took me almost an hour, but he'd waited in the room the whole time, playing on his iPad and trying to act like he wasn't annoyed when clearly he was. And I didn't blame him. He'd been dealing with a lot lately, mostly me and my problems.

We'd stayed out until about one the night before, and Autumn had rebuffed our repeated offers to stay in our extra room, choosing to drive back to Jax Beach instead. It was okay, though – I needed sleep, and I was gone from the moment Cooper transferred me from the wheelchair into bed. And sure, a hookup had been in the back of my mind, but what could I do? I wouldn't want me, either, in this condition.

Cooper pushed me into the quieter part of town, where all the antique shops were. Old Victorian mansions stood on every block, their columns smothered in faded green ivy leaves, their front yards fat with rosebushes and hydrangea. We talked and shopped for a few hours, and soon I had a red scarf, some pretty cool old picture frames that would've made my hipster friends twitch their beards with jealousy, and this battered book from 1897 that was going to look pretty cool on my shelf back home. As the early afternoon heat started to creep up on us, we left one shop called Miss Jan's Junk and crossed to the side of the road

211

that was covered in shade from the oaks. I wrapped my giant grey sweater tight, suddenly freezing, and in the reflection of a parked car we passed, I saw him run his hand through his hair rather deliciously.

"Ugh. Stop making my heart beat like that," I said. "I'm not supposed to get worked up, remember?"

"Deal," he laughed. Just then we passed a bridal shop, and inside I saw a pack of bridesmaids around my age fawning over a bride-to-be as she marched out into the showroom in a totally over-the-top dress, her mom tearfully snapping photos with her iPhone from a chair in the back. As I watched them I couldn't help but think of everything I was missing, and all the things I'd maybe never get to experience, and all the acres of organza I'd probably never get to feel on my skin, and suddenly my eyes glassed up. Then they locked with Cooper's in his reflection in the window, and I noticed that he seemed to be deliberating something again. But what?

Once again, he snapped out of some trance. He shook his head, appeared to make up his mind about something, and turned abruptly.

"Hey, where are we going?" I asked as we hit a curb a little too forcefully, and I was sent flying up three inches into the air.

"You'll see," he said mysteriously. "And sorry about that."

"It's fine," I winced. "Hey, what was it like growing up here?" I asked to change the subject.

"It was…boring, I guess. Trust me, St. Augustine is much better to visit than it is to grow up in. It's mostly retirees from, like, Connecticut, and older artists and stuff. I mean, it's pretty, but pretty doesn't keep you company after school when you wanna play baseball and there are two kids living in a ten block radius."

"That sucks," I said. "Does being back here, like, I don't know…inspire you? You know, to write?"

His shadow fidgeted on the sidewalk. "I don't know about that."

212

"Okay. And, speaking of your past, um...can I ask you about the whole pill thing?"

"I guess?"

"Okay. Well, why did you start?"

"I don't know," he sighed. "Why does *anyone* start a bad habit? I already had addiction in my genes, and things just got out of control. As soon as my dad left my family, it was just me and my mom, and we were dirt poor. She got worse every year, and I would *never* call her a burden, but – you know. It was difficult. Anyway, after high school I got hired by the Jacksonville newspaper straightaway as a writer for some reason-"

"Because you're a genius," I interrupted, and the shadow of him shook its head.

"Whatever. They saw some of my work in a local contest and hired me as a columnist who could hopefully reach out to younger readers. Anyway, I knew I couldn't afford college and I knew I couldn't leave my mom, so I said yes. But working and caring for her at the same time became too much, and taking half a Xanax every night to help myself sleep and drown out my mom's crying and moaning turned into a lot more than that, and...yeah. I just sort of cracked. I got myself together, though, and ever since then I've just been sort of drifting from freelance gig to freelance gig while helping Colleen. I have no idea what I'm going to do in this job climate without a degree, and I'm terrified of what's going to happen when my mom isn't around anymore and I have nobody to distract me from the fact that I'm lost, but...yeah. We'll see."

I considered all that as he pushed me. We really were the same: just two lost souls drifting through an uncertain world, waiting for a future we were almost too afraid to even imagine for ourselves.

"What was your dad like?" I asked for the first time, taking advantage of this rare, open moment.

"Not fun," he said.

"What do you mean? Am I prying?"

213

"No, it's fine. Hmm – how can I explain this? The thing is, women don't really understand father-son dynamics. There's this weird layer of male competitiveness a lot of the time. Or there was on his side, at least. He was threatened by me by the time I was in the fifth grade – you know, the classic testosterone-fueled pissing contest. He drank a lot, and he was a failed artist himself, and every time I'd get a good grade on a paper, win a local contest, whatever, he'd get drunk, throw a fit, call me worthless, say I'd never make it, etcetera."

"What?"

"Yeah. He never did anything, you know, *physical* or anything, but he was definitely abusive in other ways. I guess that's my biggest fear – turning into him. That's what drove me towards pills, that's the nightmare that pops into my head once a week. That's why I can't leave my mom with some part-time nurse and go start my life, you know? I would die if I ever left my mother and became my father. Literally – I'd rather just roll over and die. I hate him. If I ever saw him today, I'd spit in his face. I will *never* be him. Never."

As I stared ahead, lost in thought, he laughed a little. "God, listen to me, dragging you down on your special weekend."

"No, you're fine. I was the one who asked. You've never told me half this much about your past before."

"Yeah, but I'm not trying to be a Debbie Downer here, either. Hey, all these old houses on this road remind me of that Saviour song."

"Oh, yeah, *that* one."

"Ha, shut up – I'm talking about *Gold*. Do you know it?"

"Eh, maybe I heard it once or twice."

I recited the lines in my head as he pushed me along the cracked sidewalks under the age-old oaks:

I was thinking back today, back to when our days were golden

Back to when we were young and free, so emboldened
Running those grimy streets of town, you were King and I
was Queen
Nobody could fuck with those crowns of thorns, babe, royalty

But where did you go? Where are you now?
I'm still that girl, just older now
Just know that if you wanted me there
I'd run, run, run until I found you, I swear

Now all I see is this dying day, time flying by
Running out, flashing gold up in the sky
But will you love me in my December as you did in my July?
And would you still come to me now that I'm no longer flying
high?

(Run, run, run, I swear)

"Here we are," Cooper said as we stopped in the middle of
the sidewalk. "This is where I wanted to come. The Kissing
Tree."

"The what?"

"It's, like, 'a thing' here," he said as he leaned down,
sounding nervous for some reason, as I looked up and saw a
palm tree sticking out of the middle of a large oak. "It's
dumb, but I thought we'd stop by. For some reason a palm
tree grew right out of the heart of an oak tree, and I guess
they depend on each other now, since their roots and trunks
are linked up and everything. If they're ever separated both
of them will die immediately, and so because of that, they
say that if you kiss someone under the tree, your love will
last eternally or whatever. I don't know, it's kinda cheesy,
but still, I thought we could...I thought you'd want to...you
know...take a picture, since all the girls our age are posting
wedding selfies and everything, and..."

I cringed as I realized he'd seen straight into my
brain back at the bridal shop. The sentiment was sweet, but

215

still, he must've thought I was the biggest wedding-obsessed psycho in the world after all this.

"Cooper, it's fine. I don't care about-"

"No it's not, Summer," he interrupted. "I'm not stupid. I hear the way Autumn talks about marriage, and I see the way it makes you feel. I have eyes. And a heart. I just don't want you to miss out. I want you to be able to make the annoying Facebook posts just like all those morons, and have all those rites of passage. I know how much this situation sucks – nobody knows what's gonna happen, you know? I just feel bad that all these other girls are getting to do all this normal-girl stuff while you just sit here in a wheelchair, and I just wish I could fix it."

"It's okay, Cooper," I said, melting into my wheelchair. "I'm fine. Really."

He stared down at his feet, looking almost ashamed of himself. "It's *not* fine. It's not. I would do *anything* to make you happy, Summer, as pathetic as it is to admit that. Anything. But I'm just not ready for…for *that* right now, and, you know, it's just that, we're so young, and…"

He trailed off as my heart rate spiked. *Omg.* How could I possibly save this conversation before he decided I was a maniac bridezilla and ran for the hills?

And wait: if this trip wasn't some marriage/proposal/whatever scheme, then why in the hell were we here in the first place, anyway?

"Cooper, listen," I began, grabbing him by the shorts. "That's not…that's not what I was crying about back there. I don't want to get married right now. I swear. I just think it's sort of hilarious and embarrassing how girls these days use Facebook as a forum to throw their supposed happiness in everyone's faces and force everyone to bask in their Marriage Glow or whatever, and I wasn't…I wasn't really saying that I wanted to…you know…do that. I'm totally happy with the way things are with us. I'm grateful for every second of this, let me tell you."

Cooper didn't say anything. I looked up at his face. He was crying.

216

"What is it?" I whispered. "What's wrong?"

An old man sitting on the porch of an antique shop across the street suddenly called over to us, shattering the moment.

"Ah, the kissing tree!" he cried as he stood up, his belly stretching against his plaid button-up. "If ever a couple kisses under it, their love shall last forever! Would the young couple like a Kissing Tree shot?"

I looked back at Cooper. Keeping his glassy eyes on the old man, he clenched his jaw, bent down, and then whispered this through his teeth:

"I just want you to know that I am so sorry about all this, and that even sick and skinny and stuck in a wheelchair, you still have more dignity in one strand of your hair than any woman I have ever known."

"Really!" the man yelled, splitting my attention yet again. "Let me take a shot of you two!"

I swiveled in the chair and saw his smile twitching from under his bushy white beard. Finally, Cooper sniffled and blinked the tears from his eyes.

"Ugh. We can't just turn the poor guy down, can we?" I shook my head. "Yeah, why not, then?" he told the man as he stood tall and wiped his face. "We'd love to!"

Cooper pushed me over to the sun-dappled driveway beneath the Kissing Tree as the old man followed. After handing him his phone and explaining how to snap a picture, he came over and sank onto one knee beside me, rendering holy ground this patch of oil-stained asphalt in sticky northern Florida. As Cooper wrapped his arm around the back of my wheelchair and gave the old man a proud, dazzling smile, I closed my eyes and suddenly became enveloped in a happiness I'd never felt before. I didn't know exactly what the nurses had wanted me to accomplish on this trip, but I guessed this must've been a step in the right direction. I didn't care if we weren't at the beach, under the pier, summer-ing it up anymore – this was all I'd wanted. Just him.

217

And maybe I was just like this town. Maybe I was a mess underneath, being kept together by a coat of paint and a smile, and I was doomed in the end. But right then and there, under that weird tree, I prayed that even if I was destined to die, even if I'd never get a wedding and a baby and a minivan and the dozens of annoying Facebook statuses to go along with it all, I'd still be able to package this moment away and take it with me, wherever I was going, and keep it forever.

"Ready for your love to last forever?" the old man asked the sick girl and the healthy boy. I looked up at the branches of our very own Oak Tree of Love fanning out above us, blocking the midday sun, and realized I'd become someone from my nightmares – and had had an absolute dream of a time doing it.

"Ready," I said, and as the old man grinned and pressed the screen, Cooper leaned in and whispered something else: "Fuck all them and their weddings. We don't need an overpriced gown and a crying mom to make this thing last forever."

Eyes wide open, I smiled and said another prayer: a foolish, somewhat desperate wish that the tree's stupid powers would actually work this time.

~

On the way back to St. George Street we passed a sort of rat-faced boy in a pair of faded jeans and heard him whispering about "the cripple" to someone who looked like his brother. I held up my hand, but Cooper dismissed me and clenched his jaw: I could tell there would be no politeness this time.

"Hey, Farmer Joe," he called, and both of them immediately looked over. "My girlfriend may be in a wheelchair, but she's still way better looking than your fugly ass will ever be, so unless you want to come over here and let me beat you into the dirt you crawled out of, why don't you keep your monosyllabic thoughts to yourself?"

They turned the color of the strawberry ice cream cones they were eating and quietly disappeared into a nearby candle store.

19

Later that night I sat alone in our room while Cooper
tinkered downstairs. We'd spent the rest of the afternoon at
that Oldest Schoolhouse place, and truthfully it was kind of
boring. We'd pretty much grasped the whole concept – that it
was, indeed, *a really old school* – within the first five
minutes, and then we'd spent the rest of the hour listening to
some weird guy in a pirate costume talking about the history
of the building. After all the Oak Tree of Love intensity I
may have even dozed off once or twice, actually, as it was
getting harder to stay awake even on the most exciting of
days.

  Suddenly Cooper sauntered into the room wearing
only a towel, which hung deliciously from his torso. He had
a Heineken in his hand and held it out, offering me a sip, and
I shook my head. He smirked, tossed his backpack onto the
bed, and turned into the bathroom, and suddenly an evil idea
came to me regarding the Mystery of the Jewelry Box. I
leaned over, reached into his bag, and rooted around while
he brushed his teeth. Finally I found the jewelry box and
lightly pushed it open, and what was inside flummoxed me.

  It was a pen. It hadn't been a jewelry box at all, but a
case for a fancy fountain pen. A notebook was in the bag,
too, a battered one with a black cover. What on Earth was
Cooper writing? Was it that book he'd mentioned? And if so,
why would he be covering it up?

  "Check your phone," Cooper said over his shoulder,
cutting my surveillance mission short.

  "What?" I asked as I snapped the box shut and
dropped the bag.

  "Check your phone. By the way, did you ever post
that oak tree photo?"

  "Nah, I decided to keep it to myself – some things are
just better left unshared, in my opinion."

  "Atta girl."

  I reached into the pocket of my wheelchair for my
phone, which somehow I hadn't checked since the

schoolhouse – guess I'd been too tired. In between Facebook messages from cousins and coworkers about the surgery – thanks to Shelly's big mouth, the cat was fully out of the bag now – there was a longish text from Cooper from three hours ago. I held my breath and opened it:

We're sitting here in the oldest schoolhouse in America and I'm in love with you. You just nodded off a little and got yelled at by the weird tour guide for not paying attention and now we're both laughing like crazy under our breaths and I'm in love with you. I don't really know how to put all this into words, the fact that you're golden and dazzling and triumphant and that you're the best person I've ever met and that you sank into my being and scraped my dirty soul clean and that you make me smile all day like a total fucking maniac, so I'm just gonna text you this: I'm in love with you.

I looked up at him. I didn't care about marriages or proposals or rings anymore. I wanted him, exactly as he was, immediately.

"Come here," I said as the oldest feeling in the world rose up into my chest.

"What?"

"Come here."

He padded back into the room in a pair of basketball shorts and nothing else, looking *delicious*. Raising an eyebrow, he sank onto the bed next to me, and I sang a silent hymn of thanks that I was at least wearing cute-ish pajamas – it seemed that not even a death sentence could curb my vanity.

Cooper blushed when he saw my phone, the rosy glint giving his dark eyes this wonderful boyish quality. "Sorry for not just telling you all that in person," he said, "but I was already wiped out from that stupid tree. And besides, what kind of millennial would I be if I had social skills?"

"Touché."

221

Suddenly the intensity of my feelings for him (along with the mild painkillers Steinberg had prescribed for my throat, probably) started messing with my brain, and I didn't know why, but I started feeling *really* turned on. Sure, I acted Spunky and Upbeat and Plucky and all those other things that Sick People were supposed to be, but the truth was that I was a human just like anyone else, and I had needs. And sitting a foot away from Cooper for days on end, watching the muscles in his forearms flex and unflex, had made me experience those needs more than ever.

I put my hand on his thigh and squeezed, and it was just as firm and delicious as I'd imagined. He peered down, eyes expanding, and I could tell he knew just what I wanted.

He looked at me, and I looked at him. This was it. Just us. No phones or texts or Facebook statuses or tangled headphones to drown out the pain and mask the quietly aching voices in our minds – just the humming silence of humanity filtering in, sinking into the shallow pools in our souls to remind us that we were alive and human and hurting and reaching for more.

"Summer," he asked, "really? *Now?*"

I nodded.

"But how do you, like, feel? Are you well enough to…?"

"Yes. I want to."

He set his jaw, and the light in his eyes changed. "Good. Because I want that, too. Badly. You have no idea how badly, actually. I used to be afraid of hurting you, but not anymore."

"You do, really?" I asked, my resolve melting for a moment. "You want me?"

He put a hand on my leg. "I do."

For one last time, I wanted to wreck this for myself. "But I, I look terrible," I said, "and I don't know if I can give you what you want, and…"

"Oh, Summer." A desperate, animalistic sheen came to his brown eyes, and he scoffed up at the ceiling. "Just like Saviour said in *Strange Fiction*, enough with the fucking sunshine and rainbows and happy endings. I want what you're hiding from me," he growled, loosely quoting her again. "I know there's more. Give it to me. Give it all to me. I want your ugly, your broken, your twisted; I want the monsters that pick away at your soul while you lie awake at night thinking of us. Let's burn each other to the ground in all the best ways, until there's nothing left but you and me and love and the future."

Something deep within me coiled up and then lit aflame. I was ready.

Finally I looked him in the eye one last time, brown to hazel, heart to heart. A girl who didn't deserve love, asking a boy for it nonetheless. *Don't break me down*, I silently quoted Saviour as I tried to look past his eyes, at whatever was underneath. *Don't let me down now.*

"Cooper?" I asked.

"Yeah?"

"You might want to take off your shorts now."

"I want to see you, too," he said after I laid myself out, his ab muscles resplendent in the soft light from the lamp in the corner. "Take off your dress."

I reached underneath and wiped at my stomach tube. Thankfully it was clean of the bile that sometimes leaked out of it and dried into a brownish film that caked around the plastic tube, and so I lifted off my dress and tried not think about what a skinny, bony, pale mess I must've looked like. Sure enough, he was staring at me like I was an apparition.

"What is it?" I asked. "I look bad, I know, and-"

"No," he said. "You're just beautiful."

"I am?"

"Yes, Summer. I like you, immensely, as the You that you are, the You that I see right now, the You that you hide away because you think the world wants you to be someone else. Just...*you,* without a filter. That's the You that I like."

"I...I don't know what to say."

223

"Don't say anything, then. Just feel. And you're sure you're okay?"

"Yes. Maybe a little tired."

"Well I'm about to change that." He licked his bottom lip, making some delicious feeling sink into me and then heat me from within.

"Shall we?" he asked with a dirty grin.

"We shall, Coop."

"Oh, babe." He smiled a dazzlingly crooked smile and then got going. "I *love* when you call me Coop."

Part of me knew he would always be like this, in this setting. There was this intensity, this wildness swimming beneath his dark eyes that spoke of some beautiful inner turmoil, and I'd seen it rise to the surface and flash a few times – but *never* like this. It was clear that he was somewhat experienced, and although I wasn't sure how to feel about that, I enjoyed the effects of that experience nonetheless. It was like getting to know a completely different Cooper – a Cooper that I wanted to continue to get to know as often as possible, for the rest of my life, actually.

"You know, I love every bit of you," he said as he kissed his way down my stomach a minute or two later, veering a bit around my feeding tube. "Even the plastic parts," he laughed, making me giggle a little.

"Why?"

"I don't know. Sometimes it's our imperfections that bring us to the next level. Would Amy Winehouse have been half as interesting without the crack?"

"Hmm," I breathed. "I guess not. But why are we talking about crack right now, anyway?"

He placed another kiss on my stomach. "Because you're mine."

I giggled again, but the look in his eyes made me stop short.

"What is it?"

224

"Don't laugh," he said.

"Why not?"

"Because I want you still for when I do this."

He pushed two fingers forward, and I gasped. His mouth followed the same trajectory, and I leaned back and clawed at my bed sheets as the attack began. I had both looked forward to and dreaded this moment for weeks, but it was more than living up to my expectations.

This was *clearly* going to be a long night.

"Our neighbors are probably terrified," he panted after a minute, breaking a hole in my own euphoria.

"Why?"

"Listen – the heartbeat. It's probably making the pictures rattle in their frames in the other rooms."

I listened: sure enough, a *bumb-bump* filled the room. "Yeah. Sorry. I guess I get kinda excited."

"No," he said, shaking his head, "you're not understanding. It's mine. I've been waiting so long to work up the nerve to do this, I think I might just explode. You have no idea how badly I've wanted this."

"Oh."

He pushed me back on the bed and continued. "I love you, Summer," he whispered into my scarred chest. "Every second of seeing you in the hospital was torture for me. I am so grateful I downloaded that stupid dating app."

"Me too," is all I could say, and then it blew into me, the grand and startling and soul-stirring realization that no matter what happened between us, whether we would last six weeks or six decades, I would never ever be the same. This love had rearranged me.

You know what happened next. The sex happened. And I say "sex" because it was sort of halfway between making love and fucking. It wasn't perfect, and avoiding the feeding tube took some getting used to, and since I was so thin and bony, there were some maneuvers that were more awkward than I would've preferred. But God, it was beautiful. And it was *hot*. It was everything I'd wanted and so much more, stupid feeding tube notwithstanding. When I clutched him by the shoulders and breathed in his perfect scent and started crying and said "thank you for loving me on my way down," he cried, too, and that's when I knew it was real and true and good and right.

Twenty minutes after the big bang, we were both trying to avoid a wet spot on the bed while simultaneously trying to pretend like we *weren't* avoiding the wet spot on the bed. I rolled onto my side and rested my head on my elbow on the rustled-up sheets between us. Getting to know him in this way, seeing this new side of him, had made me want to know even more about him. I was a cannibal with an endless appetite for Nichols.

I studied his arms, his hair raised like blades of grass as he breathed in and out, luxuriating in his beautiful silence. I noticed a birthmark on his right forearm that I'd never seen before: pretty large, but so faint you could barely see it. This was what I'd wanted with him, this quiet observant time away from Shelly and Steinberg and the nurses and whoever else, when I could study him and notice all these craggy little human details about him. I wanted to know all of him, every birthmark, every cell, every mitochondria, right now, and I never wanted it to end. Unfortunately I could already sense him transitioning from Sex Animal Cooper back to Normal Cooper, and I could feel the magic slipping away.

I looked into the darkness, and my eyes fell on my wheelchair.

"Thank you for loving me," I said as I put my head on his shoulder, sounding sadder than I'd meant to. "Like, that sounds cheesy, but whatever. I don't care. You know, this story never happens. It's always, like, the hunky bad boy who becomes disabled during a motorcycle crash while trying to save a kidnapped nun or something, and then his alluring nurse falls in love with him in the hospital and dedicates the rest of her life to pushing him around and loving him. But it never happens like this. Boys like you don't fall for wheelchair girls. I don't deserve you and I know that. So thanks for, you know, loving me like this."

"And thank you for being so lovable," Cooper said as he kissed my sweaty forehead, his voice scratchier than normal. The casual touch was a bit awkward after his aggressive display before, but I tried not to break eye contact. Fleetingly I wondered if my hair smelled good. "And it's not cheesy," he said with a sad smile. "You stuck with me through my weird meltdown thing in the garage. I will stick with you through anything. Even if you are a frustrating little knucklehead sometimes."

I couldn't think of anything to say, so I just tried to catch my breath.

"You know something?" he asked after a moment, lost in wonder. "Remember when we met, and I didn't text you for a few days after that?"

"Yeah?"

"*Well*, I was trying to save you from me. From my...situation. But I failed. It was useless, because I couldn't turn off my feelings for you even if I'd wanted to."

"I know what you mean. *Trust me*. This whole summer has been one long exercise in trying to save you from myself."

He smirked into the darkness.

"What is it?" I asked, and he rolled over and rested his head on his bicep, a twinkle in his eye.

"There was another reason I called Last Great Hope, you know."

Oh no, I thought. *Elopement. Cheesy ring. Shotgun wedding in someone's backyard the day before the surgery.* I wanted love, sure, but not *that* kind of love, the kind I knew Shelly would try to force onto Cooper's shoulders.

"There was?"

"Yep," he smiled. "The nurses told me to get laid."

"Cooper! That's why we came here? Are you serious?"

"*Hell* to the no," he said. "I still wanted to bust you out of the hospital, remember? I didn't want you to spend your only days before surgery locked up in that room." He smirked that patented Nichols Smirk. I'd seen his mom do it a few times, too, and it seemed like they'd gotten the whole business down to an art form. "But honestly, it was in the back of my mind. I think the nurses felt sorry for me and wanted to help out."

"You dick," I said, and his smirk grew into a full-on smile.

"Tell me something else, Sum: was I your first?"

I looked away. What did he think this was, some cheesy college-aged romance novel starring an impossibly naïve heroine who'd never even been kissed before? I'd never been able to lock anyone down into a relationship, sure, but still, Autumn had lots of guy friends, and she'd been stealing bottles of vodka from her oblivious grandpa and arranging backyard get-togethers since we were seventeen – get-togethers involving hammocks that were far away from any scar-revealing fluorescent lights, might I add.

"I'm sorry to disappoint you," I said, "but no. Don't worry, though, the previous guy was completely awful, and I barely knew him. He didn't know my elbow from my kneecap, and I ended the whole thing and put it out of its misery before twenty minutes had passed. Maybe I should've stayed with him out of punishment and made *him* deal with this summer instead of you, actually, since he was so bad."

Now Cooper was the one looking away. "Please don't say things like that anymore, Summer. Seriously."

"You *are* mad, though," I told him. "You can admit it. It's okay."

He stared into the bathroom, his eyes impassive. "Fine. I am. But I'm not *that* mad, and I don't want you to *think* I'm that mad, or that I regret this in any way. God knows I had nothing else to do this summer. You know, that's why I've started writing-"

Out of nowhere I started choking on my spit, since sometimes it had nowhere to go but out of my mouth.

"What is it?" he asked, propping himself up and scooting closer. "Don't cry, it's fine, let me just-"

228

"No," I said, "I'm not crying, I just have to vomit."

"*Oh.*"

He jumped up, grabbed a plastic grocery bag from the bathroom, and held it under me as I emptied the contents of my throat and stomach into it. He did his best to try to act like he wasn't grossed out, but he was. Anyone would have been. Soon I was crying, the tears mixing in with the bile dripping from my lips.

"Stop it," he said after he threw away the bag and gave me some paper towels for my mouth. "I can deal with a little vomit."

There was something else in his eyes, something he couldn't say.

"Do you want to know what it feels like, not having a throat?" I asked after I cleaned myself, and he nodded.

"I guess. It would help me understand."

"Okay. Remember those little straw tubes you'd get out of candy machines or at the fair or whatever, those Chinese Finger Traps, where you'd put in your fingers and it would contract and they'd get stuck? That's the only way I know how to describe it. It's just...too tight. Things come up, but nothing goes down."

He bit his lip, his eyes full of thunderheads I had never seen in them. "I'm very sorry you have to deal with that, Summer. Do you want to sleep?"

I nodded and put my head against the inside of his leg so I could feel his pulse. Within minutes I had started to drift away, accompanied by the cruelest irony I had ever known: only now that I knew my life was probably finite was I truly enjoying it. Here I was, gallivanting around town with the hot boy of my dreams, and I was fine. I really *could* live normally. If only I could go back, armed with the knowledge and the bravery and the love I had now. How differently things could have turned out...how happy the scarred girl with the hole in her throat could have been...

Another thought came to me, and I slowly sat up again. "And one last thing. Remember today at the Kissing

Tree or whatever? This is crazy, but I thought you were going to-"

That's when Cooper's eyes got very large and he told me I was bleeding.

"What?" I asked with a smile, his words not registering.

"You're…you're bleeding, Summer."

I looked down and gasped at the trail of bloody bile that was seeping out of my feeding tube.

20

We drove an hour straight to my hospital, back to where this had all started. Dr. Steinberg was eating dinner downtown when we arrived, so to stabilize me they immediately admitted me and wrapped so many bandages around my midsection I looked like an Egyptian mummy. When Steinberg got there I was put to sleep and they performed an endoscopy, and I awoke the next morning to some bad news. I was basically okay, but I'd done *way* too much in St. Augustine, apparently, and some internal bleeding originating from my stomach had set off a chain reaction, and...the result was not good. Dr. Dill was being called to Florida, and my surgery was being moved up. I now had thirty-six hours until the Hail Mary. So much had been accomplished with Cooper in St. Augustine, and yet I felt like it had all been wiped away in a moment again, sending us back to square one. So it goes, right?

They dressed my stomach tube with bandages again and sent me home for two nights. Cooper drove me to Shelly's, wracked with guilt all the while. Obviously my latest setback wasn't his fault, but he wouldn't listen. Still, he kissed me quietly in the driveway under the oaks before heading back to his mom's, saying he wanted to give me time alone with my family, which I understood. I spent the rest of the day at home with them. My dad dropped by from Orlando and sort of awkwardly sat there making the smallest of small talk for a few hours while Chase played video games and my mom and my aunt silently glared from the kitchen. Shelly's much older half-sister, Susan, didn't have much going on in her life, and we'd sort of absorbed her as part of my family since she was a divorcee with no children of her own. Ever since my parents' split she had shown her sisterly support by hating the shit out of my dad, and it struck me as a weird and awkward and selfish thing to do around me. Divorce: another thing that sucked almost as much as health problems. *Why* did I always have to feel like the only adult in the room, again? Why couldn't Aunt Kathryn, my dad's sister who was totally normal and respectable and dignified, have come instead? Ugh.

I ended up passing out on the couch while everyone watched *Home Alone* for some reason, and the day before my surgery arrived bright and humid, just like any other day, except it wasn't any other day. Not to me, at least. My pierced stomach was in knots from the second I woke in a panicked sweat at six in the morning. I wanted to make time slow down, but I was in such a panicked cloud of anxiety, *nothing* would work. I was on a collision course with fate, and there would be no jumping off this train, wherever it was headed.

At around ten most of the Anti-Support Group showed up and congregated in the dining room with my mom and Susan while different members came up to see me one by one. One last meeting, I guess. Because the whole surgery process had been sped up so majorly, things felt pretty thrown-together, but still, I think people knew what they had to do.

First to approach me was Hank, the one-armed veteran.

"So, I hear the chances may not be great," he said, in lieu of a greeting.

"They are certainly not astounding, no."

"Yeah," he said. "This is really shitty."

"I know. Life's just shitty sometimes, until it's not life anymore, I guess."

"Uh-huh. Listen, I want you to have something." He took a short, rusted, jagged piece of metal out of his pocket. "Um, I know this might sound weird or whatever, but this a piece of shrapnel they removed from my shoulder after my truck drove over an IED, and, uh, I wanted you to have it."

I opened my mouth and then closed it. "Um, thanks, Hank, but…*why?*"

"Because you saved my life," he said simply.

"I…*what?*"

"Six months ago I had a plan to kill myself," he said flatly as he stared down at me. "I was going to tie a cinder

232

block around my ankles and jump off the end of the pier at night. I had the block, the rope, everything. And then I met you in Publix that day and you invited me to the group, and everything changed. You were the only person in my life who ever listened to me, Summer. The *only* one. Everyone else fell away, got sick of listening to me complain, whatever, which I kind of understood, but then I found you, and you sat there and listened to me pour my broken heart out every Thursday – in my own way, at least. Anyway, feeling like you're being heard is a huge thing for a person. The hugest, probably. I can't even...yeah."

I shuddered, and he continued. "Anyway, you were the only person who made me feel like I mattered, and you made me decide to stay. So, because you saved me, I thought I'd give you the thing that almost killed me, because you need to know that people can overcome things – because you *will* overcome this surgery. I know it. Oh," he added, "and I also wanted to give it to you because I'm kind of in love with you?"

He'd added on that last part so casually, I almost hadn't noticed it. I sort of squirmed a little and then reached up to hug him, whiplashed. He returned the hug, perhaps a little too enthusiastically.

"Oh, uh, thank you, Hank!" I said as I sort of patted him on the shoulder with one hand and took the shrapnel with the other. "Thanks so much. God, I don't even know what to say, that was all so nice of you to share with me. And thanks for this, um...shrapnel?"

"No problem," he said. "Oh, and Summer?"

"Yeah?"

"Tell that pretty boy from the meeting to take good care of you, because if he doesn't, I would love to in his place."

"I'll tell him," I nodded through a fake smile as he turned and went back to the kitchen.

Kim wheeled up after that.

"Well look at us now," I said as she stopped beside me, motioning at our chairs. "We match. We're wheelchair sisters now."

"I love it," she laughed in her high-pitched voice. "Speaking of that, this is for you." She reached into her purple purse and took out a small vanity mirror.

"Um, thanks," I said as I took it. "But a mirror? What is this for?"

"I don't need it anymore," she said. "You know, before the Anti-Support Group, I used to sit in my house all day staring into that thing, hating how I looked, hating my whole life and stuff. But after I met you, I stopped. You listened to me, and you introduced me to friends, and you were the only person who ever made me feel pretty. I mean, I get compliments, but *fake ones*. Everyone else talks down to me like I'm a little puppy because of the wheelchair and everything. But you're the only person who talks to me like I'm an actual *person*, not some charity case, and makes me feel like I'm really loved by someone. My *parents* don't even make me feel like you do, Summer. I'm really glad I met you. *Really*. And just know this: whatever happens now, wherever you go, I'll be waiting."

"Oh, *Kim*."

I leaned over and wrapped my arms around her bony body. Sometimes words weren't enough. Just hugs.

The younger members came and went, unable to really say much about my situation, which was fine. Last to come over was Autumn, which was a relief, since I knew there would be no waterworks with her. I lit up as she threw her arms around me.

"Hey, bitch," she said as she sat on the coffee table and crossed her legs. "Good to see you again. Hope you had fun in St. Auggy. And sorry for, you know, nearly ruining your one great chance at love, or whatever that whole thing was."

"Yeah, about that…not your best moment."

"Ugh, I know. My mom had literally *just* told me that morning, and when I ran into Cooper, I just kind of…lost it. But honestly, it's not my journey to comment on, and I should've kept my nose out of it, as usual. *Whoops*. Sorry again." She rested a hand on my knee and let out a long, dramatic sigh. "So, the shy girl used Spark to land the hottie after all. I still can't believe it. What was it like? What happened after I blabbed and it all fell down? Was that, like, *real* the other night, or were you just acting like you weren't mad at him to be polite?"

I stared out of the window at my cat as she chased around a lizard in the bushes, just trying to get by in this too-big world. I breathed for a moment and pictured that night of chaos in the garage – the night he'd finally let me in.

"I don't know," I said. "I guess I had this vision of him as some knight on a horse, this outrageously perfect boy who never got it wrong or stepped out of line." I tried to hold in the tears. "And then he had that meltdown, and dropped all the cheesy, affected lines and everything, and I got to know the real Cooper a little bit better, and let me tell you…the reality of him was so much better than that. The version of him I found under that façade was even better than anything I knew before. The way he stuck with me in the hospital, the way he took me off for that little vacation…*ugh*. Maybe I should thank you, actually."

She started crying, and I followed suit. I'd been wrong: there would be waterworks.

"God, look at us," she finally said, "we're a mess. All I came here to do was say thanks for dealing with all of us losers every Thursday in the group."

"You're not losers," I laughed with wet eyes. "Because if you are, then I'm, like, *below* loser status, and I don't even know what that is. Part-time Taco Bell employee, maybe?"

She laughed her big, goofy laugh that made me feel like a teenager in a mall again.

"Listen," she said, "there is another thing. I know I've seen you, like, every day this summer, and will probably see you again before surgery, but since bringing a present has become, like, 'a thing' today and all, I wanted to give you something, too, since I am nothing but a brainless lamb who also uses too many run-on sentences. Hold on."

She walked to the foyer and then brought back a garment bag. "So," she said as she lifted something pink out of the bag, "like, I know I always complain about not having a fiancé or whatever, and God knows I'm not any closer to getting engaged. Like, *at all*. I've had one date lately, come to think of it, and the guy literally left the bar early because I wouldn't stop asking him what he wanted to name his firstborn, which wasn't exactly the best first-date behavior on my part, looking back on it. But anyway, whatever happens with the surgery, I just wanted to make sure you'll still be a bridesmaid at my wedding, if it ever happens, God willing. Because I am a psychopath, I already picked out my bridesmaids dresses years ago, and yesterday I got one for you." She held up the dress. Pale pink and floaty, it was actually bereft of the Ugly Curse that seemed to befall most bridesmaid dresses, and it was actually kind of pretty. "So, Summer," she said, "whatever happens tomorrow, will you take this, and will you still be in my wedding?"

"I would *love* to be in your completely theoretical wedding," I said as I laughed through the tears falling from my eyes and took the dress. "There would be no greater theoretical honor."

"Awesome!" she beamed. "And I promise not to get too emotional during the vow exchange, I know how you hate cheesy stuff. I'll keep it to, like, three crying sessions, I promise."

"Thanks," I said. "And Autumn?"

"Yeah?"

"I forgive you for the Cooper thing. Really. I don't want to be on a bad note with you, or whatever."

"Good," she said as she kissed my forehead. "And I'm sorry, once again, for being such a drunken, big-mouthed bitch."

"All is forgiven. But, actually: one *more* thing."

"Yes?"

"Please go talk to Hank and distract him," I said as I threw a glance over at the dining table. "He's basically raping me with his eyes right now, and I really have to call my Uncle Earl and pretend like I remember what the hell his homemade pepper sauce tastes like, so…yeah. I need a break."

She cast a flirty look over at Hank. "Wait – you mean he's horny?" she asked, a new light in her eyes. "Maybe I should go investigate this. Besides that whole one-armed thing, he really *is* kinda cute. I've always liked depressed bad boys, after all."

"Okay, you did *not* just say that. Are you *really* trying to pick up a dude at our final goodbye session?"

She ignored me and pranced toward the dining room with a determined smile on her face.

Night came at light speed, and soon it was time for my last supper, or maybe-not-last supper, or whatever this was. Dr. Steinberg had arranged for Last Great Hope to send me out to dinner, and I'd decided on this place called Ruth's Chris in Ponte Vedra, the fancy part of my city. This was both because I'd really liked steak on the few occasions I'd been able to swallow pieces of it, and also because I wanted to go to the most expensive restaurant I could think of and hit up Last Great Hope for all they had. (My own little way of getting revenge on the world, I guess.) And I instantly knew who I wanted to go with.

Of course, Shelly really didn't want me to leave and begged me to spend every possible moment with her, but I overruled her. In the end she relented and helped me get into my dress for the night, this golden thing I'd worn to my senior prom. I'd gone with a group of girls I barely knew who had invited me out of pity, and the whole thing was awful and miserable, but hey, at least I'd gotten a good dress out of it. After Shelly did my makeup she stood back and tried to figure out what to do with my hair. It was basically falling out in clumps now since my damaged stomach wasn't

237

digesting any nutrients from the milk, and what *did* remain was dry and brittle as a bone left out in the sun. So Shelly decided to just grease it and put it in a bun, and when she was done she wheeled me over to the mirror to see how I looked.

"Oh my God, you're a vision!" she cried. We both tried not to notice how sunken in my eyes were, and how obviously the dress hung off my skeletal frame, and how I was aging at warp-speed. We both failed.

Cooper was late, which was unusual for him, and so I buried my attention in my phone and pulled up Facebook to ~~shamelessly search for validation~~ see who was pregnant, who was engaged, and who was going nowhere fast like me. The comments had been pouring in for days, because when Shelly Johnson is involved with something word travels quickly, and I clicked on my notifications to see if anyone had said anything new. There was only one comment, from me and Autumn's old high school art teacher, a sweet older lady who had become sort of a mentor to us over the years:

So sorry about your health setback. Jim & I have been praying nonstop. Remember that in art, the brightest colors always show up next to the darkest lines. Your brightest shades are on the way, sweetie. Blessings & Love, Miss Patti.

I responded with a short little comment underneath, trying and failing to believe in her polite sentiment. I had just as good a chance at never seeing color again as I did at swimming in the stupid shades of the rainbow, and I knew it. Then I went to another messaging app and signed in under my username, *arbitraryonlineusername*. I found a message from Scott, this guy from school that I'd "talked to" for two minutes last year before he'd ditched me for some bimbo named Chrissy:

Hey, sorry we haven't spoken in a while. I've been so busy with work and everything, you know how it is.

Anyway, I heard from my neighbor about what happened, and I'm really sorry. I would say good luck, but you're a warrior and you're gonna be fine. Thinking of you. Bye.

I went back to Facebook and clicked on his profile. He wasn't busy with work, he was busy getting engaged. And his bride-to-be looked like a total nightmare, staging cheesy photo shoots for every single wedding-related event. They'd even held an elaborate photo op just to capture them putting their save-the-date notices into the mailbox. *Gag.*

Suddenly I was interrupted by Aunt Susan throwing open the front door and saying a few words to someone I couldn't see. Then she looked back at me and scream-whispered, "Sum, a boy's here for you! A *hot* boy!"

"*Susan!*" my mom scolded.

"What? He's gorgeous!"

"Let him in then, and don't say a word to him!"

Susan smirked and then stood aside. Cooper walked in, his gorgeousness dampened temporarily by confusion, looking like a kitten that had just stumbled into a lion's den. I instinctively sat taller in my wheelchair and fussed with my hair.

"Uh, hi there, ma'am," he told Susan. "I'm, uh, Cooper. A good friend of Summer's."

"Hi," Susan breathed, batting her lashes. "I'm Susan. Her aunt. Her very *young* aunt."

"Um, hi. Nice to meet you, Summer's Very Young Aunt."

He greeted my mom quietly but politely and then made his way over to me. There he was, all six feet whatever of him, dressed in a black suit that didn't quite fit him that well, a red tie with white stripes, and a bouquet of pink flowers. But he was still gorgeous. Too gorgeous for the broken girl in front of him, and we all knew it. He was strong and I was weak and he was beautiful and I was scarred and he was captivating and I was unremarkable, and that had never been more apparent than now. It all fed into this fear I

239

think all girls have, this irrational little voice that says, *Sure, my guy wants me now that we're twenty and I look okay in a bikini, but what the fuck's going to happen when we're fifty and I look like shit and he's George Clooney?* My situation was just sped-up: here I was, aging at light speed, decaying in front of his eyes, and here *he* was, apparently as devoted as ever. I could not comprehend it, so I didn't even try.

His face lit up when he saw me, giving me the fireworks I'd missed on the Fourth. Every time he looked at me was a thrill. Still. Even after all this.

"You look…I can't. Hi, Summer."

"I guess 'I can't' is a good thing?" I asked.

"A great thing. A wonderful thing. And oh, shoot, I forgot something. Hold on."

He disappeared outside again and then returned behind a sleek, expensive-looking wheelchair that he'd painted this icy, silvery shade of blue. It even said SUMMER-MOBILE on the seat in his terrible handwriting. "This is for you. My mom didn't need it anymore," he blushed, "so I grabbed it and, like, painted it for you, or whatever. I know you like that shade of blue."

"Wait, how?" I asked in disbelief. Transparent blue was my favorite color, because it was the color of the sky just before the sun rose *and* immediately after it set. It reminded me that whatever you were dealing with in the present, you had survived your past and had no choice but to face your future, so you'd might as well square your shoulders, chill the fuck out, and deal with what life has put in front of you.

"Um, I don't know. Your phone case and your comforter are both ice blue, I guess?"

I ran my hand along the wheel as tears burned my eyes. Here was the knight I'd never believed in, steering a wheelchair instead of a white horse, but still – he was here, and I was a believer.

"Cooper, it's…amazing. I'm gonna be the most stylin' wheelchair lady in town," I laughed, trying not to cry.

"Can you help me get in it? I'm sweating like crazy in this vinyl hospital contraption."

After some maneuvering, he lifted me by the armpits and set me down gently in the chair. It was embarrassing, but I didn't say anything. It's not like I had any dignity left to lose after that hospital stay and St. Augustine trip, anyway. This chair was much less clunky than the hospital chair and much easier to push, not that he let me push myself, anyway. As he led me to the foyer I tried not to think of how surprisingly strong he was, and of how good his hands felt on me, and of how much I already missed his touch.

"Shall we?" he asked.

"We shall."

"Hold on, Mr. Nichols," my mom said. They'd apparently bonded in waiting rooms and hallways during my bout of unconsciousness after the Fourth, and lately she couldn't go an hour without mentioning him. I could tell she was afraid of what would happen to him if the surgery failed, but what could she do? She was powerless against his charms, just like everyone on Earth, basically.

"Yes?" he asked, and she called him over and started whispering to him.

"Set a good example, please. Don't eat too fast or too much in front of her. She needs to pace herself or she'll be sick all night."

"Oh, wouldn't dream of being insensitive about her eating issues, Ms. Johnson," Cooper said loudly as he winked over at me. "The guilt would just eat me alive. I'd never be able to swallow all that."

"He literally wouldn't be able to stomach hurting my feelings," I chimed in. "I'm going to stand on my own two legs today, I don't need guidance."

"But if you ever need a leg up," he said, "I'll be right beside you."

Shelly stared at us for the moment and then shook her head and walked into the kitchen. "Whatever. You two are *seriously* weird."

We left my leering Aunt Susan at the little kitchen table and headed into the sticky night.

We valeted his car at the restaurant, which was a first for me. It took super long for Cooper to lift me out of the seat and lower me into the wheelchair, and we tipped the guy a little extra for waiting. There were no hostesses around, so Cooper held open the door for me and sort of awkwardly maneuvered me through the doorway with one hand. He was so attentive. Ruth's Chris looked just like any other fancy restaurant, dark and sleek and quiet, with big windows that overlooked a lake and a highway. After we sat at a table near those aforementioned windows, someone showed up with a bottle of Rosé out of nowhere, and we smiled and accepted it.

"So," Cooper said after we settled in, a foreboding sense of finality settling over our little table. This was it. There would be no more days at the beach for us; no more St. Augustine getaways. Fate had contracted our time together before the surgery to this one final night, and whatever I didn't tell him tonight would perhaps never get said at all.

"So," I said, figuring I'd start with the easy stuff.

"Yeah. God, I can't even believe we're here. Was it just me, or has this all come at light speed?"

"I know. It doesn't even make sense."

"What's it like?" he asked quietly.

"To not eat?" I asked, motioning at the bread on the table. "I don't know. Food to me is like the glass of water the waiter puts in front of you whenever you first sit at a table. You could drink some, or not, or whatever. That's how I see food."

"No," he said with hesitant eyes, "to…to know…"

"Oh, to know that I might die in a day?"

His shoulders fell. "I mean, when you say it like *that*…"

"No, it's fine," I said. "I mean, this *situation* isn't fine, it's royally fucked up, but your question was fine."

"I hate to ask," he said, "and I know you hate talking about stuff like this, but…I just want to know. Looking at you in that wheelchair, I feel so helpless, and I want to know so I can feel how you feel. I want to be right there with you. I wanna go there, too."

"Hmm. Let me think." I stared out of the window, comforted by the hum of the crowded restaurant. The day was winding down, giving me perhaps the last sunset I'd ever see. Something that was either an alligator or a large soft-shell turtle – you could never quite tell in Florida – sat on the muddy bank, and cars screamed by on A1A beyond it.

I finally turned to my beautiful Cooper. "First of all, that's a moot point," I said. "The first time I heard that song *Live Like You Were Dying,* I couldn't roll my eyes hard enough. To live with the shocking, Earth-shattering news that you're going to die one day? News flash: we're *all* going to die one day, every single one of us, be it tomorrow or a century from tomorrow, and there's nothing we can do about it. Might as well start living while you're not dead, you know? And humans' obsession with death baffles me anyway, because literally everyone dies the same way: your heart stops. A lot of different things can cause that, from cancer to old age to getting run over by an overweight bicyclist to Esophageal Intresia, but still, every human's death certificate should say 'cause of death: heart failure,' since *every* death occurs because of a heart stopping. An Internet billionaire living in San Francisco, and Britney Spears, and that homeless guy at the end of your street? They're all going to die in exactly the same way. What counts is what they did before that to make them different."

"You're different," he said quietly. "No texts this time – I wanna say this face-to-face. You're the most graceful person I've ever met."

"Stop," I told him. "Thanks, but stop. I don't want to cry tonight."

His eyes got sad. "Okay."

"But to answer your death question," I said, "well…okay. You know when you're still asleep and you're

243

at the tail end of a dream, and on some level you know the morning has come and you need to wake up, but then you pull yourself under again to get some more sleep because you're not ready to face the world yet?"

He nodded.

"This feels like that, but…backwards. That's the only way I know how to explain it. My soul doesn't want to acknowledge that it might be going to sleep soon. The whole 'death' thing is in the back of my mind, sure, but the rest of me doesn't even want to consider it a possibility yet. So it still doesn't seem that real. More *sur*-real than anything. And trust me, I've tried, but I still can't really grasp it. Ugh, I don't know – it's all so hard to put into words."

"Yeah," he said as he looked down at the table.

"And also," I said, my voice picking up, unable to shut my mouth, "I guess it's all just kind of the same fear of the unknown that any other twenty-four-year-old feels, you know? I'm not *that* special. We all think about this stuff. *Am I ever gonna find a job? Am I ever gonna get married? Am I ever gonna find a place in this world? Am I gonna die during stomach surgery tomorrow?* In a weird way, it's the same. It's all, like, peering around a dark corner, terrified of what you're gonna see, terrified to even *begin* imagining a future for yourself because you haven't even figured out the present yet. My situation is just on steroids. All I can do is just deal with it and hope for a good outcome."

"You're my best friend," he announced out of nowhere, his eyes wide and glassy and unblinking. I looked away.

"Stop. Not now. Not tonight. Put it in a text or something. I'll cry."

"You are so beautiful," he continued, his voice catching in his throat. "You are so special and important and elegant and smart and kind and worthwhile, and you are so much better than me and everyone else I've ever known in every single way, and you are the only truth I have ever found in this lying world, and I love you to the floor of me, and it breaks me to imagine a future without you in it, and I just want you to know all that, just because."

"Oh, Cooper."

I just stared at him for a while before finally snapping out of it, shaking my head, and reaching for my glass. "I'm think I'm gonna need some more of that Rosé."

"What are you thinking?" he asked a little while later, after our appetizers. I'd managed to eat a few bites of raw tuna despite Dr. Steinberg's orders, and I was proud of myself for breaking the rules.

"I don't know. I-"

We heard giggling and both looked over at the next table. A group of teen boys celebrating a birthday quickly looked away, their faces pink like my favorite roses that grew in my yard. I'd noticed them gawking earlier while Cooper had transferred me from my wheelchair into my seat, but they'd kept quiet until now.

"Hold that thought, I have to go to the bathroom," Cooper said absently as he got up and set his napkin on the table. "Be right back."

He didn't come right back.

Where is he? I wondered after ten or fifteen minutes. At twenty-one minutes, a group of waiters appeared with a large cupcake adorned with long, fancy sparklers. Figuring it was something the hospital had set up, I smiled as big as I could.

"Happy engagement to you," the waiters sang in the tune of the birthday song. "Happy engagement to you! Happy engagement dear Ashley, happy engagement to you!"

They all stared down at me, this little broken girl sitting at what might have been her last meal with the boy she loved, and I started crying. And that just made me even more upset, because I hated to be that chick who couldn't control her emotions – but this level of humiliation was just *beyond.*

"I...I'm not engaged," I said. "I'm not Ashley."

Slowly they all exchanged horrified glances.

"Oh my God, we came to the wrong table," one girl whispered, her mouth falling open. "This…this is the cancer girl from that hospital program."

"*Esophogeal Intresia!*" I snapped, the girl's words hitting me like a truck. "Get my life-threatening condition right if you're going to mention it at all! Cancer is not the only malady in this world, you know!"

They all hung their heads, equal parts chastened and confused. The host looked down at his chart. "Oh my God – we were supposed to go to table eighty-four, not forty-eight." He looked over at me as the others cringed. "We are so, so, so sorry. Oh, wow."

"Oh," another said, "we didn't…we didn't know…"

"We'll comp your meal," the host said quickly.

"It's already been comped," I told him.

"Then we'll…we'll make it up to you somehow. Oh, God. Sorry. *So* sorry."

They all turned and crossed the room, and I watched as they waved the same exact sparklers and sang the same exact song for this blonde girl who clapped her hands to the beat and jumped up in her seat so everyone could see, her fiancé watching with a politely mortified smile. I wanted to escape this horror show, but I knew I couldn't get to the wheelchair alone – Cooper had already parked it in a back hallway – and so I just sat there and sort of stared down at the table, alone as I ever was.

What a joke. What a fucking joke. As if I hadn't been marginalized enough in the eyes of society with my scar and my stomach tube, why not add a wheelchair, a desperate wish for marriage, an embarrassed boyfriend, and a death sentence to the equation? And if I *did* die, I wouldn't even get the chance to leave behind a little blonde-haired baby girl like Steinberg's girlfriend had. There would be no last-minute miracles for me. My life was a joke and everyone knew it, and I would be totally forgotten the minute I left this place.

I didn't even care if God was real or not anymore – I hated him just the same.

Finally Cooper returned with a muffled apology about his grandma calling him in the hallway and talking his ear off.

"What's wrong?" he asked as he sank into his seat. I couldn't explain, so I just glared at my plate, which was empty because I couldn't fucking eat. He looked over at the girl celebrating with her stupid engagement cupcake.

"Oh, no, I'm so sorry," he said. "That's really insensitive of her to celebrate in front of you like that."

"No, it's not," I said, looking up. "She doesn't even know who I am. She doesn't know why we're here tonight."

"Then what's the problem?"

I wanted to make Cooper hurt as much as I hurt, and so I told him what had happened, right down to every humiliating detail. I wanted to twist the knife and watch it cut him just like it had cut me. When I finished he just stared down at his feet, and instead of feeling vindicated, I just felt like a stupid asshole.

"That's terrible. I'm sorry I left and abandoned you," he said finally. "I…I hate when people look at us."

"Oh, so now you finally admit you're embarrassed?" I asked, anger winning out over goodness once again. "Why not do it a month ago and save yourself the trouble?"

He made this sound like he was sucking air in a vacuum. "Summer…*Summer*. I wasn't embarrassed. I was angry that people were looking at us, so I left, because I didn't want to fight someone and ruin your night. Because I *would* have fought them, trust me."

This just made me cry harder. He reached over the table and wiped a tear from my face, and in an attempt to stop crying, I smiled a little.

"Don't be sad," he said. "Don't. You're going to be fine. See, you're smiling, it can't be that bad."

"No," I said through gritted teeth. If love was the ultimate kaleidoscope, one glorious entity capable of refracting itself out into the world in the form of a million different emotions, the current one I was feeling was absolute rage. "I'm smiling because I'm miserable and I kind of hate you right now," I told him. "I may be dying, but I am still a woman."

He took back his hand. "Oh."

I looked over at the engaged couple again as they took selfie after selfie. They were our age, perhaps even younger, and I started thinking about how different the blonde's path was from mine. What I wouldn't give to be worrying about bridesmaid gowns and cake tastings and venue options and lighting schemes instead of broken throats and leaky stomachs and major surgeries. I rolled my eyes as I imagined the Facebook posts that were no doubt going to be uploaded later tonight. Stupid bitch.

No, I told myself. *No. Don't think like that.* I was being ridiculous. This girl had no clue that I even existed. She was simply a girl in love, following along with a society that told her to throw herself out there and get validation in the form of a big white wedding. I needed to take my own advice from the day of my surgery news and chill the fuck out.

"Let's just run," Cooper said after a while, a stubborn glint in his eyes. "We can still do it. Let's just get away from all these monsters."

"And…and *what*?" I asked. "Skip the procedure? Die in my sleep? I need this surgery, if you haven't heard."

"I don't know," he said, his voice cracking. "I…I just want to take us away. We'll escape them and we'll get away from here and we'll make our own little heaven, just you and me, maybe forever, if you want."

"Oh, Cooper," I said, the hard ball of anger in my chest cracking a little as tears pressed against my eyes. "Isn't it beautiful to think we could?"

Soon the manager arrived with a hundred-dollar gift certificate that I might never get to use. I took it with a scowl and looked outside just as a single crow took flight and disappeared into the low clouds.

248

Our last stop was the pier. *Our* pier. I didn't know why, and it's not like I could swim, but since I was so used to all of Cooper's crazy ideas by now, I didn't say anything. Just like the first night, he tipped his head at the guard, who gave us a sad smile and opened the gate. He wheeled me a little too fast, and going over the bumps on the old weathered boards was a little painful, but I didn't complain. All I could think of was the sea, and how it gave me life, and how good my prince looked in the moonlight here in the tail end of this dream.

When we made it out the end we turned around and just looked at the general gorgeousness of a shimmering Jacksonville Beach for a while.

"Are you okay now?" he finally asked. "I don't want you to be mad."

"Yeah, yeah, I'm fine. Sorry for flipping out. That was just, like, beyond mortifying." I took a breath. "I'm fine now. You know what I was thinking, actually?"

"What?"

"Last time we came here, I remember looking at the apartment buildings along the water and thinking, 'Man, I would hate to have their cleaning bills every time a hurricane came by and flooded everything.' But tonight I looked out and thought 'Shit, I'd love to have one of those apartments, how beautiful.' I think these last few months have made me less of a pessimist – is that possible?"

"I guess it is," he laughed, brushing me off, but I knew the truth. Yes, I was still dragged down by the horrors that went on in the world, and yes, there would probably always be a part of my soul that was dark with the knowledge that this life was unfair. But loving Cooper had wiped so much of that away. Love could fix a lot, it seemed.

Cooper looked over at me. "I want you to cry now, Summer."

"What?"

"I want you to cry."

"I heard that, but what are you talking about?"

249

He sighed. "You can say whatever you want, but I know you're tired. I see how the world treats people sometimes. You are so brave to act so unaffected by it, and not just show it and get it out there. But it's there. The sadness. I know it's there. I could see it back in the restaurant. And I want you to get it out."

I tried to ignore him, but suddenly I started shivering all over. Oh my God, he was so right: I *was* sad, as much as I tried to be in denial about it. Every time someone looked away from me or treated me a little differently or asked me who had slashed my face – I was sliced open by every word, and I carried that sadness down to my bones. I had never let myself acknowledge it, though. Not until now. Not until the chaos of the last few days had cracked me open like this.

I took Cooper's hand and cried tears of ancient misery into the sea.

Twenty minutes later. The wind in my ears and nothing else.

"God, it's so bizarre being here again," he finally said. "Tell me, what did you think of me, when we first met?"

I fidgeted a little, my nose still running. "Basically, I was just thinking, *Oh god oh God oh God this boy is thought-scatteringly hot oh God what do I do shit I'm gonna faint oh God.*"

"I'll accept that reaction," he smiled.

"…And what did you think of me?"

He paused. "I don't know. I thought you seemed like a good, genuine person, and after a while I started feeling like I was…I don't know. Sinking into something."

"Good," I smiled after a few moments. "I was pretty sure I was acting like a psycho and you were all freaked out or something."

"Never," he said. "I've loved you since the moment I met you, Summer. I know that now. I just wish the world would give us a million more. And I think it will."

We didn't say anything for a while. But eventually he cleared his throat again.

"You know, I'm happy with the way I spent this summer, and it breaks my heart to think you don't believe me when I say that. But are *you* happy with it, though? Did you do everything you wanted to do?"

I wanted to believe him, I really did, but I wasn't so sure. "I think so," I said. "I mean, I met you, didn't I?"

A nervous smile flickered on his face. "Beyond that, I mean. If you had, like, a bucket list or whatever, what would be on it? Hypothetically speaking?"

"Oh, God," I said as I leaned back. "That's so weird to think about. I don't even know. I've always thought about adopting a baby. But like, later in life, obviously."

"Really? Why?"

I took a breath. "Well, the prospects of me ever carrying a baby to term and everything aren't great. But if I can't make a life, I'd still like to save one."

He was silent again for a while.

"But that's not all," I continued. "I'd probably want to do all the stuff I'd never been able to do because of my health problems, too. And to live actively." He gave me a weird look. "Well," I explained, "when people talk about people with disab   I mean, about people like me – they tend to speak passively, or put the problem in front of the person. They'll say 'the wheelchair girl' instead of 'the girl in the wheelchair,' 'the cleft palate boy' instead of 'the boy with the cleft palate,' etcetera. And that just feeds into something I decided very early on – I never wanted to let my problems define me. I wanted to put them out there and then just forget about them. So many people let the circumstances of their lives drag them down – they let the world happen to them. But I wanted to happen to the world."

"You happened," Cooper said. "Trust me, you happened. What else do you want?"

"To shine," I admitted with a nod. "I feel so gross admitting that, but it's true. To be noticed. To be seen. To have grown up the way I did, to sit and watch everyone else breeze past me and fall in love and get married and the rest…it made me feel so small, so unnoticed, like nobody would care that I was ever alive."

I looked over at him. "But I was so wrong, Cooper. The way you've loved me…you know, we've posted zero selfies, uploaded no Instagram pictures, and yet I am *so* happy with the way you've loved me. I don't care if anyone sees this. This is real."

He frowned, his fresh scent catching my nostrils in the wind. There were still so many things I wanted to know about him. What lived under those chocolate eyes?

"What is it?" I asked.

"I just…like. I don't know. I don't like to hear you talking like that, Summer. Even if the worst does happen and it all goes dark, you'll…people will…"

He wiped a tear off his cheek and jumped up. "Speaking of colors, I wanted to remind you of something."

He walked over to the railing and started pulling on a rope that was tied to a post. Soon he procured a bucket that had been submerged in the ocean.

"Sorry I was a little late picking you up today, but I had preparations to make," he said as he lugged the bucket over and dropped it in front of me. "Since you couldn't go in the ocean, I thought I'd bring the ocean to you. Take off your shoes and put your feet in."

"Are you serious?"

"Totally."

I slid off my shoes and dipped my feet into the perfectly cool water. Sure enough, the bucket lit up with the beautiful blue-green glow of the plankton.

"You glow, Summer," he smiled. "You're glowing. Still. Even in that wheelchair, you're still so beautiful to me."

"I'm glowing," I breathed as I looked down into the bucket with endless and timeless wonder.

After that we just sat there for a while, enjoying the universe. It was a little cloudier than I would've wanted, and the breeze was a little chilly, but the moon was almost full and the light on the water was so beautiful.

"True or false," I said, thinking back to our first Spark date, when he'd said the same thing to me. "True love lasts forever."

"Ugh, do we really have to go there?"

"Excuse me for having it on my mind under these circumstances. And besides, that weird old dude at the Oak Tree of Love got me thinking."

"Okay," he said after a while. "Okay. Ugh, you know, I'll never forget when my grandmother died. I mean, I'll remember it for obvious reasons, but there was more than that. She had really bad Alzheimer's and she declined for a long time, and by the time she had a stroke and the end was coming, she was literally a vegetable, lying there with no clue what was going on. But even during all that, my grandpa never left her room, and he only ever called her 'his bride.' Like, even as she lay there dying, he'd say things like 'where's my bride? Has anyone seen my little bride?' and stuff. Yeah, it was tough. So then she had a bigger stroke and they called us to the hospital the day she started shutting down, and as her breathing slowed and she started taking her last gasps of air, my grandpa leaned in and whispered, 'I was so lucky to have you.' Even after all that, even after years of her having Alzheimer's and staring up at the ceiling and not knowing how to eat or talk or fucking breathe sometimes, he was still grateful. It blew my fucking mind."

I was crying now. Again. But I didn't try to stop this time.

"I'm sorry, I'm not trying to make you sad, Sum. But I definitely think love can conquer death. I mean, words are energy, and who's not to say that my grandfather's words – and his love – aren't reverberating out there in the universe somewhere right now, finding new life in some star a million galaxies away, giving new love to some alien couple sitting on an alien pier on their alien planet?"

"I don't know," I said. "The odds of soul mates and everything, it just doesn't-"

253

"You talk about odds?" he interrupted. "Us seven billion humans weren't even supposed to happen according to you, remember, Mrs. 'Life is an Accident?' My grandparents, us, *nobody*. The word 'fate' comes from an old Latin word meaning 'it is spoken,' but who spoke it? Where's the proof that someone made us happen like this? And what were the odds of *us* happening? Nothing, and nada. We are a brilliant little series of happy accidents – you taught me that. So, humans appeared on a watery rock spinning around a ball of flames suspended in the middle of an endless ocean of nothing, and yet you *still* tell me you don't believe in a miracle like the idea of soul mates? If all that can happen, and all these weird wonderful humans can accidentally pop up on a little blue ball spinning in the dark, can't you find your one and only true love? Seems like small potatoes in the scheme of things."

I didn't say anything. Soon he punched the wooden deck.

"What's wrong?"

"I just wish there was someone whose ass I could kick over all this," he said. "I mean, there's a villain in every story, you know? At least I could blame a disease, like Alzheimer's, with my grandma. But there's no bad guy in your story. There's nobody to fight."

"Oh, but there is," I said. "Life. Life is our villain."

"What?"

"You know, car crashes don't kill us. Cancer doesn't kill us. Esophageal Intresia doesn't kill us. *Life* kills us. We all die in the game of life. Every one of us. It's a game of numbers and we all lose in the end. That's why we need to get to winning while we're still here, and bla bla bla, I am impossibly full of clichés, so sue me."

"I guess," he finally said, taking a deep breath.

"Random question, but have you ever been in love before, Cooper?"

"No," he sighed. "Never been in love. I mean, I thought I'd come close, but no. Nothing compares to…this.

254

To us." He looked over and rested an arm on my wheelchair. "To you. I'm just...stuck in you, Summer."

We stared out at the water again. I was shocked at the amount of affection that could flow between us sometimes. We just...*got* each other, I guess. He was on my team.

"Why do you ask? Have you?"

"Psh. Obviously, no," I said. "There were a few little things that happened here and there, but never *love*. I actually got dumped by this one guy before we even became official. I didn't even know that was possible. It was a disaster. He said we was too busy with work and stuff to date anyone, but at a dinner party I overheard him telling his friend that he was basically repulsed by me and only talked to me out of pity."

"And when he confessed his undying love for men, were you surprised?"

"Stop! It was fine. When he sent me the text saying he wanted his space or whatever, he used this excuse that he 'didn't think I was smart enough for him,' and so I just looked up at the award I'd gotten in seventh grade for winning Florida's statewide spelling bee and felt nothing at all."

He stared at me. "See, that's the difference between you and everyone else. Any other person would've torn into him. But you're different. You operate on a higher plane."

"Whatever," I said again. How was it that he believed in me so thoroughly? How did I tell him that he made me feel so brave, I could just get out of my wheelchair and run out into a storm in my best dress and dance in the rain like an idiot? "Cooper, I didn't...I didn't know what love was until you. I didn't know how to *feel* until I met you."

"Wow, that gives me some strange sort of satisfaction," he said, and I pulled in my legs and wrapped my arms around my knees. I was always cold these days. "What's your biggest regret?" he asked next.

"Not meeting you sooner," I said, and he smiled. "And also, like..."

"What? Tell me!"

255

"It's stupid, but once again, I feel like I was never really *heard*. Like, I was always marginalized because of the scar and stuff, and I never felt like my voice mattered. You have no idea how isolating it was – there was just this barrier between the world and me, and there was nothing I could do about it. It was so hard to compete against all the Facebook girls with their weddings and everything, with my…*situation* I had going on. But that's all stupid stuff."

"No it's not," he said. "Stop talking like that. You'll be heard, no matter what happens. Trust me. And I have sort of a good feeling about this, anyway. You're young and strong – relatively, at least. This'll just be a bump on the road." He swallowed.

"Yeah," I said, trying to believe him. "You're right. I'll be fine."

"Wow, so you're not such a defeatist after all!"

"Wait – really? Do you really think I'm a defeatist?"

He shook his head. "No. I was kidding. I think you are honest, and I think realism is the best armor anyone could ever give themselves in this fucked-up world."

"Okay, good."

Suddenly a pair of lovebugs landed by my hand, and I smiled as I watched them cavort with each other – until I realized what was actually going on. They weren't playing at all, but one of them was hurt, and the other was struggling to get it flying again, and the effort was dragging both of them down.

I looked over at Cooper. "And one more thing," I told him. "I appreciate you sticking with me after that night in the garage more than words can explain, but still, I am so sorry about this summer. I am so sorry for doing…all of this to you. When you matched with me on that app you thought you were signing up for a summer romance by the sea, and it has been anything but that. I'm sorry."

"Stop," he said, but the insistence in his voice sounded flimsy somehow. "Stop. You're going to be fine, and you've done nothing to me, and-"

"No, I'm *serious*," I interrupted. "If I could go back and un-download that app and undo all of this to you, undo *me* to you, I think I would."

"So we're still on this subject, huh?" he asked after a pause. "We're really back to this again? You think I *regret* falling in love with you?"

I chewed on my lip. "I don't see many other scenarios."

He leaned back and let out a long breath. "Your parents' marriage," he said. "You liked when they were married, right?"

I stared out at the moonlit sea as the halcyon scenes of my parents' marriage suddenly stretched out before me, shimmering like the luminous waves. Oh, God, did I miss those days. I'd been thinking about them a lot lately, actually. In my mind's eye I suddenly saw my parents as the people they'd used to be, before the drifting and the separate bedrooms and the harsh words that would pass over the dinner table. I saw them holding hands during Disney World weekends in July; I saw them stealing glances into each others' eyes at the pool on Labor Day when they were supposed to be babysitting the neighborhood kids; I saw them kissing in the rows of firs under the Christmas tree tent in the Big Lots parking lot while I giggled with my friends and pretended to be grossed out but secretly shivered with the gleeful, dazzled bravery that can only be felt by a young child of two people lost in deep love. Those times were gone, and I was no longer that little girl with Daddy and Mommy at her side, but the memories remained, and whenever I felt lost in the waves of the world I would sometimes find myself clinging to those scenes with everything in me.

"I mean, yes, obviously," I whispered.

"And you're a little mad at the world about how things went down, and you kinda wish they could've remained happy and stayed together, right?"

"More than anything," I breathed.

"And did their eventual divorce make your moments as a happy, whole family any less special? Do those

257

childhood memories blaze any less brightly in your mind because of your anger about how they ended?"

"No," I said, "but-"

"There is no 'but,' Summer. You created one perfect little summer for me, and I'm grateful, and I'm gonna take it with me, no matter what happens. This summer will remain. I promise."

The wind whispered at our backs, and for the first time, I actually believed what he was saying, and felt a little better about everything. Another pause followed, and then: "Cooper, do you think you'll ever love again, if…*if?*"

"Stop," he said, the muscles in his neck tensing. "Don't even talk about things like that. That's not gonna happen."

I could tell the question troubled him, so I let it go. "You're right," I said as I shifted a little in my wheelchair, the breeze chilly on my neck. "You're right." There were so many more things I wanted to tell him, so many things I couldn't put into words because he was still too gorgeous and I was still too awkward and this was still all too surreal, but I made a mental note of how to maybe fix that when I got home. Hiding behind a keyboard one last time wouldn't kill anyone.

"But if anything *does* happen," Cooper finally whispered into the July breeze from beside me, his voice a quiet prayer, "remember this: I'm gonna be your boyfriend forever, Summer Martin Johnson."

21

Shelly woke me up at five the next morning. We held each other for a few minutes, or rather *I* held *her* while she cried, and I couldn't deny that I felt a little guilty for abandoning her this summer. But I had made my choices, and I was mostly happy with where I had placed my time. I just wished I had more to give.

Soon we started shaving my stomach and bagging up my toiletries and doing all the other last minute things that constituted getting ready for a major surgery. I wheeled myself out onto the porch at six forty and smiled as the sun started peeking over the sea down the street, illuminating my perfect little corner of the planet. The first winds of what felt like an early cold front had filtered in overnight, the coolness alien on my summer skin. Esophageal Intresia and not being able to eat fucking sucked, but still, this had been a good life. I was pretty sure of that.

I took out my phone and called Cooper. As I put my hand to my ear I noticed how different it looked compared to when I'd met him. My wrist had shrunken considerably, and my arm was now covered with the fuzzy baby hair associated with malnutrition. I was so different from the stronger, braver, tanner girl I'd been at the beginning of the summer. But I was still strong in some ways. After all, I still braved the paralyzing case of butterflies Cooper still gave me every time I talked to him. I couldn't believe I'd done it – fallen in love this summer. What had seemed like such a pipe dream had fleshed itself out into something that was so real I felt it all around me, heard it humming in the silence, saw it sparkling in the dark. Never in my wildest dreams had I expected Cooper. Never.

I thought about where I was before him, and the problems that faced me, just like anyone else my age. Was I any more mature now? Had I gotten any more of my proverbial shit together? I guess I was happier, which was some small success, but did that *really* change anything? And I decided I didn't know. I didn't know if love could save me any more than my doctors could. But wouldn't it be nice to think so? Wasn't it pretty to believe in the rescue?

"Hi," Cooper answered after four rings, his voice sleepy and comforting.

"Hi. I love you."

"And I love you."

"God," I breathed as I looked at the sunrays falling on the palms and tried to forget about this weird, non-goodbye goodbye period of the last few days. "This place is so beautiful."

"What is?"

"This life," I said. "This world."

A semi-awkward silence followed. "Oh. Yeah."

"I am so glad I downloaded Spark," I said for probably the tenth time.

"And I am so glad I didn't creep you out too much and make you ignore my messages."

"Ha. See you at the hospital?"

I could hear my mom, who had demanded to drive me there, tearfully preparing a Coffee Pot of Doom in the kitchen. I noted how similar this scene was to the day I'd first downloaded Spark and met Cooper: a porch, a phone, a girl, a wish.

"Wouldn't miss it for the world," he said. "Shall we?"

"We shall," I said. And then we prayed.

Shelly drove me to the hospital with the windows rolled down. As we hit the highway, Saviour's biggest hit, *Hellraisers*, came on, and I hummed along as the day was born:

Palms by the water, lights up in the sky
Wading in pools with you while my youth flies by

Pressing pause on our dreams, drinking in dusty basements
Sticky July days with no pressing engagements

You got one hand on the wheel, the other on my dead heart
And that's when all the bad thoughts start

I thought I was destined for something greater than this
But turns out fate, it had you in mind, kiss kiss

Fucking around out here on these streets
Ruining ourselves with Fast Car on repeat

My mom calls us hellraisers for the trouble we cause
Lighting up at the park, scoffing at stupid laws

But here with you, boy, I know why they call it 'raising hell'
Your love made the flames rise up and make me unwell

(Unwell, raising hell)

Don't know what happens next in this life, this game
All I know now, my friend, is that I'll never be the same

These feelings, they're sinking right down to my DNA

(Gotta run from what you love before it burns you at the stake)

So if history repeats itself, God knows I'll run from this love

(Unwell)

Run, run, run away

(You raised hell)

I shivered and changed the channel.

  Checking into the hospital was beyond surreal, filled with wardrobe changes and mile-long instruction lists inspected with a counselor lady and stacks of paperwork that required me to literally sign my life away to Dr. Dill. Soon I found myself lying alone on a hospital bed in a light blue gown in a small room on the second floor. This was where I was supposed to meet whoever wanted to talk to me before the surgery, which was scheduled for ten AM. They were only letting people come in one at a time, something about occupancy rules, I don't know. First was my precious little brown-haired brother. It pained me to see him so scared and nervous as he shuffled in, his dark eyes darting from side to side.

"I love you so much, stinky," I said after he came to my bed. "You're so smart and funny. I'm really lucky to have you as a brother. You feeling okay?"

"Yeah. Love you too," he said quietly. I squeezed his arm.

"Hey, do you remember when I used to take you to Sierra Grille, when you were really little?"

"Yeah," he smiled, warming up. "We'd get Southwest Burritos and sit on the benches by the window, and you'd let me get a raisin cookie even though mommy never let me have them, and then we'd lie to her when we got home and say we went to Subway."

I smiled and bit my lip. "Yeah. Never forget those days, okay?"

"Okay." He cleared his throat. "And, uh, I wanted to tell you something, too, just in case."

"Yeah?"

He took a deep breath and fiddled with his fingernail. "Thanks for being my mommy when mommy wasn't being my mommy."

"Oh, Chase..."

I couldn't say anything, so I hugged him instead. Just like with Kim, some things didn't need to be put out there. They just *were*.

Next was my dad and Nancy, his wife. She was crying. He wasn't. She just sort of awkwardly stood back while he knelt beside me, and I gave her a polite smile and then faced him.

262

This was it. No Chase around to distract us from the awkwardness; no conversations about the weather to avoid the fact that we didn't know each other. The time for the truth had come.

My father was a failure as a parent, something I had accepted with sadness long ago and quietly forgiven him for. Still, at the time I'd gleefully told myself that I'd filled in the Dad-shaped hole in my heart with dirt forever, and that whenever he'd surely come back to my porch begging for his little girl back one day, I'd sneer at him and slam the door in his face. But the saddest thing was that he never came back. He'd never even cared about my preemptive rejection, and he'd probably preferred having me out of his hair so he could press restart on his life with his new wife, anyway. It felt like seeing a creepy guy approach you in a bar and getting yourself all ready to turn him down and revel in the hot satisfaction of rejecting him, only to have him breeze by without even noticing you. Sometimes a kid just wanted their dad to sit by their bed and put a hand on their knee and tell them everything was gonna be alright, and my father's steadily increasing remoteness had taken any of this behavior out of the equation. But I was okay. I'd found my heroes in books. And a dating app.

He cleared his throat. He'd never really known the right thing to say, which was fine, because that was sort of His Thing. He was awkward, and it was kinda cute. But something told me it wouldn't be so cute today.

"Summer, you're going to be fine and everything," he began, his greying blonde hair shining in the light from the window. "And I know that, but still, I, uh, wanted to say some things to you...just in case."

"Yeah," I nodded. Lots of people said things like "just in case" in hospitals.

My dad smiled wistfully at something I couldn't see, his brown eyes creasing in the corners. "You know, Sum, one time when you were four, you were in the hospital for a while, and I had to stay with you and miss a work party I'd been looking forward to. I'll never forget this next thing:

263

after you overheard me talking to the nurses about missing it, you sat up in your bed and said, 'I don't want to be Summer anymore.' I asked you why, and you crossed your arms and said, 'Because I'm a boo boo.'"

He looked down at me. "You are not a boo boo, Summer. You never were. You're a blessing. Some people spend so much time loving the ones around them that they forget that *they* are loved, too. I am grateful for every second I get to love you, Summer. Do you understand that?"

I nodded and glanced away.

"You know, you are the most selfless person I have ever met," he continued, his voice cracking. "And I mean it. You never *ever* feel sorry for yourself about your scar and everything-" which was highly inaccurate, I noted to myself, I just didn't complain about it out loud- "and you're better than me. You're the strongest person I have ever known, but more than that, you're *quietly* strong, which speaks so much more of you. The world doesn't deserve you, and neither do I, and I'm so sorry I stepped away, and if I could replay every single second of your childhood after that day and put myself back in your life, I would, and…and…"

He trailed off. It was killing me to see him like this because of me. (Pardon my choice of words.) Finally he made an awkward, throat-clearing sound. "And also, um, you're not, you're not to blame…it's not your fault about the divorce," he spat out as Nancy fidgeted in the corner. "It…it was never going to work out between Shelly and me anyway. Do you get that? I know how you must feel, and you need to understand that none of it was your fault, and, yeah…"

I nodded again, and he rested his hand on my arm as I guiltily watched Nancy start to weep in the corner. "I am so grateful for you, Summer," he repeated. "You were such a blessing."

I yanked my head over at him.

"*Are,*" he said quickly. "I meant to say *are.*"

Shelly was next. Her dark hair was a mess and she'd probably been crying all morning, and she looked scared shitless. She just sort of stopped beside my bed and pawed at my arm, unsure of what she could and couldn't touch. By now she knew that any overt show of emotion or fear stressed me out in hospitals, and I could tell she was holding stuff in. A lot of stuff.

"I can't believe it's finally here," she finally said. "You can talk about something, you can prepare yourself for something, but when that 'something' finally arrives..."

She shook her head and looked down at me. "Are you scared?"

"Yeah. But I can deal with it."

Her lip quivered, and then she completely broke down. She bent over and sobbed against my arm.

"That's just it," she cried. "I am so sorry for all the things you've had to 'deal' with in your life, Sum. You deserved so much better than this. If I could take it all, all the pain and suffering, and feel it as my own, I would in an instant, you have no idea. I want to so badly. I am so sorry. It should've been me," she sobbed, again and again. "It should've been me."

I didn't say anything. I couldn't. I just let her cry on me. Because all at once it occurred to me that my mother was strong. I had mistaken her exuberance for weakness, when all along she had been the one propping up my family when we needed her the most. She'd literally given up her adult life to care for me, stepping into the role of mother *and* father after my dad's exit, and suddenly I found myself filled with gratitude. Empathy was worth its weight in gold, and here she was, spilling her empathy all over me in the form of her tears. And right then and there, I stopped expecting her to be the person I wanted her to be, and accepted her for the one she was.

Which all just fed into my guilt even more, actually. Guilt that I was lying here on this gurney putting everything through all this misery because, AHHHH, my stupid fucking body didn't work correctly.

She wrapped both hands around my cold face. "Whatever happens, I will always be your mommy, and you

265

will always be my little girl. Not your friend, not someone called Shelly, but your *mom*. Do you understand that? *I will always be your mommy.*"

"Yes, Mom," I said, and her eyes filled up with tears again – I'd never called her that before, not that I could remember, at least. "Okay. And thanks for everything you've done for me, too, Mom. God, why can't I stop saying Mom, Mom?"

"Don't ever stop, baby. And, oh, quit with the gratitude," she said as she dabbed a tissue at her eyes, waving me off. "I was happy to care for you."

I took a breath. "Okay. And there's something else, too."

"Yes?"

"If anything happens to me," I said slowly, "I want you to take care of Chase."

"Okay," she frowned.

"Wait. More specifically, I want you to *back away* from him. Let him breathe. Let him have a childhood. No more phantom colds or nonexistent fevers. He's not me and he never will be, God willing, so let the kid be a kid. God knows he won't have the chance when he's grown."

"Okay," she nodded again, giving a smile that did not show in her eyes. "Okay. I know what you mean. I'll cool it. I swear."

"Thanks, Mom."

"Say it again," she said with her eyes closed, smiling with everything in her, and I took her hand in mine and kissed it.

"Okay, Mom. No more Shelly. You're Mom forever. I promise."

The last visitor was Cooper. My sad, beautiful Cooper. The hospital nametag on his shirt had his name on it, and I smiled at his horrid handwriting. He appeared in the doorway and said nothing, because there was nothing to say. But even after all this time, he still made me dizzy. He was so beautiful it made my insides hurt.

He stopped beside me. A tanned god of a boy, careful not to slip into anyone and get hurt; a pale phantom of a girl, desperately lashing out to leave love behind before she left too early. He got pulled down deep. I reached out and left a mark. How in God's name would we ever make that mark last?

"Hey, kid," he finally said.

"Hi."

He put his hand on my arm, and I flinched involuntarily.

"Oh, shit," he said, pulling away, "did I hurt you?"

"Noooo, no no no. Here, put it back, I was just cold."

He returned his arm and smiled at me. "Good. I wanna be your cure, not your pain," he said, quoting Saviour again.

"Oh, gosh, Cooper. You were. Trust me."

He turned, showing me his beautiful profile: his strong chin, his soft, full lips, his stately nose like a Roman general heading into battle. He stared out of the window and inhaled through his nostrils, chewing on his lips.

"So life is not a cheesy romantic comedy after all," he finally said. "I don't remember the part in that Kate Hudson movie where she was strapped to a gurney."

"I know, Cooper. I know." *Damaged people get no stories*, I thought to myself. Nobody posted gushy love posts about them or exalted them from the heavens. They just broke and suffered in the dark. Until Cooper came along, at least.

"Are you afraid?" he asked. I looked away, towards the medical equipment across the room. This was getting so real now. Things were welling up within me, anger included, threatening to spill out.

"I wanted a forever," is what I said next. "Not this. God, I hate this world sometimes."

He put a hand on my shoulder. "Stop, Summer. Please. Every second I spent with you was a gift. I beat the odds by finding you. I-"

I reached up and grabbed him, unable to control it anymore. "Stop it, Cooper. Stop! This isn't some Hallmark Channel movie. This is real. I'm skeletal and I have a scar on my face and I might fucking die, and oh God, I wanted so much more from this life, and-"

He bent down low, took my free hand, and rested it on his chest. Two humans, tangled up in each other, for now at least. "Feel this, Summer. Do you feel it?"

His heart was thundering.

"Yes."

"I feel that every second I am around you. I love you, Summer, and you are feeling that love right now. You found a dead boy and made his heart beat again. You are the only thing in the world that makes me feel this alive. You squeeze so much life into every second I have with you, and I don't care how fucking cheesy or stupid or Hallmark that sounds – I'm thankful. A little angry at the situation, yes, but thankful underneath that. So thankful. Thank God for you, Summer."

"Look at you," I smiled after a minute. "Mr. Agnostic, thanking God in front of me. I never thought I'd see the day."

"Oh, didn't I tell you?"

"Tell me what?"

"Remember when I told you I needed something to believe in? I found it. I believe in God now."

"Wait, you did? You do?"

"Yep," he nodded. "You're God."

"Ummm...?"

He laughed in this weird, rough, breathy way. "Wait, let me rephrase that. I do worship you, but that's not exactly what I'm talking about here."

"What, then?"

He studied me, looking at me from under his eyelashes, which was my favorite Cooper Thing that he did. "Well, to me, the question of God comes back to the existence of a soul – do humans have souls? And will those souls go anywhere after this, or will we just die and cease to exist, like road kill on the side of this relentless march of time and tragedy that we call life? But there is one thing humans do that no other being on Earth is capable of: we love." He motioned down at our tangled hands. "Humans love deeply, unconditionally. Sure, squirrels boink each other and have babies for the sake of the continuation of their species, but they do hold their partner's hand while they flicker and fade from the world, like my grandpa did for my grandma in her final hours? Do they nurse and comfort their friends through sickness and injury? Do they find twin souls and grow old and silver-haired together? No. Every time I've seen you reach out and love someone, take your hand and put it on a broken person's arm and encourage them with your words, kiss me on the cheek and make me feel like the most important person in the universe, play a game with your little brother while you could be doing something else – that's holy. Those moments when we're together and we sink into that weird little world where it's just the two of us and we almost feel like we're glowing with love and then some vibrating entity that feels older than the sea filters in and hums between us   that's religion. That's us rising above our humanity – transcending the genre – and reaching a higher level, a galactic level. That's love. That's God. That's grace. That's majesty. And you love, Summer, so you're God." He laughed again, quieter this time. "To me, at least."

A wretched sob escaped from my chest. I stretched out and smiled up at the ceiling.

"*God*, we need to stop talking like this!" I said as I wiped my nose and tried to pull myself together. "It's just a surgery, not a firing squad. Maybe I'm gonna be fine. Maybe I'm gonna go to sleep for ten hours and wake up and everything will be back to normal, and I am not saying goodbye to you in this hospital bed right now."

"Yeah," he said, looking around. "I guess we could've found a more romantic setting than a dead-end room with industrial blinds and the faint smell of that damned disinfectant spray."

"Not exactly a girl's childhood dream, no."

A flurry of activity outside told us they were waiting for me. Nurses were good at that; passive-aggressively ruffling some blinds or slamming a book closed to tell you that although they respected your time, scalpels were waiting to be stained with your blood and humanity.

"Hey. You're gonna do it all, you know," Cooper said, leaning closer, but fear was blooming in his eyes, and it terrified me. "You're finally gonna be healthy and strong, and you're gonna eat all the food in the world and then adopt a kid, a whole orphanage full of 'em, and you're gonna get the most obnoxious Facebook wedding in the world, and then we're gonna go to that pier again and sit under the sky, for as long as you want, and glow again."

"Okay," I said, drowning in love and life and fear of the future. "Remember that poem *So It Goes* by Saviour, about her friend with cancer or whatever?" *She certainly wouldn't have had Esophogeal Intresia*, I noted to myself, caustic to the end.

"And so it goes," he recited, "to be a young soul trapped inside a set of broken bones. What a beautiful curse, to be young and beautiful and doomed."

"And so it goes," I continued, "that love will keep a soul alive. A person who was loved and left love behind cannot die so long as they are kept inside the beating heart of a human – or better yet, five."

He wiped his eye, laughed, and then shook his head. "God. We have *got* to find some less depressing singers to quote."

"You're right," I said. "From here on out, it's Katy Perry for me."

We both grimaced at exactly the same time, proving once and for all that I had found my one twin soul. We were soul mates, this boy on the cusp of forever, this girl on the edge of oblivion.

Finally a nurse entered and started going over charts and messing with stuff in the cabinet, chatting all the while. As I sat there saying my maybe-goodbyes to Cooper, the cheeriness in her voice hurt like hearing a Christmas song in January.

"...The scans are actually looking really good!" she said as she flipped a page in her notebook with her back to us. "There's less blockage than they thought. This might even go more quickly than we expected! So that's good! Really good, y'all!"

"*Yay!*" Cooper said in the same tone as the nurse as he looked down at me and rolled his eyes, making me giggle.

"Oh, and one last thing, Cooper," I told him quietly, and he leaned closer.

"Yeah?"

"This is gonna sound weird, but promise me that no matter what happens, you'll write a book. Just promise. I want to know that you'll fulfill your dream, or whatever. Please write one. You can do it, I swear."

"Okay," he said, but something in his eyes was sparkling, and I didn't understand it at all. "Okay. I'll do it."

"What's funny?"

"It's just that we're sitting here saying...you know, maybe goodbye, or whatever, and you're thinking about *me*. So typical, Summer. So typical. You'll never change, will you?"

"Whatever. Maybe the nurse is right, anyway," I said, taking a long, calming breath. "I'm gonna be fine. We're being dramatic. I'm gonna be fine. I know it!"

"You are, Summer," he said, tracing circles on the back of my hand. "I love you, and you have all my love. What more could you need?"

The nurse arrived behind my bed and flashed a tight smile at Cooper. It was time for him to go.

"I love you so much," he said as she started to lead him out. "I love you so much! I'm so glad I met you. I'm gonna see you in no time! Float on, Summer. And never forget that I-"

The stupid nurse closed the door, silencing him.

~

271

So now I'm in another room waiting for the anesthesiologist. I don't really know what's going to happen next. Maybe I'll be fine. Maybe I won't. Maybe this will be the last time I ever breathe, ever look around at the room surrounding me, ever live, ever *be*.

I stretch my arms out again and let out a terrified, heartbroken, exhilarated *ahhhHHHHuhhh* as I look up at the ceiling and try not to cry. But as much as I want to run away and live out my days under the palms somewhere in secrecy, I know I have to do this. I'd known from the moment Steinberg brought up the surgery, actually. I wasn't going to be a burden any longer. I wasn't going to have Shelly fuss over me or have my dad be depressed about my life prospects or have a team of aging doctors sit around once every six months and elegantly debate the prospects of my mortality. I was going to try to normalize myself, and if I undid myself in the process, then so be it. I was going to be Healthy Summer, or I was going to be Dead Summer. Either prospect would be better than the humiliating half-life of my first twenty-four years. Every rude comment from random people on the street, every time I'd been left alone at home during a middle school dance to stare at walls while the pretty girls twirled in their dresses under the lights, every time people had gawked and laughed at me in the lunch room, every time I'd stared at my computer watching those same girls twirling down an aisle, bouquet in hand – I just couldn't do it anymore. Oh well. You never win a match you don't sign up for.

A thought struck me, and do you know what I did next? I took out my phone to clear my head, which I was still allowed to have until the last possible moment. (Okay, maybe I'd snuck it in. Whatever.) I opened up my Facebook and scrolled through the goings-on of all the people I'd met in my life, all with dreams and goals and problems so different from mine, and I tried to be angry, but mostly I just felt sad. I remembered something and kept scrolling, and sure enough, soon I saw her: Misty the Pen Thief, that human manifestation of a Bud Light burp, that girl who'd inspired me to download Spark all those weeks ago, who lived to brag about her fiancé and how he cherished the ground she walked on. And ultimate plot twist: she'd just been dumped.

I couldn't believe it. There she was, posting some furious status about how she'd already sent out the invitations to her bridesmaids' luncheon when the fiancé had decided he "needed time to think." I guess the pretty lies had fallen away, and Misty and her man had been left with a truth neither of them could deal with: they were not a match. And I couldn't help it: I laughed, fully and completely, with everything in my broken body.

And then I thought about where I'd be right now, what I'd be doing, what my summer would've been like, had I not seen Misty's Oak Tree of Love photo and been spurred to download Spark and swipe "yes" on Cooper and lead him down this path of lies and love and death and Funfetti cake. Would my health have nosedived as quickly? Would the surgery still be months away? Had I been hurtling towards disaster ever since that first day at Joe's Crab Shack?

And what did Cooper think about all this, *really*, and his role in it? As I lay there I tried to dig inside his mind, to see whatever waiting room he was seeing, but since I did not have some Patented Mind Reading Machine, this was impossible. I guess I'd never know for sure. But if something did happen, I hoped he'd get over his anger one day. More than anything, actually. He deserved it.

As I waited, I wondered if I would ever again get to smell the marshes of Jax Beach and see the canoes paddle by in the coffee-colored water while the crickets sang; watch the leaves on the oaks in my yard ripple in the Atlantic breeze as the clouds gathered; wake up at ten on a Sunday and walk to the beach access at Fourteenth Avenue, my toes burning on the hot pavement under the dazzling sun, to sit on the sand next to Cooper until the storms filled the sky. Maybe this was all I'd ever get with him, this summer of beautiful risk, these last three months when he had loved me so perfectly by the sea. Or maybe we'd get forty or fifty or sixty more years. Or maybe I'd survive and he'd come to his senses and dump me in a week. But whatever happened, I knew I'd always have this summer, and that first night on the pier under the stars, with the waves surging around us, when we both glowed. And armed with that, I was not afraid. This summer, and this life, had been a privilege. I was sure of that.

For a moment I got giddy with excitement imagining what would happen if the surgery worked, and I woke up with a fixed stomach and a throat that functioned, a normal girl for the first time ever. Oh, God, I'd be so thankful. I'd do everything I never could before – I'd run marathons and eat seafood feasts and wear bikinis and live spectacularly for all the support group kids I grew up with who had either died or hadn't been fixed and would never get the chance. I would live and eat and run for them and I would love every minute of it; I would savor every activity that healthy people wasted away and squandered. I'd play softball for Hank and go to Key West for Autumn and drink all the beer in the world for poor Ethan, bless his heart. Then I'd swallow a Funfetti cake a day until I got big and fat and happy, I promise. Nobody would have ever been happier to get fat, I can tell you that much.

I shivered and told myself to relax. All that would have to wait. First I had a surgery to get through, and the ultimate enemy to face: time. Nobody could ever escape time. Just ask Cooper Nichols.

Finally, as I waited for the doctors and nurses and specialists who would spend the morning deciding my fate, I zoomed out and imagined looking into the room from a stranger's perspective, seeing what they would see. A blonde girl in a filmy papery gown, free at last but broken and trying to be fixed, who'd somehow gotten over herself for the first time in her life and reached out into the madness and opened herself to love, whatever it was, in all its bruising glory and otherworldly horror. Would these strangers take my example and do the same in their own lives? Would they get over the fear that kept them alone and told them they were inferior;

would they step outside the borders of their own bodies and take another human's hand? Would they shatter their own barriers and choose the scary thing, the hard thing, the worthwhile thing, the burning thing?

I crossed my legs on that cold bed in that cold room in this very wide and varied world and hoped that they would, whoever they were. I hoped they would choose love. They owed it to themselves – that much I knew.

Okay, the anesthesiologist just came into the room. I don't know what else to say now, other than that I am so grateful for you, Cooper. I am so grateful. I am so grateful. Wish me luck, if it exists at all. God and fate and numbers know I need it.

PART II
COOPER RISING

22
Cooper Nichols

I spent the morning pacing in a freezing hallway by the waiting area, too nervous to sit down, too nervous to eat, too nervous to do anything, really, other than pray to a God I didn't believe in and bite the inside of my cheeks. Why did hospitals have to be so cold, anyway?

For some reason I kept thinking of that moment on the pier the other night, and of how badly I wanted Summer to believe what I was saying, that she glowed. She was glowing. My girl glowed.

I sank onto an awkward padded blue chair and went back, back, back, in my mind, back before the days by the sea and the quiet evenings at Shelly's had transitioned to long afternoons spent staring at televisions in this very hospital, and suddenly it was almost like I was back at Joe's Crab Shack again. (I'd only just started thinking vividly and dreaming in color again for the first time since my teens, and Summer was to blame.) I'd been so pathetically lonely on my birthday back in March, friendless and depressed, and on a whim I'd downloaded the app and matched with her. The first thing I'd noticed was how funny she seemed. Her sense of humor was this fascinating mix of hard and soft, strong and vulnerable, and so I'd messaged her straightaway.

As I shuffled my legs on that uncomfortable chair in that cold room I could almost smell the salty ocean air again, hear the children screaming on the restaurant's playground, see her walking up to me. She'd been so nervous about her looks, but I hadn't even noticed her scar until she'd pointed it out to me – compared to my mom's situation, it was nothing. Instead, I'd noticed her black dress, her golden hair, her hazel eyes burning amber in the sun, the way she kept laughing and looking down at the sidewalk. The gentle curve of her cheekbones, the elegant way her eyelashes seemed to watch guard over her eyes, so sunken into her head. And God, that smile, the one that played my soul like a violin. Her presence was indescribably soothing, and for the first time in a very long time, I'd felt like I was home in some weird way – or at least somewhere very near home. I could see it all so clearly, it was like the sun had never set on that evening. After all, there were only a few moments in a human's life that came along and changed everything, little fireworks that popped in your skies and shifted the winds in your sails and put you on a new course and pushed you to new heights and horizons you'd never even dreamed of before. Mine was at six in the evening, the twenty-fifth of March. Humid breeze, golden sunset. The moment I'd met Summer.

Right away, I could tell that this Spark girl was *something*. A leading lady, not a supporting character. I didn't know what, exactly, and I didn't know how big she'd become, but immediately I sensed that this small brave beautiful girl would loom large on the landscape of my life. If only I'd known just *how* large.

I stared at a bulletin board on the wall and tried to look past it, to see where she was, exactly, within the maze of this place, and guess what was happening to her. I didn't necessarily have a *bad* feeling, I just had no feeling at all. Where were all the Feels? So to pass the time I took out my phone and started playing Scrabble, thinking about odds all the while. I looked at my game with Summer. The day before, I'd spelled STAR for thirty-three points, and now it was her turn to make a move. In her absence, I pulled up my game with Kevin and saw that all I had to choose from were useless vowels. To free up some space and get some consonants, I used some E's and O's to connect two preexisting letters and spell GEODE, and then I sat back and waited for luck to strike and give me some all-powerful consonants.

My phone pinged and refreshed. Five E's stared up at me.

At around eleven I felt a hand on my shoulder. I looked back and saw Summer's mom standing behind me.

"They said no news will be good news, so I'm assuming things are going fine," she said in her vague Southern accent. "Why don't you go out and get lunch or something? Drive around?"

"Thanks, but I'm not leaving. I'm fine. I'm just steeling myself for later."

"You brought the diary?" she asked, and I nodded and patted the lump in my pocket. "Now *there's* a surprise she'll like. Your first real book!"

I smiled a smile that went down deeper than deep. As soon as I'd seen that copy of *Eighty Eight* sitting in my garage that night, I was inspired to write, and I knew just what I'd write: her. And that's what I'd done. Sure, all I'd done was chronicle our time together to the best of my recollection, but still, I thought she'd like to see herself, and this summer, through my eyes. My diary had reached the length of an extremely short book, and after getting it bound at Office Max I'd hatched a plan to present it to her in the recovery room after surgery. I couldn't believe I'd managed to keep it under wraps for this long, and I couldn't *wait* see her face light up and show her how her influence had brought me back to life and made me dust off my dreams and bring them out to play again. I'd never been so excited about anything, actually. Hopefully this would finally erase her doubts about this summer and make her realize just how grateful I was, despite everything.

Shelly looked over at me. We'd gotten over all the awkwardness of the beginning of the summer, and now she was sort of like a goofy, highly emotional, and slightly immature second mom to me. But when I noticed the tears in her big brown eyes, I groaned inwardly and wondered if I had the stomach to deal with the Shelly Show while I was already so worried.

"Cooper," she sniffled, "I have to tell you something."

"Please, Ms. Johnson, it's okay. You don't have to go there, it's-"

"It's *not* okay," she said. "You need to hear this."

"Okay?"

She took a long, deep breath. "At the beginning of the summer, when Summer told us she wanted to fall in love, everyone laughed at her and acted like she was crazy. *Everyone*. Even me, as much as it hurts to admit. We were being *so* cynical. I thought she'd fallen off her rocker, let me tell you. And it wasn't just the surgery. You know, the thing about the…you know, her scar, and her issues and everything, I just wondered if she would ever find…"

She trailed off and stared at nothing, and I could see years of bottled-up motherly concern in her eyes. Finally she looked back at me. "All I can say is that I am *so* grateful that you came along, Cooper. I'm sorry you weren't filled in on certain things, but still, I'm thankful. You were sent from heaven above, that's for sure."

"Don't be sorry," I said, patting her shoulder. "This summer has been a privilege. I promise."

"I should've known, though," she said wistfully. "She's always been so focused, so determined, so strong-willed. No matter what was going on in her life with her health issues, she's always been able to rise above and set her sights on whatever she wanted and get it. And I guess she wanted you."

I shifted in my chair. "Um, I know what you mean, but she didn't 'go after' me," I said after a moment. "It wasn't like that. We just sort of…fell into each other. I don't know. Loving your daughter is easy, Ms. Johnson."

"Ugh, Cooper. I know it is. Trust me. And please, you know I'm Shelly."

"Okay, then, Shelly."

She slapped me on the knee, laughed, and returned to her magazine.

~

"Do you think it's weird that nobody's come out to give us an update yet?" Shelly asked about an hour later, looking up from an issue of *Southern Living* that I suspected she had not read a word of. I'd been thinking the same thing, actually, but I didn't want to say it. Saying it out loud would make it real. But this definitely wasn't going to plan. If the doctors had found that they weren't able to fix her throat and stomach like they'd hoped, they were going to sew her up and tell us the next step. They weren't supposed to just leave us out to dry like this.

Something was wrong. I could sense it everywhere. But I tried to stay calm. I was probably just overreacting, anyway, as usual.

"Nah," I said, wiping my sweaty palms on my shorts, as I tried unsuccessfully to get lost in a shark fishing article in *Void* magazine. "They said no news was good news, remember?"

Hang on, Summer, I thought to myself as I got the sickening feeling that somewhere within these walls, she was in pain. I didn't know if I was being dramatic or what, but I just wanted to hear myself think the thoughts in my head, just in case. *Be strong. Get through this. You've got the light, remember? You glow.*

"Yeah," Shelly said, blinking down at her magazine as if it was the first time she was seeing it. "But I thought they said no news, not, like, *no* news."

~

By two PM, worry was descending into vague panic. Passing nurses were completely avoiding us, spotting us and then crossing over to the other side of the hallway, an almost animalistic fear in their eyes. I didn't even want to think about why this was happening, but it obviously wasn't a good sign.

"*Where are they?*" Shelly called out from the corner of the waiting room, where family members were starting to congregate, as yet another nurse darted away. "Why haven't they said anything?"

"It's fine," I assured her, as something deep within me boiled and rocked. "It's fine. She's fine." I missed her

281

already, and I wanted to hold her hand and have her melt away my worries, like she always did. But she wasn't here.

Just then, one of the nurses finally acknowledged us. A tall, skinny girl with dark skin and braided hair almost down to her waist passed by in the hall and noticed us, clutching her notebook tighter as she walked up.

"You're the Johnson family, right?" she asked, apparently unaware that we hadn't been briefed yet, and several people jumped up and nodded. I will never forget what she said next:

"I'm gonna pray that they can start her heart again."

~

They called us down a hallway about ten minutes later. I was pacing back and forth again, switching between getting lost in the waves of worry that were swamping me and absently playing my phone's stupid Scrabble game to keep some semblance of sanity and normality, when a hospital administrator with light brown hair and an artificial smile waved us over. She turned and led us into some weird room off the waiting area containing a few rows of chairs and a podium, and the moment I looked up and saw a large plastic cross lording over us from behind the podium, my knees almost went out from under me.

We had been called into a chapel.

"Drs. Dill and Steinberg will be here to see you in a minute," the lady said as everyone went dead quiet. "Please, sit. Would you like some water? Pepsi? Anything?"

Shelly shook her head vacantly and sunk onto a chair. She held out her hand. I took it and sat next to her.

We waited in silence. Nobody wanted to say out loud what this probably meant, but the realization was filling up the room like the floodwaters of a hurricane, the quiet slowly suffocating us.

Finally Dr. Steinberg and a man I did not know walked into the room. Steinberg was sobbing, and the other man was impassive. Instantly, I knew.

282

Oh my God, I knew.

I stared down at the cheap industrial carpet, trying not to drown in the waters, as he spoke.

"I am so sorry for the delay," the strange man said, his words flat and hard like a stone at the bottom of a stream. "We ran into some unexpected complications during surgery. The thing is-"

"What happened?" Summer's dad asked frantically. "Where is she? Did they fix her throat? Can she eat now? Is she being transferred to Gainesville? Where is she?"

Dr. Steinberg started crying harder and looked away, refusing to participate in the other guy's bullshit. The man leaned forward and tried to appear serene and removed, but the muscles in his temple kept clenching and unclenching.

"Her throat is not exactly the issue today," the man said. "There were…other things that happened. But the important thing to know is that she fought so, so hard. She was so sick for so long, and she knew she just couldn't live like that anymore, and she was so brave, and she made the ultimate sacrifice, and eventually we had to let nature run its course, and-"

"Horse shit!" I shouted. "I ate a steak dinner with her last night! She was fine! This isn't how it was supposed to happen! Where is she?"

A big black panic rose up within me, but I tried to push it down. This wasn't happening. I'd perhaps expected a failed procedure and a decision to keep her throat as it was, but not *this*. Never this. It just wasn't a possibility.

"Summer's alive, right?" Aunt Susan sort of screamed, her voice a manic cackle, as Summer's stepmom started wailing and then collapsed onto a side table, knocking over a lamp. Suddenly Shelly jumped to the floor and desperately grabbed both of the doctor's arms, staring up at him with everything in her.

"IS MY BABY ALIVE?"

The doctor took a shallow breath and then looked down at her.

"No."

23

I was eleven years old when my mother was diagnosed with multiple sclerosis and got left by my father on the same day. I came home from soccer practice one blazingly hot Wednesday evening and walked into the bathroom to find her slouching in a pool of water on the dirty tile floor, staring blankly at the sink in front of her. I have flashbacks to that day a lot, especially when I'm depressed. I knew Summer only thought I could love her because I was used to dealing with health issues due to my mom's condition, but that wasn't exactly true: this awful day had set my fate into motion more than anything. After I fell to my mother's side and asked her what she needed – if she wanted me to call the cops or walk her to the doctor or whatever else – all she did was reach over and grab me by the arm.

"I just want you to do one thing," she said, suddenly serious. "Find the best person in the world and marry them. I am serious, Cooper. Treat your heart as carefully as dynamite, because when placed with the wrong person, it can explode your life. Don't settle for anything less than someone with an absolute heart of gold. When you meet someone who is kindhearted, sweet, honest, and levelheaded, I want you to marry them and never look back. It is the most important thing you will ever do. Don't end up like me, ruined by love. Do you understand me? Can you do that for me, Coop?"

I nodded.

"No – promise me," she said.

"Okay. I promise."

This is what I'd thought of when I'd forced Summer from my home that night in the garage and then gone looking for her, only to hear of her collapse soon after. This is what I'd thought of before walking into her hospital room a few days later to tell her I'd forgiven her, and that I wasn't leaving. And this is what I thought of as my life fell apart in front of me, as the future I'd envisioned for myself eroded into dust and then tumbled to the pits of the Earth before me, as Summer's father vacantly collected his ex-wife off the floor and started leading her down a hallway to say goodbye to their only daughter together. As it all melted away and I sank into an ocean of panic, for some reason all I could think of was my late grandmother's sparkling wedding ring sitting in my mother's safe back home – the ring I'd promised to give to the best-hearted person on the planet. To Summer. I'd known she'd wanted marriage, of course, but just like any twenty-five-year-old who was terrified of the future, I'd dodged the subject every chance I'd gotten, hoping to delay the matter – but now it was too late. I'd looked long and hard for the best girl in the world, and now that I'd found her, I'd let her slip through my fingers before making her mine forever. I had failed the woman I loved, and the thing I'd been running from my whole life, avoiding with the help of pills and booze and all the rest, had happened.

I had become my father.

Things were happening too quickly for me to fully understand, but I tried. After Shelly had been peeled from the floor, they led us up a flight of stairs to a quiet room on the second floor where Summer had been taken for the goodbye. *Oh God oh God oh God.* As I climbed, a primal black fury whipped up within me, dizzying me, threatening to overwhelm me at any moment, but I tried to stay with it. Some age-old voice from somewhere deep down told me to be calm, to be the rock that everyone needed, and that if I kept it all together, everything would somehow be okay and everyone would end up fine. I was simultaneously hyperaware and yet completely removed from my body, watching the scene with a zoomed-in precision and a zoomed-out detachment all at once. Outside, the world was raging – a summer thunderstorm had descended upon this place and was bending the pines outside the staircase window nearly in half. The universe was angry at what was happening to Summer – I could just *feel* it, in the strangest way.

As I walked down that sterile second floor hallway, every door I passed made me even more panicked and confused. Summer's gathering family was just sort of falling all over each other outside the entrance to her room, wailing like animals, as the nurses stood off to the side, some crying silently, others checking their phones and trying not to act like they were witnessing a death. For some reason it instantly infuriated me that the world wasn't stopping for her, but then I remembered that these nurses probably saw people die all the time and therefore this wasn't anything special to them, and that just infuriated me more. Oh, God – die. *Death*. The word made a new panic rise up in me again. A death. I couldn't face a death.

But I had to. And I would. For her.

"Come in," a nurse said with an oddly stiff formality, and I turned the corner and entered the room.

I couldn't process the next few minutes. I just couldn't. It didn't make sense that the same human body that had been alive in front of me that morning was not alive anymore; that Summer wasn't Summer anymore. They'd cleaned her body to let us say our goodbyes, and all I knew was that there was lots of sobbing and touching and kissing and feeling the last warmth we would ever feel on her skin. For all the world, it looked like she had gone to sleep. She looked like herself, but not like herself, and it was simply not making sense that this was happening and that there was nothing I could do about it. Soon my body started to shut down, my brain getting fuzzy around the edges, but I held on. A random hospital priest showed up and started praying by the bed, but I shoved him away and told him that it was our time with her. He very politely said, "Well, I'm sure she was a wonderful girl," and then left, and that word slammed into me and broke me:

Was.

My girlfriend was now past tense.

Actually the *worst* part was when I noticed a clear plastic bag against the wall containing her personal effects, some toothpaste and hair ties and a hairbrush that she would never get to use. For some reason this little bag jumped out at me with the fury of ten thousand typhoons. *Oh my God the love of my life will never get to use that stupid toothbrush oh my God oh my God oh my God what the fuck is happening oh my God.* But no, that wasn't the worst part. Soon Summer's mouth started to droop open, and because it really upset Shelly, the nurses had to come and close it, and *that* was the worst part.

Actually, no: the *very* worst worst part was the nurses finally came and asked us to leave so they could send her to the morgue for an autopsy. Morgue! Autopsy! *Morguemorguemorguemorgue.* Just thinking of the word made some primitive moan-scream escape from my mouth. I was collapsing and I was losing my mind. The thought of my girlfriend lying cold and unfeeling in some dark little refrigerated drawer while her family congregated twenty miles away made my heart fall into my stomach and my head fill with a blaring, shimmering panic. And that's when I fully disassociated.

Some strange, funny, cackling voice in my head said *Nope, this isn't happening. She didn't die, she's still here, this isn't possible, young people don't just die out of nowhere for nothing*, and I wanted with everything in me to believe the voice. So I put my hand on her arm and said in a soft, pleading tone, "Come on, Summer. Wake up. Get up for me. It's beautiful outside and we've gotta go to the beach. Wake up, it's still summertime, get up. This isn't over yet. This can't be how it ends."

I pushed back the sleeve of her gown to touch her skin and gasped. It was already ice cold.

That's when the nurses asked me to leave again and told me it would be better to just let her go see Jesus, but I didn't want to, and finally they got together and grabbed me and started pulling me away, but I turned around and it occurred to me that I would never again see her like this, with blood in her veins and some color in her cheeks. I was angry and broken and confused and overwhelmed and I was drowning. I shouted that I needed to go find the surgeon because I was going to rip his heart out of him while it was still beating, and a flurry of activity at the nurses' station resulted in a pinprick-y feeling blooming in my left shoulder. Then Summer's mom wailed something like "…but I wanted to live to see my daughter have daughters," and that just decimated me and took all my fight away, and that's when everything within me faded and then fell in on itself, and I slumped against the wall.

But still, I did get to see one last glimpse of her before it all went black. And she was so beautiful.

My God, Summer was so beautiful.

24

Summer died on the eleventh of July.

    I don't remember much about that first day or so, and not just because of the lingering effects of the sedative. It exists in my memory only as a deep, murky pond. The doctors called it a grief blackout. I just called it the worst fucking thing ever. I remember shouting into pillows, staring at walls until I wanted to die, rolling over and over and over on my bed until I had nothing left to cry out anymore. Except it wasn't so much "crying" as just this wild, guttural, furious sound that bubbled up from somewhere deep and dark within me, a sound I didn't even know I could make, a sound that would come until I'd forget I hadn't taken a breath in thirty seconds and would nearly pass out. I did that until I drained all my tears, and then I just started shaking and dry heaving while my mom sat by my bed trying to reason with me. And that was the saddest thing, that I was out of tears. Because there would never be enough tears for Summer.

    The pain was literally physical – every inch of me ached and wished and missed. It was a pain that burned. A hole had opened up within me, and I spent every second creeping around it, sometimes falling in, sometimes not. Sometimes the hole fooled me into thinking it had disappeared for a moment, but then I'd remember that Summer no longer existed and I'd be tossed in again, and then I'd hit the concrete with everything in me and find myself back at square one.

    I felt everything and nothing. I was so numb and so angry. I felt so bad for her. I wanted to take her place. I wanted to join her, sail off the edge of the pier at low tide, to meet her in the vast sea of nothingness and not feel this pain anymore. And the only thing that kept me from doing that was knowing how thoroughly it would destroy my mother.

~

No matter how I looked at it, it just wouldn't make sense to me, the concept of her being gone. It wasn't supposed to be so sudden. I knew she'd always talked about numbers and Scrabble and odds and all that, but that was hypothetical – this was real life. *And this wasn't supposed to happen.* Maybe she'd been preparing us – maybe she was letting us know anything could happen, and in her case, "anything" meant the worst. The anger was the worst part. Okay, the thousandth worst part. I just couldn't fathom how such beauty, such grace, such perfection, could just die on an operating table so pointlessly. Her death had been a crack of lighting on a perfectly clear day. It was such a waste. She was fun and interesting and elegant and she made everything better. And she was so funny – the world was so much less funny without her, that's something I noticed immediately. I wanted to reach out and touch her, but there was no Her to touch. It became this horrifyingly simple urge, impossible to understand but wholly sensible at the same time, totally alien and almost primitively deep, a shallow panic that hinted at a deeper chaos: *I want to touch her I want to touch her I want to touch her I can't I can't I can't Oh my God oh my God oh my God Where is she where is she where is she where is she She's gone she's gone she's gone.* She was everywhere and nowhere and nothing and she was gone.

I do remember bruising my knuckle. After twenty-four hours or so I thought I finally felt like eating again, if for nothing else than my own survival, and so I dragged myself into the kitchen and looked into the refrigerator and saw a Powerade I'd put there the week before. That made me think of how in that one week Summer had left, but that stupid fucking bottle was still right where I'd put it, and then I thought that maybe if I touched it again everything would go back to how it had been the last time I'd touched it, and that if I could retrace my steps I could somehow unkill her and make her undead. So then I touched the bottle and thought of how fucking awful it was that the placement of a Powerade had outlasted the love of my life, and then I punched the fucking wall, because like golf balls to the head and flu cells to the mouth, sometimes it was the little things that hit you the hardest. A knuckle was nearly broken but I didn't care. Summer was gone. All the life had left Summer, and all the light had left my life. It was like the surgeon had killed two people instead of one.

I knew I deserved the pain, though. The *worst* of the worst parts was that I felt complicit in her death. I couldn't get rid of that thought, actually. My relationship with Summer had no doubt added stress to her body during her last months. After our fight had come her collapse; after our trip had come her blood. Would she still be around had she never met me? Had her desire for love consumed her and killed her? Had the Spark app been Summer's version of Princess Diana's dark Paris tunnel or Marie Antoinette's guillotine? Had love been her road to death?

Death. Even the word had claws.

So after visiting the ER for my hand – at a different hospital than the one that had killed Summer, don't worry – I went back to the refrigerator with a manic burn in my throat and headed straight for my mom's occasionally-used alcohol shelf. After swallowing a pain pill I'd been given in the ER I ripped the cap off a bottle of cheap white wine and drank the whole thing, the sweet sweet liquid meeting my tongue and exploding into a million rays of sunlight that finally soothed me, dancing with my taste buds in a heady golden reverie. And then I took another bottle and drank *it*, too, and then I drank another, and then I took a Xanax and drank even more, until I couldn't feel anymore.

Until I couldn't think anymore.

Until my girlfriend wasn't dead anymore.

25

Two days without Summer turned into three. I grew mad at time for daring to distance me from her, because every day that came was another day further from when she'd been here; every sunrise just threw her deeper into my past. And the hangover just compounded my misery and confusion.

After the blunt force trauma of the initial days, I found that the hardest part was missing her. Just the simple, devastating sensation of wanting to hang out with her and not being able to do so. I missed her golden hair and her hazel eyes that always looked like they knew something the world didn't and the adorably awkward way she always fidgeted with her hands. I missed it all. I wanted to reach into my medicine cabinet more than ever, but I shut myself in my room and somehow forced myself to abstain.

Here on the edge of sanity, I could see it all: I was haunted by the summer. Every moment I hadn't spent with her over these last few months struck out at me like a viper; every opportunity I'd had to give her love and failed jumped out at me from the quiet. And I couldn't stop thinking about the wedding thing. I pictured how longingly I'd seen her looking at other couples' photos, the bitter edge that would come to her voice when discussing their Facebook posts. And I knew that deep down, all she'd wanted was to shine for the world like they had. Sure, we'd known each other for way too short a time to get married, but still: why hadn't I just fucking gotten over myself and let her load some fucking selfies of us? Why hadn't I at least *hinted* that I wanted marriage down the line, since that was all she wanted in the world? What was wrong with me? The invisibility and futility of it all made it even more devastating. Oh, and what made me even more miserable was the fact that the only copy of *Eighty Eight* was gone. I'd somehow lost the book during my blackout at the hospital, and after thirty calls from my mom, they'd finally admitted that it had probably been thrown away by a janitor. The Word file containing the book was on a computer that had burned up weeks before, and the book that Summer had made me, my only shot at a future, was now rotting in a landfill somewhere. The thought was unendurable.

One of the most pathetic things was how friendless I suddenly was. Before, every little thing that happened, I'd store it away in my brain and tell Summer later that night. Now, whenever I saw a cute dog or a funny commercial or whatever, I had no one to tell. It was so sad, let me tell you. And the only person I wanted to vent to was her. Sometimes I even found myself having long conversations with her in my head – or at least the version of her that was stored away in there somewhere. Once I jolted upright in bed at midnight and realize I'd been stuck in twilight sleep for an hour, having a completely one-sided talk with her about how much I hated my annoying neighbor Mr. Richards. Was I cracking up?

It was also surprising to me that I still loved her just as much as when she was alive. I was in love with a memory. Nothing had faded in the slightest, and I hoped it never would. When I envisioned my biggest, most golden moments with her, I still got zapped by the electricity that came with her touch, felt the goodness of her smile, saw the light in her eyes. I missed those moments so much it made my chest feel like a sinkhole again. Whenever I thought of her laugh, so goofy and silly, my hair still stood on end and my stomach collapsed into a nervous mess on the floor of me. I guess it spoke to the power of our love that she held that sway over me even in death. Did she know the effect she had on me when she was alive? I hoped to God she had.

~

Because of allegiance to Summer at the hospital, details of the surgery started leaking quickly. In fact, only two days post-Summer, a nurse pulled aside Summer's aunt's friend at a grocery store and confided that people were furious behind the scenes. A wrong slide had been put up in the operating

294

room, and Dr. Dill – I couldn't even think of the name because I would literally drive to his house and kill him if I let myself – had gone into her body on false information. When her vitals started plummeting and it became clear something had gone wrong, the nurses begged him to stabilize her and life-flight her somewhere else with a more equipped operating room, but he refused out of arrogance and kept trying. I could sense it the moment he'd walked into that chapel, so nonchalant and casual: he had done this. Rumors were swirling between nurses that he was already hiding documents and covering his tracks, and because the world is slanted towards rich white men with nobody to answer to, a future lawsuit was looking more impossible by the day. Nobody was even thinking about that yet, but still: someone, somewhere down the line needed to pay for this, *deserved* to pay for this, if only to give the Johnsons closure, and I was already getting the unspeakably awful feeling that they never would.

The mountain of anger in front of me stretched to the heavens, but in this story, there was no clear-cut villain. Summer had been killed by a chain of accidents and negligence and unchecked ego, not a masked criminal with a gun in the middle of the night. There was no villain. Life was the villain. She was just *gone*. It was absolutely infuriating that something so accidental had led to something so final. It just didn't make sense, and that made *nothing* in my life make sense. The monsters in this nightmare story weren't evil men with guns or ghouls and goblins lurking in the night, but tenuous, intangible things like numbers and odds and percentages and careless hospital employees. In the end, the girl who was obsessed with odds had been taken from this Earth because of a silly, easily avoidable fuck-up. The most elegant and articulate and profound voice in the world had been silenced for nothing. The love of my life was dead because of a simple doctor's mistake.

Summer had been dead for two hours before they'd even come out to say anything to the family.

I couldn't stop thinking about that day, and what she'd known during the surgery and her death, if she'd known anything at all, God forbid. I'd like to imagine that she sank into a peaceful sleep, and that was it. But I wasn't so sure. She was so strong for her size, and I knew the sedatives probably wouldn't have worked as well on her as some others. Oh, God...just the thought of her being aware of her own death ripped me in half. And little things about the surgery haunted me endlessly; dark little remarks she'd made about her own mortality that had come off as gallows humor at the time but seemed like eerie premonitions in the rearview. How did she know she was going to die? She must've known, right? Why didn't she say anything? Why would she have willingly gone to her death? I knew I'd have to give up on most of these questions eventually, because they were unanswerable, and this fight was unwinnable. But still, I *wanted* to be mad. I savored the madness. I deserved to wallow in this misery, because I should've been there to save her. I should've done *something*, anything at all. But I didn't.

And now it was useless.

When a little boy in my hometown disappeared near a train station and was found rotting in a ditch a week or two later, my town quickly filled with hot, yellow outrage. The killer was tracked down within days, though, and sympathy for the family and devastation for the victim filtered in where the anger had been. Ribbons were tied to lampposts and group prayer meetings were held in coffee-stained cafes and whispery memorial vigils were held two weekend sunsets in a row, paper cup candles flickering in the Florida wind for Little Boy Lost. Summer had been killed just as thoroughly and as concretely as that boy, and yet I knew that none of that would ever happen for her. Nobody would ever sing a hymn for her beside a marsh while the crickets welcomed the night, and her killer would never be captured beside a quiet gas station at the break of dawn and then have to stare down the lights at a big front-page trial before roasting on an electric chair after the verdict came in. This crime was suspect-less, this story villain-less. The tragedy of it all was as big and as open-ended as the sky.

~

I had not known true horror until now. To distract myself from the fury whirling within me, I took out my phone and pulled up the only photo Summer had ever taken of me. That day under the pier with Kevin she'd taken a Snapchat of my back as I'd reeled in what had turned out to be a gigantic catfish, the waves stretching out beyond me as my puny back muscles strained in the sun. At the time I'd been so struck by her caption – "FIGHT" – that I'd taken a screen shot and saved it.

Fight. That word suddenly struck me like a swordfish and started spinning around and rhyming in my head.

Fight...
fight...
write.
And then it hit me.

26

In the still misery of that night three days after it happened, the idea came to me: *a book. Write a book.* A real book, not just a diary. Summer's book. The one I'd promised her. So what if *Eighty Eight* was gone – I'd start all over again. I had to. I would take the thoughts clawing out of me and turn them into something real. I would expand my diary for Summer, which I still had, and elaborate on it until it was a full book, a *real* book, a complete document of our summer together, through *my* eyes. I'd be fulfilling my promise to her *and* hopefully immortalizing her in one fell swoop.

Part of me thought I was crazy to even try. I could barely walk to the bathroom without collapsing to cry a new surface – how in the hell did I think I was going to write an entire *book*? But I fought on. Ernest Hemingway said to write one true thing and start from there, and so that's what I did. I took out my laptop and wrote the following sentence: *I love Summer Johnson.* Because I did. And I do. And that fact will rule my entire existence.

My blood warmed as I sank into writer mode. Yes, this was going to be something, alright. I didn't know what yet, but *something.* A Summer level of something. I would make absolutely sure of it. I would spin this tragedy into gold or die trying. I owed her that much. She had fought this world like hell, and so what if she'd made all the right moves and still lost? It was my turn to head into battle.

They say that if a writer falls in love with you, you can never die. Summer's name would never be carved in stone in monuments or tributes, but she had still carved her name onto my soul, and she deserved the same to be done to her legacy – but in a much larger sense. And so, with the windswept notion that I was hurtling toward destiny, I held my hands over my keyboard and prepared to etch my vanished girlfriend onto the storm-scraped surface of history – one keystroke at a time.

~

Hundreds, sometimes thousands of words an hour flowed out of me, and in remarkably good form, too. I hadn't written like that in years, actually – maybe ever. I felt a sense of purpose sink down into my every pore as I wrote every detail of her, every detail of me, every detail of *us*; every flaw every facet every moment until she felt almost real again. Because she was real, she was broken and she was gorgeous.

As I wrote I soon discovered that as an artist, she was the ultimate muse: there was so much to work with, so many peaks and valleys to explore. She wasn't some one-dimensional cardboard cutout character of a human; she had flaws and quirks and weird little habits that drove me nuts sometimes. She could be cynical to the point of being jaded, she never met a curse word she didn't like, and no matter how close we got, there was still this side of her that felt unknowable, unreachable, like when you peered into a dark lake and saw its muddy bottoms descend into murky black nothingness. I always got the sense that there was much I would never know about Summer, and I was right. Basically, she was touched by fire – lightning in a bottle. She seemed to know something the world didn't, and everything from her thoughts to her eyes seemed to burn with that secret. Her spitfire radiance warmed me up for the first time in my life, and soon I became addicted to that heat.

I should've known she burned too brightly for my broken world. All I knew for sure was that I would've done anything to sit by her fire again for just one more hour. But in the meantime, the least I could do for her was write.

Soon I found that it wasn't the bad memories of her that pulled me down, the fights or the tears – it was the good times that stuck out at me. It was every moment I'd touched her skin and saw my future; every time she laughed that hall-of-fame laugh in the car with me; every night she'd called my name in the heat of the July air. I was haunted by happiness, because every glimpse of her glory was just a reminder of what I'd lost; a peek of the castle in the sky that never was; an echo of the love I'd never feel again. A passing chill from the ghost of what could've been.

I wrote on and on, but like vomit, the words burned on the way out, and when the pain became too much I grabbed my laptop for a break. I don't know why, and I knew Summer would probably never see it, but suddenly I got the need to message her. I knew she didn't believe in heaven with a capital H and all that, but I missed the fuck out of her, and this seemed as direct a line of communication to her as any. The prospect of calling her voicemail absolutely terrified me for some reason, and reading her texts – the digital remains of her life – was out of the question. The set of letters and emojis sitting in my messaging folder had outlived my girlfriend, and that was something I could not deal with. So I figured Facebook would be the next best thing.

After I reactivated my account, the website asked for my relationship status. Without thinking, I entered "In A Relationship with Summer Johnson," because I was, and always would be.

"Thanks," my screen said. "This information will be displayed once Summer Johnson logs in and approves your relationship request."

Needless to say, Summer would never log in and approve my request.

I wiped my nose and clicked on her profile. Holding my hand over her photo because I still couldn't bring myself to look at it, I opened up the messaging feature and wrote this:

I'm still in love with you. Come back

I sniffled and sent the message. And call me a masochist, but after that I scrolled down her page to see what people were saying about her – and the Facebook crowd was saying a lot, surprise of the century. Her closest friends had been quiet, of course, as they knew Summer was mortified by public displays of emotion or affection, but that had not stopped

300

every random acquaintance and classmate and former coworker from crawling out of the woodwork to moan and wail and air-dry all their grievances online.

I bit my lip and scanned the dozens of comments and posts she'd been tagged in, and the first unexpectedly broke my heart. It was from some girl who'd gotten married right after the surgery, and instead of doing a bouquet toss, she'd thrown the flowers into the lake behind her wedding venue. She'd posted a picture of white petals floating on the still surface of a dark pond, along with this caption:

This is for you, Summer, wherever you are. We just wanted you to catch it for some reason. Love and miss you. Wish I could walk through that door at work and see that million dollar smile one more time.
–Love, Brianna from work.

I "liked" the photo with tears in my eyes and scrolled down, but the posts just got more and more annoying and attention-seeking. In fact, most of the kids had mentioned their *own* names, and how *they* were coping, more frequently than they'd mentioned Summer. The way people in my generation ran to their phones to post about the dead had always perplexed me, but in this case it was infuriating. Why were we such whores for attention? These were probably some the same girls who had made Summer feel so inferior with their showoff wedding posts, she'd downloaded the Spark app to keep up with them. What was wrong with us?

I put on a Saviour song and thought about it as I sank back into writing mode. As children we were obsessively rewarded and praised and doted upon – *you mean you finished second-to-last in the race in P.E. class? Here's a golden star. You're a star! You're all stars! And oh, shit, now there are towers falling from the sky and white powder is being sent to news networks? Your world is falling apart, so take ten more golden stars!*

So as we grew up into a broken world that had no place for the monsters it had created, we'd transferred this deep-seeded lust for kudos and acknowledgment online and chased our broken American dreams onto social media, broadcasting our grotesque need for validation through the ever-expanding network of Ethernet cables quickly unfurling across the land and encircling the Earth like prison bars. We were a billion little celebrities – a billion little Brangelinas in our own minds – smiling for the selfies and sending them out for a brave new world to gawk at. We had stars on our report cards and stars in our eyes and we were stars in our own minds. We were all lost and searching and drowning out the silence and the pain with the noise, because like Saviour had said, the truth of our burned-out America meant nothing as long as the lie was pretty enough. We were the new American nightmare, so snap some photos of our bulbous wedding cakes – we'd arrived, validate us with your love and your likes.

But I wanted the cycle to end. I wanted people like Summer to stop being immortalized without her consent on a fucking Facebook wall; I wanted girls like her to stop being made to feel inferior because of a few people begging for some stupid marriage spotlight. And in a way, Summer *was* her generation: a girl coming into the light of love; a generation coming into the light of the Internet. How could I prove once and for all that true love lived in the darkness; that human dignity really existed in the shadows?

Soon I got bored with writing and went back to Facebook, as any Millennial would, and within minutes I found the worst post of all, from some redhead I'd literally never even heard of before:

This still doesn't even seem real! Only the good die young. RIP, Summer. Cancer is such a monster. Please pray for me, y'all, I'm not taking this very well. But at least her death is teaching us so much. Miss ya, girlie, but I am so comforted to know that you will remain in our hearts forever, until...

I couldn't read anymore. *No,* I thought with a frown that suddenly twisted up from the bottom of me. *No. No no no no no. No.* This was a level of narcissism I could not tolerate. Summer had lost her fucking LIFE, and THIS girl wanted prayers?

Okay, hear me out on this one: after being raised around my mother, I'd formed this theory that all healthy people secretly held the outrageously patronizing and megalomaniacal belief that all sick/flawed/challenged people were put on this planet to Teach Them Lessons and Be Shining Examples Of Triumph In The Face of Doom. All this Facebook nonsense was just corroborating that hypothesis. Like, every time a sick person died, healthy people went around saying things like "her life was not in vain, since it taught us all so much about ourselves" and "aren't you thankful for what you learned from her death?"

No. Summer Johnson was not an experiment in humanity, and she did not die to teach me some corny lesson about Life and Love and Loss and Angels Finding Their Wings. She died because she died. She was a person who had thoughts and dreams and fears and fetishes and failures and glories just like anyone else, and she also happened to get sick and die. Sick people were not put on this Earth for any more or less of a reason than healthy people were, and to imply anything else was both infuriating and just plain stupid. She was not a dancing monkey whose sole purpose was to teach me shit, and I really wished people would get that, but I didn't know how to tell them without sounding like a dick.

And the saying "only the good die young" was the ultimate disservice to her, too, because it made her no better than any other young person who bit the dust. Like, this one kid I knew who accidentally shot himself while showing off his new gun to his friends at a party? It sucks that he died, but he was a *total* asshole. He would taunt freshman in the halls and call people names and shout four letter words at people for daring to make eye contact with him, and just because he died at nineteen didn't mean he had anything to

303

do with Summer. She was better than him. A lot of good people died young, that was true, and it sucked. But a lot of idiots died young, too – it was just that no one was allowed to mention it, because that would be cruel, right? Nobody wanted to be the one shit-talking a dead kid, so they washed everyone in the same angelic tones and called it a day. They called death the great equalizer, and it was – because in the rearview mirror, everyone was a hero.

But Summer really *was* a hero. In every sense, she was mine, at least. I wanted everyone in the world to know it, but I didn't know how to talk about her in a way that wouldn't embarrass her or seem condescending. It all went back to her modesty: she deserved recognition, but shunned attention. I knew I had to do something to let the world know how golden she was, and I knew I wanted to try to put a period on the end of the abbreviated, unresolved sentence that was her life. I thought that maybe the book could do that, but I still wasn't sure.

As I reached up to close my laptop, the page refreshed and two new posts popped up on her wall. Amanda was praying for Jesus to meet his new angel with open arms, Bekah was hoping that we would all remember the lessons of Summer's death forever, and I was headed to my fridge for another beer.

~

The next day I was writing like a madman while listening to a Saviour track, *Say Anything*:

Out of the silence, it rises up
That voice, reminding me that this life will never be enough
So I grab my phone and stare at the stars
But these distractions, they never get me very far

So say anything, kid, take me anywhere
Just get these monsters outta my hair
And say anything, just take me anywhere

I'm slowly gettin' killed by all this dead air

If I was in those hills of Beverly, it wouldn't be like this
Fame, sex, white lines, glamorous misery, give me all of it
Stuck in a life I never planned for, with problems I don't
even care about enough to fix
This set of bones I've been given, I could do without – I just
wasn't born for this

(So say anything)
(Take me anywhere)

That's when I got a call from Aunt Susan. It seemed that Shelly, in a fit of angry grief, had torn apart Summer's room looking for a goodbye note, a diary, some kind of last words to give her some sense of closure, but had found nothing of the sort. (It did strike me as odd that someone so analytical and obsessed with little details as Summer would not have left something behind, but I tried not to dwell on it.) Shelly did, however, find Summer's secret chest, that corner of every human's bedroom where they hide from the world the things that revealed their most quietly desperate desires. Susan wanted me to know that in the chest was a specials menu from Joe's Crab Shack dated March 25th.

I said thank you as everything in me broke apart again, and then I asked if she could tell me anything else about the stash. The only other thing of substance she'd found was a photo ripped from an Intresia pamphlet that had said *I DON'T CARE ABOUT SOCIETY'S APPROVAL, BUT I **WILL** GET ITS ACKNOWLEDGEMENT*, which I found very interesting. Then I asked if there was anything else in the chest, anything at all that she remembered seeing, no matter how insignificant.

The only other thing Susan remembered noticing before ushering Shelly out of the room and into a hot bath was a stack of wedding magazines.

27

After the death of a loved one, only two things can be absolutely counted upon: misery and casserole. I had finally regained a bit of my appetite and was picking at a green bean variety of the dish that had been dropped off by a neighbor when I decided to write down the inscription for my girlfriend's headstone, which was actually a reworking of a eulogy Ernest Hemingway had written for a friend. It had popped into my head a few days before, but since Summer's book was quickly and miraculously nearing completion at forty-five thousand words, I hadn't had a chance to actually write it down just yet.

It went like this:

SUMMER MARTIN JOHNSON
Die in Love and Live Forever

"And most of all she loved the sea
Those golden sands beneath her feet
That water blue, that salty breeze
Now she will swim in it
Forever"

WE LOVE YOU SO MUCH, SUM
YOUNG FOREVER

I typed up the final poem, attached it to an email to Shelly, and added a short message in the body:

Hey, here's the inscription for the stone. Sorry I'm late, I haven't really been up to writing this, as you can probably understand. Hope you're doing better than you were. And please remember to reserve the plot next to Summer in the cemetery like we talked about. I don't care how much it costs – I wanna lie next to your daughter forever.

When I stopped crying, I punched a spot into the mess on my bed and got ready to fall asleep and wake up alone. That was another worst part, waking up every morning and remembering what had happened all over again. In my dreams I'd imagine taking a shower and then walking into Summer's house and seeing her sitting in that wheelchair and being shocked by how much I loved her, blown away that I even *had* that much love in me at all after my disastrous childhood, and then I'd take her hand and lead her away. But then I'd rise out of the oblivion of sleep, all groggy and confused and sort of excited to face the day and see her, and suddenly I'd remember that she was dead, gone, not coming back, and then the weight of it all would just fall on me and smother me, and every time it was as bad as the day it had first happened. It was just the worst. It was all the worst.

And I felt so guilty to admit that her face was *already* becoming harder to picture in my mind. The parts were there, but sometimes they just wouldn't add up to a whole, and sometimes all I could conjure was a fuzzy image of her basic essence. She existed now only in my memory, a silvery phantom of dissolving love, gorgeous and ghostly and gone, drifting away into the dreamland of my fantasies more and more every day. It was so hard not to follow her there, too. Sometimes it was so difficult not to sink into the horror within me and go back to that special place we'd shared when Summer was alive, even though it was now cloaked in darkness and despair and misery. I had to stay, and not just mentally speaking: I had to be there for my mom and Shelly and all the other people who needed me out here in the light. That's what had kept me writing the past few days, against all odds: Summer's reminder to fight. I wasn't going to give up just yet.

Just as I slipped into sleep, though, my phone pinged. I rubbed my eyes and reached blindly for the glow. It was an email from an app called TimeSure, a service that let you pre-write a message and set it to send whenever you wanted, be it in one day or one year. Everything in me jumped when I saw the sender.

It was from Summer.

My surroundings bled together as I sat up, crossed my legs, and hunched over. The timestamp said she'd written the email the night before the surgery, and picturing her sitting on her bed and leaning over her laptop, just like this, made me want to not exist anymore. She must've known she was going to die – oh, God, she must've known.

As my heart thundered inside me, I pushed aside the pain and prepared to read this digital fossil of a human life.

From: summerhateswinter1215@gmail.com
July 10, 11:52 PM

My darling Cooper:

So: I am a marriage-desperate psycho. Let's just get that out of the way. I realized it the other day under that oak tree: I have officially flown the coop and joined the crazy club, and I can't hide it anymore. I have become the people I used to make fun of, and I am completely embarrassed about it. But if you are reading this, it means that I wasn't there to stop this message from being sent, and that I am gone, and that my dream wedding is no longer in the cards for me, and that you probably hate me for all the pain I have caused you, and will continue to cause you. But if I've learned anything about this endless ocean called life, it's that if we don't forgive, we're as fucked as a boat without a propeller. So whether I am looking down on you right now, looking up at you, or if I am nothing and nowhere, I want you to know that I am sorry for all this, Cooper, and that I want you to move on. In a perfect world I will wake up in the clouds when this is all over and walk through my front door and see some dream-version of you laughing at that little yellow table with my mom and Chase and Autumn, and then you and I will wander down the street under the oaks hand-in-hand and have an endless summer on the shores of Jacksonville Beach together. I do not know if that will happen, though I can pray.

But this is not about me. It's about you, the boy who lived. Dying is easy – anyone can die. (And I would know, since I'm supposedly dead and all, LOL.) But living is the grandest and most challenging adventure of all. So because it is now up to me to guide you on the path of life that I have complicated so much for you by dying, and because like many people in our generation I am immensely awkward in person due to the majority of my correspondence taking place via iMessage, here are my last words to you, in an email. (God knows I'll probably fuck all this up in the morning when I say goodbye before surgery, so I won't even try. My thoughts are pretty but won't translate into the spoken word, so I'll speak to my laptop instead.) So, anyway, since I am a crazy desperate bitch, like I said before, here are my last words in the form of a long and meandering speech I would give at the wedding we will never have, that you never even AGREED to have, because I am crazy:

My name is Summer Johnson, and I did nothing particularly heroic during my lifetime. My name will not be inscribed in any history books to be skimmed through and then discarded by the middle schoolers of the future, I probably will not be remembered beyond a few immediate family members and that great aunt in North Carolina whom I really should call more often, and I cannot even successfully balance my own debit account without getting my card turned down at Starbucks twice a week. But I love Cooper Nichols with everything within my broken body, and for that, I know my life will not have been in vain. I still love him, even after all this. I love all of him, with all of me, all one hundred and six pounds of me, right down to the large scar running up the right side of my face, that he healed. (And no, I know what you're thinking, and it's not a cancer scar. It's a Life Scar. 'Twas life that killed this girl, not cancer.)

Our story wasn't like some cheesy romantic comedy that you'd hate-watch on TBS on a Sunday night. I didn't trip over a leaf and fall into his buff arms, and we didn't go back to my improbably large loft apartment in New York City and post selfies of our beautiful love together. At one time I very stupidly wished for someone to love me like that, but Cooper loved me better. Our road was tough and frustrating and filled with obstacles and twists and all the other annoying bullshit that makes up life, but he loved me through all that. So I guess I just want you to know that there was a boy named Cooper, and that he loved a girl who wasn't beautiful until she felt like she was.

We come from a generation that measures itself against the world. Every Facebook status and Instagram photo and Twitter post digs under our skin and tells us we're not living and loving grandly enough. If you're not seen or heard, you're nothing. But for every epic love tale splashed out in lights for the world to see, there were ten million more couples that loved each other in the dark just as beautifully. Maybe no one will ever know the story of Summer and Cooper. Maybe no one will ever know that on the shores of a town just like many other towns, on a beach just like many other beaches, during a summer just like many other summers, a boy named Cooper Nichols loved a girl named Summer Johnson in every way that a person can be loved until she floated up and joined the sun. But that doesn't mean he loved me any less deeply, or that our love was any less magnificent than those couples who throw their names under lights. And at least I know. No matter what happens, at least one human being – one Me – knows our story. I think I like those odds.

And I know what people might say. "It was just a few months – why are you both so changed by a couple of months?" But a lot of things happen in a matter of months. You should know that better than anyone, Cooper, you master of useless facts. And thanks to Wikipedia, here are a few examples. The Spanish-American War: three and a half months. The construction of the Empire State Building: fourteen months. The creation of a human life: nine months. One summer when Cooper Nichols gave a dying girl a hot breath of eternal love that she will take with her forever: three months and a few weeks, give or take.

You know, being human is weird. Our lives are endless stretches of forgotten days broken up by only a few moments of burning clarity that stick out to us. Chances are I will probably forget everything I did on any given day, and all will be swept into the vast ocean of nothingness broken up by the few islands in the stream of time that we will actually remember. But the memories of these three months will stick with me for the long haul, Cooper. Remember those Neptune Beach nights, the hipster girls dancing with the feathers in their hair? Those lazy afternoon walks down Cedar Street to the sea, those golden days when the mess was made? I am so grateful for that mess. You gave me a roaring July in the winter of my life, and I'm thankful.

So here we are, Cooper. The end of me, and the beginning of you. I wish you an adventurous heart. I hope you never lose the ability to marvel at the world. I hope you look down at the tops of the clouds from between two roaring engines, and I hope you have quiet moments at home with the ones you love most. I wish you forgiveness and empathy and understanding, because you're going to need them, and when you love someone again, I want you to love them with all of you. I hope you find someone who looks at you the way you looked at me. (BTW, just make sure she's not one of my friends, or I will haunt the fuck out of you guys.) I wish you bruises and triumphs and glory and disaster, and I hope you laugh and cry and win and lose and dream and love, all those things that make up a great big adventurous life, and when faced with the choice between jumping and staying put, I hope you jump with everything in you, every time. You are either busy being alive or busy getting dead – pick one before death picks you. The last thing anyone ever wants to say on a deathbed is "it could have been" – fight the world like hell and do everything in your power to never have to say that sentence.

And if you ever do find yourself living a life you're not proud of, Cooper, I pray you have the bravery to walk away and become whoever the hell you want to be. I believe in you like I believe in sunsets and sweet tea and the country America used to be. Even though I may never get that big white ceremony in front of my family and my friends that I could rub in the virtual noses of a thousand of my closest Facebook frenemies, I want you to know that this was enough for me, these last few months when we loved and wrecked each other by the sea. You *were enough for me. Thank you for being my island in the stream. Wherever the odds lead me now, this is my vow: I will take this summer with me forever.*

And if you ever feel yourself losing your way again, Cooper, and find that you just can't get your shit together, just reach out and love someone. Love is the most adult action anyone could ever carry out in this emotionally stunted world, and once you love, the rest will fall into place. It has to.

(Just make sure the person you choose to love listens to Saviour and posts to Facebook as sporadically as possible – you'd better believe I'll be judging you from heaven.)

Your girl always,
and please forgive me for how goddamned cheesy this was,

Summer

PS: I made this email address when I was seventeen, don't judge me for it.

And PPS:
I know you never asked me this, and I have no idea if you were ever even going *to ask me this, but just in case you were wondering:*
I do.

I broke all over again as I read, falling across my bed with great, heaving, retching sobs. A fissure opened up somewhere deep within me and pushed me apart as it exploded upwards, leaving me in pieces as I erupted.

Oh, Summer.

Her forever had lasted five minutes. She knew – she'd known she was going to die. How unspeakably terrible. Seeing her words, her humor, her personality, made me miss her so much I couldn't breathe. And I remembered then just how much I had loved her: with every organ in me; that hall-of-fame type love. She was so important. She was so special. She was so remembered. And the fact that she'd left this Earth feeling like some kind of forgotten failure or something was just…well, the *new* worst thing.

I wished so many things. I wished she hadn't loved so perfectly and died so young. I wished she'd known that she was beautiful, truly beautiful. I wished she'd known the way the world lit up when she laughed. I wished she'd known the way the air crackled and popped and sizzled around her when she entered a room. I wished she'd known she was vital and important and precious. I wished she'd loved herself like I had loved her. But she'd never gotten the chance to, and that absolutely wrecked me.

I tossed my phone deep into the abyss that was my comforter, took some melatonin my mom had given me, and prayed for sleep.

~

The night dripped by, and soon morning broke over the ocean, warm and cruel. The viewing and funeral were both being held in a tacky brown funeral home off Third Street on a cloudy, humid Saturday morning just like any other. A queen was being honored in a dump. So it goes.

I woke slowly, filled all the way up with a dark, solid, heavy dread. This was the last thing in the world I wanted to do, go sit in a hall full of strangers and listen to them air out their grief for their own selfish purposes, but I knew I had to rise to the occasion. Summer was daring me to be okay. Even her sentence, *"everything will turn out okay –*

313

it has to," was practically goading me to be alright, and so I decided to get out of bed and go through the motions, if only for today.

Before I left, though, I grabbed Summer's book, printed out her letter, and slid it into the beginning, as an introduction. Nobody was fit to introduce Summer but Summer. Then I hand-wrote and inserted a short note in front of the letter:

When you grow older, your heart dies. This was true in The Breakfast Club *and it is true now. Your bones get bigger and your toys lose themselves in closets and trunks and cardboard boxes and your dreams become buried under more pressing matters like exams and bills and engagement parties and life insurance policies and before you know it you've let go of your desires completely, your soul collapsed, your dreams burned out like the embers of a day-old campfire, and you become content with mediocrity. But for the first time since my bones got big, you made me feel small and new and excited to get out of bed in the morning, Summer. You made me dream again, and I will never be able to repay you for that. This book is at least one small initial step in that direction, though.*

So, to whoever is reading this: this is the story of Summer Martin Johnson and the eternal summer she spent with Cooper Nichols on the shores of Jacksonville Beach, Florida, soon after the dawn of a new century. No one has ever been more grateful for three months. Words alone cannot do her justice, but love can try.

All my love,
C

Then I closed the book, took out my laptop again, and typed up a new book cover inspired by Saviour's last album. I smiled to myself as the printer roared to life and spit out my new cover.

On the way to the funeral parlor, my mom looked over at me from the driver's seat with the same worried frown she'd had on her weathered face for a week. She could drive with the help of these special hand pedals that attached to the steering wheel, but she'd never quite gotten the hang of it, and this was the first time I'd let her take me anywhere in years.

"Cooper, you know I-"

"Don't ask again," I said as she jolted to a stop at a red light. "I don't want any wine before the funeral. You know that drinking is a slippery slope that leads me straight to pills. I'm fine."

My mother drank often and even dared me to join her sometimes. This shocked people, as they wanted to believe that the disabled were faultless saints who sat there smiling all day, thinking about angels and babies and kittens, when in reality they were normal people who maintained their own faults and habits and neuroses and monsters just like everyone else in the transition from Well to Unwell. And sometimes their bad habits became even worse when thrown through the prism of disability, actually, because what else could harden a human more swiftly and thoroughly than being erased from the eyes of ninety percent of the world? My mother saw the world, but it didn't see her back, and sometimes that just made her wheel towards her liquor drawer even faster. She broke my heart every day, but I wouldn't have lived with anyone else in the world. Well, besides Summer, obviously.

"I'm not asking if you want wine," she said after a moment. "What are you going to do with that book you wrote?"

I fidgeted a little. My mom was always trying to do this; make me envision and prepare for the day when she would no longer be here. That time would come, obviously, and I'd eventually have to deal with being set out on my own, but right now I was trying to deal with one crushing heartbreak at a time. I was a kid in a man's body, maybe forever.

"I don't know yet," I said. "Why?"

She rearranged her shoulders in a way that had nothing to do with her condition. "Well, don't be mad at me, but I read some of the book when you were in the shower this morning, and it was gorgeous. Absolutely beautiful. I cried on the first page, actually. Your teachers were right – you really *are* a genius."

I shifted a little. "Oh, um, thanks, but that wasn't my – I wasn't trying to make people cry, Mom."

She shrugged. "Life makes people cry. The truth makes people cry. Reality makes people cry. It happens." She threw a glance at me, testing me. "You know, you could always turn it into an Amazon book and use it to start your career as an author. I'm sure Summer wouldn't mind. It could be like one of those popular cancer books or something, and-"

"*Esophageal Intresia!*" I shouted so loud, she slowed down and looked over at me. "Oh, uh, sorry," I said. Another long moment passed, and she cleared her throat.

"I want to know something else about her, too."

"Yes? What?"

"Are you angry?" she asked, searching me with her brown eyes. "With *her*, I mean? You know I loved her, but this is all so…complicated. I know she never told you about the surgery – I could see it in your eyes, that day you found out. She knew what was happening when she signed on to date you, and yet she said nothing. She knew where the cards were going to fall. She had to."

My stomach turned over as I looked out of the window again. I'd thought about this, obviously, as I'd known everyone and their moms would be wondering about it, but I was still forming a response that conveyed everything I felt.

"I could never be angry at a dead person," I began. "Summer deserved love, just like anyone else, and she tried to find it in the only way she knew how. I'm just sorry that she felt like she had to resort to lying, and that she thought it was the only way. I would've loved that girl healthy or sick, broken or whole. I just wish she would've known that."

316

"Oh, Cooper," Colleen said, and for a minute she just stared at me while we waited at an intersection. But then she snapped back and cleared her throat again. "But, still: you bore the brunt of those decisions. Here you are, in pieces, on the way to her funeral. Who knows – maybe your father was correct in doing what he did to me, severing ties before they sank too deeply and-"

"*Don't* bring up that man on a day as holy as this," I said through clenched teeth, lifting a hand. "I'm not done yet."

"Okay?"

"Am I angry at the *situation*?" I asked. "Am I angry at certain *decisions* Summer made? Am I angry that she didn't share certain things with me? I don't know. I guess I'll find out in the years to come, in the way I deal with this." I paused and bit my lip, something big and blubbery crawling into my throat. "But God, did I love that girl. I was so lucky to get wrecked by Summer Johnson, let me tell you."

I didn't know where that last part came from, I just sort of added it on. My mom couldn't say anything anyway. She was crying too hard.

"I know she thought I was angry, though," I said as she shakily wiped her nose. "That's why she was always pushing me away. But at the same time she'd also wanted to leave something behind. She watched her friends post about their weddings and all their nonsense and she started to feel so small, like she'd be forgotten if she died. And that's the *worst* thing. I just want to prove to her that she did leave an impression, that she was successful, and that my gratefulness outweighs my anger, by a million to one. A *billion* to one. She was a numbers girl – she should understand that.

"And you know, I'm so proud of her," I said as a smile escaped to my face, my tear ducts pumping again. "She was so pretty and nice and sweet and smart, but not smart in some bullshit, smart-kid-in-the-corner-with-no-social-skills kind of way. Her intelligence was so real and concrete and useful – she could look right into any situation and cut through all the bullshit and see it for exactly what it was. I hope I can become more like that one day."

My mom sort of shrugged in a sad, weird way as she cried – this was all way over her head – and focused on driving.

"Don't worry about this, Coop," she finally said. "You'll find another girl one day, and get married, and-"

"I don't want another girl," I interrupted. "I just want Summer. I'm going to see that girl's face in every crowd I get lost in for the rest of my life."

She stared ahead and bit her lip.

"You are better than me," she said next, shaking her head. "That's all I know. You are better than me. If I died tomorrow, my life will have meant something, because I improved the world by bringing you into it. I tried to raise you to be good and kind and strong, but you have exceeded my expectations in every single way. I never even *dreamed* of having a son like you, because I didn't even know it was possible. I am so proud of you, Cooper. I just…God. Wow."

I didn't really know what to say to that, as I'd never really been good at taking compliments. Some people considered me self-centered, but what they didn't understand was that I was only "self-centered" in the sense that all my thoughts revolved around how inferior I was as a human. Still, I reached over and took my mom's hand, and she smiled and let me.

"I thank the good Lord every day for you, kid."

"Yeah," I said. I had a God now, and she was a girl with a scar who wasn't here anymore, but still, I squeezed my mom's hand a little harder. Things like this had gotten easier since Summer's death for some reason, and I hoped I would never go back to that cold boy I'd been before. Old Cooper would've maybe smiled in my mom's direction and looked away, but New Cooper was all too aware of how careless Old Cooper had been with love, letting relationships fizzle out and loved ones drift away. I treasured love now, and I was not about to let something so precious slip away. So I leaned in and kissed my mother on her bony shoulder for the first time in years, making her smile down at me with every muscle in her beautiful and ravaged face.

And speaking of Summer: Saviour's brand-new song called *The Summer Remains* came on the radio as we headed south on Third Street – a song Summer would never hear, I realized with a stifled sob that came out of nowhere. I stared out of the window again at my sepia-toned town as Saviour's creepy voice pierced the silence:

Ankles in the emerald waves
Hand in hand, hip to hip, trynna be brave
But what we can't say, we both know
Our love won't make it past this horror show

Looking for heaven under these palms, finding hell instead
Getting closer to the fire with every fight, every sip, every breath
Got lost in your glow, thought it was a halo
Turns out that elixir was poison, and those devils, they gotcha on the down low

Now we're side by side as the day breaks, 'bout to face the sun
Golden hair, golden skin, the golden ones
Angels headed straight to hell and we both know it, here in these waves
'Least I got you beside me while we face the flames

But hold up, babe, take my hand
Diamonds, platinum, wedding bands
What we had, it's gonna stay
Even though this world, it's headed for the grave

The summer remains

I bolted up straighter than a sunray at dusk. The song blew my brain open, and all sorts of words started flying out at me and revolving around in my head, including a few key phrases from Summer's email...

Rings...

Remain...

Say our vows in front of our family and friends...

No one will ever know our story...

I may never get that white wedding...

And all at once, I knew exactly how to make Summer remain.

I grabbed *This Is Not A Cancer Book* from my bag. "Turn around," I told my mom, who snapped out of some dreamy state and stared over at me.

"What? But the service starts in-"

"Turn around!" I shouted, throwing up my hands again. "Do not disagree with your poor grieving son! *Turn the damned car around!"*

"Alright alright alright," she said as she U-turned into a Krystal parking lot. "But where are we going?"

I set my jaw and willed myself to do what I had to. For Summer. For us.

"Home," I said. "And then Summer's house. And hurry – we don't have much time."

My mom gave me an uneasy look and then turned and bled back into traffic. We passed the pier, already crawling with people, and I just watched them. I'd been doing that more lately, too, just noticing things. I couldn't help myself. A middle school soccer team was walking home from the practice fields on the sidewalk along the road, and an overweight girl hung back behind the other chattering girls, staring at the ground as she trudged along. I looked at her face and saw Summer – everyone had a little Summer in them, actually. Isolation, disappointment, the futile hope for a better future. This girl just had more Summer than usual, and so I leaned out of my window and called "Hey, you!"

The other, popular girls thought I was looking at them and started giggling, but I pointed at the one behind, the one they had cast from their group. When I got her attention, I yelled, "You're beautiful. Truly beautiful. Just hope you know that. Never forget it, either."

The girl in the back blushed furiously and started walking faster, a new spring in her step, and I returned to my seat. Now that I knew a loss this searing, never again would I take for granted a day I had been given under this burning star of ours. Never again would I fall prey to fear and insecurity and self-doubt and busyness and distraction and all the other things that kept us from loving the people in our lives in the way they deserved. Never again would I overlook outcast teens and widows and orphans and old men and next-door neighbors and the disabled and all the other people in this chronically unloved world who deserved to be noticed and appreciated. Because the best kind of love, even if it ends, pushes out the edges of your heart, expands the dimensions of it and leaves space to let more in later – and that's what Summer had given me. I was full of her love, and I couldn't fucking wait to start spreading it around.

As I watched all those varied Jacksonvillians by the pier I remarked to myself how fucked up it was that most of them would never know or care that Summer Johnson existed. She was anonymous to them as the waves that came one after the other, all day every day, eternally. But at the same time it was sort of beautiful to know that there was a big wide world out there, filled with cliffs and oceans and hills and bays and humans, all with their own dreams and agonies and hopes and vices and Summer Johnsons – or their own knockoff versions of her, at least.

But still, I didn't like that they didn't know of my girl. Not at all. Summer needed to be acknowledged. After all, she had said it herself – she didn't care about getting the world's approval, but she *would* get its acknowledgement.

And why not acknowledge her in the way modern society had deemed most significant?

Summer Johnson was never incorrect about anything. She was smart and wise and impossibly self-contained and never made a misstep. But many times I'd heard her say that she would never get a wedding because of her circumstances, and therefore she would never be remembered. And for the first time, I wanted her to be wrong.

And maybe *I* was wrong, too. Maybe I wasn't my father. Maybe I could still fix this.

"So why are we going home?" Colleen asked as she turned back onto my street. I took a breath.

"I have to stop by your safe. There's a ring I want to grab."

She looked over at me, her brow creased into a deep *V*, a trait I had inherited from her.

"You mean your Grandma Nash's ring? But I thought you were saving it to give to your wife whenever you got married one day?"

"I was," I said. "And I am."

Her breath caught in her lungs as her eyes increased by ten sizes and her mouth fell open.

"Oh my God – *Cooper*."

28

We crept into the service fifteen minutes late and sank into foldable chairs at the very back of the overcrowded, musty-smelling hall. I guess because the crowd was so big, the service was running behind, too, and there was still a line waiting to see her. Summer didn't want anyone to worry and had kept the surgery news pretty quiet, but still, little bits and pieces of information had trickled out to her extended family and friends over the past few months, so they'd known *something* was coming – but nobody had expected this. It was like we'd braced for a thunderstorm and gotten a blizzard instead. An air of quietly stunned confusion surrounded the random assortment of second cousins and distant friends and former neighbors as they stopped at the casket, awkwardly looked down at Summer's remains, and said a few quiet words, looking totally unsure of themselves the whole time. I almost got up to say something when some blonde lady stopped at the casket and said what a shame it was that "Sarah" had died so suddenly "from her cancer," but my mom grabbed my arm.

The funeral home people started to clear out the crowd and ask everyone to sit, and my stomach churned harder than ever as an organ started playing from the corner. I still didn't know exactly what I was going to say, and how I was going to say it. The thoughts were swirling around in my head but I couldn't stick them together in any way that made sense, and so I just stared at the edge of the casket, thinking about life, and how much I still loved her, and all the things she would never get to do, and all the things I would get to do, and how both of those things infuriated and devastated me all at once.

I noticed Kevin's teenaged sister typing away on Facebook a few rows up, posting God only knew what in an attempt to drown out the noise. *Noise*, I thought. Just *what* were we drowning out? Why were we running from our human-ness and masking our beating hearts with Beats headphones? What was so wrong with, as Summer had put it, "living in the dark?" What was so good about shouting about yourself from the heavens? Did that really make your feelings deeper, your relationships more important, your life more vital? Why did my generation have to throw our lives under lights to make them feel real?

I thought of how poor Summer had always stuck earphones into her own ears to drown out what she herself was feeling: *I am alone. I will die young and lonely, leaving zero obnoxious wedding posts to signify that I was here, since love seems to be my era's main signifier of life.* So upon hearing her diagnosis she'd finally fought against her instinct to isolate herself and had made one last dash to reach out and find love. In reality this was a rash and ill-thought-out decision, but at the time, it had made perfect sense. Not that I regretted her actions – I was hers and always would be – but not according to the standards of a society that demanded you tie up your love in a white ceremony in front of the world. Maybe I could rectify that, though.

When I was in the seventh grade, my favorite teacher ever, Mrs. Gregory, came up to me and told me the story I was writing was getting away from me. "Too many random things are happening," she said, her red hair shining in the light from the windows facing the bus loop, "and you're losing control. Take back the narrative, Cooper. Take charge. I know you can."

Summer was dead. Her story had been written for her, her narrative overtaken by odds and ends and careless doctors. But that didn't mean I couldn't take back control of her story and write one final chapter. I knew she didn't believe in happily ever after – it was the "after" portion that had always scared her – and yet here we were, After Summer, and it was time for the Ever part. Two out of three wasn't bad. After all, who'd ever said that both parties needed to be alive for the "ever after" part to ring true?

My leg shivered with a gathering adrenaline as I sat in the back of that sweaty funeral hall. This wasn't over. Not yet. Not until the fat lady sang. Not until the sad-eyed boy gave Summer her last speech.

After we listened to a hymn about walking through some
flowery meadow or some bullshit, Autumn read *So It Goes*
by Saviour, which just killed me. Pun intended: Summer
liked dark humor. The poem, written for Saviour's friend
who had died of cancer at fifteen, went like this:

you are a
Dandelion wish

A prayer sent out into thin air,
a hymn that came back cold

A sunset sinking into treetops too early in the day,
blurring greenery

A whisper on the surface of time

all too brief.

you were
Love between bones:
dust to bone, bone to love, love to dust

as it came,
So it goes:

drenched in love.

Then some pastor dude said a few words about how she'd
never stopped fighting and kept her dignity until the very end
or whatever, which was all true, but still – *bullshit*. Then he
asked the eulogizers to get ready. The first was Autumn, who
told some funny stories about Summer's past to try to lighten
the mood. I guess she *could* be counted upon to do that. Then
a few more people from Summer's group came up, and after
the one-armed army guy Hank started his speech by saying
"Summer Johnson's compassion saved my life," I started

325

crying too hard to listen, and focused my attention on a plastic tree in the corner until he stopped talking. After Hank was Kim, who had to have the microphone handed down to her because she couldn't get up the stairs in her wheelchair. "Summer was the only person in the world who ever made me feel pretty," she began, and then I stopped listening to her, too, because I was breaking inside.

But nothing could prepare me for Shelly. I hadn't seen her since the day of the operation, but I'd heard she was in bad shape. She'd already lost a good deal of weight, and her skin was as pale as her whitish-pinkish dress, which I knew she'd worn because of Summer's roses in her front yard. And I don't know if this will sound mean or even make sense, but this was the first time I had seen her and thought that she looked like an adult.

She stopped at the podium and cleared her throat, her eyes sullen but determined.

"You know, a lot of people are angry today," she began, sounding surprisingly strong. "A lot of people are frustrated. A lot of people are confused. My daughter's death feels senseless. It feels random. It feels pointless. It feels like we are being manipulated by the world. But Summer of all people knew that sometimes the most senseless mistakes can teach us the most about the world, and about who we are in the world, and about what to do with who we are in the world." A few people gasped.

"According to a good friend of mine who is going to be a very famous author one day, madness is going to strike," she said, and that's when I realized she was partly reading from *Eighty Eight*. She glanced at me, and I swore to God, I thought I saw her wink. I blushed, but when a few people in the crowd assumed she'd been talking about me and looked my way, I shook my head and listened in. This was Shelly's moment.

"Things will fall apart," she continued, "and you will get some bad letters in Scrabble and, hey, maybe your doctor will even put up the wrong chart before your surgery and kill you. But this is why you must start living today. People often fear the future until they realize the future is now, and that they are living in it. Time will come – that's what it does. You can push against it, run from it, fight it like you fight the snooze button on a groggy morning, but still, it will run at you like it stole something. It's how we react that counts. And damn it, my daughter made the most out of her short little life."

She wiped her eyes as her voice cracked. Everyone waited for her to gather herself, and finally she glanced up at the ceiling one last time, as if pleading for Summer's help, and then returned to her notes.

"Everyone is scarred on the way to adulthood, but my daughter had to wear her scars on the outside, and she wore them honestly and openly. She didn't live long, but she did live wide, leaving no stone in the field of life unturned, and all of us in this room were touched by her open arms. She was brave enough to dream her fantasies into reality, and that is human triumph."

Shelly swallowed hard. "You know, I will never get over the way Summer was taken from us, but I do know I know I will get *past* it. Because she left me with the strength to walk forward. She was the most fearless person I ever knew, but that doesn't mean she wasn't afraid. It means she was brave enough to set her shoulders back and walk straight towards what scared her. She took the card she had been dealt in this life and played it to the best of her ability – no whining, no fussing, just quiet acceptance and progress."

Rage bubbled up into her voice, but I saw her shift her shoulders and swallow it.

"I know that no amount of words can make this any easier or better. My daughter is dead. But we can still try. I know some of us would like to place blame on certain people and let the fury consume us, but I am here today to tell you that the second you let the monsters see you cry, you lose, and that living well and standing tall is the bravest form of revenge of all. There is unspeakable horror out there, that is true. There is heartbreak and loss and misery and loneliness and disability and hatred and Monday mornings. But there is also beauty and goodness and innocence and generosity and sweet tea, and those are the things we must focus on – the world demands it of us. They can take everything away from us, but they can never take away our spirit. Summer had the worst of the world thrown at her, and she shrugged and walked on – I wish the same for all of you. Also, I urge you all once again not to be angry at the people who took her from us. God knows they will live in the hell they have created for themselves." She paused. "I love you, Summer. I miss you, and I will spend the rest of my life thanking God for the twenty four years I had with you."

She glanced at me. "And to Cooper: thank you for granting my daughter her one last wish, and thank you for your unwilling help on the eulogy I just read. Colleen did a great job raising you, and I am going to love you forever. I will do everything in my power to get your books published, I promise. And by the way, you should stop leaving manuscripts in hospital chapels for doctors named Steinberg to find two days later."

She faced the general crowd. "And to the rest of you: carry on. That is all any of us can do in this very large and messed-up world. As I read in a book called *Eighty Eight*, the only two choices humans are given are to sink or swim. I, for one, am about to swim for my life. Thank you."

She nodded and left the podium. This was it. It was time. My vision tunneled and my heart contracted in my chest as I gave myself one last chance to back out. The task before me was impossible.

But then I saw Summer smiling big and proud in her wheelchair and stood up. I wouldn't run like my father. I would face this.

Life is a game of odds. I knew that much by now. It is Scrabble on steroids. There is no order, symmetry, or destiny. We are on our own. Sometimes you win dazzlingly and sometimes you fail spectacularly. That's just how it is. I learned all that from someone I loved a lot. But that doesn't mean you can't find order in the numbers; miracles in the odds; magic in the madness. Summer was the miracle I found in the random chaos of the world, a spirit in the dark. I don't have to wonder about God anymore, because I found my own religion on the streets of Jacksonville Beach this summer. And now it was time to send her off in style.

As I got up and walked up the aisle, though, I thought of something strange I'd noticed: everyone had talked about Summer in the past tense, with pity in their voices, when there she was, right in front of us in that casket, flesh and bones and love, for one last time. Why not talk *to* her instead of *at* her?

So I tossed my little speech aside as I approached the podium, my surroundings blurring together again like the air was melting. I felt hundreds of eyeballs on me, and I could hear the murmurs spreading through the crowd as I turned and leaned into the microphone. I spotted *Eighty Eight* under me on the lectern, winked at Shelly, and straightened my coat.

But as I did so, the crowd erupted into whispers. "There he is," I knew they were saying. "There's the dead girl's boyfriend. Poor thing. I can't believe she led him on like that."

Just love, I told myself in Summer's voice, to combat the fear welling up within me. *If you ever lose your way, just love someone. The rest will fall into place. It has to.*

"Summer Martin Johnson was and is the love of my life and the best person I ever knew," I said as I reluctantly faced the crowd, pushing down the ball of terror rising into my throat. "Her love changed me, and made me push myself up on my feet and wish for more, and bla bla bla, you know how these speeches are supposed to sound. But here's the thing: too many people talk *about* the dead, and not *to* them. So I'm gonna talk *to* you, Summer."

I swiveled a little until I faced her casket. Seeing her like that brought up the anger again, but I did my best to swallow it.

"Hi, Sum," I said. "I hope it's nice where you are. Weather's fine here, maybe a little muggy. I suspect you may be somewhere, based on something you once told me.

329

You know, that little thing about how people create their own heaven and their own hell by the way they live their lives? I know you'd be somewhere beautiful, because *you're* beautiful. So beautiful. You were an Earthly paradise. You were good and honest and lovely and sweet and empathetic and you transcended your humanity and rose to the highest level of being by loving unconditionally and, oh God, it sucks so much that you're gone. But you're not nowhere. I know that. And I know what *my* heaven looks like, actually. You're there. So is beer and my dog and the sea. I hope to see you all there one day."

I choked down an angry sob. It was so hard not to be mad, but I was trying. By this point I was totally crying, the tears mixing in with the snot draining from my nose, soaking my white Oxford and the lapels of the black tuxedo jacket I'd just changed into.

"I don't know why I'm here, Summer," I said once I'd regained myself. "I don't know why I'm so lost or why I can't grow up or why everyone is so awful or why I can't find anywhere that feels like home or why this place is falling apart or why I even try anymore sometimes. But I do know you were the first thing I thought of when I woke up every morning into this burned-out world, and that you were beautiful, and that as long as I had you by my side, I didn't care that I was lost. I would've wandered with you anywhere."

I breathed.

"Don't ever be mad about what happened, Summer. Let it go, baby. We're fucked without you, I can't lie – please excuse my language, children and Jesus – but eventually we are gonna be okay. We're okay down here, you hear that, Summer? I forgive you. *I forgive you.* I'm gonna take good care of your mom, whether she wants me to or not, and even though I've only met your brother a few times, I can already tell he's gonna be a better man than me. I'm gonna make sure of it. I hope I can teach him about you, and how perfect you were, and the summer we spent together, and how you lit up Jax Beach with your grace."

I found Chase in the front row, chubby and shy and broken in his collared shirt, desperately in need of a father figure, and an idea came to me.

"By the way, Chase, that room you liked at my house when you came by that one time, that storage room overlooking the pier? We cleared it out for you, and it's yours, whenever you wanna come over and have a weekend with your new big brother. Got it?"

Chase gave me the biggest smile I had seen since before Summer's death. Smiles – I missed those.

I paused to look up at the damp ceiling tiles.

"You know, I'm pissed, Summer, and I want to punch a lot of people in the face right now. But it's also a time to be happy, because you won at life. You won at life, you hear me? You *won*. You were good and beautiful and pure and I am standing in a room full of people who loved you, and in the end there is no greater testament to a life than that." It was getting hard to speak, but I shoved down the tears. "I know you died young and unnecessarily and that it's the most unfair thing I've ever known, but don't ever think your life didn't change things, Summer. You left love behind – that's all anyone can ask for. And *I* love you, and you made *me* happy, and if a human makes even one other human happy and leaves love behind, their life was a success."

I cleared my gravelly throat. I knew I was totally rambling now, but I didn't care – this was my last chance to get all this out, and I wasn't going to let Summer down now.

I gestured towards the casket proudly. How could I *not* be proud of that girl, and want to show her off? She was mine.

"I wrote my first book about that girl, you know," I sort of smiled. "Because people like Summer deserve to have books written about them. She was a hero in every sense of the word, but she wasn't like the rest of them, nope. Most heroes throw their good deeds under lights and expect praise to be lavished upon their glories, but Summer was different. She loved people in the dark and rescued them in the silence,

331

never asking for recognition, never even *telling* anyone of her deeds, and in the end, there is no greater act of heroism than that. Oh, God, I'm gonna miss her."

I wiped the snot off my lip, an angry lump rising into my throat as I thought of her scar. "You know, I'm sure you've all seen someone like Summer," I said, a new idea in my mind. "You pass them every day: they've got a scar, maybe a touch of disease, a cleft lip, a hint of a limp. Something is just *different*, and what do you do? You veer away, because that's another thing humans do, a shitty thing – we run from what is different. We are all middle schoolers walking down a hallway and nervously laughing while the weird kid with the funny voice gets made fun of by the class bully for having a rolling backpack. We join in and laugh because the backpack kid is Different, and making fun of him makes us Just Like Everyone Else, and God, the worst thing in the world would be being left out of the pack, right? So we cut our eyes and close ourselves up to the plight of the underdog. I know that, because I used to do the same thing – until my mom, bless her heart, became paralyzed and taught me that skin was nothing but a flaccid membrane encasing a human soul. Summer was the most remarkable surprise of my life, that is true, but she was a surprise I would've overlooked had I not learned that lesson. After this loss I will make doubly sure to never again avoid the eyes of someone whose body was born different from mine, even though God knows I will *never* find another Summer again. Which brings me to this."

I chewed on the inside of my cheek as the energy in the room shifted and deepened somehow. "You know, like Shelly said, accidents and anomalies and mess-ups can strike whenever they want, but love is not conditional. The fact that Summer is lying in a casket does not change a thing. I have screamed at the heavens and cursed the ground I stood on and shouted at the gods, if they exist at all. But I do not, nor will I ever, regret the summer I spent with Summer Martin Johnson. And to prove that to her, in front of her family and

332

friends and maybe God himself, I'm gonna do this. If everyone will excuse me, I've got a wedding to attend."

I grabbed my book and stepped away from the microphone as a stunned silence fell over the room. I watched as Summer's group, Kim included, left their seats and arranged themselves in a semicircle around me and the casket just as I had instructed in a text on the way here, forming one last meeting of Summer's Anti-Support Group, creating a barrier between us and everyone else in the room – except this time, the freaks would be on the other side.

Just like Shelly had said, everyone had laughed at Summer when she'd shared her spring wish of finding love by autumn. *Everyone.* And here it was, happening a few weeks early, in front of her family and her friends – Summer's last wish, come true in a way Summer could have never imagined, but fate had ensured. And fate: what *was* fate, anyway? Who spoke the stories of our lives? Did the universe really smile on goodness, or was it all just a shot into the darkness of this doomed galaxy?

I looked at Autumn and thought that maybe some people were born to laugh and make jokes and spill secrets and puncture clouds of sadness. I saw my mother in the crowd and knew others were born to wheel around a kitchen and cook casseroles and smoke cigarettes on a porch and be mothers. Shelly's face reminded me that some people were born to fret and fuss and smother you with comfortable love. Frank's grimace reminded me that others were born to frown and complain and be there for people, quietly and relentlessly. And then I glanced back at Summer in her casket, the miracle I'd found in this probably-godless universe, and knew that some people were born to make people happy. Summer was born to love and be loved, and her death had not changed that.

So, to answer a question I'd asked Summer herself many times: *we* created our own destinies. Our actions did. Maybe you didn't have to die Facebook famous to leave a legacy. Maybe we did that ourselves through the ways in which we lived and loved and died; writing our own inscriptions for our gravestones, leaving only the dirty work for the stonemason. But what was I going to write for *my* stone? What would people say at *my* funeral? Would I be frowned upon as a once-promising failure, or would I be admired as a normal man of normal heart who had gathered his strength and risen to the occasion?

I walked up to Autumn, who wiped her face and gave me a quietly devastated smile. She'd been holding hands with Hank when I approached, and it made my guts feel warm. "I got your message," she said. "We're all in wedding attire, just like you asked, or as close to it as we could find in twenty minutes' notice, anyway. And also, the Funfetti cake we were planning for the wake at Shelly's house is in the corner – we figured it'd be a nice wedding cake," she said with tears on her cheeks and stars in her eyes as she motioned at the towering white cake in the corner. Then she reached over and patted my shoulder, and I could feel love in her touch. "Send our girl off in white, Coop."

"You got it, kid."

I turned and approached the wooden box that contained the love of my life. I stopped, squeezed my eyes shut, and then opened them and looked down at Summer in her long ivory dress. My unsinkable Summer, too young and too beautiful to have met this fate, sunken at last. She looked cold and still and stiff, and her face was different and hard to look at. It was impossible for my brain to comprehend that she was there, but not *there*. I didn't get the sense that she was Watching, you know, in some big dramatic heavenly sense, but I told myself it would be nice to believe she was. They'd arranged her mouth into an unnatural smile and hidden her scar under way too much white powdery makeup, just as she had in life, but still, she was my Summer. She would always be my Summer.

"You are so beautiful," I whispered as I leaned down and ran my finger along her scar to wipe off the makeup. "You still are. Please believe me this time."

The crowd's murmuring grew into a dull roar. I could see them craning their heads, trying to look past the Anti-

Support Group in front of me, but I didn't care that they couldn't see me – the real measure of a human was what they did in the dark, when nobody was watching.

"I'm sorry, but I lied to you during our last night together," I told Summer. "When I said I would be your boyfriend forever, I didn't mean it. I want to be your husband." I reached into my pocket. "This is for you – and no pulling away this time," I said as I slid my grandmother's heirloom wedding ring onto her left ring finger. She was stiff with rigor mortis and it took a little pushing, but it roughly fit. Then I took the bouquet of pale pink roses I'd just picked from the bushes in Summer's front yard and placed them atop her clasped hands. "Please don't be mad at me, but I just wanna make this thing official." I straightened the bouquet and smoothed my bride's golden blonde hair in her coffin, where she would lie for eternity in her bridal best. Death couldn't take this from me. From us. This love was timeless.

"I know this isn't your ideal wedding situation, but you look beautiful," I told her. "And there is a bright side – no selfies will ever be posted of this ceremony." Then I placed my hand, warm and living, atop hers, cold and dead. "I, Cooper Nichols, take you, Summer Johnson, in the presence of a God that may or may not exist, our family and our friends, to be mine. I offer you my solemn vow to love you unconditionally, to honor and respect you, to laugh with you and cry with you, and to cherish you for as long as we both shall…"

I couldn't go on. But I knew it was enough, even though I was kneeling at a casket instead of an altar. Love was enough. It was all so clear to me now. Summer was in me, every bit of me, and as long as I remained, this boy she had put back together, so would she. And maybe these were the remains of the loved ones we lost – not the bodies their souls cast aside on the journey to the other side of things, but those wonderful little bits of them embedded into all of us like stardust floating in the Milky Way, every smile every laugh every tear every whisper every shout every bit of love they ever emitted, little slivers of them that sank into us and reminded us that they were here. They may have been gone, but as surely as the dead of winter gave way to the sun-soaked glory of spring every year, they were here once, and Goddamnit, they had lived.

Summer Johnson's remains were Cooper Nichols. This union was just making it official. I would go on to win and lose and laugh and cry and die, and although I had no idea if I would succeed with my writing or find love or start taking pills again or even recover from this, I knew I'd have one hell of a time finding out. Summer was so right – dying was easy, but living was the grandest and most challenging adventure of all. And I was about to put that theory to the test like nobody in the world before. I'd lost my way over the years, sure, but Summer had made me find it again, an angel drifting elegantly through the chaos of the world, doling out ruinous and redeeming love, love that had blown me open and stitched me back up again. It was the "redeeming" part that I was going to focus on. It was time to swim.

"Gotta kiss the bride, right?" I sort of laughed through my tears as I leaned down and gave Summer one last kiss. "Thank you for giving me something to believe in," I whispered. Then I slipped in the vial of glowing seawater from our pier that I'd collected that morning, my own little version of an eternal flame for my wife. As it jostled against the satin wall of the coffin, the bioluminescence flickered a little and then extinguished for eternity – but that was fine. Summer glowed enough on her own. Then I took out her last eternal memento, the photo of us under the Kissing Tree, along with a quote of my own – no more Saviour quotes – that I'd written on the back of the picture in my awful handwriting:

Life is brief but love is long. Somewhere between anger and love is an ocean of eternal tranquility. It is there that I will see you again.

I didn't need the picture anymore, because the old man and his legend had been dead wrong about the two trees dying at extrication – even though we'd been separated, that didn't mean I needed to die, too. Quite the contrary. I couldn't wait to see Summer again one day, but that didn't mean I wasn't fine for a while. I had quite a bit to do now that she'd changed my path a little. She'd *created* my path, actually – if she was Jesus, I was Lazarus by the sea.

"Forever," I whispered as I gave her the photo. "I'm gonna love you forever. I promise. You can be angry at a person's choices and still love them – you should know that better than anyone. I don't care if you were sick or broken or damaged – you deserved love. You deserved love because you were a human, and that's what humans do: we love." I let out a funny little chuckle. "I mean, hell, if we're stuck on this little blue ball spinning in the dark and we can't reach out and feel another beating heart, fall into another soul and claim it as our own, then what in the hell is the point of it all? The love you left behind is so much greater than the regrets your departure created. You were more than worth the trouble. I pray I was too."

I took a breath and then reached up to close the casket and close the book on us. Our story had been written this summer under the oaks, and there was nothing else for us to do. It was over.

I rested my hand on the lip of the smooth mahogany casket and took one long look at my wife, knowing it would be the last time I would ever lay eyes on her. I leaned down and placed one final kiss on her eyelashes, but this wasn't the fairy tales she had never believed in, and a Snow White kiss would never wake her. She had been frozen by fate, twenty-four and beautiful forever. As my tears and my love spilled onto her wedding dress I smiled at her and saw a roaring montage of our Jax Beach summer together: I saw us jumping off the pier into the waves as the ocean lit up; arguing in my dim garage under the harsh glare of my ceiling lights; kissing under oak trees, the canopy of leaves protecting us from the brutality of this cruel world; wheeling through the streets of St. Augustine, happy and broken and free at last. Those moments were gone, washed away by the seas of time, but the memories remained. The summer remained.

I stared at her and took a deep breath. "I love you, Summer, and I am about to do everything in my power to make this world deserve you. See you in the stars – I hope. Float on, Sum. Float on."

I closed the box and turned to the crying crowd. As I stepped away, however, I glanced down and noticed *Eighty Eight* and *This Is Not A Cancer Book* hanging from my coat pocket. In all my emotion I'd totally forgotten about them. Autumn caught my eye and, seeing my hesitation, reached for the books with a look of longing in her eyes like I'd seen before. I knew she'd want to read the story of the last few months when Summer and I had loved and wrecked each other by the sea; when she'd found a broken boy and loved him back together. Lots of people would, probably. I thought of my mom's suggestion to turn it into an eBook, and for a fleeting moment I saw myself sitting at some author's convention signing copies for mournful readers who'd read the story of my summer on the beach with Summer, and how it'd changed me forever, and bla fucking bla. I'd put it out online, it'd get posted and re-posted on social media as the latest summer read, and my dream of becoming an obnoxious bestselling author would finally be fulfilled. Summer would remain, and I'd be on the right path again, my road to adulthood finally secure.

I smiled a funny little smile, slipped our books into the casket with my bride where they would be our little secrets forever, and walked away. I would find my own way in this world without Summer, and write my own books, about the life I would live after her. But some things, I decided, were just better left unshared.

THE END

~

AUTHOR'S NOTE
This book is dedicated to my brother Martin, who
remains in his son, Island
July 11, 1981 – May 31, 2012
"An honest man from where the palm trees grow"
My Summer

*Note to readers: I can't write about Martin. Just thinking about him right now makes me want to cry. I will die with my brother's story locked safely away in my soul. Maybe I'll see him surfing on the edge of the world when I leave this one, maybe I won't. This book isn't about him – it's just inspired by him. As a special thank-you to readers, though, I *would* like to share the Facebook post that inspired this book, ironically enough. In the spring of 2014 I wrote a short note to friends to mark the two-year anniversary of his death (and to preemptively address what I knew everyone would be awkwardly asking me about anyway), and posted it along with the above photo. The book quickly exploded out of that idea in my mind, spinning sorrow into something real. Here it is:

Today marks the two-year anniversary of my brother Martin's death during a botched surgery at age thirty. His demise was sudden and awful and senseless and final, but in my dreams he still looks like this, frozen in his prime like an insect suspended in amber for the ages, with sun on his shoulders and sand under his feet and a breeze at his back, young and brave and free forever. And though he left us far too early, it is an injustice to human life to measure it solely by the years we spend on this Earth. Years are one yardstick, but so are the souls we sink into, the smiles we create, the people whose lives we alter. Time is relative but impact is not, and by that standard Martin fit a little eternity into those three decades. He was the best man I ever knew, good and honest and true, and he changed me. His death turned my life upside down and remapped the road of it forever, but I am unafraid, because with the lessons he left me I am confident in every step of this new course. It breaks my family anew every day to watch his three small children grow up without him, but with the fortitude he instilled within us we will see them through and make sure they know just who brought them into this world. Because he deserves it. He was Martin. His life was so short on time, and yet so incalculably grand on impact. I am so grateful for those thirty years.

If time is the ocean in this photo, most footprints left on the sands of it are temporary, washed away soon after they are cast. Many people leave damage or heartbreak in their wakes when they leave this Earth, or even worse, nothing at all. But Martin's strength and power and resilience were the amber that cast his footprints into stone.

He left me a road map. I will follow in his steps forever.

This book is the first step on that journey, Martin. These words alone cannot do you justice, but love can try. You will never know about this book, just like you never knew about your surprise daughter who was born eight months after you died, in whose eyes and smile and spirit you remain, reincarnated in love. When your wife approached me with a positive pregnancy test a few days after your funeral, I smiled and cried simultaneously as the oldest feeling in the world rose up within me: *life goes on.* And when we brought the baby to your beloved grandfather, Dondaddy, who had been so shattered by your death, he put a hand on her little arm, nodded, and died twelve hours later.

Neither fate nor circumstance nor the scalpel of a careless doctor could stop the timeless and relentless cycle of love being born into love, dust to bone to love to dust again, and this book is the fruition of that truth. I hope I haven't let you down. It would've been so easy to sink down deep after your death, where things were safe and dark and simple, but thank you for leaving behind a legacy of human survival so powerful, I was inspired to pick up my arms and start swimming.

   Your children are so beautiful, and every time I hug them, I can feel your heart beat. I promise I will move heaven and Earth to help give them the futures they deserve. We miss you so much down here, but we are not alone: we have each other. So sleep well – I've got this. Please give Dondaddy a hug for me, though. A full, hard, honest hug. A Cooper hug.

And to whoever is reading this: the topics of physical and intellectual disabilities were very close to my brother's heart, and are now very close to mine. The disabled aren't sainted caricatures, they're real people – they're Summer. They're you. They're me. They like Funfetti cake and trashy reality shows and sometimes they get mad and shout curse words. So next time you encounter someone who was born differently than you, I hereby challenge you not to smile vaguely and look away, but to nod, say hello, mention how great the weather is, do something, ANYTHING to let them know you're listening. Their issues don't make them any different from anyone else on the inside, but still, you never know who could be aching for love; you never know who could be a Summer just waiting for her chance to be heard. So go hug somebody. Go talk to somebody. Go love somebody. I dare you. What's the worst that could happen?

I wish you love, and I hope you hope.

Float on forever,

Seth
2015

ABOUT THE AUTHOR

Seth King is a twenty-five-year-old American author and former journalist. He can be found at sethkingbooks.tumblr.com.

54431473R00190

Made in the USA
Lexington, KY
15 August 2016